YORK

—BOOK ONE—
THE SHADOW CIPHER

LAURA RUBY

WALDEN POND PRESS
An Imprint of HarperCollinsPublishers

Walden Pond Press is an imprint of HarperCollins Publishers.
Walden Pond Press and the skipping stone logo are trademarks and registered
trademarks of Walden Media, LLC.

York: The Shadow Cipher
Copyright © 2017 by HarperCollins Publishers

www.harpercollinschildrens.com
ISBN 978-0-06-230693-7
Typography by Aurora Parlagreco
17 18 19 20 21   PC/LSCH   10 9 8 7 6 5 4 3 2
❖
First Edition

For Zoe and Oliver, my favorite adventurers

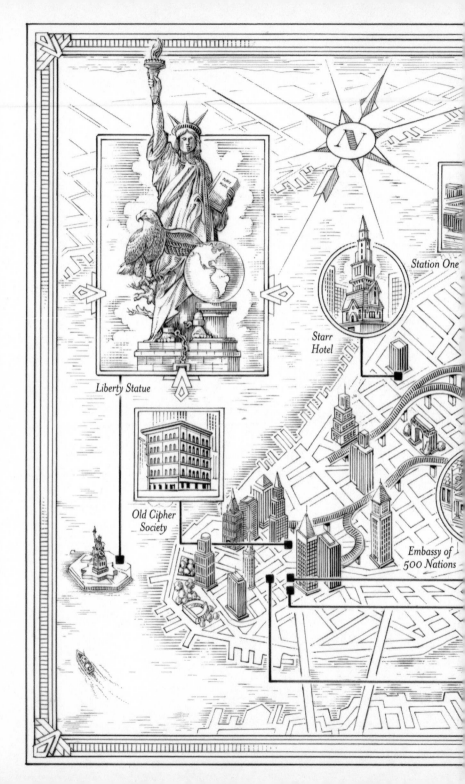

Station One

Starr
Hotel

Liberty Statue

Old Cipher
Society

Embassy of
500 Nations

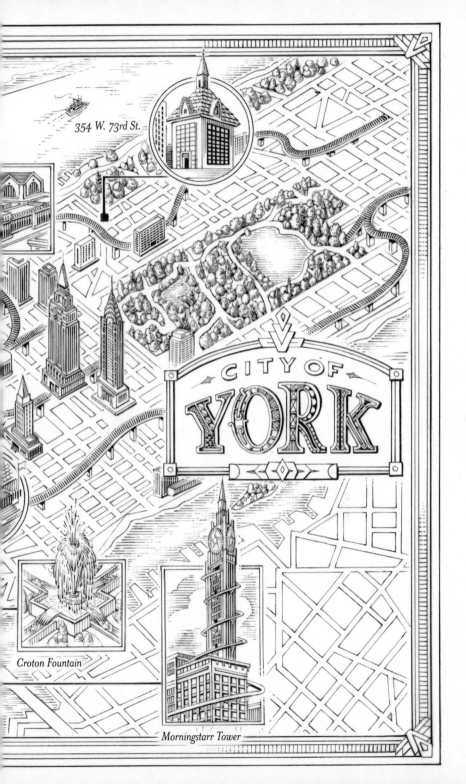

354 W. 73rd St.

CITY OF
YORK

Croton Fountain

Morningstarr Tower

The roaring street is hung for miles
With fierce electric fire.

—WILLIAM VAUGHN MOODY, "In New York," Part I
of "Song-Flower and Poppy"

What is the city but the people?
—WILLIAM SHAKESPEARE, *Coriolanus*

THE SHADOW CIPHER

New Year's Eve, 1855

The true story of any city is never a single tale; it's a vast collection of stories with many different heroes. But most storytellers believe that theirs is the *only* true story and that they are the *only* true heroes.

They are surprised to find out they are wrong.

Just a few hours before midnight, a brief hush fell over the streets of New York City, as if someone were about to tell a grand tale of mystery and adventure and needed quiet to begin. William Covington Hanover didn't like the sudden quiet, and he already knew the story of New York City—his story. He had been in this city for barely a fortnight and had concluded it was teeming with ruffians, murderers, and thieves. That he himself was a murderer and a thief was beside the point.

(And he would thrash the daylights out of anyone who called him a ruffian.)

No, the point was that William Covington Hanover didn't *look* like a murderer or a thief. He had pride. He had standards. On this fine winter evening, the air aflutter with new snow, he wore a crisp white shirt with a pleated front, a white cravat, a dark tailcoat, and clean trousers. His top hat added to his already considerable height, and his fine wool greatcoat swept behind him like the regimentals of a British general.

Which was why pretty Miss Ava Oneal had no idea he'd been shadowing her for seven blocks.

And why would she? His was a stylish ensemble pinched from his last employer, the profoundly near-sighted Lord Something-or-Other of Somewhere-upon-Avon, who never seemed to notice when the candlesticks and silverware went missing. Until the day he *did* notice, causing an ill-advised tussle over a serving fork. William was forced to stuff his spoils into a pillowcase and steal aboard a packet bound for this strange city with its even stranger inhabitants. Ruffians, murderers, thieves . . . and fools. When the ship had docked in America, and he'd informed the immigration officials at Castle Garden that his name was "William Covington Hanover," he was joking. Who would believe a man who had spent months crammed into a boat with shoemakers and potato farmers was a member of the House of Hanover, same as Queen Victoria? But they had merely scratched his quip in a ledger and waved him on.

And on he went. Through Battery Park and into the cauldron of the Five Points neighborhood, where he found lodging in a cramped tenement that reeked of gin fumes and rancid cabbage. Not much to steal in the Five Points, and far too much to drink. It didn't take long for him to migrate into the heart of the city, where the shining Morningstarr Tower stood like a beacon to everything that he had desired his whole life and all that he deserved: riches and power beyond his wildest imaginings (though, honestly, just the riches would do).

Now he was on the upper west side of the island, where the wealthy had recently built rows of fine houses as well as some grand estates complete with lawns and forest. Most of the coppers stayed south near the Five Points, but a few wandered north to protect the wealthy from, well, people like William Covington Hanover. William nodded at the coppers on the corner, tipped his hat to the groups of ladies gathered to climb into horse-drawn carriages that would bear them to this ball or that one.

"Good evening, ladies," he said, in his best upper-crust English accent. "You are the picture of loveliness this magical night."

"Good evening to you, sir," said the boldest. The ladies giggled as he passed, eyes darting over his fine coat, his fair hair, his ready smile. As long as he didn't get close enough for any of them to notice his cold-and-whiskey-reddened nose or the knife scars on his white cheeks, he was safe. He would appear to be like any other gentleman making his way to a New Year's Eve celebration instead of a man pursuing a dream in the form of Miss Ava Oneal.

Miss Ava was dressed less opulently—and more strangely—than the other ladies. Despite the festive occasion, she wore a plain jacket buttoned all the way up to the neck, a long dark skirt and cloak, and a mannish hat nearly as tall as William's. But her outfit was not the most remarkable thing about her. Nor was it her small stature, her flawless brown face, or the fact that she walked unescorted through the swirling, sparkling snow. It wasn't even that she was reading a book in the dim light of the streetlamps as she went. No, it was Miss Ava Oneal's employers who most intrigued him.

Employers by the names of Theresa and Theodore Morningstarr.

Miss Ava reached the corner and floated across the street, never lifting her gaze from her pages, though more than one coachman had to haul on the reins of his horses to keep from trampling her. The coppers watched her go, twirling their clubs, whispering amongst themselves. And the others watched her, too. William spied them everywhere; only the coppers could miss them. Rough men in gangs like the Dead Rabbits—or was it the Dead Roaches?—men who called themselves ludicrous things like Slobbery Jim and Patsy the Butcher, et cetera, et cetera. They lurked in alleys and in doorways, behind walls and trees, clad in oversized sack coats and tiny bowler hats the size of thimbles. William shook his head in disgust. In such a costume, you might as well stand in the middle of the avenue and shout: "Rich citizens of the city! Prepare to be bashed over the head and shaken like apple trees!"

William Covington Hanover would never make such an exhibition of himself. An Englishman valued subtlety; a Yank wanted spectacle. As if this city didn't have enough spectacle. The Morningstarr Tower, for one. The Liberty Statue. The oddly named Underway, a dizzying nest of above- and belowground trolleys whose workings were so mysterious that only members of a secret guild were permitted to mind the system. The rich kept their horses and carriages just for show.

At that moment, William Covington Hanover would

have been grateful for a ride in a carriage or on the Underway, as Miss Ava Oneal seemed determined to march the entire length of the island of Manhattan this cold winter's evening. Or perhaps she simply wanted to finish her book. The newspapers said she was a very smart young lady; Miss Morningstarr met Miss Oneal while both were working at a hospital for sick orphans and hired the girl on the spot. William Covington Hanover couldn't imagine why either lady would waste her time on sick people, let alone orphans. Not shocking that someone eventually burned down that hospital.

But in addition to being smart, William was irritated to note, Miss Oneal was also a very brisk walker. William sighed and increased his pace, taking only a moment to glare at a man with a face like a pickax, who was eyeing her with a little too much interest. The man took William's measure and wisely retreated into the shadows.

Miss Ava Oneal walked another block and pivoted right. William trotted to keep up, turning the corner just as a coachman barked, a horse whickered, and another carriage full of ladies rumbled off to a midnight party. The sharp odor of fresh manure cut through the chill. Almost as suddenly, a round hatch opened in the middle of the street and two beetles crawled out—if beetles were the size of sheepdogs and made of shimmering, iridescent-green metal. The beetles skittered across the snow-frosted cobbles toward the pile of manure and, working together, packed the scattered pile into a neat, round ball. Then one of the beetles turned around and used its hind legs to roll the ball backward into the hatch. Both beetles vanished after the ball, and the hatch closed. The entire process took only a few moments.

William Covington Hanover had seen the Rollers many times, but he still wasn't used to them. Unnatural, they were, those glittering, skittering machines. Another invention of the Morningstarrs: brother and sister, twins, geniuses. They had designed the shining Morningstarr Tower, the incandescent Starr Hotel. Built impossible bridges and the greenest of parks. Engineered the Underway. Paved the streets in strange, silvery cobblestones that somehow absorbed the power of the sun, spun shimmering window glass that did the same, and forged the Lion batteries that contained it all. Created all manner of Morningstarr Machines, including the Rollers that tidied the roads, mechanical snails that washed the windows, whirring dragonflies that did everything from drying shirts to cooling people in summer. For fifty-seven years, the Morningstarrs had performed architectural and mechanical wizardry to make New York City the most dazzling city in the world, or so New Yorkers claimed. And after seeing the gleaming metropolis of the future for himself, William begrudgingly had to agree. (Though he was certain Theodore, not Theresa, was the true genius behind all this invention, as ladies were much more suited to embroidering cushions and giggling at tall men.)

But, four weeks ago, Theresa and Theodore Morningstarr had disappeared into the labyrinth of the Morningstarr Tower, and hadn't been seen or heard from since. Before they vanished, the twins deeded all their land and property to a trust in the city's name and left the city a parting gift: a sort of puzzle, or treasure hunt. The first clue, some string of incomprehensible gibberish, was printed in the newspaper. That clue would lead to another clue, the newspaper headlines howled, and another and another and would eventually reveal the greatest treasure known to man. The treasure only waited for a treasure hunter clever enough to discover it.

Well, William Covington Hanover was clever enough to know a joke when he saw one. A treasure hunt! What nonsense! Some great game the Morningstarrs played with an unwitting public, a public currently poring over the paper and then racing from one building to another on a wild-goose chase.

But the Morningstarrs had also left not a small sum of money in trust to Miss Ava Oneal, the young woman they had hired as help but looked upon as a granddaughter. And if anyone knew the secrets of the Morningstarrs—if anyone knew where the *real* treasures were hidden—it was her.

And because William Covington Hanover was a gentleman—or, at least, dressed like one—he would ask her nicely.

After that, he intended to bleed her secrets out of her.

Subtlety could take a man only so far.

Miss Ava Oneal continued walking until the elegant houses grew farther and farther apart, hidden by thickets of trees. When she reached West 73rd Street, Miss Ava finally slowed in front of a tall building with a light gray facade and surrounded on either side by two more nondescript buildings. He might not have known the center building to be a Morningstarr building except for the letters "TTM" etched into the cornerstones. Perhaps this was Miss Ava's home, bequeathed to her by her benefactors. It was a pretty enough structure, so far west that William smelled the rich, oily stew of the Hudson River even in the cold. But William Covington Hanover had his sights set on bigger things, gold and silver and shiny—

"May I help you?"

William stopped walking so abruptly he slid on those odd icy cobbles and had to pinwheel his arms for balance.

Miss Ava Oneal stood staring at him. "Are you looking for someone? You've been following me for some time."

William shaped his voice into that same plummy accent. "Following you? My dear lady, I assure you that I—"

"That's quite a coat. Who did you steal it from?"

"I beg your pardon! I was a general in the queen's army and—"

"No doubt," she said rather rudely, just like an American. But she was very pretty. Doe-eyed, full-lipped, that brown skin so smooth. She had to be at least twenty-five years old, but she looked younger. Seventeen? Eighteen?

He switched tactics, smiling and spreading his arms. "I confess. I couldn't help but notice that you traveled unescorted. And even this beautiful city can be a dangerous place for a young woman."

"So I've heard," she said, returning his smile. "And you mean to protect me?"

"Indeed," he said, warming to the part. "Let me introduce myself. My name is William Covington Hanover."

"William Hanover!" She tucked her book beneath one arm and clapped her hands. "You don't say!"

"I do say!"

"Marvelous!"

"Well, yes. I mean, thank you, dear lady." He took another step toward her, then another, in order to loom more properly.

"Did you have a disagreement with a cat, Mr. Hanover?" Miss Ava murmured, peering up under thick lashes at his scars.

"War takes its toll on us all," he said. "Please allow me to see you inside. I would rest so much more easy knowing that such a handsome young woman arrived safely at her destination."

"You are delightful," said Miss Ava Oneal.

He couldn't help it; his smile deepened to a grin. "Thank you again."

"Much more delightful than the others."

His smile wavered. "The . . . others?"

"The other men who have followed me. The ones

given to clubbing people over the head and dragging them into dark alleys. Do you know one of them had the nerve to propose to me *after* he threatened to cut out my eyes? I said no."

William's jaw dropped. Ava Oneal withdrew her book from the folds of her cloak, placed the book beneath his chin, and gently closed his mouth.

"Gentlemen don't threaten to cut ladies' eyes out. It simply isn't done. Not even in this book, which is quite scandalous. Have you read *Penelope*?" She tilted the book so that he could read the cover.

But unless he needed kindling, William Covington Hanover had no use for books. "I can't say I've heard of it, Miss Oneal," he said, holding out his elbow. "Now, let's get you out of this chill."

"Ah, you know my name."

"Pardon?"

"My name. You know it." She tapped his chest with her book. "You *were* following me."

Enough of this, he thought, and slapped the book from her hand. It slammed into the stone of the building and dropped into the thin crust of snow on the ground.

"Oh," said Miss Ava, eyes widening.

"Oh," he said, taking another step closer. "I have a

few questions for you."

"Oh?" she repeated, reaching up and laying a small hand on his shoulder. She ran that hand down the length of his arm, curling her slim fingers around his pinky. Her full lips parted. As if she wanted to kiss him.

Then he heard the snap of his pinky as she broke it.

He only had time to emit a strangled squeal before she kicked him in the kneecap and swept his feet out from under him as easily as if she were tumbling a puppy.

"That," she said, with a click of the tongue, "is no way to treat *Penelope*. Or me, for that matter." Her eyes shifted in the dim light, pupils shining like gunmetal.

He scrabbled backward, pinky burning, shattered kneecap screaming. How could such a slight girl have wounded him so badly, and so fast? "Wait . . . wait . . . you can't . . ."

She advanced on him, floating in that strange way of hers. "And yet, I did."

"This cannot be real."

"Oh, I'm as real as anyone. And I am always and forever a lady." Miss Ava bent close, smiling at him with gleaming pearly teeth. "Would you like to see what kind of lady I am, Mr. William Covington Hanover? The others didn't like it, but perhaps you might."

"No," William huffed, barely able to get the words

from his throat because his heart had crawled up inside it. "No. Leave me be. I won't bother you anymore."

"It's no bother."

"Please," William said, exactly what Lord Something-or-Other had said before the serving fork had found its mark. "Please."

She opened her mouth wide and William squeezed his eyes shut, sure she would tear him to bits, roll him up, drop him in a deep dark hole.

Instead, she screamed, a loud, piercing, ladylike shriek. "Help me! Oh, won't somebody help me!"

His eyes flashed open in confusion.

Miss Ava Oneal scooped up her book and slapped his face with it, punctuating each word, "Cad! Beast! *Ruffian!*"

One minute the street was dark and empty; the next, coppers boiled out from the alleys and the woods and poured down the streets, as if they'd expected some trouble, as if they'd expected *this* trouble.

He was wondering how far one could run on a ruined knee when a copper shouted, "Get him, lads!"

It was no use, they were coming, they were here. William Covington Hanover—murderer, thief, and not much of a ruffian—threw his arms over his head. As the clubs rained down, the last thing he saw was Miss

Ava Oneal. She brushed the ice from the cover of her book, straightened her skirt, and stepped through the doorway of 354 West 73rd Street, taking with her all the secrets of the Morningstarrs, and every one of her own.

NEW YORK CITY
Present Day

CHAPTER ONE

Tess

The city had many nicknames: Gotham. Metropolis. The Shining Starr. The Big Apple. The City That Never Sleeps. These nicknames were not always accurate. For example, why would anyone refer to a city as an overlarge piece of fruit? Also, the city *did* sleep, but it slept the way a cat does, eyes half open, watchful, ready to spring at the first sign of fun, or danger.

That morning, a very different kind of cat was getting ready to spring. The cat in question lived in the Biedermann family's cluttered apartment at 354 W. 73rd Street and kept her sock collection underneath the Biedermanns' coffee table. This was not normally a problem for the Biedermann family, except when they had guests or when their feet were cold.

Today, they were having guests. They were also having a problem.

The cat—a large spotted animal that would have looked more at home on a South African savanna than in the living room on the Upper West Side—had the business end of a striped sock gripped firmly in her teeth. She was growling. The lanky girl sitting on the floor gripping the other end of the sock growled right back.

"Seriously, Tess?" said Mrs. Biedermann.

"This . . . is . . . my . . . favorite . . . sock . . . ," Tess said, her dark braid whipping like a tail against her olive skin. The cat's striped tail lashed in kind.

Tess's twin brother, Theo, who was standing at the kitchen counter, poking at his favorite alphabet cereal with the back of a spoon, said, "The cat's winning."

Tess said, "Yeah, well, I wouldn't need to clean up the stupid socks if those people weren't coming to see your stupid tower."

Mrs. Biedermann rifled through a briefcase the size of a suitcase. "It's not a stupid tower. And stop saying things are stupid."

"It's the *wrong* tower," Tess said.

Theo Biedermann had built a scale model of the Tower of London—a model that took up the Biedermanns' entire dining room—for a national Lego contest (he won). Now, a week into summer vacation, school officials were finally coming to interview Theo, to congratulate him for his prize (even more Legos) and to photograph the tower for the school website. Mrs. Biedermann thought they should clean up the cat's sock collection before the people arrived, but the cat, Nine, had other ideas. So did Tess.

Theo still didn't look up from his cereal. "You don't have to wear your favorite socks, Tess. No one's going to interview *you*."

"You should have built the Morningstarr Tower," Tess insisted, bending her legs and putting her weight on her heels for leverage.

Theo looked up from his cereal. "Hey! I spelled *Fibonacci*! Oh, hold on, the *i* is floating away."

Nine—who, oddly enough, didn't seem much interested in the names of mathematicians spelled out in wheat products—flattened her striped ears and nearly yanked the sock out of Tess's hands. Tess held fast. Behind them, the morning news hosts on the TV blah-blah-blahed about new parking regulations, about Great Britain negotiating with China for more all-weather solar panels after an especially rainy spring, about new water pipelines, about the best work-to-evening outfits for women, about a new guacamole recipe with peas.

"Peas," said Tess to the cat, "do not belong in guaca-mole."

"Mrrow," said Nine, pulling harder.

"Next up on the program," yapped the TV host, "we'll be headed to a surprise press conference with philan-thropist and real estate developer Darnell Slant. A man with a plan to move New York City into the twenty-first century!"

"We're already *in* the twenty-first century, duh," Theo said.

"Darnell Slant has been linked to some of the world's most beautiful women, including performance artist Lora Yoshida, pop star Cath Tastic, and supermodel and entrepreneur Mink. But just last week, things took a more serious turn in his life. He pledged a hundred million dollars to biological research that could lead to cures for cancer and numerous other diseases. And that, he says, is only the beginning. In a recent inter-view with Channel 8 news, Mr. Slant talked about the importance of progress over stagnation, especially when it comes to the continued development of our city. 'The Morningstarrs were geniuses, the earliest architects of New York,' he said. 'But the world in which they lived is gone. There is a point at which preservation becomes fossilization. We can love our heroes too much.'"

Tess dropped her end of the sock, surprising Nine. "Turn up the TV, Mom."

"Why? What's on?" said Mrs. Biedermann.

"'Maybe some of you are thinking that all these old buildings in and around our city hold clues to the Old York Cipher. But I want you to focus on the word *old* instead of the word *cipher*. The old must make way for the new.' And now, let's turn to our own Amber Amberson, who is live at the Slant press conference."

As soon as Darnell Slant's boyish face popped up on the screen, American flags flying behind, Mrs. Biedermann pressed a button and the TV went black. "I wish they'd stop giving that guy a microphone. He's not smart. He only seems smart."

Nine brushed up against Tess's leg before slinking under the coffee table with her prize. "I wanted to watch that," Tess said.

"I can't even look at his nasty mug," said Mrs. Biedermann.

"Why can you say things are nasty and I can't say things are stupid?"

"Because they're not the same thing. Plus, I am a grown woman and I can say whatever I want. It's one of the few perks of adulthood." Mrs. Biedermann shoved the briefcase aside. "Has anyone seen my keys?"

Tess hauled herself off the floor, scooped a set of keys from the seat of the tattered recliner her dad refused to donate to Goodwill. She dangled the keys in front of her mother. "I don't know how you keep losing stuff anyway," Tess said as her mother took them. "You call yourself—"

"A detective, yes," said Mrs. Biedermann, flashing her badge. "Everybody does."

"Not everybody," said Theo. "We call you Mom."

"And we call *you* Mr. Literal," Tess snapped.

"Okay, Tess, what's bugging you?" said Mrs. Biedermann.

Tess bit her lip, considered not saying it. But, in the end, it just popped out, the way many things popped out of her mouth even when Tess didn't want them to. "It's just that Slant is on the TV again and I'm worried that . . ."

As soon as she started talking, as soon as she said the word *worried*, she could almost feel her brother's eyes rolling as he scooped up his cereal bowl and dumped Fibonacci and the rest of his alphabet friends down the drain.

"I thought they were talking about the money he donated to cancer research," said Mrs. Biedermann.

"And then they said, 'And that is only the beginning.' What if it *is* only the beginning, Mom? He's a real estate developer. He buys real estate."

Mrs. Biedermann took a deep breath. "Tess, Darnell Slant has been trying to buy up every building in this city since *I* was a little girl."

"No, he isn't—just the important buildings. The Morningstarr Tower. The Starr Hotel. *Our* building. He won't stop talking about it. There are all these interviews all the time and—"

"Technically," said Theo, "it's not our building. The city owns it."

"Not everything is technical, you robot," said Tess. Their mother's family had lived at 354 W. 73rd Street for more than a hundred years. A hundred years! Her grandfather, Benjamin, had the apartment on the top floor and had taught Tess and Theo everything he knew about the structure, and about the Morningstarrs who had built it. He had even talked her parents into naming them "Theresa" and "Theodore." It was completely unfair that anyone else could lay claim to her home, even the city both she and the Morningstarrs had loved.

Especially not Slant, a man who bought beautiful old buildings and replaced them with shiny cracker boxes no one could afford. A man who only dated super-models and actresses from reality shows.

"Slant doesn't want our building, Tess. It's a decent enough building with a bit of history, but it's hardly the Morningstarr Tower. And what did I say about calling your brother a robot?" said Mrs. Biedermann.

"If he doesn't want to be called a robot, he should stop acting like one," said Tess. "Humans have feelings."

"Spoken like a crybaby," Theo said.

"A crybaby who can beat you in an arm-wrestling match."

"Your arms are longer," said Theo.

"And a running race," Tess added.

"Your legs are shorter."

"And a climbing contest."

"In summation, you're built like a gibbon."

"And tug-of-war."

"You can't even beat the cat."

"And—"

"Tess!" said Mrs. Biedermann. "You know he only says those things to wind you up. So, who's the robot?"

"But—"

"I think it's time for you and Nine to take a walk. Go

to the post office and pick up Grandpa's mail for him. And you, Theo, need to get ready for your interview."

"What do you mean?" Theo said. "I am ready."

Mrs. Biedermann shook her head. "You are most certainly not ready. I should have gotten you a haircut. How about wetting it so it doesn't look so . . . large."

Theo fingered his dense curls. Tess said, "You know it will only dry bigger."

"Okaaay," said Mrs. Biedermann, drawing out the word, as if the riotous dark hair of her children was too tangled a mystery to solve. "How about changing your shirt?"

"What's wrong with my shirt? It's new!"

"It says 'Schrödinger's cat is dead.'"

"I know."

"It has a *cartoon* of a dead cat."

"It's a thought experiment demonstrating what Schrödinger saw as a problem with certain interpretations of quantum mechanics when—"

Mrs. Biedermann held up one palm. "Now that you've cleared that up."

"Not really," said Tess. "Turn around, Theo." He did. The back of the T-shirt said "Schrödinger's cat is ALIIIIIVE" and had a picture of a zombie cat.

Mrs. Biedermann threw up both hands. "Look,

Theo, 'Schrödinger's' sounds like some sort of medical condition to me. Plus, the front of your shirt still has a dead cat on it."

Theo said, "Technically, so does the back."

"People will see it, and they're going to think you're weird."

"Too—" said Theo.

"—late," finished Tess.

Mrs. Biedermann gave Tess a flat mom stare. "I thought you were going to the post office."

"I'm going, I'm going," Tess said. She grabbed Nine's leash from a hook on the wall, and Nine bounded over like any dog might have. Tess hooked the leash to Nine's harness. She checked her back pocket for her keys, slung a messenger bag over her shoulder, and then walked to the door. Paused. What she did *not* do, would not do, was turn and glance around the spacious, sunny apartment as if it were the last time she'd ever see it. She would not make a comment about rent control, or about how they'd never be able to afford another apartment this size or any size in Manhattan or any other borough, or how they'd be banished to the wilds of New Jersey or maybe even Idaho if Slant got his way. She didn't say a word about her mother being forced to commute two or three or seventeen hours on a train to get to her job as a New York City detective, or complain that they would never see her and therefore forget what she looked like. And Tess did not worry aloud that her dad might be unable to find a new job as a school counselor in the suburbs of Idaho and would likely dissolve into a morass of self-pity during which he wandered around their ugly split-level, wearing the same pair of Cheeto-stained sweatpants for weeks on end, his hair getting larger and larger until they were forced to shear it and knit scarves for cash.

Because if she turned and glanced around the apartment and voiced any of her fears, Theo would roll his eyes again, and call her a girl—as if that were a bad thing to be—and her mother would take her by the shoulders and tell her she had nothing to be anxious about, and her dad, who had gone on a coffee run and was due home any minute, might tell her she was "catastrophizing."

Well, maybe she *was* catastrophizing. But catastrophes happened every day, didn't they? A person ought to be prepared. And to be prepared you had to imagine all the possibilities. Tess was very good at imagining the possibilities.

Nine nudged her hand. Tess stuck her tongue at her brother, and then she and Nine slipped out of the apartment and into the hallway. Mrs. Cruz, the building manager, worked hard at maintenance, but the building was showing its age: the plaster crumbling a bit in the corners; the decorative tiles with their distinctive star patterns chipping; the solar glass in the hall windows wavy enough to shatter the sunlight into rainbows; most of the Morningstarr seals, plaster medallions stamped with a star within a sun, missing from the window moldings.

But even with its flaws, this was not just any building. This was one of the five original buildings built by Theresa and Theodore Morningstarr, and therefore it was like no other building in the world (the Tower of London included). It contained all sorts of memories, all sorts of stories. She pressed her ear against the plaster as if to hear them.

Behind her, a small voice said, "You're not talking to the walls again, are you?"

Tess turned. A little girl, about six years old, stared at her from her perch on her oversized tricycle. She had bronze skin and black pigtails that stuck out like antennae. Her mouth and chin were smeared with something purplish.

"Hi, Cricket. You're not pretending your finger paints are lipstick again, are you?"

"Why would I do that?" said the girl.

"Well, why would I be talking to the walls?" Tess said.

"My mom says you act funny because nobody pays attention to you but that I should always be nice."

"Okay."

Cricket slid the heart charm on her necklace, *zip-zip, zip-zip*. "I do not enjoy being nice." She flipped a switch on the handlebars and *beep-beep-beep*ed the trike in reverse, all the way back down the hall till she disappeared around a corner.

"Who enjoys being nice?" Tess said to the now-empty hallway.

Nine chirped at Tess, then glanced at the elevator.

"Right. Sorry, Nine." She stabbed the down button. The elevator opened, and Tess and Nine stepped into the car. She pressed the button for the first floor, the marking so worn you couldn't read the number anymore. The elevator twitched slightly and then began to move. The building itself might be plain, but the elevator was anything but. It was an electromagnetic elevator, which meant it could go horizontally as well as vertically, and did. Every time she got on, the elevator took a different path to its destination, sometimes going straight up and down, sometimes taking a series of lefts and rights, sometimes zigzagging all over the place. Theo said the building was as big as it was simply to accommodate the strange paths of the elevator, a terrible waste of space, even if the elevator itself was cool. But Tess thought it was more than cool—it was magical. What if the doors opened onto a floor she had never seen? A *world* she had never seen? The elevator could go very, very fast, too, dropping straight down from the top floor to the first so quickly that the passengers experienced a moment of weightlessness, though this happened rarely, as if the elevator somehow understood that this wasn't going to make everybody happy.

Tess braced herself just in case, but the elevator was in a leisurely mood and took only one left and two rights before dropping straight down and setting itself gently on the first floor. The calm ride settled her nerves, and she was smiling when she walked toward the double doors, happy to see the same inlaid tile floors and cameo walls that her mother had grown up with, and Grandpa Ben had grown up with, and so on.

And she smiled wider still when she stepped out into the summer sunshine. Tess even smiled at the little clots of tourists taking pictures of the cornerstones and the address plaque, checking their guidebooks and maps, trying to figure out the Old York Cipher for themselves. They always came to one of the original buildings first, not that it would help them. No one had ever found a clue in one of the original buildings; that would be way too obvious, and the Morningstarrs were anything but obvious. But Grandpa Ben said that when he was a kid, you could barely get in and out of the building with all the tourists everywhere. Now there were just a few scattered groups, and most of them looked bored.

"It says here that the Old York Cipher was a gift to the city of New York from Theresa and Theodore Morningstarr, and that the first clue is at the Liberty Statue," said a white woman in white pants and a terrifying Hawaiian-print shirt.

The portly, pasty man with her grunted. "Then why didn't we go to the statue like I wanted to?"

"Because they already solved that clue. And a bunch after that. And then they got stuck."

"I just wanted to see the darned statue. And who's they?" said the man.

"People."

"What people?"

"People! The Old York Puzzler and Cipherist Society."

"Cyclist Society? I'm not getting on a bicycle. We just had breakfast."

"Cipherist."

"What's a cipherist?"

"It's someone who solves a cipher—what do you think?"

"Cipher," said the man, mopping his pink brow with a napkin. "Why does everything have to be so fancy? Why don't they just call it a code?"

"A cipher isn't the same thing as a code," Tess said. "It's way more complex, substituting words or numbers or even symbols in a message. Like the book cipher that the Morningstarrs used for the first clue in the Old York Cipher."

The portly man beetled his brows at her. "It's the same thing."

Tess said, "But it's not! Ciphers are much harder to crack, because—"

The woman pointed at the leash in Tess's hand. "Wild animals are illegal."

"This is Nine. She's a cat."

"She looks like a jaguar. Or a leopard. Or a jaguar-leopard."

"She's just . . . long."

The couple stared down at Nine, all forty-five pounds of her. Nine flicked her tail and offered a friendly chirp, as if to confirm, yes, regular cat, no jaguars here! Still, the couple backed away.

Not surprising. Nine definitely wasn't a regular cat. Nine was a mix of Siamese, serval, and who knows what else. A sprinkling of wolf, maybe. One day, Great-Aunt Esther showed up at the Biedermanns' apartment with an oversized spotted kitten. "I have brought you an animal," she said. "This animal is called Nine Eighty-Seven. I have also brought you some Fig Newtons. But not for the animal."

Aunt Esther, like a lot of people in Tess's family, was more than a little eccentric. And Nine was probably a little more sabertooth than Siamese.

The woman with the terrifying shirt said, "Normal people don't walk cats."

"Normal?" said Tess. "Was Einstein normal? Marie Curie? Ada Lovelace? Ida B. Wells? Wonder Woman?"

"Your cat is growling at me," said Terrifying Shirt Lady.

"She's purring," said Tess. Tess didn't tell her that Nine had a ten-foot vertical leap.

"You city people are so strange," the woman said.

"Thank you!" Tess tugged at the cat's leash, leaving the tourists to the torture of each other's company. Down the street to her left, the trees of Riverside Park beckoned, the weedy smell of the Hudson curling an inviting finger. But she took one last look at 354 W. 73rd—the familiar, unassuming gray facade, the windows like so many eyes watching over her, always watching over her—and headed east. It was early enough that the metal Rollers were out emptying garbage cans, scraping up bits of trash, and rolling them into hatches between waves of traffic. Sleepy people shambled to cars with cantilevered solar panels on top like the folded wings of locusts. As Tess got closer to Broadway, the Underway rumbled under her feet, as if she were walking on the back of some great murmuring beast. Everywhere, the city was waking up.

She reached the corner and turned onto the avenue. Horns honked; voices rose and fell. Buildings loomed on either side of the sleekly cobbled road, cliffs of jutting stone and vast pools of shimmering glass drinking in the sun. In front of her, newcomers stopped to gape while harried New Yorkers streamed around them. A teenager on a Starrboard darned in and out of the crowd. No matter how many times she walked these streets, she always felt as if she were walking at the bottom of a canyon, a part of a great river of humanity carving out a path.

These were the sorts of things she wished she could tell Grandpa Ben: that she felt like the buildings were cliffs, that she was a part of a river of humanity carving out her own path, that she both liked and hated that even strangers thought she was strange. Grandpa Ben had been the president of the Old York Puzzler and Cipherist Society for as long as Tess could remember and had been working to solve the Old York Cipher for even longer.

But not anymore. Nothing about Grandpa was the same.

Nine whined and nipped at Tess's fingers, snapping her back to the real world. Another thing Theo would say: "That cat always knows when you're *cat*astrophizing. Get it?" She got it. Probably why Mom and Dad let Tess keep Nine, had her trained and registered as a therapy animal. People had gone mad for genetically altered and hybrid animals—fox-dogs, bunny-cats, cat-coons, fer-otters—till the city cracked down, especially on the larger hybrids, sometimes called chimeras. A cop on his beat took one look at Nine and the silver city tag dangling from her collar. He shook his head and muttered, "What's next? Horse-bears?"

Next was the post office, and there were no horse-bears there; the place was nearly empty. The only noises were the soft whisper of Nine's paws on the marble floor, the low talk of the employees, and the faint *shoop! shoop!* of mail canisters shooting through pneumatic tubes in the walls. Tess pulled the keys from her pocket and unlocked Grandpa's box, and the usual avalanche of envelopes fell out. Nine pounced and chomped, caught one in her mouth and refused to let go, which was fine with Tess, as she could see it had TRUST NO ONE TRUST NO ONE TRUST NO ONE written all over it. Most of the mail came from other cipherists, but some of it came from paranoid conspiracy theorists. Grandpa Ben didn't mind the conspiracy theorists; he used to say that people thought *he* was one of them simply because he thought the Old York Cipher was real. So many assumed it was a fairy tale, a silly story that brought in the tourists, nothing more. Her parents thought so, even if they never said it out loud. Sometimes, Tess caught her mother's impatience whenever Grandpa Ben came for dinner and launched into one of his theories. Tess couldn't blame her father or her mother for not believing in the Cipher, or even for their relief when Grandpa Ben and the society parted ways. Mr. Biedermann had to counsel hundreds of kids at the school where he worked, some who didn't have parents or even enough to eat. As a detective, Mrs. Biedermann had her own mysteries to solve, and they weren't one hundred sixty years old.

But Tess still wanted to believe. What if the Cipher

was just waiting for the right person to solve it? Grandpa Ben once said that this was exactly how the Cipher snared a person in the first place; as you were trying to solve it, the puzzle made you believe that it was also trying to solve *you*.

"You make it sound like it's alive," Tess had said. "A puzzle can't be alive."

"Doesn't this city seem alive to you? Doesn't the air crackle? Don't the streets hum? Lots of things are alive," he said.

"Then how can you quit?" Tess said.

"I'm not quitting, *Gindele*."

Gindele. His name for her. Little deer. "Grandpa, you quit the society. You're giving up." She'd tried not to sound mad. So, he had some memory problems. Lots of people had memory problems. Maybe the doctors were wrong.

He said, "Accepting things for what they are isn't giving up."

"*Far kinder tsereist men a velt*," Tess said, one of Grandpa Ben's favorite sayings. For your children you would tear the world apart.

"And I would," he'd said, laying his still-strong hand on the top of Tess's head. "One day, you'll understand what that means."

Now Tess scooped Grandpa's mail from the floor and stuffed the pile into her messenger bag. She paused to inspect the envelope still clenched in Nine's teeth. The TRUST NO ONE message wasn't scrawled in red marker or crayon the way those sorts of messages usually were, but carefully scripted in black ink. The whole thing was sealed with gold wax, too, which was a nice touch, and which likely meant that the contents were especially banana-pants—especially since the address had been crossed out and rewritten three times. Tess tried to take the envelope to put it in her bag, but of course Nine wasn't having any of that. The cat lowered her head and growled.

Ah well. Who cared if Nine wanted to gnaw on some random letter from some random person? Grandpa Ben couldn't worry about such things anymore. And maybe Tess shouldn't worry about them, either. Maybe she wouldn't think about all the infinite possibilities, at least not the bad ones. She had the whole day, the whole week, the whole summer. Theo loved the precision of his blocks, but Tess loved building with things that warmed up in her hands—metal, plaster, clay. She could finish the model of a sphinx moth she'd been working on, one that would eventually hover in the air like a humming-bird. Or maybe Theo would come to Central Park and they could play Frisbee; she wouldn't mind if he spent the whole game calculating the angles of her throws. Maybe her dad could take them out on a river cruise, and they could watch for schools of fish darting through the clear blue water of the Hudson. A trip to the top of the Morningstarr Tower, Underway tracks whirling around the rocket-shaped spire like the largest, fanciest party favor. Grandpa's warm and gravelly voice echoed in her head: "Of course the Morningstarrs would build a tower; they were luftmenschen, dreamers, always with their heads in the clouds. It's a shock they ever made any money at all."

As Tess made her way back to 354 W. 73rd Street, she resolved to stop catastrophizing for once, to be a luftmensch dreaming up all the infinite possibilities—good ones—of a summer afternoon.

But by then, the Old York Cipher—alive as the city, alive as Tess herself—had already made a choice.

For its children, it would tear the world apart.

CHAPTER TWO
Theo

Later, much later, Theo would think about how a single day—and a visit from two creepy strangers—split his whole life into *before* and *after*.

But, at that moment, Theo didn't have a second to think. He sat against the wall, snapping blocks together so fast he pinched his fingers. A sheet of paper with a rough design and some quick calculations lay on the floor next to him. He probably wouldn't be able to finish—the school people would be there soon—but maybe they'd be late. Really late. Drastically, dramatically late. And then his Tower of London model would be perfect. It would be complete. Even a person with no knowledge of history or architecture would recognize it.

As Theo worked, his mother glanced up from the

stack of files she was reading. "That is amazing, Theo."

"Thanks, Mom."

"You built the whole thing, grounds and all."

"Yep," said Theo.

"And you won the contest."

"Um-hmmm."

"And the school people will be here any second now."

"Yeah."

"So, what are you doing?"

Theo snapped faster. He'd built all the structures that comprised the Tower of London, including the White Tower, the Salt Tower, the Broad Arrow Tower, the Bloody Tower, and the Tower Green where the wives of Henry VIII had lost their heads. He'd built the Royal Chapel, Traitor's Gate, the Tower Wharf, and the remains of the Lion Tower Drawbridge. He'd even built the moat around the entire compound, and the Thames River along one side.

But he hadn't built the Tower *Bridge*. It was only the most iconic bridge in the United Kingdom. And it was right next to the Tower of London. Why hadn't he built the bridge? He should have built the bridge.

So, he was building the bridge.

To his mother, he said, "Since we're just sitting here, waiting, I figured I'd keep busy."

"That model already takes up the entire dining room. And now you're building into my living room."

"So?" said Theo.

Mrs. Biedermann pinched the bridge of her nose. "It would be nice if you kids got into miniatures."

"Technically, this is a miniature."

"Technically, your family is going to end up living in the hallway because our home will be filled with the entire city of London."

"Um-hmm," said Theo. He could live in a hallway. Plenty of room in a hallway. Wasted space, really.

The hallway outside their apartment suddenly produced Theo's dad, who opened the apartment door and backed inside. He had a tray of coffees in one hand and a large white paper bag in the other.

"I come bearing coffee for all!" Mr. Biedermann announced.

"You're the only one who drinks coffee," said Mrs. Biedermann.

"You drink coffee, Mom," said Theo.

"I gave it up," Mrs. Biedermann said.

"Three days ago," said Theo.

Mr. Biedermann put the tray and the bag on the kitchen counter. "Correction: I come bearing coffee entirely for myself!"

YORK: THE SHADOW CIPHER ◆ 45

Mrs. Biedermann tapped a pen on her case files. "I thought you were going up to Absolute Bagels?"

"Eh, the lines were full of snotty college kids."

"Tell me that you didn't go to Sam's to buy a jelly doughnut."

"I didn't," said Mr. Biedermann. "I bought a dozen jelly doughnuts. And some blintzes, too. Maybe a lot of blintzes."

"Larry!"

"What?"

"You're supposed to be watching your cholesterol!"

Theo said, "I guess he'll be watching his cholesterol go up."

"Ha-ha," Mr. Biedermann said. He dug around in the bag, pulled out a cardboard container and a fork. He opened the container and forked up a bite of blintz. "Where's Tess?"

"Walking the cat," said Mrs. Biedermann.

"Good. She'll work off some of that anxiety."

Theo said, "No, she won't. Tess is like a Lion battery. She can't walk it off or run it out."

Mr. Biedermann laughed. "Oh yeah? What does that make you, kid?"

"Her extremely calm and well-adjusted brother," said Theo.

"Ah," said Mr. Biedermann, chewing, swallowing. He nudged a stray Lego with his toe. "I thought the school people would be here by now."

Mrs. Biedermann said, "Yeah, me, too."

"Though I suppose it could be all the commotion out front."

"What commotion?"

Mr. Biedermann shrugged. "I don't know. Someone filming a movie, maybe? I saw a crowd and some cameras and went around back to the service entrance."

Theo kept snapping furiously, liking the idea of a commotion. Maybe the principal would be forced to postpone till the afternoon. Or next week. Next month. Actually, September would be great, because then maybe he could build the whole city of London just like his mom had suggested. Or something else entirely. The Great Wall of China. The Shah Mosque in Iran. The Tower of David in Jerusalem. The Great Library of—

"I still don't get why you didn't build the Morning-starr Tower," Mr. Biedermann said through a mouthful of blintz.

Snap, snap, *ow!* His dad sounded just like Tess. Or Tess sounded like his dad.

Theo said, "I just wanted to do something different."

Mr. Biedermann nodded as if he understood.

Then he said, "Why?"

Before Theo ever started the Tower of London, he had tried to build the Morningstarr Tower. The Morningstarr Tower had twelve elevators that could move in any direction, escalators that zigzagged up the middle of the building, entire rooms that could be rotated and recombined to form new rooms of any shape or size. And that was only the beginning. It had taken the Morningstarrs fifteen years to complete. Theo could have worked for months and months and still not gotten the model right. Not even close to right. Sure, he could have built a serviceable representation of the building's facade, but that would be like making a mannequin and saying you'd created an actual human being. He would never have finished the whole thing soon enough to enter the Lego contest, which offered scholarship money in addition to more Legos. And hadn't Grandpa Ben used to say, "Is your work finished or is it just *due*?" So, Theo had tried to build something easier, something faster. And he'd won! Yet here he was, still building, almost out of time.

A sudden pounding on the door made him fumble with his blocks.

"The school people?" said Mr. Biedermann. "How did they get in?"

"It's probably just Cricket careening around the halls with her trike again," said Mrs. Biedermann.

Mr. Biedermann said, "Or her little brother practicing his karate kicks."

"I'm not sure that putting Otto into martial arts was the best idea."

"Remember the damage he did with the Wiffle ball bat? At least he can't knock the bulbs out of the fixtures anymore."

More pounding.

"No," said Mrs. Biedermann, "but he might just kick down the door."

Mr. Biedermann scooped another bite of blintz, threw open the apartment door. But instead of a six-year-old on a trike or a hyped-up four-year-old wearing his father's necktie for a headband, there were two men in suits, fists raised. One of the men was so tall, his head reached the top of the doorway, bright red hair buzzed close enough that he looked as if his scalp had been scalded in hot oil. The other man was a foot and a half shorter, light brown hair slicked back from a pallid, pockmarked brow. As the taller man ducked his head in order to see into the apartment and the little one bared gray teeth, the bit of blintz fell from Mr. Biedermann's mouth to the floor.

"You dropped your lasagna," the short man said in a flat voice.

The tall man said, "That's not lasagna. That's a blintz."

The short man said, "What's a blintz?"

"A crepe, usually filled with cheese and fruit," said the tall man. "I have to admit I prefer a savory blintz. No sweet tooth, I'm afraid." He smiled brightly, blandly. "The ones with caviar are my favorite."

"Caviar is fish," said the short man. "I don't like fish."

"Technically—" Theo began, but his father cut him off.

"Who are you people?" Mr. Biedermann said to the men. "Who buzzed you into this building?"

"We buzzed ourselves in," said the short man.

"And how did you do that?" said Mrs. Biedermann, and swept her own jacket aside so the men could see the badge on her belt.

The tall man held up a large and bony hand. "Let me back up a bit. I'm Mr. Stoop and this is Mr. Pinscher. You must be Mr. and Mrs."—he consulted his clipboard—"Biedermann."

"Mr. and *Detective* Biedermann."

"Detective. I'm sure you know why we're here, so I'm

just going to give you these documents and we'll move on to the next apartment." He held out a packet of papers. When the Biedermanns didn't take the papers, his smile drooped at the corners. "You didn't watch the press conference this morning?"

"What press conference?" said Mrs. Biedermann.

"It was all over the news. There are crews out in front of this building right now interviewing people."

"Interviewing who? What was all over the news?"

"That explains it," said Mr. Stoop, smile back on his face. He pressed the clipboard to his heart. "I myself believe it's important to keep up on current events, but not everyone agrees."

Mrs. Biedermann snatched the packet of papers away from the man. Theo stood and walked over to his parents. Up close, the tall man's skin was so white his freckles looked a bit like cereal floating in milk.

"You'll find all the relevant dates and numbers on the documents," said Mr. Stoop. "Don't hesitate to call should you have a question. Have a great—"

Mrs. Biedermann didn't look up from the papers. "Don't move. Either of you."

Mr. Pinscher rolled creepy, colorless eyes. Theo wondered if there was a scientific name for them, then decided *creepy* covered it.

Mr. Stoop heaved a great sigh. "Detective, we do have other documents to deliver."

"You can wait," said Mrs. Biedermann.

Mr. Stoop's attention moved from Mrs. Biedermann to Theo, to the blocks he still had clutched in his hands. "Those were my favorite toys when I was a child," said Mr. Stoop.

Child? Theo swallowed his annoyance. "They're not toys."

Mr. Pinscher snorted. Mr. Stoop's lips twisted in amusement. "Of course they're not." He gestured to the Tower of London with his chin. "Did you build that by yourself?"

"Yes," said Theo.

"No help from anyone else?"

"No."

"Not even your dad?"

"Why would my dad build my model for me?"

"And what's it supposed to be?"

"What?" said Theo.

"Is it a fantasy world? A school for wizards, perhaps?"

Theo stared up at the milk-skinned man and his cereal face, moles and freckles that spelled out nothing good. "I should have built the bridge."

Mrs. Biedermann touched Mr. Biedermann's arm.

"Larry, these papers say that they sold the building."

"Which building?" said Theo.

"This building," said Mr. Stoop.

Theo must not have heard the man right. He thought he said *this* building, but—

"That's impossible," said Mr. Biedermann.

"I'm afraid not," said Mr. Stoop. "I have to say that this wouldn't be such a surprise if you kept up on the news."

Theo looked at his mom and his dad. He looked at the Tower of London, at the unfinished bridge in pieces in the corner, at the blocks in his hands. Tess was just talking about this before she left, but Tess always worried for nothing, didn't she?

"This is a Morningstarr building," Theo said.

"Yes."

"So, it's impossible."

"Oh, it's possible," said Mr. Pinscher.

Theo felt his lips move, his mouth shaping the words. "Who did they sell to?" Even as he asked, he knew. He knew because Tess had somehow known all along.

"So, Slant is our new landlord?" Theo asked.

"I don't think so," said the short man.

Mrs. Biedermann said, "We have thirty days to vacate."

Theo took a step back as if someone had just shoved him. Vacate? In *thirty days*? It had taken him twice as long to build the model in the dining room. How would they pack everything up in thirty days?

And where would they go?

The tall man, Mr. Stoop, glanced over their heads, eyes darting around their apartment. Theo didn't have to turn around to see what the man saw: the well-worn furniture, webbed in cat hair; the books spilling out of the mismatched bookcases they'd bought at a flea market; the palm plant that had gotten so big that it grew in crazy loops at the top; Theo's sprawling model encroaching like a rising tide on the living room. A strange heat crept up Theo's neck into his cheeks. It wasn't grand, it wasn't even tidy, but it was their home.

To his mother, Theo said, "What will happen to this place?" But her face had gone stony, unreadable.

His mother tapped the paper in her hands. "I'm going to need confirmation of this."

"As you can see," said Mr. Stoop, "that is a legal document, signed, notarized, and served. But you can call the mayor's office if you'd like."

Theo squeezed the blocks so hard, the edges bit into his palms. He should have built the Morningstarr Tower like Tess had wanted. But how could he have known what was going to happen? That was Tess's thing, the what-if game she always played with herself, driving everyone else crazy. What if a great white shark swam up the Hudson River? What if a tornado touched down in the middle of Broadway? What if boys were girls and girls were cats? What if a greedy jerk bought your house right out from under you?

No, he shouldn't have built the Morningstarr Tower. He should have built 354 W. 73rd Street.

"Mom?"

In the doorway, Stoop and Pinscher parted to reveal Tess, frizzy hair coming loose from her braid, Nine hunched like a sad gargoyle beside her.

"What's going on?" she said. "There are all these people outside. They're saying . . . they're saying . . ."

Nine lowered her ears and hissed at Stoop and Pinscher, dropping some kind of paper she'd had clenched in her teeth. Mr. Pinscher bent to retrieve the paper, and Nine lunged with a yowl. Tess fought to control her cat, and everyone started shouting. Mr. Pinscher told Tess to call off her monster, Mr. Biedermann told the two creepy men that it was time for them to leave, and Mrs. Biedermann said something that Theo couldn't hear because a thin buzzing noise had filled his head, drowning everything and everyone out. His legs pivoted him, robot-marched him back to his model, stepped him over the wall. Like the debtors and disgraced royalty that had crossed the gates into the Tower of London before him, he stood in the courtyard, wondering how he had gotten there.

Tess, still wrestling with the cat, watched him from the doorway, frowning at him as if he were someone she'd met before but couldn't quite place. *Look at that boy in the dead-cat T-shirt. He seems so weird.*

The blocks dropped from Theo's hands and landed right on the Tower Green where the wives of Henry VIII had lost their heads.

And Theo—who, as it turned out, was neither calm nor well adjusted—lost his. He cranked up his foot and put it through the new bridge, the sound of the crash not nearly loud enough.

CHAPTER THREE

Jaime

While Tess Biedermann was trying to keep her monster cat from eating Mr. Stoop and Mr. Pinscher and Theo Biedermann was losing his head, Jaime Cruz remained blissfully unaware that anything had changed. Despite the commotion in the hallway and Mozart's Fortieth Symphony blasting inside his own apartment, he was fast asleep, big brown feet hanging over the edge of his twin bed. And he would have stayed asleep if his grandmother hadn't thrown open his bedroom door, waded through the piles of clothes and comic books, and given one big toe a hard pinch.

Jaime shot up. "WATCH OUT FOR THE ZOMBIES!"

His grandmother, who he called Mima because she

was like a mother to him, put her hands on her hips, raised one brow. "I am looking at a zombie right now."

"Mima?" Jaime said, blinking away dream-images of the shambling undead.

"No," she said. "It's the secretary of state. I'm declaring your room a disaster area."

Jaime found his glasses on his nightstand and put them on. His grandmother came into focus—short and wiry, thick dark curls shot with silver, her expression the usual mixture of fondness and exasperation.

"What time is it?" he said.

"Time to admit to your long-suffering grandmother that you spent the entire night playing video games. Again."

"Not the *entire* night," Jaime said, yawning.

"Jaime," she began, pronouncing his name the Cuban way, the *J* curling like smoke from the back of her throat. In addition to her native Spanish, she spoke five other languages fluently and another three well enough to make polite conversation, and she could ask for the ladies' room or a cup of coffee in a dozen more.

"Mima, it's the first week of summer vacation," Jaime said. "Kids are allowed to stay up playing video games during summer vacation."

"Says who?"

"It's in the Bill of Rights."

"Not the one I read. After breakfast, you can clean up all these books and papers and junk. It's a fire hazard. I won't have a fire hazard in my building, let alone in my own apartment."

"Okay, Mima."

She turned to walk out, stopped, and picked up a drawing from Jaime's desk. He had a Lion-powered tablet his father had sent him but preferred drawing on paper. The tablet had a stylus and all sorts of fancy settings, but the smooth, pliable screen seemed so indifferent to his efforts. Paper soaked up the ink, drank it in as if it were thirsty for it.

"Is this a zombie fighter?" said Mima, inspecting the drawing.

"Yeah," said Jaime.

"Not bad. I like the sword. And these are some fancy boots he's wearing."

"See, I told you I wasn't playing games the whole night."

"No, you were drawing cartoons," she said, putting the sketch back on the desk.

"What's wrong with that?"

She looked at that *Spider-Man* movie poster over his bed—Miles Morales leaping from top of the Morningstarr

Tower, shooting webs in both directions. "As long as you keep your grades up," she said, "there's nothing wrong with it."

Jaime didn't answer; he didn't need to. They had this conversation all the time. Jaime would stay up too late with his computer games and his drawings; Mima would worry he was wasting his brains on foolishness and more foolishness; Jaime would point out his straight As; Mima would say that foolishness always catches up to a person sooner or later. Usually, she would launch into a lecture about his mother and the groundbreaking work she had done so many years ago, and his father and all the sacrifices he'd made. But not today. Maybe because it was summer vacation. Maybe because she knew that his best friends, Dash Ursu and Eli Avasthi, were both already at camp and Jaime would be alone till school started again. Maybe she really did like the zombie fighter and his awesome boots.

"Come on, lazy boy. Get out of bed and I'll make you some eggs," Mima said, and swept from the room.

Jaime climbed from the bed, stretched. He fed his hamster-hogs, Napolean and Tyrone, both girls. Napolean curled up in his palm the way she always did, naked little elf feet sticking straight up. Her "quills" had been rendered filmy and fluffy by the genetic engineering, and she emitted little happy squeaks as he rubbed her soft belly. Tyrone, on the other hand, squealed indignantly when he tried to catch her. She took to her wheel and ran like she was trying to power the entire cage for liftoff to a more just universe. Tyrone was not to be messed with.

"That's right, Tyrone," said Jaime. "Don't let anybody get you down."

The delicious smell of eggs and peppers wafted down the hall and into his room, so he put Napolean back in the cage. He pulled on his favorite painter's pants and a Mister Terrific T-shirt, washed up, and slouched toward the kitchen. The short hallway was lined floor to ceiling with photographs of his whole family, his grandparents when they were young, long before his granddad passed. But mostly the pictures were of his parents—his mom splashing in the surf with her brother and sister on a beach in Trinidad, his father running on a soccer field in college, his mom again working in her first laboratory. As he did every morning, Jaime paused in front of his favorite, a picture of his mother holding a chubby little boy on her lap, both of them laughing, bright silver smiles in happy brown faces. She looked so young in the picture, too young for the chubby little boy to be hers, but she'd been thirty-two and a doctor when the photo was taken. It was the last photo his father ever took of his mother. It seemed impossible that a woman whose smile was so radiant had died just a few weeks later and that the little boy was now as tall as she was then.

"If this food gets cold, I will be forced to feed it to your Franken-rodents," Mima called.

He touched the frame of the photo once, then tore his eyes away from the picture. "Coming."

Jaime sat at the table just as Mima scooped some eggs, onions, and peppers onto his plate. "What's up for you today, Mima?"

Mima exchanged Mozart's Fortieth for Tito Puente's "Oye Como Va." She waved her spatula to the beat. "Oh, Mr. Perlmutter complained that the moldings around his window need to be caulked, that the Morningstarr seal is coming loose again. And the Hornshaws have a leaking bathroom sink. And the Ms. Gomezes are having trouble with the air-conditioning."

Mima had been the building manager of 354 W. 73rd Street for more than thirty years. Delicate as she looked, she could snake a drain, plaster a ceiling, replace a lock, refinish a floor, rewire a washing machine, unclog a toilet, get out a juice stain, install a ceiling fan, operate a jigsaw, douse a kitchen fire, program a cable box, and probably survive in the wild with only a nail file and a thimble. Jaime's dad said he got his mechanical aptitude from Mima and not Jaime's grandfather, who could barely operate a toaster without injuring himself.

Jaime took a bite of the eggs. His dad would be in Sudan for three months, working to start up a new solar power plant. The money was too good to pass up, he'd said. But Jaime couldn't help wishing he'd passed it up anyway.

"Did Dad call this morning?"

"No," said Mima, "but you know how busy he gets."

"He's always busy," Jaime muttered.

"Your father has sacrificed a lot for you, mi vida."

Jaime nodded and shoveled more eggs into his mouth so he wouldn't get another lecture on hard work, sacrifice, respecting one's elders, and cleaning one's plate after one's grandmother toils over the stove to feed you, lazy boy. Besides, he was starving.

He was halfway through a second helping of eggs when he finally heard the voices outside in the hallway, a sort of hum that got louder and louder, cutting into Tito's drums. Mima must have heard the hum, too, because she turned off the music. By the time she did, however, the voices had gone quiet.

"Cricket and Otto?" Jaime said.

"Those two have worn their mother out," Mima said. "She stays inside her apartment, slumped in front of the TV like one of your zombies. And this is why I didn't want that TV."

Jaime didn't bother explaining that zombies wouldn't exactly appreciate TV. He took one last bite of eggs and went to the door. He opened it to find a man so short that Jaime looked straight over the top of his head before even registering anyone was there. The man thrust a packet of papers past Jaime to his grandmother, who had come to the door. "Have a nice day," the man said, his voice toneless as the whine of an insect.

Mima took the papers and said, "What are these?" but the man was already whirring away.

Jaime stepped into the hall. At one end of the passage, an impossibly, unreasonably, insanely tall man waited at the elevator. He nodded at Jaime as if in greeting, but Jaime had never seen him before. The little man reached his companion. The elevator opened and the two stepped inside, turning around to face Jaime. The pair of them seemed like something out of a comic book, one so stretched out and hollow cheeked and mole specked, the other so punched down and razor burned and lizard lipped. Jaime itched to draw them. As the elevator doors closed, the little man waggled his fingers. *Bye-bye.*

"Did you hear?"

Jaime turned his head toward the other end of the hallway. Tess Biedermann stood in front of her open apartment door, her hand tugging at the leash of her ginormous spotted cat, her face greenish and crumpled like a tissue.

Jaime didn't know Tess well, but he knew her well enough to know that it would take something awful to make her look like that.

His own throat felt strangely tight when he said, "Hear what?"

Jaime sat on the Biedermanns' couch, chewing on some sort of pastry that Mr. Biedermann called a blintz, which sounded more like something that happened to you rather than something you ate. *That guy? Oh, yeah, he was totally blintzed. Look at him. He's just a zombie now.*

Mima, as blintzed as Jaime was by the news that their building had been sold right out from under them, was doing what she always did when she was stressed: cleaning. She'd found an ancient hand vacuum shaped like an anteater and methodically removed the cat hair from every piece of furniture in the Biedermanns' living room. When she was done with the furniture, she followed Mr. Biedermann around making odd gestures in the air behind him, as if she were trying to figure out how to vacuum his pants without being rude.

But then, Mima wasn't the only one behaving oddly. The Biedermanns' apartment was packed with people—all of them blintzed out of their minds. It was as if the entire population of 354 W. 73rd Street had decided that a police detective like Mrs. Biedermann would surely be able to rescue them from this disaster. She could call in some favors, help them fight city hall, and they wouldn't be forced from their home.

So, Mrs. Biedermann was making calls. From the look on her face, she didn't seem to be getting the answers she wanted, but she kept calling. Mr. Biedermann had put up a big pot of coffee and was passing out cups. Mr. and Mrs. Adeyemi huddled with Mr. and Mrs. Yang and Ms. and Ms. Gomez. The Hornshaws talked to Mr. and Mrs. Moran while the Morans' daughter, Cricket, darted through the apartment on her tricycle. Her little brother, Otto, demonstrated a blur of "karate" moves on top of the coffee table until his father plucked him off it. Under the coffee table, the giant spotted cat sprawled on what looked like a pile of laundry. Mr.

Perlmutter, who had lived approximately a thousand years so far and didn't seem too happy about it, brandished his walker at no one in particular. Tess Biedermann went around the room, asking various adults if they should band together and sue the city. The adults did what adults usually do to kids during a crisis: they ignored her.

Most fascinating to Jaime was Theo Biedermann, who was stomping through a huge, sprawling Lego castle like a slow-motion Godzilla destroying a fictional Tokyo. He'd reel back his foot and send it through a wall. Reel it back again and knock out a tower. Kind of horrifying, kind of awesome. Even Otto stopped wriggling in his father's arms to watch the blocks flying in every direction.

Watching Theo got a lot less awesome and way more horrifying when Mr. Moran pointed at the blocks and said, "That's exactly what Slant will do to this building. Knock it down to the ground. He'll build condos that cost millions apiece and we'll all end up in Staten Island."

"Try Idaho," said Tess Biedermann, who elbowed her way into the conversation.

"Are you sure there's nothing we can do?" said Mrs. Hornshaw.

"The detective is making some calls."

Mr. Moran said, "She's not going to be able to do anything. The city owns the building; the city can sell it."

Mrs. Yang said, "We're nothing to any of them."

The taller Ms. Gomez agreed. "We're bugs."

Otto yelled, "I'M NOT A BUG I'M A NINJA!"

"But I thought this place was a historical landmark," said Mrs. Adeyemi. "I thought it was protected."

"The motion never passed. Who do you think is on that board?" said Mr. Yang.

Mr. Moran nodded. "Bajillionaires."

Theo paused midstomp. "There is no such number as 'bajillion,'" he said, and then brought his foot down. Blocks sprayed up.

"Can't we sue?" said Tess, "I mean, if we all band together . . ."

Mrs. Biedermann laid her phone on the kitchen counter. It hadn't even made a sound, but everyone stopped talking. Theo Biedermann stopped stomping. Cricket zoomed around the room on her trike till her dad caught her.

"Well," Mrs. Biedermann began. And that's all she had to say for every face in the room to fall.

"What?" said Tess. "Well, what?"

"I'm sorry," said Mrs. Biedermann.

"You're sorry," spit Mr. Perlmutter. He brandished his walker again, then hobbled out the door.

The rest of the people took a last sip of coffee, a last bite of blintz. Mrs. Moran took ahold of the trike while Mr. Moran gathered one kid under each big pink arm.

Cricket, dangling in her father's grasp, looked at Jaime. "Your hair looks like little worms."

"Be nice, Cricket," said her mother wearily.

"My hair *is* little worms," Jaime told Cricket. "They dance when no one is looking."

"Mommy, I want hair worms that dance when people are looking. I want *famous* hair."

"Sure you do," her mother said, patting her own short and tidy black 'fro.

"I'M A NINJA!" shouted Otto.

"You're just a dumb baby," said Cricket to her brother, who had Cricket's bronze skin but limp hair. "You're not famous at all."

Jaime sat on that couch, feeling like a dumb baby, not famous at all. Slant, Inc., had offered everyone relocation money, but not nearly enough to keep everyone in this borough, let alone this neighborhood. And who would find Mima another job? She loved this building. She loved the goofy elevator and the old windows

and the ancient plumbing and the plaster that always
needed fixing. For Mima, there would never be another
building like this one. She had stopped following Mr.
Biedermann around and was now standing alone in the
middle of the room, frowning at the vacuum as if it had
failed her.

Plus. Plus.

His mom had lived here.

Mrs. Biedermann scooped up her phone and made
another call. "Ronnie? Yeah, it's me. Great, thanks.
You? Glad to hear it."

"Mom, I just need to talk to you for a minute," Tess
Biedermann said. "If we could—"

Her mother held up a hand, kept talking. "Listen,
your sister's a real estate agent, right? She any good?
Be honest! Okay. Can I have her name and number?
Something's come up and we might have to find a new
place. Yeah, I know. I'll explain later. I have a pen, go
ahead."

Tess Biedermann finally gave up. She slumped on
the couch next to Jaime, the two of them watching Theo
knock down the last wall standing. Tess said, "He never
does stuff like that."

"Like what?"

"Never freaks out. Never messes things up."

"Oh," said Jaime. He didn't know what else to say. Everything was already messed up.

The Biedermanns' apartment emptied out. Mr. Biedermann gathered the plates and coffee cups. Mima put the little vacuum back wherever she'd found it. Jaime stood to follow her out, but she said, "Why don't you stay with your friends? I have some calls to make, too."

Friends? He'd gone to grammar school with the twins and knew them a little. But they were like a set of salt and pepper shakers; they didn't seem to need anyone else. Jaime wasn't sure what *he* needed. He wanted to crawl under the coffee table and curl up with the cat till the whole thing was over, but what kind of chicken did that? He should march his famous hair to the mayor's office and stage some sort of protest. Make speeches or chain himself to a radiator or go on a hunger strike or all three. Something. *Something.*

Mrs. Biedermann covered the phone. "Tess? Did you sort Grandpa's mail yet?"

"What? No. Who cares about—"

"Why don't you bring it upstairs and put the new batch with the rest?"

"But—"

Mrs. Biedermann's eyes landed on Jaime. "Maybe

Jaime wants to go with you. And the cat. And your brother, before he decides to start kicking our furniture out the window."

"What does it matter?" Tess grumbled. But she whistled for Nine. The cat crept out from under the coffee table and Tess slipped her into a harness.

"Come on, Theo," Tess said. "Mom wants to get rid of us."

Mr. Biedermann put a stack of plates in the sink with a rattle. "Tess, you know that's not what your mother meant."

Tess didn't answer. She marched toward the door. Turned. Glared. At both of them. "Are you guys just going to stand there, or are you coming with me?"

Theo blinked, focused on Jaime for the first time since Jaime had arrived in the apartment. "Well? What do you think?"

"I think you look a little blintzed to me," Jaime said.

Theo smiled, a tiny smile that disappeared as fast as it had appeared. "We're all a little blintzed." He stepped over the destruction and followed Tess out of the apartment.

"Thanks, Mr. and Mrs. Biedermann," Jaime said, though he wasn't sure what he was thanking them for, really.

Mrs. Biedermann waved, continued her phone call.

"Bye, Jaime," said Mr. Biedermann absently. "Hope you'll come by again."

"Sure," Jaime said, the word thick on his tongue. "We have a whole month."

In the hallway, as Jaime was shutting the Biedermanns' door behind him, he noticed something white and crumpled on the floor. He picked it up. An envelope with a gold seal and what looked like teeth marks. How upset had Mima been that she'd missed a piece of trash littering up her building? That she didn't stop and pick it up? That none of the other tenants had?

He turned the envelope over, smoothed it out. The words TRUST NO ONE TRUST NO ONE TRUST NO ONE screamed at him. "Now you tell me," he muttered.

"Jaime?" Tess called. She was holding the elevator with a stiff arm and a furious expression, wispy tendrils of hair standing out in a corona all around her head. She reminded him of Tyrone the hamster-hog trying to power her way to a more just universe.

Don't let anybody get you down.

Jaime folded the envelope and slipped it into a pocket. "Coming."

CHAPTER FOUR

Tess

The major symptoms of shock: weak pulse, clammy skin, shallow breathing, dizziness, light-headedness, confusion. To this list, Tess added numb lips, itchy toes, gnashing teeth, and a deep desire to toss the nearest real estate developer into the Hudson. Maybe *all* the real estate developers. And their creepy minions. Where does a person find minions anyway? Was there a job board online somewhere? How would an advertisement for minions read? *Have you ever been told your smile makes people uncomfortable? Does your voice sound like a dentist's drill? Does your gaze cause others to break out in hives? Have you misplaced your moral compass?*

"Tess, are you okay?" Jaime asked.

Right. She wasn't alone in the elevator. Sometimes

she forgot she wasn't alone, like when she walked down the street and realized she'd been mumbling to herself for blocks.

"Tess?" Jaime said, pushing his glasses up the bridge of his nose.

"Yeah?" said Tess.

"You were mumbling to yourself," Theo said.

"I don't mumble," Tess said.

"I wasn't talking about the mumbling, I was talking about your eye," said Jaime.

"My eye?"

"It's sort of . . . twitching."

"My eye is really, really angry."

"Makes sense," said Jaime.

But the twitching was contagious, Tess noticed. As they rode to the penthouse, Jaime's fingers typed out manic messages against the leg of his jeans. Theo's foot tapped as if he was reliving the way he'd destroyed the Tower of London. Nine paced the length of her leash, pausing only to sniff at their sneakers. Even the elevator was twitchy; it lurched forward, stopped, jerked back, retraced its path, then lurched and jerked again.

Finally, they reached the seventh floor and the elevator released them into the corridor, which smelled of oatmeal, musty newspaper, and just the tiniest bit of lavender. Tess dug around in her messenger bag, pulled out the keys to her grandfather's apartment, and unlocked the door.

Grandpa's apartment had three bedrooms, a kitchen, a living room and dining room, even a library. He'd offered to switch apartments with the Biedermanns once, but Mom said there was no way that Grandpa would be able to fit his stuff anywhere else.

"I've never been up to the penthouse," said Jaime.

Theo grunted. "My mom says a more accurate name would be 'the fire hazard on the top floor.'"

Which was true. The apartment was packed with books and maps and parchments, strange gadgets designed by the Morningstarrs and others, piles of newspaper that formed little chimneys all over the place. How would they sort it all? And where would they move it?

Tess let go of Nine's leash and the cat pranced between the chimneys. Huge windows lined one wall, motes of dust dancing in the bright sunshine. Nine leaped up to catch them like a bear snapping at spawning salmon.

"Wow," said Jaime. "This is . . ."

"A mess?" said Theo.

"Amazing," said Jaime.

Clanking sounds erupted from the kitchen, followed by some high-pitched squealing that pasted Nine's ears to the top of her head.

"I thought your grandpa wasn't here," said Jaime.

"He's not," Theo said.

"Then who—"

A man dressed entirely in silver armor complete with helmet clomped into the living room. He held a tray with a plate of cookies and three overfull glasses of water that sloshed all over his chain-mail gloves.

Jaime's mouth dropped open. "Is that what I think it is?"

"It is," said Theo. "A Lancelot. Servant model. Built by the Morningstarrs, based on designs by Leonardo da Vinci. Something they did when they were young, but the machines caught on."

Tess said, "In the early eighteen hundreds, everybody had a Lance—well, all the rich people had a Lance—but they went out of style more than a hundred years ago."

"Maybe if you got him a different outfit," said Jaime.

"Lances can get destructive when left alone too long," Theo said. "My grandpa's always finding the toilet paper pulled off the rolls and dragged around the house."

Jaime nodded. "So they're like big metal kittens?"

Lance held out the tray to Jaime, metal arms squeaking.

"He makes the cookies himself," said Tess. "Oatmeal.

They're pretty good, usually. He must have made these before my grandpa . . . well, before he left. They might be a little stale."

"Stale cookies are still cookies." Jaime took a couple of cookies and a glass of water. "Thanks, uh, man."

Tess wasn't hungry, but she took a cookie, and Theo did, too. Lance clomped back into the kitchen, where he started banging around pots and pans. If he had the ingredients, Lance could make cookies, beef stew, vegetable soup, or pancakes; you never knew which. Normally, just the thought of an empty suit of armor whipping up a batch of pancakes would make Tess laugh, but now . . .

She put the water and cookie on top of a stack of papers, her stomach clenching and unclenching in its own interpretative dance of catastrophe. When she went back downstairs, her parents would tell her to stop worrying so much, that worrying didn't solve anything. But worrying was supposed to keep bad things from happening—that was the entire point of worrying. You said to yourself, I hope I don't die in a bizarre accident with a revolving door, and you didn't, see? *Because* you worried about it.

She felt as if she had been smacked in the face with a revolving door. A stale cookie wasn't going to fix that.

But what would?

What could?

Tess said, "Well, I can't say I didn't expect this."

"That your Lance would need some oil?" Jaime said.

"That Slant would eventually get our building," Tess said. "That he'd want to destroy it."

"I didn't expect it," said Theo. "Not in our lifetime. It's . . . it's . . ."

"An affront to decency?" Tess said. "An affront to humanity? An affront to every living creature in the known and unknown universes?"

"It's pretty bad," Jaime said. He took a bite of a cookie, raised his brows, and popped the rest of the cookie into his mouth. "I wish we could do something."

"Like what?" said Theo.

The cat banked off the window, flipped in the air. Jaime wandered around the apartment, sipping his water, picking up framed photographs and putting them down again, pressing middle C on the baby grand piano that Grandpa used to play before he got sick. Tess almost explained about Grandpa, about where he'd gone, but Jaime was examining a Duke map of New Amsterdam, 1664. Next to that was another map that showed New York City under British occupation from 1776 to 1783. And then a drawing of the Tombs, a fortress prison on

Centre Street built around 1830 in the style of ancient Egyptian architecture, right next to the Five Points neighborhood.

Jaime leaned in to look more closely. "What is this place?"

"That's the Tombs courthouse and prison," Tess said. "The building's still there. It's where my mom works. But the neighborhood around it was torn down a long time ago. It was mostly immigrants living in cruddy buildings that were sort of sinking into the ground. Lots of crime and stuff. The Morningstarrs were immigrants, too, and when they first came, that's where they lived. Later, they fought to get the place cleaned up, the people fed, schools built, things like that." She nodded at a portrait of the Morningstarrs on the opposite wall. In it, the twins looked like two cotton swabs—long faced with wispy tufts of white hair.

"Not everyone wants poor people fed and educated," said Jaime.

"Or living in decent housing," said Tess. Again her stomach accordioned in, accordioned out. She imagined the people of the Five Points who had just arrived in America, whole families crammed into a single hot and dirty room, the stink of Collect Pond, fouled with factory runoff and waste, seeping in through the racked walls. She hoped that Idahovians were against fouling ponds with factory runoff. She hoped they supported decent housing.

Jaime moved from the drawing of the Tombs to a framed newspaper clipping hanging lopsided. "'*New York Sun*, 1855,'" he read. "'Morningstarrs leave first clue in city-wide treasure hunt.'"

Theo recited, "42, 1, 2; 42, 20, 7; 42, 1, 10; 42, 2, 17; 42, 2—"

"Stop showing off, Theo." Tess waved her hand. To Jaime, she said, "He remembers every number he hears and likes to remind everyone."

"I remember studying the first clue in grammar school," said Jaime. "It's a book cipher using an Edgar Allan Poe story."

"'The Purloined Letter.' From a magazine called *The Gift*. My grandpa has a couple of copies of that magazine, too," Tess said, pointing. "Right on that shelf."

Jaime wandered over to a nearby bookcase, scanned it, and pulled out the magazine, the pages of which were laminated.

"The first number is the page number, the second number is the line number on that page, and the third number is the word in that line," Theo said.

"'It begins, as everything does, with a lady. Her

book holds your keys,'" said Tess. "We know. Everybody knows."

Theo said, "But did you know the word *begins* doesn't actually appear in the story, only the word *begin*?"

"What does it matter?" said Tess.

"Details always matter," Theo said. "Like the fact that the Morningstarrs used that story in the first place. They could have used the Constitution. The Bill of Rights. The Bible. Something by Dickens or Melville or even a recipe for a cake. They could have used anything. But they used a detective story about something hidden in plain sight, which pretty much describes all the clues they left."

"They used a detective story because they had a sense of humor," Tess said.

"I wouldn't go that far," said Theo.

"I thought they were real sticks in the mud," Jaime said. "Never laughed. Never smiled." All three of them looked again at the portrait of the Morningstarrs, who seemed to be glowering at them the way eagles eyed their prey.

Tess crossed her arms. "It's just a theory my grandpa was working on. He said that anyone who designed machines the way they did had to have a sense of humor."

"They designed the machines the way they did

because they thought people would accept them if they looked more like natural creatures," said Theo.

Tess waved him off. "You sound like a history book."

"Thank you," said Theo.

Jaime leafed through the magazine, counted down the lines on the pages. Then he said, "That's your grandpa's thing, right? Studying the Morningstarrs? Trying to solve the Cipher?"

"It was his thing," said Tess.

"What happened?" said Jaime.

"He just gave up, that's all."

Remarkably, Theo still had the energy to roll his eyes. "It's not like he could help it."

"Yeah, well," Tess said, knowing she was being unfair, even awful, but still wanting to argue. Her mind raced with what-if questions, each worse than the last.

"Stop catastrophizing," Theo said.

Jaime looked from Theo to Tess. "Is that a real word?"

"I am *not* catastrophizing," snapped Tess, annoyed that Theo could read her so easily.

A loud crash echoed from the kitchen. Theo said, "You're not the only one who's mad, you know."

"I know," she said. But sometimes it felt like it. The therapist her parents brought her to see liked Tess to do a lot of drawings. The therapist was a nice man with a bushy mustache; he looked like a portrait from another century. He said, "It's interesting that you drew yourself with this little golden crown on your head. What does the crown mean to you?"

"That's not a crown," she'd told him. "That's a nimbus of outrage."

Lance clomped back into the living room with the tray of stale cookies. Jaime gave him the empty glass, took two more cookies. Theo stuck a hand in his thick hair and held it there, his thinking pose. The cat stopped leaping and sat in front of the window, staring out at the middle distance. Tess let out a sigh, and with the sigh her outrage leaked away, leaving her with a hollow in her gut the size of a city. She slumped in the nearest chair, pulled the strap of her bag over her head, and set the bag on the floor. A stack of Grandpa's unfinished crossword puzzles sat by the chair, as if Grandpa had been paging through the endless clues. "Almond capital of the world." "Bug bite." "Wrong."

"Look at this place," she said. "Where's Grandpa Ben going to put it all when the building is gone? Where are any of us going to go? There has to be a way to stop this."

"We could stage a protest," Jaime said. "Go on a hunger strike."

"My mom would never let me go on a hunger strike," said Theo.

Jaime sighed. "Now that you mention it, neither would my grandmother." He glumly ate another cookie.

"If we can't keep Slant from knocking down a building he owns," Tess said, "I wish we could find a way to buy it back."

"Okay," said Theo, "but where are any of us going to get that kind of money?"

Jaime finished the cookie, found an antique monocle sitting on a shelf. He took off his glasses, blew the dust off the monocle, and held it up to one eye, making that eye look twice as large as the other, deep brown with a ring of gold around the edge of the iris. "Wouldn't it be great if we could find a treasure? We could buy back the building."

"Well, if we could solve the Cipher, we'd—" Tess began, and then stopped. If they could solve the Cipher, then maybe they'd find treasure. More than treasure. The secret of the Morningstarrs. The reason for all these buildings, all these things they made. That had to be worth something.

It had to be worth *everything*.

"People have been trying to solve the Old York Cipher

for one hundred sixty years," Theo said. "I'm not sure there is a solution."

Of course there was a solution. There had to be a solution.

"There's a solution," said Tess.

"How do you know?" Theo said.

"I just do."

"I don't," said Theo. "The Morningstarrs valued process over product. Or maybe the process is the product. The puzzle is its own reward. That's what Grandpa Ben said, anyway."

"Yeah, well, Grandpa Ben's not here," said Tess.

Theo extricated his hand from his unruly hair. "What's your point?"

"What if we did solve the Old York Cipher?"

"Tess . . . ," Theo began.

"I'm serious!" Tess said. "If we solved it, we'd get the treasure and we'd also prove it wasn't a hoax. It would be news all over the world. The city couldn't sell this building or any of the other Morningstarr buildings, either. The buildings would be too important to sell."

Jaime stared at her with his giant eye. "I'm not so sure about that," he said. "A lot of things are for sale that shouldn't be for sale." He put the monocle back on the shelf and used the bottom edge of his T-shirt to polish his glasses. "What if your brother's right and the Morningstarrs just wanted a whole lot of people running around trying to figure out clues? What if your grandpa was right and this is one big joke?"

"This is no joke," said Tess. The top of her head was twitchy, itchy, as if her nimbus of outrage were getting too tight for just one person. "This is our home."

Jaime slipped the glasses back on, blinked. Theo shifted in his seat. Nine padded over to Tess, laid her chin upon Tess's knee. Even Lance went quiet. Tess knew what they were thinking. How could a bunch of seventh graders solve a mystery that people had been trying to solve for more than a century? People including her own grandfather? Grandpa Ben had tried; he had tried his entire adult life. Up till now, it hadn't mattered that Grandpa hadn't found an answer. The important things couldn't be rushed. You had to dream your way to them, like a luftmensch, like the Morningstarrs themselves. She touched a page of Grandpa's unfinished crossword puzzle. Tempus fugit. What if you had no time left to dream?

"It's not just about us, guys," Tess said. "A lot of people live in this building. People who don't have the money to just pick up and move because some megalomaniac says we have to. We can't sit around waiting for Slant to send his wrecking balls." This wasn't catastrophizing anymore. This was telling the truth. A lump hard as a pebble tumbled in her throat, and she couldn't seem to swallow it back no matter how many times she tried. "We can't just sit here, Theo. We can't. We *can't*."

"Okay, okay," Theo said, one palm up like a traffic cop. He gave her that look that said he just might go along, not because he thought it was a good idea, but because Tess needed him to, because he was her brother, because he was not a robot. At least not today.

Tess turned to Jaime. They'd gone to elementary school with him, they'd seen him around the building for years, but they didn't *know* him, not really. He had his own friends and always seemed way too cool to hang out with them—the nerd twins, those fuzzy-haired weirdos. And yet Jaime was here, and he was listening, not pointing, not laughing. Tess cocked her head, a question.

"It's my home, too," Jaime said quietly. Through the dancing dust motes, something passed between them. A decision. An agreement.

Theo's hand dropped to his lap. He frowned, his shaggy brows meeting in the middle just the way they had when he was smashing the Tower of London to bits.

"Let's say for a second that we are going to try to solve the Cipher," he said. "We have to do it right."

Jaime nodded. "We should start at the beginning."

They were humoring her or maybe they were humoring themselves, but Tess didn't care. She smiled. "'It begins, as everything does, with a lady.'"

"Right," said Jaime. "So let's go see her."

CHAPTER FIVE
Theo

A what-if question: What if everything you're doing is pointless?

This was what Theo was thinking as Jaime texted his grandmother and Tess called their parents to tell them they were going out for the afternoon. And it was what Theo was thinking when the elevator looped in confused circles before depositing them in the lobby. He was still thinking it as they walked over to 72nd Street, and then headed toward the Underway entrance on Broadway. Pointless, pointless, pointless. Like building the entire Tower of London plus the London Bridge, only to kick it to rubble.

But Tess was bouncing on her toes the way she did when she was excited, and Nine bounced alongside her.

Maybe this trip wasn't so pointless if it could make Tess bounce like that, at least for a little while. He just hoped she wasn't too devastated when it all came to nothing. Because it would.

Grandpa Ben growled in Theo's head: *The only thing that's truly pointless is kvetching about the pointlessness of things. What is the real point: the destination or the journey?*

So, Theo tried to focus on the journey, which helps when you're trying to run for the train without tripping. They shoved their tokens into the turnstiles and burst onto the platform just as the Number 1 arrived. The cars were the same sleek, silvery steel they had been in the time of the Morningstarrs—the cars never broke down and so never needed to be replaced. They could travel below- or aboveground, with some routes suspended high over the city, wound like vines around the buildings.

But today's ride would be belowground, so they settled into the spotless, plush red seats. No one dared eat or drink on the immaculate trains, because if you did, you would be thrown off at the next stop, no questions asked. In the corner of the car, a uniformed Guildman, sallow and sullen, sat in a glass box, glaring at the passengers as if every single one of them were an interloper, an intruder in his clean and perfect world. The Guild-man's gaze lingered on Nine the cat, but the cat was wearing her service-animal harness and was perched still as a sphinx. No out-of-control behavior, no gacked-up hairballs, no reason to toss them all off. Nine didn't even chase the delicate metal caterpillar parading up and down the train car, scouring the dirt left by so many shoes, as it did every hour. The Guildman watched Nine lifting one paw, then the other, to let the caterpillar clean beneath, and frowned. Theo couldn't be sure, but the Guildman seemed disappointed.

Theo wasn't the only one to think so. Jaime pulled a small notebook and a pencil from one of his many pockets and did a quick sketch of the Guildman, giving the guy a blue cape, a mouth like a nutcracker, and a thought bubble that said, *"No vermin on the train."*

A good sketch, if you liked comic-book kind of stuff. Theo said, "Where's the vermin?"

Jaime shrugged. "We're the vermin."

They were, sort of. Scuttling underground, not very different from the rats that used the Underway tunnels to get from one place to another. But Theo had also seen lower Manhattan from above during a solarship tour, seen the way the tufted green carpet of Battery

Park spread at the feet of the winking glass towers of the financial district. Grandpa Ben had been okay then. Mostly.

"Look, Theo," he'd said, pointing out the window. "Aren't humans capable of the most amazing things? Isn't nature? Look how blue the grass is!"

"You mean green?"

Grandpa laughed. "Yes, green. Of course."

Theo didn't know whether it made him feel better or worse that Grandpa Ben would never know how truly rotten humans were. Or maybe he had known all along and tried too hard to forget it. Grandpa remembered everything until he didn't. What kind of journey was that?

Tess nudged his knee.

"What?"

"You're doing that thing with your lip."

"I am not."

He was, though. Pinching and pulling on the bottom lip like he trying to yank it over his head. He let go. Next to him, Jaime ignored the Weird Things Theo Was Doing to His Face and kept drawing. He added the outlines of passengers and a picture of Darnell Slant in the middle of his drawing. Cartoon Slant announced that he'd just bought the Underway and they all needed to get off the train forever. The speech bubble said, "Walking is good for all you commoners!"

A half hour later, Theo and the rest of the commoners walked out of the station and onto the esplanade that bordered the park. Sunbathers and Frisbee players dotted the lawns while the sun blazed the nearby Hudson silver. They dodged Starrboarders and bladers and hordes of giggling teenagers all punching one another for no good reason. They hauled Nine away from all the curious babies who wanted to hug her and away from all the parents afraid that Nine wanted to make snacks out of the babies.

They passed a group of girls, black and brown, jumping double Dutch and singing the Cipher song:

> *"Lady Liberty was number one,*
> *Clue, clue, who's got the clue?*
> *City hall where George had fun,*
> *Clue, clue, you've got the clue.*
> *A diary in a library,*
> *Clue, clue, who's got the clue?*
> *Puzzle out the penitentiary,*
> *Clue, clue, you've got the clue.*
> *John Bowne House, Quaker, Quaker,*
> *Clue, clue, who's got the clue?*

Prison Ship, gonna meet your maker,
Clue, clue, you've got the clue. . . ."

The rest of the song faded away as they walked. At
Castle Clinton, Theo and Tess and Jaime lined up to
get tickets for the ferry. When this place was still called
Castle Garden, Theo's great-great-grandfather Emil
Adler had lined up here, too, with only the change of
clothes and a pocket watch—all he'd brought with him
from Germany—to sell for food and lodging. Theo had
never been that desperate, never been that hungry. He
tried to be grateful for that the way his parents and
grandparents always reminded him to be, but today,
gratitude seemed impossible.

They bought their tickets and boarded the ferry,
squeezing their way through the crowd to the railing.
He'd ridden the ferry so many times with his grandparents that the press of the wind and the smell of the
water made him feel less weird, more like himself. In
the distance, the Liberty Statue rose out of the water, as
familiar as a member of the family. Made out of copper,
still gleaming bright and reddish brown because of a
special treatment that kept it from oxidizing, she stood
on a pedestal, a book curled in one arm, a torch held
high in her other hand. On her right, an eagle perched

on a tree branch, its wings just beginning to spread. On her left, a globe topped a short pillar. One foot was chained, the other had broken free.

"The last time I came here I was in kindergarten," said Jaime. "I forgot how big she is." He turned to a fresh page in his book and drew the statue. In his version, she was grinning. Her speech bubble said, "Yo!"

Yo, Theo thought, as the ferry docked on Liberty Island. *Yo,* as they powered past tourists to get to the statue. *Yo,* as he craned his neck to take the whole of Liberty in.

"Okay, the puzzle," Jaime said. "I remember this one from that video about the Morningstarrs we had to watch in third grade. You apply the sequence of numbers that was printed in the *New York Sun*—"

Theo recited, "42, 1, 2; 42, 20, 7; 42, 1, 10—"

"You just can't help yourself, can you?" Tess said.

"Right, and you apply those numbers to that Poe story," Jaime continued as if Theo hadn't interrupted, "and get 'It begins, as everything does, with a lady. Her book holds your keys.' I checked the magazine back at your grandfather's apartment, and it worked, so at least that part of the Cipher seems right."

Tess said, "And the chance of any other text giving a coherent riddle using that same sequence of numbers is . . . well, I don't know what it is but it's really low."

Theo said, "I know what—"

"Shut up," said Tess.

"Okay. So, the real question is whether the 'lady' in question is *this* lady?" Jaime pointed at Liberty.

"I think so," said Tess. "Not only is she a lady—*the* lady—with a book commemorating the signing of the Declaration of Independence, but it was the Morningstarrs who secured this island for the statue."

Jaime was still staring up at Liberty. "'July IV MDCCLXXI,'" he read. "July 4, 1776." He wrote the date into his sketchbook. If Theo had to guess, Jaime wasn't humoring Tess. He seemed to be taking this seriously. And of course Tess was.

Is it the destination or the journey, Theo?

Theo cleared his throat. "At first people thought the word *keys* meant literal keys."

"Yeah," said Jaime. "I remember there were people who insisted that a set of keys must be hidden inside the book."

"Someone even sued the city for the right to open the book with a blowtorch," Tess said. "But the word *keys* obviously meant 'keys to a puzzle.'"

"It's only obvious after the fact," said Theo, who, again, couldn't help himself.

A voice called: "You kids trying to solve the Cipher or something?"

They all turned, even Nine. A sallow guy trailing behind a large tour group smirked at them.

Theo tugged at his lip, let go. Why adults felt comfortable interrupting the conversations of people they didn't know was the most annoying sort of mystery.

"A regular bunch of Nancy Drews," the man said. He held a brown bottle, swirled the liquid inside it. Root beer? *Regular* beer? "That's cute." He chuckled to himself and took a sip.

Nine growled but Tess smiled sweetly the way she did when she was angry enough to bite. "Just a bunch of Nancy Drews, that's us all right."

The man chuckled again. Or maybe it was a chortle. Who could tell the difference?

Jaime had his sketchbook out and he was sketching a two-panel comic. In the first panel, the man was doubled over with the words *HEH HEH HEH HEH* all around him. In the second, he laughed so hard he dropped his bottle on his foot. *YEEOUCH!*

"Guys, let's go inside," Tess said. "If we're cute out here, I'm sure we'll be *super* adorable in there."

They left Guffaw Man still chortling and walked around to the other side of the statue, where glass doors led into a dark, damp gallery. Because it was so nice out, the gallery was completely empty but for them. All around were photos and plaques and posters about the history of the United States and about the making of the Liberty Statue. Tess and Jaime kept talking about the Cipher, how everyone figured that the date on Liberty's book was the key to another book cipher, so applied the number 741776 to the Declaration of Independence. When that didn't work, they applied it to the Bill of Rights, and then to all the plaques and displays in this gallery. And when *that* didn't work, people started thinking about women with books, writers like Harriet Beecher Stowe or Phillis Wheatley.

"It wasn't the date that was important," Jaime said. "It was the fact that it was talking about the Declaration of Independence."

"And George Washington first read the Declaration in front of a crowd at city hall in 1776. And that's where they found the next clue, in the cornerstone of the city hall built in 1811."

Theo sat on the nearest stone bench and tuned them out. In front of him, the original design of the statue was preserved behind glass. He didn't have to read the description to know that the Liberty Statue was erected in 1851 at a time of increasing turmoil. He could hear his grandpa telling him: "The Lady was meant to represent the hopes and dreams of a struggling nation. The hope that everyone in America could be free."

Free, sure. Free to have your home ripped out from under you. Free to be laughed at by jerkface tourists. Free to—

"Hey!"

Nine had some kind of white paper in her mouth and was hopping around like she'd caught herself a whole tuna and wasn't about to give it back.

"She grabbed it right out of my pocket," said Jaime.

Tess bent down and held Nine's harness to keep her still. "Isn't that my grandpa's letter?"

"It is?" Jaime said. "Oh, sorry. I found it in the hallway outside your apartment, then forgot I had it."

"Nine must have dropped it when Slant's minions came," Tess said. "She doesn't want to drop it now, though."

Jaime bent down next to Tess. He scratched Nine between her ears and under the chin until the cat purred like an Underway train. The letter fell to the ground.

"How did you do that?" said Tess. "I can never make her let go of anything!"

"I have a way with monster cats," Jaime said. He held the letter up to the light. TRUST NO ONE TRUST NO ONE

TRUST NO ONE was written all over it. He held it out to Tess. "You probably want to open it."

"It's probably from some goofball. My grandpa still gets loads of letters like that. And all of them say 'trust no one' or 'top secret' or 'for your eyes only' or 'the FBI is watching' or whatever."

"This one looks kind of old, though," said Jaime. He held it out to Theo. Theo shook his head. He didn't need to read a letter likely written by a guy who lived in his mom's basement and dressed entirely in duct tape.

"You can open it if you want, Jaime," Tess said. She stood and yawned. "I'm getting hungry. Maybe we should find some lunch before we go to city hall. A pretzel at least."

Theo should have figured that once they started, Tess would not stop until she'd reinvestigated every known clue. This was going to take forever, and it was still point—

"Guys?" Jaime said.

He had opened the envelope and was holding a worn and yellowed piece of paper, burned around the bottom edge. "So, the name of that Edgar Allan Poe story was 'The Purloined Letter.'"

"'Right,'" said Theo. "So?"

"Purloined. As in stolen."

"Yeah," said Theo. "And?"

"You also said that the Morningstarrs wouldn't do anything random, right?"

Because of the way Jaime held the paper and the envelope, only one word showed through his fingers: TRUST. Theo's heart hiccuped. "Right," he said.

"So," Jaime said, glancing up over the top of his glasses. "How funny would it be if I were holding a letter stolen from one of the Morningstarrs right here?"

CHAPTER SIX
Jaime

Jaime scanned the letter again and again, then sat down on a stone bench so abruptly that he bruised his own butt. Long before Jaime became Jaime—when he was just little James Eduardo with his big black glasses and the red cape his father bought him one Halloween—he was obsessed with superpowers. He stood in front of the microwave to absorb the rays; he tickled spiders in the hopes they'd bite; he chewed mint and bay leaves so he'd become immune to toxins; he made his own Cerebro using one of his grandma's colanders; he searched the sky at night sure a green lantern would find him, or maybe even the Green Goblin. There was no end to the ways a regular boy could become a super boy; his comic books were filled with them. Sometimes, a single superhero could have so many different beginnings that their stories were hard to keep straight. No, it didn't happen like that, it happened like this! No, this! Now, this! Wait . . . this!

Which one was the right story? Which one was the *real* story? And how would you ever be sure, when everything could always start all over again?

He told himself that one day something special would happen, something amazing and surprising and unexpected—a lightning strike, an alien invasion, an experiment gone wrong—and he would have to be prepared. He practiced ninja moves, sword thrusts, scissor kicks and uppercuts, speed running, wall climbing, and cat crouching, driving Mima crazy in the process. She would say, "Why do you not stop moving for one single second?"

And Jaime would say, "I am getting ready for my next beginning!"

Mima would say, "And I am getting ready to tie you to your chair!"

When he got to third grade at Charles Reason Elementary, he had to stop wearing the cape—because it wasn't a part of the uniform and because the other kids made fun of him. But the cape wasn't the only reason. They also made fun of him because he was tiny—the smallest, skinniest boy in the class, barely the size of a kindergartner. "Just one of your 'locs is bigger than you are," the other kids said.

Worse, what boy named Jaime Eduardo Cruz understood some Spanish but couldn't speak much beyond hola and gracias and uno, dos, tres? It didn't seem to matter that kids named Wagner couldn't speak German, or kids named Maccarone couldn't speak Italian. It didn't seem to matter that his mother spoke English, and had studied Latin at her high school in New Jersey, or that that his grandmother was fluent in so many languages that she occasionally sounded like translation software.

The two kids who didn't make fun of Jaime were the two kids who got made fun of *more* than Jaime. Because they didn't speak Spanish or German or Arabic or Chinese or Latin, they spoke some loopy, made-up language. And they spoke it a lot, mostly to each other.

"Whabat abarabe yaboabu drabawabing?"

Jaime looked up from his purple workbook. "Huh?"

A girl with a braid nearly down to her waist turned his purple workbook around so she could see. "Whabo abis thabis?"

He knew who she was, of course. She lived across the hall from Mima. He scanned the room and found her twin, who sat in the corner, reading a hardcover book with no pictures on the front. His normally huge, bushy hair had been shorn, and he looked sad and naked without it, as if someone had stolen his magic staff or his rocket car or lasso of truth.

The girl tapped the figure of Miles Morales he'd drawn on the inside of his workbook and asked again. "Whabo abis thabis?"

"That's Ultimate Spider-Man. He's different from the other Spider-Man."

She regarded the drawing. "Drabaw maborabe!"

"Huh?"

"Drabaw maborabe! Drabaw maborabe!" Even though she was speaking very fast, he got the gist. He thought a minute, then drew a quick picture of the Wasp.

She clapped. He was so surprised, he looked around to see if anyone else was looking, if this was a joke. Most kids thought his drawings were okay, but nobody had ever clapped for them before. So he drew her a picture of Iron Man. Captain America. The Falcon. The Falcon when he became Captain America. The Morning Star, whose powers came from a malfunctioning

Lion battery. Storm. Sunspot. And then, because she sort of reminded him of her, Kitty Pryde.

"Tess Biedermann!" the teacher barked. "Are you done with your workbook page?"

"Yabes!"

"English, please."

"Yes. I finished the whole book."

"You . . . excuse me?"

Tess said, "It was kind of fun. So I kept going." Tess grabbed her workbook and held it up, smiling.

The teacher was not smiling. The teacher stared at her; then her eyes slid to her brother in the back of the room. "Theo? Did you do your whole workbook?"

"Nabo," he said.

"English!"

"No."

"Did you finish your page?"

"No," he said.

"Why not?"

"The directions don't make sense."

"You didn't understand them?"

"I understood what they wanted me to do, but they weren't clearly written. I thought I should read this book instead. It's about nuclear fusion. Harnessing the power of the stars."

The teacher slumped at her desk, covering one half of her face with her hand, so that one eye was visible through the V between her pinky and ring finger. It made her look a little like a pirate, and a little like a really annoyed third-grade teacher. "What about you, Jaime? Are you reading about nuclear fusion?"

"No," he said. "I finished my page. I'm drawing superheroes."

"What else would you be doing." This was not a question.

Jaime said, "Tony Stark uses cold fusion. For his Iron Man suit."

"Even if you could create a reactor that small, you'd still have storage problems. And side effects," Theo said.

"He does," said Jaime.

"Hmmm," said Theo.

The teacher rested her elbows on her desk and put both hands over her face. "I want everyone in their seats. Those who have not completed their worksheets, finish them now. Everyone who has completed their entire workbook can sit quietly and practice meditation."

Before she sat down, Tess Biedermann leaned down and whispered, "You should create your own superhero.

A brand-new one nobody's ever seen before."

"I am," he said, wondering how she knew.

Later, when his grandmother found him scribbling away, drawing one superhero after the next—different outfits, different talismans, different powers—she asked him what he was doing. He said, "I am trying to find the right beginning." Mima clucked her tongue and told him that he was clearly a cuckoo boy, because anyone could see he had already begun.

Now Jaime sat on a bruised butt in the gallery of the Liberty Statue holding a letter about a letter, a letter about so many things, and had the strangest feeling that this was its own kind of beginning.

"Jaime!" Tess stomped her foot.

"Sorry, what?"

"The letter! Are you going to read it or not?" said Tess.

The twins squeezed next to him on the bench and peered over his shoulders as he read aloud:

Dear T:

I'm writing this to you now only to have to burn it later, as I must burn everything. I know we have to keep our secrets but it does grow tiresome.

Wasn't it lovely of Miss King and Mr. Munsterberg to join us at our little soiree? And when I say "lovely" of course I mean excruciating. Who keeps inviting these people? Perhaps I do. But I wish you wouldn't argue so much about politics once you've realized there's simply no point. I agree that the natives must keep their land east of the Mississippi as per our treaties with those nations, I agree that Jackson is a nightmare, but by the time we finished the soup course it was clear that we were dining with monsters. It would have been more productive to simply pelt them with roasted potatoes till they ran away. They were worse than that horrible woman who rummaged through your desk at our last dinner party. I can't remember her name, but I remember her face when she looked in her reticule and saw that the letter she'd stolen from you had been replaced with some spiders I'd been working on. She did pinwheel about rather spectacularly, no? You keep telling me that I've lost my sense of humor, but I believe that incident proves I haven't. Or perhaps I have regressed.

In any case, I hope that none of these people will go to the Tredwells'. I would like to say that the occasion would be enlightening for all who need it, a fresh start, a new perspective, but some people do not wish to be enlightened. It pains me to say it pains me.

Are we doing the right thing? Are we doing enough? Are we the right people to be doing any of it? Will we ever know? Maybe I have lost my sense of humor after all, but when I tell you that I don't feel like myself anymore, I'm the only one who laughs. What have you lost?

Never mind. I'm speaking in riddles again. I know how much you hate that.

Let's hope that no one fishes this nonsense from the fire.

—T.

When he finished reading, Tess's eyes got so big that whole planets could have fallen into them. "That's Theresa Morningstarr's writing, but I've never seen this letter before. I've never *heard* of this letter before. And my grandpa has read everything the Morningstarrs have ever written. There are entire archives of their correspondence. Almost all of it is just boring business stuff."

Jaime scanned the letter again. It wasn't boring at all. It was actually sort of funny and sad at the same time.

"We can't be sure it's a Morningstarr letter," said Theo. "It doesn't sound like a Morningstarr letter."

"It's written to 'T' from 'T,'" Tess said. "She talks about keeping secrets, about the spiders she's been working on. And what it says about burning letters explains why so few of their personal papers exist."

Jaime said, "But who could have fished it out of the fire? And who would have sent it to your grandfather all these years later?"

"Who would have sent it *today* of all days!" said Tess.

"It could have been sent a week ago," Theo said. "It could have been sitting in that mailbox for a month."

"Still," Tess said. "It's a clue. I know it is." She practically hummed with excitement. It was like sitting next to a beehive. Nine rubbed Tess's knees with her face as if to calm her.

"Okay, let's think about this for a minute," Theo said, hand stuck in his hair. "It seems important, but what if it's some bizarre coincidence?"

"This can't be a coincidence," Jaime said.

"Nope," Tess said. "Way too adorable."

"What's that supposed to mean?" said Theo. "How can a coincidence be adorable?"

"When it's too much of a coincidence to be a coincidence," said Jaime.

"Maybe it's a hoax," Theo said. "The cipherist world is full of hoaxes. Someone could have written this letter, dipped it in coffee and burned it a little to make it look old, and forged Theresa's handwriting just to mess with Grandpa. Happens all the time." Theo got up and paced the gallery, his footsteps echoing. "Everything in that letter could be made up."

"Not everything," said Jaime. "Jackson was pushing legislation to force the Cherokees and other nations to leave their homes and move to some lands in the middle of the country or some random place. Didn't pass, though. I made a diorama about it in fourth grade. Did you guys ever try to make a diorama about legislation? It's not that easy."

"I love making dioramas," Tess said.

"*Everything else* in this letter could be made up," Theo said.

"But isn't this exactly what the Morningstarrs would do?" Tess said. "Bury a clue in a letter sent to a person who's never even identified, *a letter that talks about a stolen letter* just like the Poe story? And this line, here, that's underlined: *would be enlightening for all who need it*. It's like they're messing with *anyone* trying to solve the cipher."

"Okay, but someone had to send this to Grandpa Ben. If you had a real Morningstarr clue, why would you send it to anyone? Why wouldn't you check it out yourself?" Theo said.

"Maybe whoever sent it tried to figure it out but couldn't," said Tess. "Or maybe whoever sent it wanted Grandpa to solve it."

"Tess—"

Tess shook her head so aggressively her braid whacked Jaime in the arm. "It has to be a clue."

"Who are Miss King and Mr. Munsterberg?" said Jaime.

"If this is a Morningstarr clue, the names aren't important. Most of the other clues were codes or ciphers," said Theo.

"So all we have to do is figure out what kind of puzzle it is," Tess added.

Jaime had solved puzzles before. The rules always seemed random until one of them worked—then they made perfect sense. "Maybe we're supposed to apply the numbers from the very first clue that appeared in the newspaper in 1855 to this letter?"

Theo frowned, then shook his head. "I don't think so. Those numbers were 42, 1, 2; 42, 20, 7; 42, 1, 10, like that. There aren't even forty-two lines in this whole letter."

Tess said, "The solution to the very first clue was the date the Liberty Statue's book. 741776. Try numbering the lines in the body of the letter."

Jaime took out his sketchbook and started scribbling. "So, if we don't count the greeting as a line, we get

'Mississippi as per our treaties with those nations, I agree that Jackson is a'

'And when I say "lovely" of course I mean excruciating. Who keeps inviting these people?'

'I'm writing this to you now only to have to burn it later, as I must burn everything. I'

'Mississippi as per our treaties with those nations, I agree that Jackson is a'

'Mississippi as per our treaties with those nations, I agree that Jackson is a'

'there's simply no point. I agree that the natives must keep their land east of the'"

"Well," said Theo, "That doesn't look like much of anything."

"But even if the key refers to certain lines, we don't know which word is important in the line," Jaime said.

Tess said, "Sometimes there's a pattern. Maybe it follows the 741776 code? Seventh word, fourth word, like that?"

But when they tried using the seventh word of the first line and then the fourth and first, they didn't get anything useful.

"This doesn't feel right," Tess said. "We're missing something."

"That's what I was trying to tell you back at Grandpa's apartment," Theo said. "People have been trying to solve this mystery for more than one hundred fifty years. Even if this is a Morningstarr clue—and we have no idea if it is—it could take decades just to figure it out."

Jaime didn't say it, but they didn't have decades before Slant would take possession of their building.

He went back to the letter. "What if the names *are* the

most important thing about this letter? Miss King. Mr. Munsterberg. Tredwell."

"I guess we can go to the library and use the computers to look them up," said Tess.

Jaime stuffed the sketchbook in one pocket, the Morningstarr letter into another, and he fumbled for his cell phone in a third. "I can look it up right now."

"You have a phone?" Theo grumbled. "We're not allowed to get one till next year."

For the name "Miss King," Jaime got so many results that nothing stood out. "Mr. Munsterberg" yielded an entry about one Hugo Munsterberg, a psychologist who wrote a book about the film industry in 1916. But the name "Tredwell" was different. "'The Seabury Tredwell House, built in 1832,'" Jaime read aloud. "'The Tredwell family lived there for a century. It's a museum now. Everything inside is preserved just as it always was.'"

Nine the cat started to pace and Tess's knee started to bounce. "What if there's something important hidden at the Tredwell House?" she said.

Jaime read from the letter in his hands: "A fresh start, a new perspective." He lowered his voice to a whisper. "Guys. What if . . . what if there are *two* trails of clues? The one that people have been following for years, and this one. Like a secret cipher?"

Theo's hand hovered in the air, as if he didn't know where to put it. "Huh."

Jaime wanted to chortle and to chuckle and to roar. He felt like laughing the way you do at a surprise birthday party, the way you laugh when they bring out a cake shaped like Spider-Man.

They got up and shot through the gallery doors, almost mowing down Guffaw Man and his tour group.

Guffaw Man snorted and said, "Are you kids still trying solve the Ciiiii—"

The rest of the word was swallowed up by the wind as they ran right past him and into the bright sunshine.

CHAPTER SEVEN
Cricket

The morning after Darnell Slant—or rather, his creepy minions—told the residents of 354 W. 73rd Street that they were officially homeless, six-year-old Zelda "Cricket" Moran woke up the same time she always did: 5:22 a.m. on the dot. And she did the same thing she did every single morning: she climbed out of bed and selected her outfit for the day. She was very particular about her outfits, which she matched very carefully to her moods. (This didn't always please the adults around her, especially on class picture days or family reunions when she insisted on wearing a skeleton costume or a gas mask.) That morning, she put on a pink tutu, striped tights, red sparkle high-tops, her favorite heart necklace—the one that the building had given her—and a black T-shirt with a picture of a skull and crossbones and a snake head poking through the eye socket, because this was the most metal outfit she owned and she was feeling particularly metal.

Since no one else was up, she marched into the kitchen, poured herself a bowl of her favorite cereal—no milk, because milk made everything soggy and soggy was not metal—and ate in front of the TV. When she was done with her breakfast, she spent the next fifteen minutes practicing her crowd-surfing in the front foyer, which was a little difficult because she was by herself. After a while, Karl trundled into the room and tugged on her pigtails as if they were handlebars and he was trying to steer her. He was always trying to steer her. *Stop trying to steer, Karl!* Or else he was spinning the lock on the pantry door, scrambling to get at the Cheez Doodles. He loved Cheez Doodles.

Cricket got up and unlocked the pantry—silly Karl, the combination was 1, 2, 3—and grabbed a handful of Cheez Doodles. Karl ate them while Cricket put on his harness. Then she walked him around the apartment. Well, Cricket walked. Karl was on his back with his legs in the air, getting dragged along. He looked a little bit dead. That was pretty metal.

Her mom finally shuffled out into the living room.

"Cricket, please don't drag your raccoon around like that. You know how dirty he gets."

"He likes it, don't you, Karl?"

Karl scrubbed the cheese from his masked face with his tiny hands but didn't try to get up.

"Right," said Cricket's mom. Her hair was mashed down on one side of her face and her eyes were bloodshot. It wasn't a good look for her, but it was also too early in the morning for Cricket's UNBRIDLED HONESTY. At least, that was what her dad would have said. The first time he said it, she had to look in her special word book for the meaning of *unbridled*. Then she spent the next two weeks galloping around like a horse.

"Who are you today?" her mom asked.

"Isn't it obvious?"

"Not to anyone over the age of seven," her mother said.

"I'm a ballerina-spy-deathmetalhead."

"Lovely," said her mother, walking into the kitchen area. She opened one cabinet after another, using bad words under her breath. Cricket had looked up some of those bad words in her special word book. She wondered if her mom knew what the words meant. She thought not.

Cricket said, "If you're looking for the coffee, I used

it for my experiments."

Her mom's head swiveled toward Cricket like a bobble toy. "Experiments?"

"I was a supermodel-scientist-archvillian yesterday, remember?"

Her mother closed the cabinets, slumped at the kitchen table. "It should be a crime to mess with a woman's coffee."

"Are you going to have me arrested?" said Cricket.

"Of course not."

"Call Detective Biedermann! I would like to be arrested!"

"No, you wouldn't."

"Would, too!"

"Cricket, it's not even six in the morning. It's too early for this. It's always too early for this."

"Too early for what?"

Her mother made a tiny sound like a cross between a sigh and a sob and put her head down on the table. She did that a lot—sighing and sobbing and putting her head down on the table. She did it so much yesterday that her dad told her that she had to stop BURSTING INTO HYSTERICS at the drop of a hat. Cricket's special word book defined *hysterics* as "a fit of laughing or crying or yelling." But Cricket's dad was the one yelling and nobody had dropped any hats anywhere. When Cricket informed him of all this, his face got as red as a riding hood. She was going to tell him about being as red as a riding hood, too, but she decided to bridle her honesty.

Anyway, all the adults in the building seemed to be BURSTING INTO HYSTERICS, one after the other, like the first graders in Cricket's class passing around the sniffles. Her mother tried to explain why. She said all the adults were upset because some man named Dermal Plant bought the building where they lived and didn't want them to live there anymore. Daddy was especially upset because they'd probably have to go stay with Cranky Cousin Gordon in Bayonne, New Jersey. Cranky Cousin Gordon's whole house smelled like nachos even though Cricket had never once seen him eat nachos. PECULIAR.

Once Dad got out of bed, her parents would probably start arguing about Cranky Cousin Gordon again and Dermal Plant and nachos, and Dad would flail around accusing everyone of BURSTING INTO HYSTERICS.

Cricket had better things to do.

"I'm going to take Karl for a ride."

Her mother didn't lift her head from the table. Her

voice was muffled when she said, "Don't you want to wait for your brother to wake up? Maybe he can be your side-kick."

"Otto is just a dumb baby. Karl is my sidekick. He has a bandit mask and tiny monkey fingers."

"Monkey fingers," said her mother to the wood of the table. "Right."

Cricket tucked her necklace under her shirt so no one would be tempted to steal it, put Karl into the basket at the front of her three-wheeler, and rolled it toward the door.

"Stay on this floor, okay, Cricket?"

"Hmmph," said Cricket, what she said when she didn't want to lie but was totally not telling the truth.

Out in the hallway, Cricket and Karl made laps around their floor, going faster and faster each lap. Karl made happy chirping noises the whole time, like a good sidekick. He probably needed his own outfit. What would a deathmetalhead raccoon wear? A helmet, of course. Probably one with antlers.

They got on the elevator and punched the letter L. The elevator groaned, the sound a lot like the sound her mother had made while slumped over the table. The elevator went up first, then down, then up, left, right, then finally headed for the lobby. Cricket's dad said that the elevator reminded him of Cricket, which made no kind of sense.

A shrill *ding!* and the doors opened. The lobby had miles of smooth, slippery tile, perfect for a race. Because it was so early in the morning, it was completely empty, completely quiet. Cricket started slowly but sped up, rounding the corner so fast that she almost tipped over. She was about to say, "That was close!" but before she could say it, someone else did.

"That was close."

Cricket stopped pedaling and looked up and up and up. A giant of a giant was standing in front of her, his big, white, speckled face hanging like a moon.

"You should be more careful when you play, little girl," the man said. "You could get hurt."

Cricket did not enjoy being spoken to as if she were a dumb baby. "You are the color of ranch dip," she announced.

"I prefer the term *alabaster.*"

She stared.

The man smiled.

It was not a good look for him.

Cricket pressed a lever on the handlebars and backed

up the tricycle, *beep-beep-beep*. That was when she noticed the ring of yellow tape around his wrist. "What's on your bracelet?"

"This is caution tape. Do you know what the word *caution* means?"

"Hmmph," she said.

The man stepped forward right into Cricket's personal space. "It means that there are certain things in this building a little girl shouldn't touch. And certain places in this building that are too dangerous for a little girl to go."

Behind the tall man, another much shorter man had his ear pressed to a small brass door that hung high on the lobby wall, his gloved fingertips tapping here and there, *tap-tap, tap-tap*. Cricket wondered if the door talked to the short man the way the walls talked to Tess Biedermann, if the man was also ECCENTRIC. The short man looked up when he felt Cricket watching. He smiled, too.

And it wasn't a good look for him, either.

The tall man said, "This is what they call a dumb-waiter, a little elevator people used to deliver items or maybe send trash down to the basement, but it doesn't work anymore. And the door seems to be stuck. Do you know how to open it?"

Cricket shrugged.

"Do you know anyone else who knows how to open it? The building manager perhaps?"

"Hmmph," said Cricket.

The little man stopped tapping and stepped away from the wall. It was then that Cricket saw that the tapping hand wasn't a hand at all, and it wasn't even attached to the short man. The man whistled, and the leathery brown creature—a spider? A lizard?—scuttled down the wall and into a waiting bag.

"We don't want anyone playing with this door," said the tall man. "It's broken. And if you got it open, a little girl could fall down the shaft."

"A *little girl* could," said Cricket.

The man's watery eyes fell on Karl. "Or her raccoon could fall. A little girl wouldn't want anything to happen to her raccoon."

Cricket felt her face go as red as a riding hood. Nobody talked about Karl falling down anywhere.

"I think we understand each other," said the tall man. He patted Cricket on the head.

Nobody patted Cricket on the head.

But today, Cricket was a ballerina-spy-deathmetalhead, and she knew what was what. She bridled her honesty. She smiled her sweetest little-girl smile. Karl chirped his cutest raccoon-cat chirp. The man nodded and walked back to his short friend. They put an X of CAUTION tape on the brass panel of the dumbwaiter.

Cricket motored her trike back to the main elevator. She would never tell the men that she knew how to open the dumbwaiter. Or what she'd found inside. She would never tell anyone.

But she would keep an eye on those men from now on, because that's what a spy would do.

So. Very. Metal.

CHAPTER EIGHT

Tess

The morning they were supposed to go to the Tredwell House, her mom took one look at Tess and said, "One of those nights?"

It had been one of those nights, and it hadn't. Yes, she was so wired and tired that her nerves felt like a marmoset-mongoose had been chewing on them, but it was a small price to pay if they had actually found a new branch of clues to solve the Cipher. But of course she couldn't say that. Not yet. Today they would try to find the next clue, if there was one. Only then could they be sure they were on to something new, something no one else had found before.

"I'm okay," Tess said to her mom.

"Did you try meditation?" her father asked.

She'd tried her favorite guided meditation video for an hour. She'd organized her underwear drawer by color. She'd tried counting backward from one million. When the sun rose that morning, she was on number 937,582.

"I tried," said Tess. "But sometimes it just doesn't work."

"If it makes you feel any better, I couldn't sleep either," said Mr. Biedermann. "Your mother, on the other hand, was snoring up a storm."

"I wasn't snoring," said Mrs. Biedermann.

"How would you know?" said Mr. Biedermann.

When they finally harnessed Nine and met Jaime in the lobby, Jaime was the one who seemed sleepy. Even his short 'locs looked a bit droopy.

"My grandma was online this morning looking for jobs. She already has an interview for next week. And my dad texted and said he was calling a friend to see if he can get us another apartment. In Hoboken."

"Nobody's moving to Hoboken yet," said Tess. "Or Idaho."

"What's with you and Idaho?" said Theo.

"What's that?" Tess said.

"Idaho?"

"No, that." Tess pointed at the strips of yellow caution

tape X-ed over a metal panel by the mailboxes. "Who put that there?"

"I bet it was those two creepy guys who served the eviction notices," said Jaime.

"Stoop and Pinscher," Theo said.

"Don't tell me those are their names," said Jaime.

"I won't, then," said Theo. He was silent for half a second, then blurted, "Stoop and Pinscher really are their names."

"Ignore him," Tess said. "Do you have the letter?"

Jaime patted his side pocket. "Right here."

To get to the Tredwell House, which was now called the Merchant's House Museum, they walked over to 72nd and Broadway to catch the number 2 to Times Square. Today, the Guildman in the glass box was gaunt as a skeleton but with eyes like precious stones. He scanned the car, looking for rule breakers and troublemakers. For a second, the Guildman's amber eyes seemed to lock on Tess's. She held her breath, but he quickly moved on. Nine nudged her hand. She exhaled slowly and then took three more deep cleansing breaths.

At Times Square, the train stopped, and the three of them ran up the stairs to catch the N. This train started underground but climbed steadily upward into the air until they were riding high above the city streets. Below the tracks, people and cars darted like silverfish, but everyone's eyes were on the Morningstarr Tower, glass panels gleaming, spire needle sharp and poking into the clouds, Underway tracks curled around the base. Tess didn't say what she was thinking, what they all were thinking, that it was only a matter of time until Slant got his hands on the Tower, too. What would it look like with the word SLANT slapped on the front of it, blinking in neon? Nothing that Tess ever wanted to see.

They got off the train at 8th Street and walked five minutes to a four-story redbrick row house with green shutters and a door painted a dignified cream. An elegant wrought-iron fence matched the railing leading up the stairs. Two fixtures that maybe once held lightbulbs stood on either side of the entrance. It was a pretty house, but nothing on the outside screamed "clue!" Unless you were a student of history—or one of Benjamin and Annie Adler's grandkids—you wouldn't know that 29 East 4th Street was one of the few remaining nineteenth-century structures still standing in New York City. The building right next door was plastered with demolition notices. Which made Tess mad all over again, the nimbus of outrage buzzing in and around her head. She marched up the steps, threw open the door, and burst inside.

Dozens of people already crowded the narrow front hallway, including an entire troop of Morningstarr Scouts, all wearing matching red shirts and beanies, all looking like a flock of birds. Everyone turned to stare first at Tess, then at Nine, then at Jaime and Theo behind her.

"Welcome to Tredwell House," said a beige young man in a boxy beige suit like an envelope. His name tag said Colton. "As I was saying, Tredwell House was purchased in 1835 by a wealthy merchant named Seabury Tredwell for eighteen thousand dollars. That's about half a million dollars today."

"Not a lot for New York City," grumbled a middle-aged man with a fake orange tan and the kind of smooth, unwrinkled face Tess's dad liked to call "well preserved" and her mom liked to call "pickled."

Colton, the tour guide, said, "It used to be that there were many, many row houses of this style here and all over the city, but what makes the Merchant's House unique is that it's the only one left standing."

One of the Morningstarr Scouts, a short girl wearing a patterned headscarf under her beanie, said, "Are there any ghosts in here?"

"Ah, I'll get to that in a minute," said Colton. "First, I want to tell you about Seabury Tred—"

The girl said, "Everything is better with ghosts." The other Morningstarr Scouts nodded.

"Seabury Tredwell," said Colton, perhaps just a little too loudly, "came to New York City in 1798 when he was eighteen years old. In 1820, when he was forty years old, he married twenty-three-year-old Eliza Parker."

"Ew!" said the Morningstarr Scouts.

"Ew?" said the middle-aged man. His wife socked him. Or maybe it was just a random woman who found him irritating.

"They had eight children—Elizabeth, Horace, Mary, Samuel, Phebe, Julia, Sarah, and finally Gertrude, who was born in this house in 1840. Only three of them ever married," said Colton. "The oldest daughter, Elizabeth, wedded a prominent lawyer named Effingham Nichols in 1845. He was one of the people involved in the Union Pacific Railroad before it collapsed due to the competition from the Morningstarrs."

And there it was, a connection with the Morningstarrs! Theo elbowed Tess, Tess elbowed Jaime. Nine meowed. Some of the Morningstarr Scouts giggled. Some of them edged away from Nine and her Nine-sized teeth.

"By the 1860s, this area was packed with bars and cheap hotels, riddled with unsavory characters, but the Tredwell sisters refused to move and didn't change anything in the house except for adding modern plumbing and electricity. Phebe, Julia, and Gertrude lived out their lives in this house. When Gertrude, the youngest member of the family, died in 1933, she left this house completely intact. So, why don't we have a look around? If you'll all follow me, we'll go downstairs first, where we'll find the family room and the kitchen." Colton waved them down the hall toward the back of the house.

When most of the crowd was out of earshot, Tess whispered, "Let me see the letter again. What was the bit that Theresa Morningstarr underlined?"

Jaime pulled the letter out of his pocket and read, "'would be enlightening for all who need it.'"

"That has to be a clue," said Tess. "*Enlightening* as in a book is enlightening?"

"Maybe," said Theo. "Or maybe it's a pun." He glanced up and stared at a fixture hanging overhead. "Maybe instead of *enlightening* as in 'instructional,' she meant something that actually sheds light? Like a lamp or something?"

"Or a fireplace," said Tess.

"Or a candlestick," Theo said.

Jaime put the letter back in his pocket. "I'm sure there

aren't more than a million candlesticks in a nineteenth-century house."

They hurried to the back of the house and into the kitchen, where Colton was talking about how all the meals were first cooked over an open fire by the Tredwells' four servants, and then later on the stove that stood in the fireplace. "A house and a family this size could not have run smoothly without someone to do all the work."

"Why didn't they do the work themselves?" said one of the Morningstarr Scouts.

"It was a lot more work to cook dinner in the nineteenth century, when you didn't have running water or modern appliances. That stove wasn't even there in 1832."

Tess sidled over to the large open fireplace, where the stove sat. Nothing seemed unusual about it. There were no strange markings in the bricks, there was no loose mortar to hint at a secret compartment. She looked behind the stove and even under the stove. She risked opening the oven.

"Please don't open that!" said Colton, gripping his own tie in alarm. His voice went up about three octaves.

"Sorry," Tess said. She closed the door. A little flutter of worry flapped in Tess's gut. How were they supposed to know where to look? How were they supposed to know what to look *for*?

From the kitchen, the group moved into the family room. While Colton was talking about the furniture, Jaime and Theo examined some candlesticks on either end of the mantel and Tess fiddled with a lamp sitting on nearby table.

"Hello! Please! Hello, don't touch that!" said Colton, startling Tess so much that the lamp tipped and almost fell over. She caught it just in time.

"Sorry, sorry," said Tess, righting the lamp.

Colton clutched his tie so hard that he made it longer, his overlarge Adam's apple going up and down. The Morningstarr Scouts went wide-eyed. The middle-aged couple shook their heads, the woman murmuring, *"Where are her parents?"*

"Okay!" said Colton, getting control of himself. "Let's move upstairs. Please don't touch anything."

"Did you hear that, young lady?" said the pickled man to Tess, plumped lip curling.

"Dabid abi habeabar whabat?" said Tess.

The man blinked. "I thought you spoke English."

"Abi dabo."

The man huffed in confusion until his wife dragged him away.

Jaime said, "What language was that?"

Tess said, "It's Turkish—"

"Irish," Theo finished. "You put an *ab* in front of every vowel in a word. If you talk really fast it sounds like gibberish."

"And it annoys the heck out of people," Tess added.

"Nabo, rabeabally?" said Jaime.

"Ha," said Tess. "You guys see any clues?"

"Not so far," Theo said. "We should probably get upstairs."

"Yeah," said Jaime. "There are probably a billion more candlesticks and lampshades to look at."

Up on the next floor, Colton was telling the group about the front and back parlors. "If you look up, you'll see beautiful matching chandeliers, or in this case, 'gasoliers.'"

"What's a gasolier?" said the girl in the headscarf.

"It's a chandelier powered by gas!" said Colton.

The Morningstarr Scouts glanced at one another. In unison, they said: "Gas? In a *house*?"

"Well, in the earlier part of the nineteenth century, scientists and engineers were trying to find the best way to provide power—light the city, move the trains, all of that. They were trying to figure out what kind of fuel was best. The Morningstarrs invented the solar glass and solar cells that we now use to pave the streets, so we get our energy from the sun. But back then other people were experimenting with burning coal and oil and gas. Burning gas could be dangerous, though. There's an old story that one of the gasoliers burst into flames. There's even a burn mark on this sideboard."

Colton kept talking, but Tess was too focused on the gasolier. It was bronze and had six burners, mounted to the ceiling with an ornate medallion. The other Cipher clues were mostly mathematical puzzles, but what if this new Cipher worked differently? What if the clues were riddles or even mechanical clues, hidden writing and secret slots? Maybe one or the other or both of the gasoliers could turn like a clock? But how would she possibly be able to test that without anyone freaking out, and without breaking anything or setting the place on fire?

She could wait until the group was touring the floors above, sneak back down here, climb up on a chair—a priceless chair—and try to turn or pull or otherwise operate one of the gasoliers. If her mother knew what she was planning, she'd be grounded for months.

Tess swallowed hard. Nine rubbed against Tess's legs. While Colton warbled about sideboards and tables and priceless rococo whatevers, Tess walked Nine to the marble fireplace to look at the argon lamps on the mantel. They had etched glass domes and crystals that hung from them, but she didn't see anything remarkable about them. But that was the point, of course. And what if the next clue had nothing to do with lights or lighting? What if they had this all wrong?

She wished she could talk to Grandpa Ben. The last time she'd seen Grandpa, he'd—

Nine mrrrowed and nibbled on Tess's fingers. Colton stopped talking and narrowed his eyes at Tess. "Why don't we head upstairs. All of us! Together! Looking at the furniture but not touching any of it!"

Tess sighed. And then she noticed that the girl in the headscarf suddenly appeared *behind* Colton. Colton jumped.

"Hello! Where have you been?"

"Exploring," said the girl. "I went to the attic to see where the servants lived."

Colton's smile went tight. "Most people like to stay with the tour."

The girl shrugged. "I'm more interested in the servants. They're the ones who had to do all the work. These other people sat around playing cards and having cotillions. What *is* a cotillion, even?"

Colton said, "It's a ball or a dance that—"

"That was a rhetorical question," said the girl. "Also, I went up to the attic because I wanted to see ghosts and ghosts live in attics."

"Well, since you're so interested in the lives of the servants," Colton said, "let's all go to the top floor to see where they slept!"

Tess decided that she would wait until the group had reached the attic to sneak back down here to try to get a closer look at the gasoliers. She joined Theo and Jaime at the back of the line. By the time they reached the top floor of the house, everyone was winded.

"Can you imagine being a servant here and having to carry water and laundry and food up and down the steps every day, twelve or fourteen hours a day?" said Colton.

No fancy furniture up here. No crystal lamps or chandeliers. Just a couple of beds, a table, and a heating stove.

"We don't know exactly what happened here in the Tredwell House," said Colton, "but we do know that a lot of domestic servants in New York City homes were poor, uneducated girls, many of them immigrants. Unfortunately, some of these girls suffered all sorts of mistreatment from their employers."

The Morningstarrs had employed servants, too, but Tess didn't like to think about the Morningstarrs treating those people badly or paying them so little. But Grandpa Ben always warned that they couldn't romanticize anyone from the past, even those who had done great things. "Remember," Grandpa said, "history is filled with horrors as well as wonders. And so are people."

Horrors and wonders. Wonders and horrors. Tess closed her eyes and imagined sleeping up in this attic room, which was probably boiling during the summer and freezing in the winter. Getting up in the gray light of dawn, going downstairs to light the kitchen fires, and then all the other fires in the house so that everyone else would be warm.

Lighting the fires.

Lighting *all* the fires.

Enlightening for all who need it.

Theresa Morningstarr had been making a pun. But she'd been serious, too. The servants were the ones who "enlightened" those that needed it. Without their servants, the Tredwells would have to sit in the cold and the dark. And so would all the other rich folks in New York City. Maybe even the Morningstarrs themselves.

So, would the clue be in the expensive lamps and

fixtures on the main floors . . . or right here, in this room, where no one would think to look for anything—or anyone—valuable?

On the dressing table, there was one simple candlestick. When Colton turned to point out a rosary hanging from one of the bed frames, Tess quickly picked it up. Again, she found no markings. It didn't twist or fold into a different shape, or telescope into a . . . telescope. There were no tiny scrolled messages curled in the spot where the candle was inserted. She put the stick down quickly before anyone noticed what she was doing.

Meeting a ghost might be easier than this.

Then her eyes fell on the little heating stove. She needed to look inside it, underneath it, but she couldn't get near it because Colton was standing right there, jawing away about the Tredwells' summer house in Rumson, New Jersey, where they went to escape outbreaks of cholera and yellow fever that regularly swept New York City in the hot months.

Nobody seemed to be listening. Poor Colton, stuck with a tour group full of ghost-obsessed Scouts, self-obsessed tourists, and Cipher-obsessed seventh graders, disrespectful all.

Finally, Colton declared it time to head downstairs

to see the bedchambers of Mr. and Mrs. Tredwell, and the group dutifully followed. Tess bent and pretended her shoelaces had come untied. Theo and Jaime waited with her.

"What is it?" Jaime said as soon as everyone else had gone.

"Help me look in the stove. Hurry!"

He didn't ask questions and neither did Theo. As Nine danced around them, they opened the door and checked inside. The interior was spotless, no levers or letters or code. They checked the top and the back and the sides, looking for anything that seemed unusual.

"Hello!" a voice called from the bottom of the stairs. "Where is the rest of my group?!"

"Coming!" Jaime said.

Tess lay on the floor and felt around the underside of the stove.

"Anything?" Theo whispered.

"Hold on." Tess moved her fingers slowly over metal. Totally smooth, except . . . What was that? Some sort of serial number? No. Writing. Writing etched in one corner of the metal. Four lines. A maker's mark? Or something else?

"Give me a piece of paper and a pencil!"

"He's going to come up here in a second," said Theo.

"Go down then," Tess said. "Stall him."

Theo didn't move. Jaime handed her the paper and pencil. She could barely see what she was doing, but she placed the paper over the writing and quickly rubbed the pencil all over it.

"Hello!?" called Colton.

Footsteps marched up the stairs.

Tess thrust the paper and pencil at Jaime and leaped to her feet. He shoved the paper in his pocket just as Colton's beige suit appeared at the top of the steps, grinning in that overly cheerful way that said he suspected them all of trying to ruin the Tredwell House forever.

"What are you guys doing?" he said.

"I thought I saw a ghost!" Tess blurted.

"What?" said Colton.

"Um, there was a guy. Standing in that mirror over there. Dressed in old clothes. He looked like the guy in one of the paintings down in the parlor."

Colton gripped his tie, then released it. "You mean Seabury Tredwell?"

"Yes!" Tess said.

"I can't believe it," said Colton. "I've always . . . it's just . . . no one has ever seen a ghost on one of my tours before!"

"Well, I did. And it kind of freaked me out."

"Yeah," Jaime said. "She almost fainted, like one of those nineteenth-century ladies. I was about to call for the smelling salts."

"I bet!" said Colton, smile wide and genuine now. "Did the ghost, um, say anything to you?"

"He did," Tess said, grinning right back. "The ghost said, *'Everyone else is wrong.'*"

CHAPTER NINE
Theo

Of all the possibilities that Grandpa Ben had considered—that there were dozens of clues in the Cipher, maybe hundreds, that the only treasure worth seeking was knowledge, and this was what the Cipher was trying to teach—he'd never mentioned the possibility that the Cipher could have another branch of clues. That the Cipher wasn't one puzzle, it was *two* puzzles leading in two different directions. Were there even more branches? Three? Four? Ten? Did they ever converge? And where?

And the question that had kept Theo up the whole night before: Who could have sent Theresa Morningstarr's letter in the first place?

Now Theo sat hunched with Tess and Jaime at Bug's

Burgers, the Loco Burger in front of him untouched. Tessa's rubbing of the etching from the bottom of the Tredwells' servants' heating stove lay in the middle of the table:

> When coming here from Watertown,
> Soon after ent'ring Cambridge ground,
> You spy the grand & pleasant seat,
> Possess'd by Washinton the great.

Keeping her voice low so that no one else at the restaurant would hear them, Tess pointed at the top of the etching. "Watertown, Cambridge, that's all about the Boston area, where the first battles of the Revolutionary War were fought." She took a bite of her burger. Loco Burgers tasted a lot like chicken and toasted sunflower seeds, both nutty and crunchy, but Theo was too hyped up to eat. He was a little surprised Tess was eating; sometimes she claimed she felt bad for the bugs.

"Do you think the next clue is in Boston?" Jaime asked. "I don't think my grandmother is going to let me go all the way to Boston."

"Congress met in New York before they established Washington, DC, as the capital."

"Narrows things down," said Jaime.

Tess said, "What about this, the word *spy*? The Morningstarrs hid the other clues in plain sight. Spies are hidden in plain sight, right? So maybe this verse refers to one of Washington's spies?"

"Dope that Washington had spies," Jaime said.

Tess wiped her lips with a napkin. "A whole ring. It was called . . . um . . . what was it called, Theo?"

"The Culper Ring," Theo said.

Jaime took out his phone and typed in the name. With a French fry, Theo traced the Bug's Burgers logo on his soda cup. The logo was a grinning locust in a top hat and tap shoes. If this locust knew it was going to be ground into a burger, Theo didn't think it would feel much like dancing.

"Okay, here it is," said Jaime. "Under the leadership of Benjamin Tallmadge, the Culper Ring provided valuable information to General Washington, such as information that the British planned to counterfeit American dollars and that a high-ranking American officer—later revealed to be American Major General Benedict Arnold—had been plotting with the British to surrender the vitally important American fort at West Point."

Theo said, "Benedict Arnold used secret writing. Could be referring to him. But I don't think Arnold spent a lot of time in New York City. And he ended up in London."

"And if we can't get to Boston, we absolutely can't get to London," said Jaime.

"Right," Theo said. He didn't mention the fact that if any of the clues required them to travel outside New York City, they probably weren't going to be the ones to solve them.

Tess chewed, swallowed. "So, is the verse referring to Benjamin Tallmadge? Or someone else?"

Jaime said, "I'd say Washington, even with the jacked-up spelling."

"Spelling didn't become standardized till the late eighteenth century," Theo said.

"Thank you, Robot Theo," Tess said. "But maybe that means this was not written by the Morningstarrs in 1855, but by someone else a lot earlier."

Jaime typed the verse into his phone.

"I wish Mom had gotten us cell phones for our birthday," Tess grumbled. "Every other thirteen-year-old has one."

"Did you guys have one of those blowout bar

mitzvahs?" Jaime said. "Like with dancers and a DJ and everyone dancing the hora and stuff?"

Theo said, "Oh no. Just a small ceremony. We don't like big parties."

"Our parents don't have that kind of money, anyway," Tess said. "And we don't have that many friends. I mean . . . .um . . ." Tess's face flared red. "What did you do for your thirteenth birthday party?"

"Haven't had one yet. I turn thirteen in September. I got this phone when I turned twelve," Jaime said, grinning. "Benefits of having a dad who feels guilty about taking a job overseas." He held up the phone. "We should have done this search first. The verse on the stove was written by Nathan Hale around 1776."

Theo nibbled on the fry. "Hale was a part of the Culper Ring."

"He was seen wandering around New York City taking notes whenever he passed a British barracks. He was caught by the redcoats and hanged," Jaime said.

"I didn't say he was a very good spy," said Theo.

"There were other spies who got away. Cato, an enslaved man who worked for a dude named Hercules Mulligan. Cato was questioned, but nothing was ever proven."

"*He* was a good spy," said Tess.

"And it looks like there were some lady spies, too. Anna Strong. And another lady who was never identified. People still call her by code number: 355."

"She was a *very* good spy," said Tess.

"The number 355 could mean something," Theo said. "Or maybe 355 was a woman the Morningstarrs knew?"

Tess frowned at her burger, mumbled, "I feel bad for the bugs." She gave the rest of it to Nine, who swallowed it in one bite. "Researching this could take forever. I wish we could ask Grandpa."

"Well, we can't," Theo said. "We'll have to keep reading."

Tess bit her lip. "You know who else might know about the spies of George Washington."

"We can't risk it," said Theo, knowing immediately who she was talking about. "If they knew we'd found something they'd start investigating, and if they start investigating, then everyone will start investigating. Even Slant."

"We'll have to see them sometime."

Theo dropped the fry to his tray. "We should go to the library, find what else they have on the Culper Ring, and—"

"We don't have time for that, Theo. Not when our

home is on the line. Not when there are people around who already know all this stuff."

"Which people?" said Jaime.

Theo watched a mechanical snail make its lazy way across a window, leaving a sparkling rainbow on the glass in its wake. How could he tell his sister that one or two small discoveries didn't mean that they'd be the ones to solve the Cipher? How could he tell his sister that, even now, he wasn't sure that the Cipher *had* a solution? And that Grandpa had never been?

"But we'll have to be careful," Tess was saying. "Really careful. We can't let on we've found something. They'll be all over us. In a nice way, but still. We could pretend that one of us has a summer project about Revolutionary spies or something."

"Careful around who?" Jaime asked again.

Tess had already made up her mind. She grabbed the rubbing, folded it neatly. She handed it back to Jaime. "Don't show this to anyone."

"I wouldn't. But are you guys going to tell me who we're talking about?"

"My grandpa Ben's old friends."

Jaime finished his burger, crumpled the wrapper into a ball. "I'm guessing you're not talking about his pals at the bingo hall or the bowling alley."

"No," said Theo. "His friends at the Old York Puzzler and Cipherist Society."

They caught the M103 solarbus. It sat up high enough that they could look down on the solar "wings" folded neatly on top of each passing car. Jaime was sitting diagonally in front of Theo, so Theo had a great view of his latest sketch; a superhero-like character balanced on top of the nearest car like she was riding a surfboard. She was wearing a T-shirt, jeans, and what looked like a bandolier of sledgehammers.

Tess peered between the seats. "I thought that lady superheroes wore high heels and short shorts."

"Here we go," said Theo.

Jaime said, "You *want* me to draw her in short shorts?"

"No! I just thought when boys draw lady superheroes, they put them in dumb outfits."

"Hey, now," Jaime said. "Plenty of girls draw them that way. And the guy superheroes wear tights and other dumb stuff."

"Not as dumb as the outfits the girls wear. Metal bikinis or whatever. I hate that. Unless the women have skin made of diamonds, any idiot could stab them in the femoral artery with a pencil and they'd bleed out."

"That's why she's wearing the armor," Jaime said.

"Stylish yet practical."

Tess laughed.

Jaime tucked his sketchbook away when they got closer to the Old York Puzzler and Cipherist Society, located in what was once the Five Points neighborhood and the site of the Morningstarrs' first home when they arrived in New York City in 1798. The bus dropped them right in front of the massive circular Croton Fountain with its four "rivers"—streams of water in waist-high marble troughs flowing east, west, north, and south. Behind the fountain was the Embassy of the Five Hundred Nations, flying the colorful flags of First Nations from the Abenaki to the Comanche, Pawnee to the Sioux. A man with two neat black braids and a sharp blue business suit sat on the edge of the fountain, eating a vanilla ice-cream cone. He nodded a greeting as they walked by. They nodded back.

A few minutes later, they arrived in front of a largish building that looked more like a warehouse than the home of one of the oldest and most secretive organizations in New York City.

"Big," said Jaime.

"They need the space," Tess told him.

"For what?"

"You'll see," Theo and Tess said at the same time.

"Do you guys practice that?"

Together, they said, "Ha."

Next to a pair of heavy wooden doors there was a small plaque and a buzzer.

THE OLD YORK PUZZLER AND CIPHERIST SOCIETY
BY APPOINTMENT ONLY

He didn't miss this place, that's what Theo had told himself when Grandpa quit the society, what he kept telling himself when it became clear Grandpa wouldn't be coming back. But it was strange to be standing outside the building, contemplating the buzzer, strange to be standing without Grandpa—Grandpa, who used to stroll right in, who used to consider this old building a second home, Grandpa, who never needed an appointment.

"Theo, are you calculating the volume of the building or are you going to ring the buzzer?" Tess said.

Theo pressed the button.

After a few moments, a bored female voice said, "Yes?"

"It's, um, Theo and Tess Biedermann? We don't have an appointment, but were wondering if maybe we could—"

"Theo and . . . SWEET MOTHER OF KITTENS, STAY RIGHT THERE, I'M SENDING HIM UP," said the voice, then cut out.

They waited. And waited. After about five minutes, the door flew open and a large white man with thinning wheat-colored hair, bright blue eyes, and the kind of muscular physique ideal for violent sports or movie gladiators stood there, breathing as if he'd just come in from a run. He looked from Tess to Theo back to Tess, then opened his arms wide.

"Hi, Uncle Edgar!" Tess said, flinging herself into them.

Edgar Wellington caught her, laughing. "I wondered when you two would come knocking. How long has it been?"

"Almost six months," Theo said. *I don't need this place, I won't miss this place.*

"That's way too long. How are you?"

Tess blurted: "Darnell Slant bought our building."

Uncle Edgar held Tess by the shoulders. "I heard."

"We're not going to let anybody take our home."

Uncle Edgar nodded. "I believe that."

"We're not going to live in a car!"

"Excellent news."

"We don't have a car," said Theo.

Uncle Edgar let go of Tess and clapped Theo on the back. "Which is just as well. You can't live in your car if you don't have a car." He turned to Jaime. "And who is this?"

"Jaime Cruz, sir."

Uncle Edgar shook his hand firmly. "Jaime! Nice to meet you! Have you ever been to the archives before?"

"No, I haven't," Jaime said.

"Come in then, and take a look."

They walked into a small, oak-paneled lobby with a few couches and chairs arranged around a low coffee table. Except for the newspaper articles about the Old York Cipher framed on the walls, it could have been the waiting room at the dentist's.

Uncle Edgar strode across the small room to a plain wooden door on the opposite side. It seemed ordinary in every sense of the word, but when he opened it, he revealed a steel wall with a keypad in the middle of it. He punched in some numbers and the door slid open. Behind the door was a steel box that appeared to be an elevator but was really a sort of holding area. Edgar motioned them all inside. As he waited for the door to close behind them, he said, "I suppose your grandfather couldn't drop by?"

Theo didn't have to look at Tess to know the expression

she must be making. Her whole face screwed up tight, balled fist banging on the side of her leg. "Grandpa isn't traveling much these days. Not even in the city."

"Ah," Edgar said, as if he had known exactly how Grandpa was doing, which he probably did. Edgar Wellington had been friends with Grandpa Ben for decades. Plus, the cipherists seemed to know everything, even things that didn't have anything to do with the Cipher.

Once the steel door had closed behind them, Uncle Edgar moved to the back wall, where another keypad was mounted. He raised his hand to punch in more numbers, but before he did, he turned back to Theo, Tess, and Jaime. "Are you guys ready?"

"Yes!" said Tess and Jaime. Theo said nothing. He was telling himself that he didn't need this place, didn't miss this place.

Then a hole opened up in the steel, dialing bigger and bigger until the hole had erased the steel, and the only thing Theo could tell himself was that he was a liar.

CHAPTER TEN

Jaime

The first glimpse of the archives punched the word
out of Jaime: "Whoa!"

Instead of being on the ground floor—the way
you'd expect to be—they walked out onto a large platform where they could look at the cavernous spaces
both above and below. The building had all its interior floors removed, leaving only four narrow walkways
ringing the perimeter. The walls of the entire structure
were lined floor to ceiling with shelves, those shelves
packed with books and manuscripts. At the bottom of
the structure, tables and chairs were arranged around
cases displaying artifacts, scrolls, puzzle boxes, and giz-
mos. Though the shelves lining the walls and the tables
and chairs were wood, much of the rest of the structure

was metal—metal guardrails around each balcony, a wheelable filigree staircase that curled from the uppermost balcony to the ground floor three stories below. In one corner was a single birdcage in which a large black mynah bird whistled and flapped. A bunch of people sat at tables and in chairs, talking and bickering.

The mynah suddenly squawked: "Cat! Cat! Cat!"

Three stories below, more than half a dozen faces looked up, all of them grinning like clowns. "Wellington! Why are you dawdling up there? And why are you all grinning like clowns?"

Jaime didn't know if he was grinning like a clown, but he did feel like leaping out of his own skin. He had never seen anything so close to the secret lair of the superheroes he'd spent so much time drawing. If Batman's Batcave and Dr. Strange's Sanctum Sanctorum had a baby, it would be the Old York Puzzler and Cipherist Society's Archives.

They took the tiny staircase one at a time, the whole thing vibrating with each step. Jaime wondered if they had picked this whirling staircase to make the trip into the heart of the archives doubly dizzying, so you never knew where to look as you made your descent.

A woman with a light brown face, bright pink hair, and a flowered dress like something out of the 1950s stood at the bottom of the staircase, beaming. She elbowed Edgar Wellington out of the way.

"Hey, Ms. Sparks," Theo said.

"Ms. Sparks, Ms. Sparks, who are you calling Ms. Sparks? I'm Imogen, you little fuzzball," she said, and gathered him up in her arms. "And you, too!" She squeezed Tess. Then she turned to Jaime. "And who is this handsome young man?"

"Jaime Cruz, ma'am."

"I'm a *ms.*, I'm a *ma'am*—you kids are killing me. Nice to meet you, Jaime," she said, and gave him a squeeze, too, so tight that it could have doubled as the Heimlich maneuver. Then she placed both palms on her knees and made her face level with Nine's. "And hello there, kitty. How are you? How many lives do you have left? Eleven or twelve, I bet." Nine mrrowed and rubbed against Imogen's combat boots.

Another woman charged over to them, a nose ring glinting against tan skin. "I'm Priya Sharma," she said, giving them another round of hugs. "You can call me Priya," she told Jaime.

"Keep hugging them like that and they'll need an oxygen tank," a white man with salt-and-pepper hair said from his wingback chair.

"Oh, just because you're a cold fish doesn't mean

everyone is, Gunter," said Imogen Sparks.

"Just because I don't feel the need to squeeze the life out of children doesn't make me a cold fish. I'm Gunter Deiderich." He nodded at them all. "I'm sorry about your home."

"We all are," said another man, whose bushy beard began right under his dark eyes. "Do you remember me? I'm Gino Ventimiglia."

"And that," said Priya, "is Gino's beard, which is making a bid for world domination."

"This is Theo's hair," said Tess, "which is giving Gino's beard a run for its money."

"Maybe they can all join forces and defeat Slant," said an olive-skinned and elegant man who introduced himself as Omar Khayyám, and gave everyone brief and elegant handshakes. After that, they said hello to Adrian Birch, Flo Harriman, and Ray Turnage, and got a shoulder clap, a fist bump, and a high five, not necessarily in that order. The only society member present who didn't greet them with a hug or a high five or a handshake was a yellowy-pale woman Edgar introduced as Delancey DeBrule. The woman said nothing, simply sucked her teeth in disapproval.

Tess leaned over and whispered, "I once compared her to a walking stick. I don't know why she was so insulted; phasmids are amazing insects. To escape predators, some give up a limb, some feign death, and some release a foul-smelling fluid. What's not to like?"

Delancey stood up from her chair with an operatic flourish, turned the chair around so that it faced the shelves instead of the people, and then flounced back into her seat, ignoring them all.

The mynah said, "So there!"

Jaime said, "What's the bird's name?"

"Auguste Dupin," said the bird, cocking its head and fixing Jaime with a remarkably intelligent looking eye.

"Auguste Dupin is the name of a detective invented by my namesake, Edgar Allan Poe," Edgar Wellington said. "Poe had an interest in secret writing. We thought it would be a little less obvious than naming our mascot Cipher or Code, right, Auguste?"

"Cipher or code," said the mynah.

"Speaking of ciphers and codes," Jaime said, tapping one of the glass display cases, "why do you have an egg in a case?"

"You can write a message on a hard-boiled egg using ink made from vinegar," said Theo. "The ink leaches through the shell and leaves the message on the egg underneath without a trace on the outside. It's called

steganography. Hiding messages rather than encipher-
ing them."

Jaime said, "Well, that's—"

"See this little ball? Did you know that the ancient
Chinese wrote secrets on scraps of fabric? And they
balled up the fabric and dipped it in wax? And then the
wax balls were swallowed?"

"How would they deliver . . . oh, uuugh," said Jaime.
"I would not want to be the one to get that message."

"Sometimes Greeks would shave the heads of their
messengers and tattoo messages on the scalp. Then they
would wait for the hair to grow back, and send the messengers on their way. When the messengers arrived,
their heads would be shaved and the messages read.
That is, if the messengers didn't die of blood poisoning
first."

"Not in a big hurry, then?" said Jaime, staring at a
curling scrap of leather with a strange tattoo in one of
the cases.

Edgar Wellington said, "Invisible ink on paper is
another way to hide a message. Benedict Arnold, the
Revolutionary spy, wrote messages in invisible ink
between the lines of letters his wife wrote to John André
of the British army. We've found invisible writing in

books and even on paintings. But that's not the only way to hide messages. Here, take a look at this letter in this case. This is a letter from World War II. Look at the hidden message!"

Jaime squinted at the document. "I—"

"Fourth line down, twelve words to the right," Theo announced. "A microdot. Germans could shrink a page down to a tiny dot and then drop it into some random letter. The first one was found in 1941 because of a tip that—"

"Okay, Theo," said Tess. "We've all heard about this stuff."

Theo sort of gulped, as if the entire history of cryptography were backing up in his throat like a bezoar, as if he just couldn't help himself. "People have been speaking in code, writing in cipher, and hiding messages in all sorts of ways for thousands of years. This whole case has papers and manuscripts and books from the Arab cryptanalysts, who were working in the golden age of Islamic civilization. They basically invented cipher breaking."

"Theo," said Tess, "slow down. "The last time you got this excited, you trashed the Tower of London."

"The Arabs made all their important discoveries in cryptanalysis—they invented it—but this was *after* they made all sorts of advances in math and statistics and linguistics, after they translated books from Egyptian, Hebrew, Chinese, Roman, Babylonian, Indian, Farsi, and a bunch of other languages."

"My people made many, many advances," said Omar Khayyám, nodding.

"Up there on the second level are books on medieval secret writing, including books on Mary, Queen of Scots. The archives also have recordings of Navajo code talkers—Windtalkers, some people called them— who used a code based on their language to transmit messages during World War II. The language is so hard to learn, and so few people knew it, that the Japanese couldn't break it."

Imogen Sparks said, "Do you think Theo missed this place?"

"Nah," said Jaime. "He's a cold fish."

"I'm going to get our friends here some refreshments. Ray brought some of his famous chocolate chip cookies," Priya Sharma said. She went to the bookshelves and pulled out a red volume nestled in a line of green volumes. The bookcase swung wide. Behind it was a full kitchen.

"This place is so awesome!" said Jaime. "When was it built? *How* was it built?"

Edgar said, "This neighborhood was originally known as the Five Points. Rough slum. The Morningstarr twins lived here when they first came to the country from Europe. All of the buildings were eventually torn down and other buildings popped up in their places, this warehouse being one of them."

"This city tears down more buildings in a single month than most cities still have standing," said Ray Turnage, a tall black man with a shaved head. "New York City is one giant boneyard."

"Anyway," said Edgar, "one of the original Cipherists bought it for a song and began the conversion into these archives. Over the years, we've expanded to include other artifacts."

Jaime gestured to a bunch of papers strewn across a nearby table. "What are these? They kind of look like tic-tac-toe games."

"That's Rosicrucian cipher. Sometimes called a pig-pen cipher," Edgar said.

"That's not a Rosicrucian cipher," said Gunter. "I've never seen a Rosicrucian cipher that used sets of dots in that particular way."

"It's a *variant* of the Rosicrucian cipher," said Edgar. "A lot of secret guilds used ciphers like these. But it's

really rather simple. Each letter is represented by a dot
or set of dots in a particular location. This is the key."

"So," he continued, "if I wanted to write your name,
I would write it like this." He scribbled a series of lines
and dots on a clean piece of paper.

"Cool," Jaime said.

"Anyway, someone found the key and some enciphered messages hidden behind a map at the public
library."

"Wow!" Jaime said. "What did the messages say?"

"They're about hiding a kitten from the master of the
house," said Gunter. "So not very interesting."

"Kittens are always interesting," Tess said, scratching Nine.

"And what's that?" said Jaime, pointing at a board,

about ten feet by three feet, hanging from thin chains going all the way up to the ceiling. On the board was a strange arrangement of brickwork in the shape of three pyramids.

"Oh, that's the latest clue in the Old York Cipher," said Edgar. "The symbol from the wall of 211 Pearl Street, built in 1831."

"Another building we just lost to developers," said Ray Turnage, shaking his head.

"What does the symbol mean?" Jaime asked.

"We don't know yet," said Edgar. "It's not a tradesman's mark. Nothing we've ever seen before."

"Looks sort of Egyptian," Jaime said.

"Yes," said Edgar. "We're not sure if the pyramid shape is important, if maybe there's a match hidden in another building in the city."

"For all we know its match was in a building already torn down," said Imogen Sparks.

"We have enjoyed quite good luck so far," Omar said, sitting and folding his hands over his knee. "We have not run into a dead end yet."

"Yet," said Imogen. "But this could take a while to decipher. Those Morningstarrs were something. So smart."

"And cheeky," said Tess.

"Now you sound like your grandfather," said Imogen.

"He always said that anyone who made whimsical machines like they did had to be funny, but we've never found any evidence of that."

Jaime imagined Theresa Morningstarr pelting people with potatoes, hiding mechanical spiders in purses, and hid a smile behind his hand.

Priya returned with a tray of cookies, which she placed on a nearby table. Jaime would never refuse the offer of a cookie, any kind of cookie. He grabbed a chocolate chip and took a bite. Buttery, salty, chocolatey—even better than Lance's oatmeal cookies. As he chewed, he examined the brick wall with its incomprehensible pyramids. He hadn't the slightest idea what the shapes meant. He wasn't an expert on the Morningstarrs like the twins were, but he knew the Morningstarrs *were* smart. And cheeky, if that letter was any proof.

He stopped chewing.

Smart and cheeky.

Cheeky.

Cheeky?

He didn't have to look in his pocket to remember that last two lines of the verse they'd found were:

> *You spy the grand & pleasant seat,*
> *Possess'd by Washinton the great.*

The *seat* of George Washington. The seat! Not a city with government buildings, but an actual seat?

"So, what brings you to the archives?" Edgar said. "Trying to walk in your grandpa Ben's footsteps? Solve the Cipher yourselves?"

A loud scoff came from Delancey DeBrule's direction. Everyone pretended not to hear it.

"No, not today," Tess said. "Today we have some questions about something else. You see my friend Jaime is—"

"Very interested in the decorative arts," Jaime said.

Tess frowned. Theo stared at Jaime.

"Excellent!" said Flo. "Which era?"

"Late seventeen hundreds, early eighteen hundreds," Jaime said.

"Yeeeeah," said Tess, going along. "He has . . . a summer class. They're studying pottery, furniture, all that kind of stuff."

"He is?" Theo said.

"He's doing a project about George and Martha Washington," said Tess.

"I didn't know the Washingtons were known for their taste in tables," said Imogen Sparks.

"They were, in a way," said Flo. "Martha Washington embroidered her own cushions."

"Cushions!" Jaime said. "I like cushions." Tess gave him a look. So, he wasn't a very good spy, either.

"He has to do a diorama," Tess said.

"I was reading something about a famous chair that George once used," said Jaime.

Tess's eyes widened, and then Theo's eyes widened. Flo didn't notice anyone's eyes. She said, "Most of their belongings are at Mount Vernon in Virginia. There are pictures all over the web."

"Nothing around New York?" said Jaime.

"Well, there's his inaugural chair," said Flo. "But that's not all that interesting in terms of decorative arts. But interesting enough because of the story behind it."

Tess casually inspected the cookie tray, picked up an almond biscotto. "What story?"

"Oh, just that nobody bothered to save or preserve the chair until the 1830s, when a US marshal saw it and figured out what it was."

"Huh," said Tess. Jaime was amazed that someone as nervous and about-to-explode-any-minute as Tess could also lie so smoothly. "So we could see the chair?"

"Sure," said Flo. "At the New-York Historical Society. But really, the best pieces are at Mount Vernon."

"Cool," Jaime said, "We'll definitely look at the web."

Flo said, "You should see Mount Vernon in person. It's not far by train. Ask your grandfather to take you!"

Imogen elbowed Flo. Flo said, "What?—Oh! I meant your parents. Your parents can take you."

Tess put the cookie back on the tray. "Right."

One minute they were in the Old York Puzzler and Cipherist Society's Archives, chatting about George Washington's furniture, and the next minute Tess Biedermann was stomping out of the archives, up the twisting staircase, out through the double doors, and onto the street, where she stomped some more.

"Tess, slow down," said Theo, which was exactly what she'd said to him when they were in the archives and Theo was lost in his cryptographic history—spewing trance. They did that a lot; said the same things to each other. Funny that neither of them listened.

"Tess!"

"What if we can't solve it?" Tess hissed. "What if we lose our home and have to live in a houseboat? What if there's a freak storm and we're carried out to sea? What if there are sharks? What if the sharks jump into the boat?"

Theo said, "If sharks jump into the boat, Nine will eat the sharks."

Jaime added, "And if Nine doesn't take care of them, you will."

"Yeah?" Tess said. "With what?"

"The power of your rage?"

"Oh," she said. They passed Croton Fountain, listening to the *shhhhhh* sound the water made. *Shhhh, there are no sharks here. Shhhh, this will all work out okay.*

This will all work out okay was what Jaime's father had said when he took the assignment in Sudan. And Jaime had stomped, too. He had stomped for weeks and weeks.

On the inside, he was still stomping.

Jaime cleared his throat. "About the riddle. I think George Washington's *seat* means a literal seat and not the seat of government."

"Right," said Theo. "Good thinking. We should probably go find that chair."

Tess had finally slowed to a walk. "It's getting late. We have to be back for dinner. Tomorrow?"

Jaime nodded. He wouldn't ask about the twins' grandfather, though he could picture the man so clearly, drifting through the hallways of 354 W. 73rd, a pencil tucked behind his ear and a book tucked under his arm, so lost in his own thoughts that he might not even hear you when you said hello.

It was as if everyone was a Cipher. You could look for keys and clues, but you might never figure them out.

CHAPTER ELEVEN

Tess

They decided to walk to the nearest Underway station and take the train back uptown, but when the train came, there were only two seats left in the car. Since Tess was too antsy to sit, she let Theo and Jaime have them while she dangled from one of the overhead straps and held Nine's leash. As the train stopped and started, stopped and started, Jaime sketched in his sketchbook. Theo occupied himself by thinking deep thoughts, and Tess imagined wrecking balls crashing through stone, several generations of families stuffed in cars and in houseboats, cat-eating sharks, and shark-eating cats. She wondered what Jaime was drawing—maybe another girl superhero with a bandolier of sledgehammers, a boy in a red cape or in a suit of iron, a man who looked like

Jaime's dad erecting sun castles in a Sudanese desert.

Or maybe he wasn't drawing superheroes at all. Maybe he was drawing the archives and the heroes there, the ones who had been trying to solve the Cipher forever. Tess felt a little twinge of guilt that they were keeping the new clues from Uncle Edgar and Imogen and Flo and everyone else at the society. But Theo had been right. If the Cipherists started investigating, the whole city would soon get wind of it, including Slant and his minions. Slant could hire his own cipherists, an army of cipherists. And if Slant solved the Cipher first, if he took the most valuable treasure known to man for himself, who knows how much power he'd have? He could buy all of New York City. He could buy all of the world.

The doors of the Underway car opened and a thousand or maybe a million people flooded in, surrounding Tess and Nine so that she could no longer see Theo or Jaime, or even the ever-present, ever-watchful Guildman in his box. A random elbow nudged her in the ribs, and she had to keep her face angled to the right in order to keep her nose out of someone else's all-too-fragrant armpit. Nine huddled against her leg.

At her feet, the caterpillar was maneuvering between people, scrubbing the floor. It reached Tess, suddenly stopped. Which was weird. The caterpillar never stopped for anything or anyone.

"Hey, could you stop nuzzling my pit, please?" the skinny guy next to her said, so pale he was almost gray. He was in his early twenties and was sporting floppy hair, a ratty T-shirt, and what her dad called an Artisanal Hipster Mustache.

"I am *not* nuzzling your pit," Tess said. Nine growled. The caterpillar rose up on its back legs, swaying like a snake. Tess could have sworn the thing was *looking* at her. But she didn't think it had eyes. It had pincers, though, and the pincers were clicking.

"Why is it doing that?" said Mustache, also watching the caterpillar. "I've never seen it do that before."

An Asian woman with a purple Mohawk seated nearby said, "It's looking at you."

"It's not looking at me," the man said. "It's looking at *her*." He jerked his mustache at Tess.

"Why would it be looking at her? She's just a kid." The woman's eyes narrowed as she examined the man. "What did you do?"

"I'm just standing here."

"You must have done something. Did you kick it?"

"No," said the man. "Why would I do that?"

The woman raised a brow. "Why would you walk around with that stupid thing on your face?"

"Is that supposed to be funny?"

The caterpillar swayed back and forth, back and forth. Nine's head followed the movements as if she'd been hypnotized.

And then the door to the Guildman's box opened, and the whole car went silent except for the sound of the wheels on the tracks, and the thud of boots on tile. The Guildman appeared in front of Tess, a boxy man with tan skin and sharp brown eyes. Tess gripped the strap tighter, her heart beating in her palms.

The Guildman frowned at the swaying, clicking caterpillar and frowned even harder at the hipster.

"Dude," said the hipster, "it's not looking at me; it's looking at her."

The Guildman looked from the hipster to Tess, Tess back to the hipster.

"I didn't do anything to your pet bug, okay? Chill," the hipster said.

The Guildman tried to grab the hipster, but the guy whipped his arm away, smacking Tess in the process.

"Ow!" she said, hot pain exploding in her cheek.

The Guildman clenched his teeth and pried the hipster's hand from the pole.

The hipster wailed, "Dude! I didn't mean to hit her. And this isn't my stop! I'm going to be late for an audition! Seriously, dude, this is going to really mess me up!"

The train screeched to a halt. The doors opened. The Guildman shoved the hipster onto the platform. He said one word:

"*Bus!*"

Then the doors closed and the train started again. The Guildman scooped up the caterpillar, holding it like a baby, which was more than weird, because the caterpillar was still clicking its mandibles, as if it were talking to someone, as if it were talking to the Guildman. For one long, torturous moment, the Guildman studied Tess before moving back to his glass box, carrying the caterpillar with him.

Everyone on the train exhaled. Nine licked Tess's hand, and Tess practiced her deep breathing, in and out, in and out, but her head kept saying what was that, what was that? And she didn't know what was that, except for completely bugburgers.

"What happened?" said Jaime when they got off the train. "We couldn't see anything. There were too many people."

She described the caterpillar swaying like a snake, clicking as if it had something to say.

"Creepy," Jaime said.

"But probably just a malfunction," said Theo.

"Since when do the Morningstarr Machines malfunction?"

Theo pulled at his lip. "Good point."

By the time they reached their building, it was close to dinnertime, and Tess was totally worn out, bruised cheek aching. Even the elevator seemed worn out, and it carried them directly to their floor without any of its usual whimsical side trips. The doors opened.

Stoop and Pinscher were standing by the tiled wall with a chisel and a hammer. Pinscher held the chisel, and Stoop tapped it until a tile popped off.

"What are you doing?" said Jaime, leaping out of the elevator.

Pinscher caught the loose tile, slipped it into a plastic bag.

"We're taking samples of some of the more distinctive features of the building, of course," Mr. Stoop said calmly.

"*Samples?*"

"Yes, samples. Of the tiles, of some of the plasterwork, crystal doorknobs, that sort of thing. We'll preserve these artifacts. Perhaps display them somewhere in the new building after it's built. This is a Morningstarr building, after all. Didn't you know?"

Jaime looked mad enough to spit. "Do *you* know how hard my grandmother works to keep all those tiles on the wall? To keep everything clean and repaired? To keep this building running?"

"Well, she won't have to work that much longer," Stoop said. He smiled his bland, bland smile, and then he and Pinscher strolled to the elevator. Just before the doors closed, he said, "We're going to have to take this elevator apart, too, you know. I'm sure all the gears and buttons and things will look nice . . . in a collage."

Jaime took one step forward, one hand curled around his pencil, as if he were looking for the nearest femoral artery. Pinscher gave one of his little waves. The doors closed.

"I hate those guys," Jaime muttered.

"We all hate those guys," Theo said.

Tess said, "Next time, I'm going to let Nine eat them."

"Mrrrow," said Nine.

They agreed to meet the next morning. Jaime walked to the end of the hall, and Tess and Theo let themselves into their apartment. Inside, their father was putting books in boxes and their mother was on the phone, pacing.

"Yeah, I heard you. But we've got some things going on here. Can anyone else take this? Uh-huh. Uh-huh.

Okay. Yes. I know. I'll be there in an hour." She clicked off, laid the phone on the counter, took one look at Tess, said, "What happened to your face?"

Tess rubbed her cheek. "Nothing happened to my face."

"Which is why you have a big red mark on it. Because nothing happened."

"I banged it on the pole in the Underway," said Tess.

"Did you have a spell? Theo, did she have a spell?"

Theo said, "She didn't have a spell."

Mrs. Biedermann swept both their faces with her mom-cop laser gaze. Then she said, "I'll get you some ice."

"It's fine," said Tess.

"It's swelling," said her mother. She dug around in the freezer and pulled out a bag of peas. She tossed them to Tess.

"Is this dinner?" said Tess.

"Yes. Put it on your face."

Tess pressed the bag of peas to her cheek and kicked at the empty boxes on the floor. "What are these?"

Her father heaved a heavy, forlorn sigh. Her mother said, "Those would be boxes."

"Why do we have boxes?"

"Boxes are usually used to pack things."

"But we just heard yesterday!" said Tess. "We have a whole month!"

Her mother's eyes went soft. "We're getting a head start, honey. We have a lot of stuff, including the stuff in your grandpa's apartment, which we should have packed months ago but I couldn't manage because . . . Look. I just don't want to leave everything for the last minute."

Her father sighed again. He appeared to be packing one book at a time, placing it in the box only after he'd read the cover, the flap copy, and the acknowledgments. Nine crawled out from under the coffee table holding a sock, which she then draped across Mr. Biedermann's knee. He patted her head, and she gave a mournful chirp.

Tess edged closer to her mother. "Dad doesn't seem too happy."

"None of us are happy. I'm not happy. I don't want to leave here. I never thought I'd have to." Her mother put her hands on her hips, her gaze moving from the kitchen to the living room, to the dining room, to her husband sighing over a pile of books on the floor. "But we have to prepare."

Tess was about to spill it all, beginning to end, from the strange letter written by Theresa Morningstarr and mailed to Grandpa Ben, to the clue underneath the

Tredwells' servants' stove, Stoop and Pinscher already wrecking the place, and the need to stop them. But something in her mother's face kept her from doing it—the way her brow crinkled, the way her lids looked ever so slightly red, as if she'd been crying. Her mother never cried, at least not in front of Tess. Tess's mother wore dark suits and sensible shoes, a badge and cuffs on her belt. She didn't break down. There was nothing she couldn't handle.

Still.

Tess scratched for a topic that wasn't terrible, that wasn't loaded. "What are we having for dinner?"

"Peas."

"Come on."

"I already called for Chinese. That okay with you?"

"Sure," said Tess.

Her mother tucked a loose curl behind Tess's ear, her fingers gentle. "Things are going to fine. I promise."

Tess couldn't tell who she was trying to convince.

They ate on the coffee table. Fried rice, chicken with cashew nuts, vegetable lo mein, egg rolls. Nine loved egg rolls and spent the whole meal trying to lick Tess's lips.

"Okay," said Mrs. Biedermann after downing some food quickly but neatly, "I gotta go."

"Are you sure someone else couldn't take it?" said Mr. Biedermann.

"Some whiny important guy had a break-in. Has some connections, so . . ."

"So the brass wants the best on it," said Mr. Biedermann. He and Tess's mom stood up. They didn't touch, but the look that passed between them was like a touch, so much so that Tess felt like she was watching something she wasn't supposed to. She rammed half an egg roll into her mouth.

"You could take human bites," said her mother.

"Or ladylike ones," said Theo.

Tess chewed loudly. "I'm a lady and these are my lady bites."

"Mouth closed, please. No one needs to witness your mastication process," said Tess's father, who was more of a stickler about things like manners.

"I only do it to gross Theo out."

"Except it grosses your dad out instead," said Tess's mom.

"Not you?" said Tess.

"You have to work pretty hard to gross me out," she said. "Okay, I'm off to console a very sad, very rich man who has lost his prized coin collection."

Nobody mentioned anything about not-at-all-rich

people losing the only home they'd ever known, nobody talked about their beloved elevator stripped to the gears and used to make a bit of lobby art.

Theo said, "Go get the bad guys, Mom."

"Don't I always?" she said.

Then she was out the door. Tess and Theo and their father threw out the cartons and washed the plates and silverware. After that was done, Theo disappeared to his room, and Tess asked her father if he wanted help packing the boxes. She didn't *want* to help pack the boxes, but the sight of him packing them alone was too sad.

"I think I'm done packing for the night, sweetie," said her dad. "How about we watch a movie instead?"

"Okay," she said.

They flipped through the channels and found *Storm II*. Tess had already seen it, but it was better than any of the *Wonder Womans*; they'd rebooted that one three times and still hadn't made a version in which Wonder Woman wore actual pants. So, they watched Ororo Munroe battle a water dinosaur with her mutant weather-manipulating powers.

"It'd be so cool to have mutant powers," Tess said.

"With great power comes great responsibility."

"That's Spider-Man, Dad."

"Oh, right. How about 'With great power comes zappier lightning'?"

"I like it."

They still weren't tired when *Storm II* was over. They flipped through the channels till they found another, older movie they'd seen many times about a guy who finds out his life is not really a life, but some sort of computer-generated virtual reality, and he has to save the world from the tyranny of the machines. Tess and her father settled on the couch, Nine stretched across both their laps, purring loud enough to power the universe. When they got to the part where the main character has to make a choice—open the white box and he can live out his entirely manufactured life with all its petty joys and annoyances, or open the black box and learn the hard, cold truth about the world—Tess yawned and said, "Of course he opens the black box. Anyone would open the black box."

She'd said this before. She'd probably said it every time they watched this movie. And every other time she'd said this, her father had agreed, yes, of course, who wouldn't open the black box? Who wouldn't want to know the truth?

This time, her father said, "That's the problem.

People think they've already opened the black box."

"Huh? What you mean?"

"They think they're the only ones who understand the real truth about the world, and that it's everyone else who's been tricked."

"Yeah, but if you found out that you had been lied to, who wouldn't want to know what's really going on?"

"Most people aren't so brave."

"But—"

"The biggest problem we have is that people like to fool themselves into thinking that they could never be fooled." He took her hand, squeezed it, let go. "There aren't enough boxes in the world to fix that."

CHAPTER TWELVE
Theo

It was the sort of dream you *know* is a dream as you're dreaming, and yet, Theo couldn't wake up.

He was creeping up the stairs of the Tredwell House, wincing every time the old boards creaked underfoot. He'd brought a flashlight but didn't want to risk using it—someone outside might see the beam in the windows and call the police. So, he felt his way in the dark, sliding his hands along the walls. When he hit a velvet rope that blocked the servants' quarters, the metal clasp clanged like a bell. He snatched at it, stilling it with his hand, waiting for the echo to dissipate. The air had the same smell as before—furniture oil and must and history—but there was a heaviness to it that hadn't been there in the daytime, a weight, as if all the dead Tredwells were with him, solemn and silent, as he unclasped the rope and rounded the last flight of stairs to the attic. Which was silly, because he believed in ghosts as much as he believed in gnomes or fairies or true love between any people besides his parents and grandparents. (His dad believed in ghosts; his mom said he'd believe in love one day. They both said he'd grow out of the weird dreams.)

He stood, eyes adjusting to the moonlight that poured through the windows. The narrow beds came into view, the little stove squatting sullenly against the wall like some animal that had been robbed of its prized posses-sion, just waiting for the opportunity to steal it back.

(He hadn't grown out of the dreams.)

He stepped into the pitch-black of the closet and closed the door behind him. He found a metal panel with numbers. (What was this doing in the closet of the Tredwells?) But he turned the flashlight on and tucked the end between his teeth, light facing the panel. With the screwdriver he'd brought, he removed the metal panel, revealing the wires underneath. He pulled a wire cutter from his pocket (why was he carrying wire cut-ters?), unclipped and reclipped, cut and spliced; and soon enough, the back of the closet yawned and he was stepping into the chill air of the archives.

But this was not the archives.

(Why would this be the archives?)

This was not anywhere he recognized.

(Why couldn't he wake up?)

Instead of standing inside, he was standing outside, in the middle of a cobbled street, the gray scrim of moon shining on foul water pooled in the gutters. On either side of the street, shabby two-story taverns leaked out-of-tune piano music punctuated by raucous bursts of laughter. A horse-drawn carriage clattered down the street, splashing him with mud and who knows what else. He yelped and tried to wipe it off, getting noxious muck all over his hands.

"Well, well, well. What are you supposed to be?"

Theo whirled around. A man wearing some sort of costume—a long coat, short pants, a rumpled hat— leaned in doorway, picking his nails with a knife.

"I said, what are you supposed to be?"

Theo said, "Excuse me?"

"Excuse you? Excuse you?" The man sauntered toward Theo. He was so ripe with sweat and grime and cheap wine that Theo slapped his hand across his nose and mouth and cursed his sense of smell.

(Wake up.)

The man twirled the knife in Theo's direction. "What kind of togs are those?"

"Togs?"

"Togs! You got cole in them pockets?"

"Coal? I don't understand."

"Cole! Coin!"

Theo backed up a step and bumped into another costumed man who smelled as bad as the first one, maybe worse. "Who's this, Reggie? A new friend a yours?" the second man said. The second man shoved Theo into the first one. The first man pushed him into the second, and the second man caught him as he staggered, laughing as Theo struggled to get away.

(Wake up!)

A third man—jacket torn, hair greasy, teeth black— tottered into the road, grinning a Halloween grin. "What's this? One of the swells come to the Five Points?"

"The Five Points?" said Theo, so surprised he stopped struggling for a second. "But the Five Points neighborhood doesn't even exist anymore!"

"Five Points is all around you, boy!"

Theo thrashed in the man's arms, looking for something, anything he recognized. The closet he had stumbled out of. The Morningstarr Tower in the distance. But . . .

"Where's the Tower?"

"Tower?"

"The Tower! It should be right over there!"

"There ain't no tower! Boy thinks he's in a fairy tale!"

"I do *not* believe in fairy tales. The *Morningstarr* Tower."

"The what?"

"The Morningstarrs. A man and a woman. Really rich and important. They built all of New York City!"

"Nobody named Morningstarr around here."

"They made the Cipher! If you want cole, coin, whatever, you have to solve the Cipher! It's a treasure hunt!"

The man holding him shoved him to the stones. "There ain't no tower. There ain't no Morningstarrs. And if there's a treasure, you'd best be telling us where it is before we hush you right here."

(Wake up.)

"I don't know where it is!" said Theo.

(Wake up!)

"I'm trying to find it!"

"WAKE UP!"

"I have to find it I have to find it I have to find it—"

He sat up. He was not in the archives. And he was not in the Five Points. He was in his bed, sheets twisted around him, his mom leaning over him.

She said, "It's okay, Theo. It was just a dream."

"What . . . what time is it?"

"About two in the morning."

"Oh," he said, and flopped back down on his pillow.

"Are you okay?" she said.

Yes. No. "This has been a really weird day."

"What were you dreaming about?"

"I broke into a house."

"Really?"

"Really. I had tools and everything."

"Wonder who exposed you to that sort of criminal activity." She smiled in the dark.

"And then I was in the Five Points neighborhood and ran into a bunch of really smelly, really dirty guys."

"Five Points?" She sat on the edge of the bed. "You mean the gang area downtown, from the eighteen hundreds? I think your grandfather read you too much Dickens when you were little."

"Maybe."

His mother straightened the twisted sheets, draping them over him. "Where did you guys disappear to all day?"

"Museum."

"Anywhere else? The society maybe?"

"How did you know?'

"I talked to Edgar about donating some of your grandfather's collection to the archives. He mentioned you'd stopped by. He was worried. He said you got upset."

"*Me?* I didn't get upset. Tess got upset."

"He said you seemed upset."

"I'm fine," he said.

She nodded. "What are you trying to find?"

"Nothing," he said too quickly.

Her expression didn't change. "Uh-hmm," she said. "You can look as hard as you want for . . . whatever you want, but I don't want you guys getting hung up."

Too . . .

. . . late.

"We're not getting hung up," Theo said.

"You might need to manage your expectations."

She didn't say, *No one has been able to solve the Cipher, not even my father.* She didn't say, *The Cipher is just a story to lure the tourists and make New York seem like a place where dreams come true.* She didn't say, *What's done is done, and we need to get more boxes.* But she didn't have to. Theo picked at the plaster seal on the window molding.

"Theo, if you keep playing with that, Mrs. Cruz is going to have to spackle it again."

"If Slant is going to knock down the building anyway, what difference does it make?"

His mother gazed at him another moment, expression unreadable. Then she stood, pressed a kiss on his forehead. "I think we should both get some sleep."

"Okay."

"Good night."

"Mom?"

"Yes?"

"Did you catch them? The ones who stole the coins?"

"Not yet," she said. "These things take a while. Can't skip any of the steps in an investigation."

"But soon you'll catch them?"

She smiled. "Maybe tomorrow."

"Right. Tomorrow."

And then it was tomorrow. Another day, another society, this one the New-York Historical Society on the Upper West Side, 170 Central Park West at 77th.

The home of George Washington's chair.

Theo, Jaime, Tess, and Nine decided to forgo the Underway and walk. Though it was still midmorning, the pretzel and hot dog vendors were out in force, the steam from their carts salting the air. When they arrived at the museum, they stopped to let Jaime sketch the life-size bronze statues of Frederick Douglass and Abraham Lincoln at the entrance. Inside, a poster declared the museum's special exhibits:

The Games We Played: American Board and Table Games

Beauty's Legacy: Gilded-Age Portraits in America

Keith Haring All Over

Lion-Heart: Old New York and the Electrocell Revolution

*Ciphers and Secret Societies: The Puzzling Case of the
Underway Guildmen*

New York City Pizza: A History

They declined the map offered at the ticket window, marched past the permanent Morningstarr exhibit—complete with a household version of the Roller, about the size of a cat; an early model of the Morningstarr Analytical Engine, based on the work of Charles Babbage and Ada Lovelace, and the giant portrait of the twins themselves, all white hair and deep frowns and road-map skin—and went right for the chair, passing furniture, paintings, and other exhibits, including this sign on an otherwise empty pedestal:

THIS OBJECT HAS BEEN TEMPORARILY REMOVED
AS WE REVISE ITS FACIAL EXPRESSION, WHICH WAS
DEEMED ZOOLOGICALLY IMPROBABLE AND/OR
TERRIFYING TO SMALL CHILDREN.

They finally found what they'd come for: a plain mahogany chair with a simple design on the back. The plaque next to the chair said that on April 30th, 1789, at Federal Hall in downtown New York City, George Washington sat in this chair on the day of his inauguration.

Jaime pulled his sketchbook from his back pocket and made a quick drawing of the chair, front, back. Surreptitiously, he tested the back and legs to see if it came apart somehow. He even got on the floor and drew the underside of the chair, which got him in trouble with one of the wandering guards, who told him to get up and stop crawling around the floor like some sort of cuckoo bird.

Tess said, "I thought cuckoo birds *flew*."

The guard said, "Don't get smart."

Theo said, "She won't."

Jaime peered at the chair and back at his drawing. "I'm not seeing anything interesting about this chair."

"Well, the chair was lost," Tess said. She pointed at the plaque marking the exhibit. "Nobody even bothered to store or preserve it until this guy named William Waddell recognized it in 1831 and decided to take it home. His family held on to the chair for fifty years and even let some other presidents borrow it."

"Okay, so are we supposed to look into the other presidents who might have sat in the chair?" Jaime asked.

"I don't think so," said Tess. "I wonder if the clues are about things or even people that have been lost or overlooked."

"Maybe we should look into this William Waddell dude," said Jaime. "I've never heard of him before. Seems he's been forgotten, too."

Tess peered at the plaque again. "It says here that there's a painting of one William Waddell in this museum."

"There is?" said Theo. "Huh."

"Let's try that painting next," said Jaime.

When the guard turned to berate an old lady for getting too close to a silver bowl, Tess flapped behind him like a cuckoo bird, which was a little bit like watching a gibbon attempt to fly. Jaime started doing it, too, and dropped his sketchbook in the process. Theo picked it up, flipped through the pages. Jaime had drawn the Liberty Statue, the stove in the servants' quarters of the Tredwell House, the archives from above, bony Delancey DeBrule sputtering, Auguste Dupin peering around her shoulder.

"When did you do these?" said Theo.

Jaime stopped flapping. "Last night, after we got home."

"From memory?"

"How else?"

"Huh," said Theo, handing the book back to Jaime.

Jaime said, "I'll take that as a compliment."

"It's the best you're going to get from him," said Tess, who was already jogging to the next exhibit hall, Nine loping alongside her. Another guard told her to quit flying around like a dodo bird—which didn't make sense, as dodo birds were a) flightless and b) extinct—and made Theo think that perhaps the guards needed some lessons in ornithology. (Odd considering that most of the second floor of the museum was taken up by an exhibit called the Complete Flock of Audubon's Aviary.)

But Tess had already reached the painting. Or where the painting should have been. On the wall was a blank space with a small card:

THIS EXHIBIT IS TEMPORARILY UNAVAILABLE.
WE APOLOGIZE FOR THE INCONVENIENCE AND
THANK YOU FOR YOUR PATIENCE.
—THE RESTORATION DEPARTMENT

"Great," Theo said. "Dead end."

Tess said, "No, it isn't. We just need to get into the restoration department."

Jaime said, "Without breaking the law. My grand-mother will lose it if I break the law."

"No one's breaking any laws," said Theo, who had no idea if breaking laws would be required, though he hoped not. "My mom would not approve."

"We can't get in trouble, either, though," said Jaime. "My grandmother will kill me if we get in trouble."

"Nobody's getting in trouble," said Tess.

"Hmmm. You guys probably won't," Jaime said, but he followed them from the exhibit area. They went back to the ticket booth to consult a map, but the map didn't have any particular area marked "Restoration."

"Not helpful," said Theo. His skin was starting to itch. When he got annoyed, he got itchy.

"Stop scratching," said Tess. She shoved the map at him and walked up to the nearest ticket clerk, who was chatting on her phone.

"I don't know *when* she's supposed to do it," the clerk said. "I just heard that she is going to do it today. I know! That's her goal. The press, the police, whatever. She just wants attention."

Tess tapped her fingers on the counter until the clerk put her hand over the mouthpiece of the phone. "Can I help you?"

"Hi there! My aunt Jane works in the restoration

department up on the third floor and I was supposed to meet her for lunch?"

The clerk said, "You mean the lower floor?"

"Yeah, that's what I meant. The lower floor."

"What's your aunt's last name?"

"John," said Jaime.

"Your aunt's name is Jane John?"

"Yes."

"Okaaay." The clerk tucked the phone into the crook of her neck and typed the name. "I'm sorry, I don't have an employee by that name."

"Are you sure?" said Tess. "I know she told me that she worked at the New York Museum of Natural History."

"This is the New-York Historical Society Museum and Library."

"That's different?" said Tess.

"Uh, yes?" said the clerk.

"Oh! I was wondering why there weren't any T. rexes."

"Come on," said Theo, yanking Tess away from the clerk. They walked toward the entrance of the museum and then quickly cut right, taking the stairs. On the lower level, there were some classrooms and the children's museum. The offices were behind a frosted-glass door marked, unsurprisingly, "Museum Offices." Theo didn't have to look at Tess to know what she wanted to do. They pushed open the door, and walked into the offices as if it were the most natural thing in the world, as if they belonged there. At the end of a long hallway, there was another frosted-glass door, this one marked "Restoration." It was quite a trick to creep silently down a hallway while still trying to appear as if you're doing nothing wrong, especially when you were the son of one of the city's most prominent detectives called in to investigate the city's worst thefts. His muscles hummed with the effort of it, and that made him itchy again.

They passed individual offices, some empty, some with people working diligently inside, but no one seemed to notice them.

Until a man looked up from his desk and frowned.

"Hey!" he said. "What are you kids doing down here? You can't be down here. Hey!"

Tess pushed Jaime, Jaime shoved Theo, and Theo stumbled, then ran. Most of the nearby offices were occupied, but there was one dark door, unlocked, that said "Laboratories." Theo ducked inside, Jaime and Tess right behind him. It was a long, shadowy room packed with row upon row of lab tables. They dived underneath one of them, squished together. Somewhere, a refrigerator hummed a warning.

"We're going to get arrested," Jaime whispered.

"Shhhh!" said Theo.

The door creaked; footsteps echoed. "I thought I saw them come in here."

"Who?" said another voice.

"A bunch of kids."

"Why would a bunch of kids come down here? *I* don't even want to be here, and I work here."

Theo risked a peek around the table, saw a few sets of legs walking in their direction. He crawled to the next table, tucked himself under. He turned around, realized that Tess and Jaime had stayed put. He gestured for them to follow when the legs passed right between the tables. Theo went still. Tess slapped her hand over her mouth.

The legs kept moving toward the back of the room. Tess and Jaime crawled over to Theo and squeezed in next to him. They tried not to breathe.

"I don't see any kids."

"I'm going to have to call security anyway."

"You don't want to do that. You know what a freak Sig is. He'll just do something bugburgers like have the kids thrown in jail."

Jaime elbowed Theo and then made frantic motions with his fists like a person shaking a set of bars.

"We can't have a bunch of kids running around down here. They could wreck something or steal something."

"They were probably just looking for the cafeteria."

"Or they're thieves or in a gang or something."

"A *gang*? Do you hear yourself?"

The footsteps rounded the room and then walked out into the hallway. Theo peeked around the table. The legs were gone. And there was a door on the other side of the room with light coming from underneath it. Maybe it opened into the restoration area. Theo pointed at it, waved for Tess and Jaime to follow. They crawled from one lab table to the next until they reached the door. Theo knelt and slowly turned the handle, cracked the door, looked inside. He saw a sea of easels and work tables, each with picks or brushes or other tools. He also saw a sea of feet. Tess tried to push him forward, but he resisted.

"There are too many people in there," he whispered.

And then there were too many people out here; footsteps echoed in the hallway.

Jaime lunged back under the nearest table. Tess and Theo did the same. The lights came on. Heavy shoes thudded on the floor, then stopped. The shoes walked to the west end of the room, turned north, walked for a while, then turned south. Theo pressed his face to the floor and looked under the table, watched the feet move in straight lines. Whoever it was was walking a grid. The room was big, but not that big. It wouldn't take long for them to be caught.

They had two choices. They could crawl into the restoration room and take their chances, or try to zigzag to the door leading to the hallway so that they could make their escape.

The footsteps stopped again. Theo pressed his cheek to the floor again to see where the shoes were.

Except he didn't see a pair of shoes. He saw a cheek pressed to the floor just the way his was. And a pair of eyes. And a mouth that smiled.

Theo sat up so fast he whacked his head on the underside of the lab table. The footsteps thundered in their direction. Tess squeaked and scooted to the next table. Jaime went the other way. Meaty hands reached for Theo just as he threw himself out from under the table, slid down the empty row. He scrambled to his feet and caught a glimpse of a guard uniform before he ran, making random lefts and rights like a Morningstarr elevator. Tess squeaked again as the guard caught her, and then the guard roared as Tess's sneaker came down on the top of his foot. Jaime reached over the top of a lab table, grabbed her by the arms, and hauled her across it to the other side. The guard lunged for them and missed. They split up, pinging around the tables like some reenactment of the world's worst video game.

As soon as Theo thought, *Why is this man chasing us around tables, why doesn't he just block the door, who is this bad at geometry?* the guard gave up the chase, blocked the door. But he didn't block the door to the hallway, he blocked the door to the restoration room.

Mistake!

Theo broke for the other door.

And ran headfirst into a wall.

He fell on his butt. Which hurt.

The wall said, "Hello, children. My name is Sig."

CHAPTER THIRTEEN
Jaime

The man named Sig was built like Ben Grimm of the Fantastic Four—almost as wide as he was tall—and had no tolerance for these shenanigans. Jaime knew this because Sig said: "I have no tolerance for these shenanigans."

When Tess tried to explain about her aunt Jane John and how she worked here and how they were supposed to meet her and—

"I don't like shenanigans and I don't like fibbers," Sig said.

Fibbers?

Sig pushed them down the hallway as if they'd already been tried and sentenced and were off juvie till they were twenty-one.

His dad was going to kill him. Mima was going to kill him.

"Where are you taking us?" Tess demanded.

"My office. I'm calling the police. I'm calling your parents. None of you are leaving till both of them get here."

"We didn't do anything!" Tess said. Nine mrrowed in kind.

"I'm also calling animal control," Sig said, sniffing at the cat.

"She has a license!"

"Faked," said Sig.

"My mom got that license!"

"Your mom faked a license?"

"What? No!"

Someone behind them called: "Mr. Sigurd! Wait!"

Sig whirled around so fast that Jaime went whipping around with him. A woman in a blue suit brandished a phone. "We may have a situation."

"Take care of it," Sig barked.

"It's a pretty big situation," she said.

Sig grunted, shoved them into the nearest office, and sat them down in three chairs. "Stay!" he said, as if he were talking to a bunch of puppies. Then he stepped back out into the hallway. Jaime leaned close to the open door to hear.

"This is unacceptable. Where's everyone going?" Sig said.

"To see Lora Yoshida."

"Who?"

"The performance artist? She's staging a flash mob outside on the street. They want to watch."

"A flash *what*?"

"A flash *mob*," the woman said, overenunciating loudly as if Sig was hard of hearing. "They're dancing. At least, I think it's dancing. Or maybe it's just wiggling? I don't know. They're blocking the museum entrance."

"Super," said Sig.

Next to Jaime, Tess muttered a series of what-if questions, getting more and more breathless as she talked. What if these guys called the real cops? What if they were arrested? What if they were taken downtown and put in a cage with a bunch of mobsters? What if the mobsters recruited Theo to run numbers for them? What if Theo became the most notorious mobster in the history of the city? What if he were known as Theo "The Hairball" Biedermann? What if rival gangs put out hits on Tess and her mom and dad to get back at Theo, and they were forced into the witness protection program, and had to move to a ranch in New Mexico, where they would raise chickens, cattle, and alpaca?

"Nobody's joining the mob," Theo said absently. And then he said, "Wait . . . did you just call me 'The Hairball'?"

Nine licked frantically at Tess's fingers.

Footsteps thundered down the hallway. Jaime scooted closer to the open door to see a wave of people—museum employees?—rushing up the stairs.

"This is unacceptable. Where's everyone going?" Sig said.

"Well, Mr. Sigurd, as I was saying, everyone wants to see Lora Yoshida. She has torches."

"Torches? Why does she have torches?"

"She's erected a scale model of the city on the street. They're supposed to set fire to it. That's what I meant by 'situation.'"

"It's the middle of the day! Why would they set anything on fire?"

"It's supposed to symbolize the destruction of the city by greedy corporations. Or something like that."

"How is that art?"

The woman shrugged. "Ask Lora Yoshida."

"Why don't they do this stuff downtown and annoy the kooks at the Modern Art Museum?" Like a bull, Sig exhaled loudly through his nose, stormed over to the office. Jaime threw himself back in his chair. Sig barked, "None of you move." Then he slammed the door.

And locked it.

They stared at the locked door.

Tess stopped muttering her what-if questions. "That can't be legal."

"But he did it anyway," Theo said.

"What are we going to do?" Jaime said.

"Well, we can't stay here," said Tess. She rummaged around on the desk and found a paperclip. She straightened it out, jammed it into the lock on the door. In a few seconds, she was easing the door open.

"Do I want to know where you learned that?" Jaime said.

"Our great-aunt Esther," said Tess. "She was a locksmith."

"Among other things," Theo said.

"See anyone?" Jaime said.

Tess shook her head. "No, it looks like they're all gone."

They sneaked out into the hallway.

"We should get out of here while they're distracted," said Jaime.

"Yeah," said Theo.

"Totally," said Tess.

But instead of making their escape from the museum, the three of them turned toward the frosted door of the restoration room. It was now or never; Sig didn't seem like the kind of man who would forget a face.

Nine chirped softly as they crept down the hall, but if she was trying to tell them they were being stupid, well, they already knew that. Jaime knew that. If they got caught again . . .

But there was no one in the restoration room, either. No one alive, anyway. Faces watched them from all around the room—faces in paintings and in etchings, faces in sculptures.

"How do we know which one it is?" said Tess.

"What's the guy's name again?" Jaime said. "The dude in the painting?"

"William Waddell," Theo said.

Jaime found his phone, searched images. "Got it," he said. He glanced around the room. "There." He pointed at a painting in the corner.

They moved closer. The first thing you noticed about the painting was the pale, thin man with the high forehead and the sunken eyes, then the way his black suit was swallowed up by the foliage and the grass around him. Next to him sat a woman in a bright orange dress, a little girl in pink perched at her feet. Two other girls, one standing, one lounging on an elbow, had those odd sorts of faces Jaime had seen on children in other old paintings, tiny middle-aged-lady faces. On the other side of the tall man was a boy in a blue coat, his dark pants also disappearing into the background. Behind the family a large stone house, almost a castle, loomed.

Theo swiped a magnifying glass off the nearest table. "Let's see if there's anything hidden in the painting."

"We have to hurry," Tess said. "We have no idea how long they'll be outside."

"One minute," Theo said. But it took much longer than a minute to examine the painting, which had all kinds of detail in it—bushes and trees and grass.

"Make sure you check out all the bushes and trees, too. If I wanted to hide some kind of writing or code or whatever in this painting, that's where I'd put it," Jaime said.

"I don't see anything," said Theo.

"Doesn't mean it's not there," Tess said. "Let's flip it over."

Carefully, they lifted the painting and turned it over.

If it had once had paper backing, the backing had been removed. There was no writing on the painting.

"Nothing," Theo said, flipping it back. "Maybe it's not the painting, exactly. I wonder what that building is, in the background?"

Jaime allowed his eyes to drift over the sunken eyes, the tiny middle-aged-lady faces on the children, the looming castle, the trees, the bushes. Something about the painting called to Jaime, something about the way everyone was posed. Two of the children gazed off in different directions, but the wife and the son looked up at their father, as if waiting for him to speak, while the oldest daughter reclined in the grass and seemed to be staring directly at Jaime, daring him to figure it out. He looked from the reclining girl to the man, who must be William Waddell himself. Then he noticed something sticking out of William's pocket. Some sort of book or paper.

"Here's a question," Jaime said. "If you were going to have your portrait painted, would you stick a random paper in your pocket like that?"

"I wouldn't," said Tess.

"I would," Theo said, "if I wanted everyone to look at it." Theo pressed the magnifying glass against the tiny square of paper depicted in the painting. "I don't see anything written on it, though."

"Maybe something's written under the paint," said Tess.

"Or written in invisible ink," Jaime said.

"Maybe," said Theo.

"I was kidding," Jaime said.

"I wasn't," said Theo. "But some inks are developed by heat, and some by a chemical reaction. If there's any kind of invisible writing here or anywhere on the painting I don't know what to use to reveal it."

"This was before 1855, remember?" said Tess. "So would the ink be made of something natural—lemon or vinegar or spit?"

"The Culper spies used ferrous sulfate and water," said Theo. "Basically, iron. We need sodium carbonate to activate it."

"Where are we going to get sodium carbonate?" Tess said.

"This *is* a restoration department," said Jaime.

"So?" said Theo.

Jaime went to the wall and looked at the shelves of chemicals and solvents. "So, they clean old paintings with sodium carbonate."

"You're kidding," Theo said.

Jaime grabbed a box of washing soda off the shelf, held it up. "I wasn't."

He ran to the sink and grabbed a cup sitting on the counter. He filled the cup with water and brought it back to Theo. They mixed a bit of the washing soda with the water. Jaime found cotton swabs on the supply shelf, dipped one into the solution, and then held it out to Tess. She put her hands up. "You're the artist, I think you should do it."

"I hope this doesn't ruin the painting," Jaime said. "I mean, I don't love it or anything, but . . ." He rubbed the swab gently against the "paper" in William Waddell's pocket.

"I saw this movie once where they found invisible writing on the back of the Declaration of Independence," said Tess. "They rubbed a lemon all over it to reveal the message."

"That's so stupid," said Theo. "If the invisible ink was juice or vinegar, they would have smeared the whole thing till it was unreadable."

As Jaime rubbed, he thought he saw the faintest hint of brown underneath the white. "Holy secret writing, Batman. Give me the magnifying glass."

Theo passed the glass. Jaime centered it over the brown scratches.

The Other Hamilton shows you the shape of things.

They were staring at this new riddle, stunned, when they heard voices outside.

Jaime tossed the glass back to Theo and his phone to Tess. "Zoom in and take a picture." He pulled out his sketchbook.

"What are you doing?" Theo whispered.

"I don't trust technology," Jaime said.

Tess took a photo. "We have to cover up the writing," she said. "Maybe there's some paint or a marker around here."

"Markers? Are you serious?" Jaime poured more of the washing soda into the water and dipped the swab. He scrubbed at the painting until the writing was gone. "I hope I didn't wreck this."

"You didn't. You found the next clue," said Tess. Jaime felt the flush up to his 'locs. He could get used to being a cipherist.

The voices got louder. Nine mrrowed.

"We gotta go," Theo said. He waved at a door on the other side of the room. Jaime hoped it wasn't a janitor's closet.

They bent low and ran to the door, ducking into the

next lab just as the frosted-glass door to the restoration room opened.

Voices crept under the door. "That was incredible!"

"*She's* incredible!"

"I would watch her read from the dictionary."

"I don't think Sig liked her, though."

There was laughter, and then: "Hey, did someone already start cleaning the Waddell piece?"

Tess, Theo, and Jaime ran through the lab to the door on the opposite end, almost slamming into a group of women trying to get in.

"Oh, sorry!" said Tess. "We thought this was the bathroom."

A black woman wearing one of the biggest, most magnificent curly weaves Jaime had ever seen said, "Sure you did."

Another woman said, "Sig is looking for you kids."

Jaime's stomach sank. So they would be arrested after all. Or worse.

The one with the weave smiled. "He's tearing apart the corporate offices. If you catch the elevator now, you should miss him."

Jaime said, "Thank you. Seriously."

The woman gave him a beautiful, motherly smile.

"That guy thinks he's working for the FBI. What's the FBI going to do with an angry refrigerator?"

Jaime was still trying to picture an angry refrigerator when Tess pulled him into the hallway. They heard shouting coming from either end, coming from everywhere. Tess stabbed the button.

"The elevators don't come any faster when you do that," Theo said.

"I know," Tess said, stabbing the button anyway.

The doors finally opened and they jumped inside. When the elevator reached the ground floor, they held their breath, released it when they saw no one but tourists. Once outside, they inhaled the scent of smoke, saw the burn marks on the pavement. The Rollers were taking care of piles of spent sparklers.

"We should send Lora Yoshida a thank-you note," Tess said.

Jaime patted his pockets, making sure he still had his phone and his sketchbook. "Weird that she was the one to distract Sig the Refrigerator, though."

Theo kept looking back over his shoulder, as if he expected Sig to be behind them. "Why is it weird? I mean, it's weird to want to burn things in the street, but other than that . . ."

Jaime stopped walking. "Don't you guys know who she is?"

"An artist?" Tess said.

"Yeah, and she's also Darnell Slant's ex-wife."

CHAPTER FOURTEEN
Tess

"That's way too adorable," Tess said.

"You keep saying that coincidences are adorable when I don't see how one has anything to do with the other," Theo said. "Koala-pandas are adorable."

"*You're* adorable," Tess said.

Jaime said, "I'm thinking it's a little adorable, too. Cuddly, at least."

"You're hurting my head," said Theo.

"What I think your sister means is that this is starting to feel planned somehow," Jaime said.

Tess said, "Grandpa Ben always said that when you tried to solve the Cipher, the Cipher was trying to solve you."

Theo frowned so hard that all his features scrunched

to the middle of his face. "How could the Cipher engineer anything? It's a puzzle. A series of clues. It isn't alive."

A Roller crossed in front of them, scraping up bits of burned paper and snack wrappers. "How would you define *alive*, Theo? Is that Roller alive? Is Grandpa's Lancelot alive?"

"So you think a Morningstarr Machine talked Lora Yoshida into putting on a performance to distract museum security guards? That's nuts. You've seen the insides of Morningstarr Machines, and you know that's all they are, machines. Amazing machines, but machines."

"I'm not saying I have all the answers—"

"You don't have any answers—"

"I'm just saying that this feels weird," Tess said.

Theo sighed. "What's weird is that this has been too easy."

"Easy?" Jaime said. "A man built like a fridge just tried to send us to jail."

"What I mean is that it took years for people to solve a single clue in the original Cipher. We've solved a bunch already. The odds of that seem astronomical. As if . . . as if the Cipher wants to be solved." He tugged on his lip, as if he were about to pull it up and cover his whole head with it, wrap up his body, and roll into traffic, because what he and Tess had just said was too ridiculous, too fantastical and impossible and a million other un-Theo-like things.

A shiver danced up Tess's spine. She stepped in closer to her brother and to Jaime. "We should be more careful. We can't talk about this with anyone else. We can't let on. We can't let anyone overhear us, either." She checked behind them to see if they were being followed. Nine turned and checked, too.

"Well, that doesn't look obvious at all," Theo grumbled.

"Let's figure out what we need to do next," Jaime said.

"I'd like to figure out how Slant keeps getting all these artists and supermodels to marry him," said Theo. "He looks like he colors his hair with shoe polish."

Tess didn't bother to point out the irony of Theo "The Hairball" Biedermann talking about anyone else's hair. She was still thinking about this, her mind conjuring up everything from government spies to foreign agents to hostile aliens disguised as human beings to minions of Slant, all with ridiculous hair, when they entered the lush green of Central Park, all gently rolling hills and tufts of trees. They got three pretzels with mustard and sat on a park bench to eat them. A slight breeze lifted Tess's braid, and she smelled pretzels, hot dogs, and the faintest scent of zoo. The Rollers were here, too, picking up refuse left from picnics and impromptu baseball games and rolling it away. A bunch of teenagers played exo-ball, their metal exoskeletons allowing them to leap over one another's heads and crash into one another while laughing like hyena-wolves. Nine watched them leap, rapt.

Jaime pulled out his sketchbook, on which he had written the words from the painting:

The Other Hamilton shows you the shape of things.

"This sounds more like a riddle than a cipher," Theo said.

"Hamilton like Alexander Hamilton? Who's 'the Other Hamilton'? And what's the shape of things? What things?" Jaime said.

"I don't know," said Tess. She gave the sketchbook back to Jaime and took her pretzel from Theo. There was nothing like a New York City pretzel. She wondered briefly if she should be worried about what they were made out of—recycled cardboard? school paste?—and then decided she didn't want to know. Theo had a smear of mustard on his upper lip. Neither Tess nor Jaime informed him of it.

Jaime set the sketchbook aside and consulted his phone. "Alexander Hamilton is buried in the graveyard at the Trinity Church. I say we try there first."

"But we're not looking for Alexander Hamilton, we're looking for the Other Hamilton," Tess said.

"His other half, maybe?" said Jaime. "His wife is buried there, too. And his kids."

"Huh," said Theo. "Maybe. It's worth checking out, anyway."

"The Morningstarrs liked to be cryptic, didn't they?" said Tess. "Get it? Buried? Cryptic?"

"And you say my jokes aren't funny," said Theo.

"The mustard on your face is funny," said Tess.

It was early afternoon, so the Underway only had a scattering of people. A woman buried in shopping bags. Two more teenagers with Starrboards. A man in coveralls who was fast asleep sitting up. Jaime took out his sketchbook and drew the car and the people, simple, quick lines that somehow captured them all.

"Where did you learn to draw like that?" Tess asked.

"My dad."

"Your dad? But I thought he was some kind of engineer?"

"He is. But he also paints, watercolors mostly. He's not much of a talker, but he paints pictures of the things he does and things he sees and sends them to me. I have paintings of test tubes and landscapes and monkeys and street fairs and all kinds of stuff—wait, I have one with me." He dug around in his side pocket and took out a folded piece of paper. Tess opened the folded paper—so soft, the way paper gets when it's handled a lot. Inside was a painting of a windswept red desert, a camel trekking across the sand, reins held in the hand of a tall woman. She was wearing a long white cloak and looking back over her shoulder, dark curls escaping the hood.

"It's beautiful. Different from your stuff, but I like it."

"Yeah," said Jaime. "Me, too. He thought about being an artist when he was young but . . ." He shrugged. "Mima's parents, my great-grandparents, brought her to Florida from Cuba when she was my age. She says they had it rough for a while. She's practical. She wanted my dad to be comfortable. She wanted him to have a real job."

"Being an artist isn't a real job?"

"Not like being a doctor or scientist or engineer is."

"I guess," said Tess. "Who's the lady? She's pretty."

Jaime paused. "My dad likes to put my mom in his paintings sometimes."

"That's nice," Tess said.

Jaime nodded, refolded the drawing. On the back of the paper, Jaime's dad had written *Be good to Mima. Home soon.*

Jaime saw what she was looking at and then said, "He's never home soon enough."

Tess worried her fingers in Nine's fur. She had questions the way she always had questions: How much did Jaime miss his dad? How much did he miss his mom? Was it harder to miss someone who was forced to leave you or someone who chose to? But their stop came soon enough, and Tess shook her questions out of her head. They filed out of the train and walked the short distance to the Trinity Churchyard. According to Jaime's phone, the church had three burial sites—the churchyard at Wall Street and Broadway, the Trinity Church Cemetery on Riverside Drive, and the churchyard at St. Paul's Chapel. The graveyard itself might have been spooky if it hadn't been so sunny and warm, and if there weren't so many tourists crowding the walkways, reading the old cracked stones, the strange markers with skulls and wings.

The biggest crowd surrounded Alexander Hamilton's grave, not only because he was Alexander Hamilton—a

Founding Father of the United States, chief of staff to George Washington, face on the ten-dollar bill, and dopeface who managed to get himself killed in a duel by the vice president of the United States—but because his was a sizable monument, with four pillars and a sort of obelisk-like triangle on top, flowers and coins left all around it. A tour group took rubbings of the markings on the tomb.

Theo said, "Hamilton wasn't that old when he died. Who knows what he could have done if he hadn't dueled with Aaron Burr."

"What happened to Aaron Burr?" said Jaime.

"Ignominy!" said Theo.

At Jaime's surprised laugh, Tess said, "Sometimes Theo talks like a dictionary. Anyway, for a dude that was born in the 1750s, Hamilton wasn't the worst. He created our banks and stuff. And he was supposed to be an abolitionist."

"Hmmm," said Jaime. "Unlike Jefferson, who *talked* about people being equal but still had slaves."

"Right?" said Tess. "But Hamilton didn't trust the poor even though he'd grown up dirt poor. Which is strange when you think about it. Why would hate yourself?"

Theo said, "Grandpa Ben always told us that great people are capable of doing terrible things and that we shouldn't ever forget it."

"But I wonder if that's what happens when you grow up," said Tess.

"What do you mean?" said Jaime. "You turn evil?"

"No. And I'm not talking about everyone. Just that some people have all these convictions; they know what's right and wrong, but they get too old and too tired to follow through. They give up. Or maybe they get so scared and selfish that their convictions get twisted to serve them instead of serving the world and the people in it."

"Meaning you turn evil," said Jaime. "That's the most depressing thing I ever heard."

"Well, I could be wrong," Tess said.

"When she says 'I could be wrong,'" Theo said, "she means 'I could not possibly be wrong.'"

"My grandmother is like that," said Jaime.

"I knew I liked your grandmother," Tess said.

"Speaking of wrong, we're looking at the wrong grave," Jaime said. They turned to look at a line of grave markers near Alexander Hamilton's monument. The largest was for his wife, Eliza. The marker said:

ELIZA

DAUGHTER OF

PHILIP SCHUYLER

WIDOW OF

ALEXANDER HAMILTON

BORN AT ALBANY

AUG. 9TH 1757

DIED AT WASHINGTON

NOV. 9TH 1854

INTERRED HERE

Jaime did another search on his phone. "Says here that Eliza Hamilton spent the rest of her life after Alexander's death fighting for his legacy. She founded orphanages in New York City and Washington, DC." Jaime looked up. "Well, she doesn't sound too evil."

Tess glanced the graveyard and lowered her voice. "Look at all the people taking pictures of Alexander Hamilton's grave, and nobody's over here." But Tess still didn't know how the marker would show them "the shape of things." The stone itself wasn't unusual. So they tried the graves of the *other*, other Hamiltons, Hamilton's children, but there wasn't anything unusual about those grave markers either.

Tess drifted back to the grave of Eliza Hamilton. It made sense to her that the Morningstarrs would use this marker for a clue. Not only was Eliza overlooked, she was trying to make sure her husband wasn't. She was trying to do the right thing. And wasn't that what Theresa Morningstarr was wondering about in that first letter sent to Grandpa Ben?

Tess wanted to do the right thing, too. She wanted to solve this mystery. Not just for herself and her home, but because Grandpa Ben couldn't.

She moved closer to the grave marker. She ran her gaze over every inch of the stone but still didn't see anything unusual.

Except . . .

She dropped to her knees and squinted. Underneath the inscription was a small . . . circle? She traced it with her finger. No, not a circle.

"What is it?" said Theo.

"An octagon," she whispered. Then leaned back on her heels and frowned. "Does that mean anything to you guys?"

"Nope," said Theo.

"Nope," said Jaime.

Tess got to her feet, worried the end of her braid. "It has to mean something. I think the Cipher wants us to remember this lady. To think about the things she did, things that were important but didn't make her famous."

Jaime held up his phone. "She was known to take orphan children into her own home even though she was broke."

"Too bad she's not here right now," Theo said. "She could take us in. We're homeless now, too."

The joke just hit Tess like a brick.

Home.

Less.

She was homeless. *They* were homeless. Which of course was the reason why she was here in the first place, because Slant had stolen their home from them, snatched it away like a robber grabs a purse. Yes, she'd spent twenty-four hours imagining her family in a split-level in Idaho, crammed in a car, floating in a boat on a shark-riddled sea, and farming alpacas in New Mexico, but it was the first time she'd heard someone say it so plainly, so baldly, so *technically*. Home. Less.

Nine mrrowed and Tess patted the top of her domed head, rubbed her striped ears, tried to relax, tried to make her own joke. "Homeless orphans. We're like something out of Dickens."

"I . . . ," Theo began, then stopped, index finger

pointing at nothing, nowhere. Then he tapped his cheek, one, two, three.

"What?" said Jaime.

"What?" said Tess.

"Look up 'Octagon, Dickens, NYC' in your phone," Theo said.

"Okay," said Jaime, typing, "but I don't see— Oh!" He stared as his phone for a long moment, reading.

They should have gotten a phone for their birthday— why hadn't they gotten a phone for their birthday? "What does it say?" Tess said.

Jaime held out the phone. The first entry on the screen said, *Octagon, New York City, an award-winning Manhattan landmark.* Out loud, but not loud enough for the other tourists to overhear, she read: "'The Octagon was built as a stunning island retreat in 1841. Designed by architect Alexander Jackson Davis, and built with handsome stone quarried from Roosevelt (formerly Blackwell's) Island itself, the Octagon's signature rotunda was so striking that English novelist Charles Dickens praised it as "remarkable," and "spacious and elegant."'"

"Yes!" Theo said. "Dickens made a trip to New York in the 1840s and wrote about the Octagon in *American Notes for General Circulation.* My grandpa used to read it to me."

Jaime blinked. "My grandmother read me *The Cat in the Hat*. In five different languages, but still."

"The Octagon wasn't a retreat at all," Theo continued. "It was the entrance to the New York City Lunatic Asylum."

CHAPTER FIFTEEN
Theo

As soon as he said the word *asylum*, Tess flinched as if stung by a bee. She closed her eyes, lids twitching. Theo didn't have to ask to know what she was thinking about. The day they brought Grandpa to that new place, shiny and blue and smelling like mouthwash. *This will be better for Grandpa,* their mother said. *He'll have twenty-four-hour care. He can't manage anymore on his own and I . . . I . . . It will be better for him.* And Grandpa Ben, small and hunched on the new bed, trying to smile through it. It had been one of his rare good days, and that only made the whole thing worse. A wizened woman hobbling down the hall on the arm of a relative grinned through the open door. *Welcome to the asylum,* she'd said, giggling, until her grown daughter hushed her. *Welcome, welcome, welcome.*

In the cemetery, crumbling grave markers all around them, Nine snuffled, then chewed on Tess's fingers, but still Tess stood there, eyes closed, swaying a little. Theo should snap her out of it, he should take her arm or say something.

"Is that girl okay?" said a man standing nearby with his family. He was wearing a baseball cap and a T-shirt that said "Take a Bite Out of Gotham City," which was plain nonsensical.

"She's fine," Theo said. "She just gets headaches sometimes." He willed Tess to open her eyes, see the man's nonsensical T-shirt, say, "Thabat's sabo sabilly."

"Doesn't look like a headache to me," the man said.

Now other people in the graveyard were looking and whispering. Theo wanted Tess to laugh, to tell them that no one had paid her this much attention since kinder-garten, when she'd brought in a bone and told the class that it could be a chicken bone *or* the finger bone of a Sasquatch that had gotten into the city from New Jersey via the Lincoln Tunnel, and she was forced to have a talk with the school counselor about the difference between real life and make-believe.

Nine's meows turned loud and insistent. Theo was telling himself to say something, to do something, when Jaime lifted his hand as if to put it on Tess's shoulder.

Though Jaime didn't touch her, she seemed to feel it just the same. Her eyes flew open. "What?" she said. "What are you guys staring at?"

"Are you . . . ?" Jaime said.

Tess flushed, wrapped Nine's leash around her hand. "Me? I'm totally fine."

His parents told Theo to go easy on Tess after she'd had one of her "spells," to be gentle with her, but he knew Tess hated that.

"Are you done with your nap?" Theo said. "Can we go now?"

She made a show of rolling her eyes. "You're such a robot."

"That's me," he said, letting out a rush of breath that felt like the pulling of a splinter. "Your robot brother."

But the asylum would have to wait; they needed to get home for dinner. On the Underway, Tess dug a napkin out of her pocket and told Theo he still had mustard on his face, like nothing weird had happened. With the Guildman staring him down, he was careful to tuck the soiled napkin in his pocket. He didn't want to drop it and get thrown off the train. Nine seemed to notice the Guildman's attention and sat on Theo's feet, guarding him.

With the warmth of the cat against his legs and the rocking of the train car, Theo could stop thinking about Tess and about Grandpa and think, instead, about something that didn't make his brain and eyes feel like they were made of water.

He thought about Charles Dickens.

Dickens first came to America in 1841 to lecture Americans about international intellectual property, something Americans weren't much interested in at the time, because they liked being able to publish the work of non-Americans without paying any of the writers. But Dickens had ten children to support. Plus, he enjoyed writing about America—the gross parts of it, anyway. Like the Five Points neighborhood, which he described as "reeking everywhere with dirt and filth," with "coarse and bloated faces" peeking through "broken windows that seem to scowl dimly." That was probably why Theo had dreamed of the Five Points, because Dickens had written about it in *American Notes*, one of Theo's all-time-favorite bedtime stories. In *American Notes*, Dickens had also written about Blackwell's Island, now called Roosevelt Island. Theo wondered what they would find there, where they would go next. And then he wondered again at the way in which the clues kept coming together for them, snapping neatly the way Legos did. In 1855, the newspapers said that the Cipher was just waiting for the right people to solve it. Had it been waiting for them all this time? A bunch of seventh-going-into-eighth-graders? Grandpa Ben had always told him to never underestimate himself just because he was young. *The energy of young people powers the world. You are smart, Theo. More than that, you are curious, and that will carry you.* But Tess was the curious one. And Theo was smart enough to know there was a mountain of things he *didn't* know, and that mountain weighed on him.

When they got back to 354 W. 73rd Street, they said good-bye to Jaime and let themselves into the apartment. Which was crowded with society members. Edgar Wellington, Priya Sharma, Omar Khayyám, Imogen Sparks, and Ray Turnage were all sitting in the living room, eating oatmeal cookies. Grandpa Ben's Lance clomped around the Biedermanns' apartment, serving large glasses of milk. He seemed about as happy as an empty suit of armor could seem.

"Ah, here are the kids now!" said Mr. Biedermann.

Theo and Tess greeted everyone and took a few cookies from Lance's tray. Nine circled the room, getting scratches and pats and murmurs of *Who's a kitty, are you a kitty?*

"We decided to bring Lance down here because he

seemed so lonely upstairs by himself," said Mr. Biedermann.

"Good idea," said Theo, munching on a cookie. But Tess was eyeing the society members suspiciously.

"So . . . ," she said, trying desperately to sound casual but not sounding remotely casual, "what are you guys doing here?"

"We have to start packing up Grandpa's apartment," said Mrs. Biedermann. "Since he always wanted the society to have his collection, I asked them to come over and help, since they know which artifacts are important."

Tess lowered the cookie from her mouth. "We don't have to do that now, do we?"

Nine circled back to Tess and rubbed against her leg. Mr. and Mrs. Biedermann exchanged a look. Edgar Wellington said, "We'll just be taking inventory for a while. We won't remove anything till you're ready."

Mrs. Biedermann knocked back a swallow of milk. "Except for Lance."

"What about Lance?" Tess said.

"We don't have the room for him here, and it's not good for him to be alone anymore. He shredded six rolls of paper towels and left the mess in the bathtub."

Tess put the cookie back on Lance's tray and stalked

from the room, Nine on her heels. Mrs. Biedermann sighed.

Edgar Wellington said, "She just needs some time."

"That's just what we don't have, Edgar," said Mrs. Biedermann.

Lance stomped back to the kitchen and rattled around in a cabinet until he found the griddle.

"Well," said Mr. Biedermann, "I hope you Cipherists like pancakes."

The next morning, Theo, Tess, and Jaime met in the lobby to head over to Blackwell's Island, now called Roosevelt Island. There were several ways to get onto the island: Underway; bus; cab. And the best way to get onto the island was not under it or even across to it, but *over* it.

They got off the Underway and walked to 59th Street and Second Avenue, where they found the Roosevelt Island Tramway Plaza. Unlike the Underway trains, which ran on tracks both below and above the city streets, the tram was a trolley car suspended from wires slung over the East River from Manhattan to Roosevelt Island. For the same cost as an Underway ride, you could traverse the East River and see the city from the air.

After a ten-minute wait, Theo, Tess, Jaime, and

Nine boarded the tram, a red car attached to the wires above with a large silver clawlike contraption. Luckily, Roosevelt Island wasn't that popular a destination, so there were only a few tourists scattered about, and none with nonsensical T-shirts. The tram pitched a bit and then began its ascent. Tess was quiet, after a big fight with their mother over the fate of Lance, which she won, but only temporarily. Jaime was busy with one of his sketches, a black superhero with lightning coming from his ears. Theo's muscles and nerves relaxed as the frantic sounds of traffic—the squeals of tires, the horns, the sirens—got farther and farther away. Even the gentle sways of the tram in the wind didn't startle him. The tops of apartment and office buildings came into view, the water towers perched on top of them like spaceships drawn by children. Alongside the tram, the 59th Street Bridge was so close that Theo, not prone to imagining such things until recently, envisioned the people who had built it more than a hundred years ago sitting on the girders, legs dangling as they ate their lunches. In the distance, the spires of the Chrysler Building, the Empire State Building, and the Morningstarr Tower spiked the clouds beyond the endless rows of buildings. Below, the East River, greenish when you stood close to it, shone like a silvery ribbon.

"Remember the first time we took the tram?" said Tess finally. "With Uncle Edgar and Grandpa? What were we? Four or five?"

"Yeah," said Theo. "I remember that you asked if there were sharks in the East River and Uncle Edgar told you that story about that great white shark in New Jersey."

"Uh, what shark in New Jersey?" said Jaime.

"You don't know about the shark in New Jersey?" said Theo.

"No, I don't, and even if I did, you would tell me anyway, so why don't you just tell me?" said Jaime.

"In 1916, a great white or a bull shark—people still argue about which—killed a bunch of people on the Jersey Shore before swimming into the Matawan Creek, where he killed two more people."

"A shark can swim into a creek? Seriously?" said Jaime. He turned to Tess. "Now I understand why you're so obsessed with sharks."

"After that, Tess wouldn't even swim at the Y."

Jaime added a shark to his drawing.

The car began its descent toward Roosevelt Island. Jaime quickly sketched the view from the tram—the buildings, the Queensboro Bridge, the river like a ribbon complete with a shark fin sticking out of it. Theo remembered another story Uncle Edgar had told on that first tram trip, one about a submersible shaped like a shark, with the saw-toothed skin of a shark, built by the Morningstarrs. Grandpa Ben had laughed and said, aside from some mentions in a couple of old letters, no substantial evidence of that submersible had ever been found—no plans, no prototypes. Uncle Edgar had replied, "Maybe because the Morningstarrs didn't want it to be found."

But the Morningstarrs, as brilliant as they were, couldn't have known the future, couldn't have been certain that the clues they had so carefully hidden in the buildings and the streets and artifacts wouldn't be destroyed by progress or chance. The Tredwell House could have been knocked down for a drugstore, the Waddell painting stolen or spray-painted by deranged men wearing Take-a-Bite-Out-of-Gotham-City shirts. Blackwell's Island, a dumping ground for criminals and mentally ill people, was now a land of apartment buildings and schools and parks. It was just luck that one of the few original structures left on the island from the time of the Morningstarrs was the Octagon.

It seemed crazy to rely on luck, but one of Grandpa Ben's favorite questions was this one: *Isn't there a fine line between brilliance and madness?*

Maybe if the Morningstarrs could rely on luck, Theo could, too.

If he could persuade himself to believe in luck.

Which he didn't.

To reach the Octagon, Theo, Tess, and Jaime took a twenty-minute bus ride to the northern tip of the island. They stood in a parking lot in front of a beautiful rotunda made of blue-gray stone, two large boxy wings flanking either side.

"It looks brand-new!" said Tess.

Jaime showed them some old pictures of the Octagon on his phone, so run-down that it was barely recognizable. "How do we know what to look for when so much of the original has been replaced?"

"Remember what Slant's minions said to us when we caught them prying that tile off the wall?" Tess asked. "They said they would use the artifacts to decorate the lobby of the new building. Maybe they did that here, too."

"Anything really significant would have been given to a museum," Theo said.

"Then maybe someone can tell us which museum," said Tess. "Come on."

They walked up the steps and into the building.

Inside, the design was spare and modern, with a flying staircase spiraling all the way up the walls of the rotunda, culminating in a skylight at the very top. Everything was polished wood and marble. If there were clues or artifacts still in the Octagon, you'd never know it.

A couple that Theo's mom would have called "posh" sat on a couch looking through some documents with a man in a suit. More posh people stood staring at paintings hung on the walls of the rotunda. A blond woman smiled toothily at them from behind a desk. "Hello! Can I help you? Oh, wow, pretty tiger-lion, but we don't allow pets in the building."

"She's not a pet," said Tess. "Well, she's not just a pet. She's a service animal. And we're just looking around."

"Right," said the woman, peering over the edge of her desk. "Okay. Well. Let me know if you need anything."

They walked the perimeter of the Octagon, which wasn't big but also wasn't small. The art on the wall was the kind his mom called "schmears"—a smear of one or two colors on a white canvas, the type of painting most people claimed could be done by kindergartners. And for all Theo knew, this entire exhibit was done by kindergartners. As if to prove this, the main doors opened and two men in matching shirts that said Sunshine Daycare stepped inside, leading a group of small children. The children wore clear plastic bubble suits that made them look like giant balloons with hands and feet. They bobbed and bounced behind the men. Two little girls repeatedly belly-bumped each other until one of the Sunshine Daycare people said, "Not too hard, girls, we don't want you getting hurt!" One of the little girls promptly bumped the other onto her back, where she spun in lazy circles, flailing like a turtle. Nine's head spun in kind.

Tess jerked on Nine's leash, hauling her away from the little kids bobbing like buoys in a stream.

"It would be great if we knew what we were looking for," said Jaime. "We don't even have a hint. This whole place has been forgotten, in a way."

After that, they climbed the staircase that wound itself up to the skylight. They spent at least an hour scouring the walls and the stairs and the floors for a sign of something cluelike.

"There must be something," Tess said, once they had reached the skylight and couldn't climb any farther. "Let's go back downstairs and ask the woman at the desk."

"I doubt she knows anything," Theo said.

"Maybe she knows someone who knows something," said Jaime.

When they got back to the front desk, the bubble-suited children were gone. The blond woman said, "Hello, again. What can I help you with?"

"We're interested in the history of the Octagon," said Tess.

"Great!" said the woman. "I have some brochures right here that give you the whole backstory." Up close, she was a lot younger than Theo first thought. Not so much a woman as a college girl. Her fingernails were blue with little floating clouds.

"Thank you," Tess said, taking a brochure. "We were wondering if you found any artifacts when you were renovating."

The blond girl tipped her head, birdlike. "What kinds of artifacts?"

"Oh, I don't know. Records or letters or doctors' notes. Loose keys. Personal effects. Jewelry. Maybe bits of brick or stone with messages scratched into them by desperate patients. Like that."

The girl kept smiling, though her eyes cut to the posh couple on the couch. "What? Why would you think we found anything like that?"

"This rotunda was the entrance of the New York City Lunatic Asylum," said Theo.

The girl said, "This building opened as a retreat in 1839."

"I'm not sure I'd call a lunatic asylum a 'retreat,'" Jaime said, eyes on the sketch he was making.

Theo said, "Charles Dickens once visited here."

Jaime read a quote from Dickens off his phone: "'Everything had a lounging, listless, madhouse air, which was very painful. The moping idiot, cowering down with long disheveled hair; the gibbering maniac, with his hideous laugh and pointed finger; the vacant eye, the fierce wild face, the gloomy picking of the hands and lips, and munching of the nails: There they were all, without disguise, in naked ugliness and horror.'"

"If you could keep your voices down," the blond girl said, again glancing at the couple seated on the couch nearby.

"The patients got rotten food, scurvy, cholera. And when the asylum first opened, they were supervised by inmates from the penitentiary instead of nurses," said Jaime.

The blond girl's smile dimmed. She leaned forward and whispered, "Look, that's not stuff my boss likes us to emphasize, especially when people are in the market for apartments." She jerked her chin at the posh couple. The couple frowned.

"How much are apartments here, anyway?" Jaime asked.

The blonde slid a price sheet over to Jaime. Jaime regarded the sheet, then the blond woman, then the sheet, then the woman. "I think there are too many zeroes written here."

"No, that's the right number of zeroes."

"You'd have to be Darnell Slant to afford a studio."

"Tell me about it," said the blonde.

"Tell *me* about it," said Tess.

"Right?"

"No, I mean, really, *tell me about it*," said Tess. "You guys had to have found something during your renovations. Things you donated to museums maybe?"

"The place was pretty much cleaned out when we got it. A pile of broken-down bricks. But not, like, significant bricks or whatever."

Tess's face fell. "Okay. Thanks anyway."

"Except for some junk down in the storeroom."

Theo's skin prickled. "What kind of junk?"

"Stuff that we've been meaning to give to the local history people. We've been holding on to it while they're working on getting funding for their own building. But I'm telling you, there's nothing interesting. Some old boxes of garbage. A broken wheelchair. It's not like we're talking Morningstarr relics here."

"Is there any chance we could see that stuff?" Tess said.

"Oh no," the girl said. "My boss would kill me if I took people to the storeroom. Besides, it's nothing interesting, like I said."

"You know," Jaime said, "my grandmother is in the market for a new place."

The girl raised her eyebrow. "Seriously?"

Jaime said, "Oh, my grandma's loaded."

"Made her money in commodities," Tess said. "And futures."

"Yep," said Jaime. "Both of those. Do you have a map that shows the grounds?"

The girl let go of her hair. "I bet you guys think you're slick. You want a map to see where the storage room is, right? Do you think we'd put the storage room on the map?"

"We had to try," said Jaime. "Thanks anyway." He ripped a page out of his sketchbook. "For your time."

The girl looked down. It was a picture of her twirling a curl around a little cloud finger. Even though Jaime had sketched only a few lines, he'd somehow captured the girl's spirit. Theo hadn't known such a thing was possible. He might have called it magical, if he believed in magic.

"Oh," the girl said in a small voice. "This is . . . Oh."

"Well," said Jaime, slapping a hand on the counter, "we'll get out of your way now."

The girl bit her lip. "Hold on." She ducked behind the desk and came back up holding a set of keys. "Bernard?" she called to the man in the suit speaking with the posh couple. "Watch the desk for a few minutes?"

Bernard's smile was tight. "I'm with clients, Apricot."

"Great, thanks, Bernie!" said Apricot, scooting out from behind the desk.

Bernard barked, "Apricot!"

Theo was thinking that, if her parents were that determined to name their child after a piece of fruit, that "Quince" or even "Gooseberry" might have been a more interesting choice, or at least more fun to say, when Apricot gestured for them to follow her to the bank of elevators. Once they were all inside, she stuck a key into a keyhole on the wall and turned it. She pressed a button marked B2.

"I don't want you guys to get your hopes up or

whatever," Apricot said. "But I'll let you look."

"Thank you," Tess said.

"You'll have to be fast, though, because Bernard will have a complete cow if he has to answer the phone even once. Bernard doesn't do phones."

The doors opened onto a dim hallway painted the sort of pee yellow that someone had mistakenly assumed would cheer up the place. They followed Apricot down the hall into a small storage room with metal shelving. Apricot pointed to some water-stained boxes, a pile of stones and bricks, a rusted-out wheelchair missing a seat. "That's all that's left. We only saved this stuff because the museum people asked us to."

"Thanks for letting us take a look," Theo said.

Apricot didn't even glance Theo's way. "No one's ever drawn me a picture before. I mean, no one's ever drawn me a picture of *me*. That was, like, really cool. So, you guys have ten minutes." Apricot disappeared into the hallway.

Since ten minutes wasn't much time, they each took a box and began digging around. Theo found old discharge papers from random patients, spectacularly illegible doctor's notes, and what looked like a handle for a gardening spade.

"Anything?" Tess said.

"Nothing stands out," Theo said.

"When you don't know what you're looking for," said Jaime, "nothing is going to stand out."

"Or everything will." Tess flipped her braid, attacked the pile of stones and brick, examining each. "Nectarine said that none of the stones and bricks were significant, but . . ."

"Apricot," said Jaime.

"Pineapple," Theo said.

"Raspberry," said Tess. "None of these bricks are important bricks." She moved on to a stack of dusty papers.

"Um," Jaime said, holding up a tattered grayish coat with too-long sleeves. "Is this what I think it is?"

"Yep. Straitjacket," said Theo. "This stuff really should be in a museum. Water could get in here, bugs, thieves, whatever."

"We're the thieves," Tess said.

"Only if we take something," said Theo. He flipped through a list of supplies, a bunch of crumbling bills, and a letter about something called a "zoological garden," which argued that allowing the patients pets like bear cubs and goats could help with patients' therapy.

"Not if the bear cubs ate the goats," he muttered.

"What?" said Tess.

"Nothing," said Theo. He pulled out a faded sheet of paper. A patient list?

NO.	AGE	ETHNICITY	MARITAL STATUS	CHILDREN	DIAGNOSIS
2116	17	Bohemian	Single	None	Insane by religious fantasy
2117	50	German	Married	Eleven	Insane by domestic troubles
2118	39	Unknown	Married	Eight	Insane by overexertion
2119	33	Unknown	Married	Two	Insane by mental excitement
2120	59	Unknown	Married	Eleven	Insane by overwork and domestic trouble
2121	Unknown	Unknown	Unknown	None	Insane by heredity
2122	22	Unknown	Married	One	Insane by loss of property

Insane by mental excitement? By domestic trouble? By loss of property? Those didn't sound like reasons to send anyone to an asylum, Theo thought.

A waterlogged book with its cover missing sat at the bottom of the box. Theo picked it up, idly turned to the title page. *Penelope*, by A Lady. An old book but a famous one, written sometime before the Civil War.

Theo was about to put the book back in the box when he saw the faded, barely there scrawl of brownish ink along the bottom of the page:

Is it insane to defend yourself against disreputable men, Doctor, or insane not to? I'm going home to find my heart. I hope you find yours.

—Ava O.

All around the inscription, someone had drawn a border made up of tiny stars within suns, the seal of the Morningstarrs.

His brain itched. Ava. It was a common enough name. Lots of people named Ava wandering around.

Yet, he knew that name. Everyone who had ever heard of the Morningstarrs knew that name.

It was the name of Theresa and Theodore's closest companion. Their secretary, emissary, friend . . . and heir.

Miss Ava Oneal.

CHAPTER SIXTEEN
Jaime

Theo was holding up a dusty old book like he was angry at it for something, but before he could tell them what was special about the book and why it made him so mad, Apricot-Pineapple-Raspberry appeared in the doorway. "Time's up!" she said. "Bernard is totally pitching a fit."

"But—" Tess began.

"No buts!" said Apricot. "He's threatening to have me fired if I leave him upstairs by himself five more seconds."

Out of the corner of his eye, Jaime saw Theo tuck something behind his back. Jaime stepped in front of him so that Apricot wouldn't see what Theo was doing. "Sorry," Jaime said. "We didn't mean to get you in trouble."

Apricot shrugged. "Oh, Bernie can't get me in trouble. I just don't want to listen to him screech anymore. Goes right up my spine."

They quickly put everything back in the boxes. Tess kept up a steady stream of chatter as they rode the elevator back to the lobby. Nine sniffed at Apricot's shoes and licked her knees. Theo stood rigidly against the wall of the elevator, his legs crossed like a little kid who had to go to the bathroom. As they walked through the lobby, they ignored Bernard's icy stare, which, Jaime noticed, seemed to be focused on *him* rather than the twins, waved good-bye to Apricot, and burst out into the heat of the afternoon.

Once they were a block away from the Octagon, Tess said, "Okay, Theo. Show us what you found."

Theo glanced around, then reached behind his back and pulled the book out from under his T-shirt. *Penelope.*

"I know that book," said Jaime. "It's one of my grandmother's favorites."

"Is that the one about the woman kidnapped from New York City and forced to work on a plantation? And then she escapes and fights her way back home to her fiancé?" said Tess.

"Yep," Jaime said. "There's a six-hour miniseries

that Mima's made me watch at least ten times. She loves the actor who plays Samuel Deerfoot."

"Forget about the miniseries," said Theo. "Look at this inscription."

Tess said, "Ava O? *Ava Oneal?*"

Ava Oneal, Ava Oneal, Jaime thought. "Wait . . . *the* Ava Oneal? The Morningstarrs' assistant? I thought she was just a legend!"

"Nope, not a legend," said Tess. "They have some of her correspondence at the Old York Puzzler and Cipherist Society. And plenty of other people wrote about her in their own letters. There just aren't any known pictures of her. Not even drawings, which is odd."

Theo tugged so hard on his lip, Jaime worried he'd tug it right off. "There are a million Avas in the world," he said. "That message could have been written by anyone. Also, we can't be sure if it's just a note or a clue."

Tess began, "That's too—"

"Do not say 'adorable,'" Theo said.

"But—"

"It's not adorable, it's ridiculous!" He tried to kick a rock and missed, nearly landing on his back. "Why would the Morningstarrs leave a clue in some random book left to rot in an old building?"

"Why not?" said Tess. "The Morningstarrs didn't

know that the book would end up in an old building."

"Right! They didn't know!" Theo yelled.

"Shhhh!" Tess said. "Someone will hear you."

Theo lowered his voice. "If you want people to solve your Cipher, why wouldn't you at least try to put clues where people could find them?"

"Maybe they thought they were," said Tess. "Or maybe they thought it would make it harder to solve."

"And anyway," Jaime said, "didn't you also say that you weren't sure the Morningstarrs wanted the clues to be found? And didn't you say that the clues all seem to be about forgotten things, forgotten people?"

Theo uttered sounds that might have been words and might not have been.

"What did you just say?" said Jaime.

"He said, 'I'm so *farblunget,*'" Tess said. "Yiddish for 'lost or confused.' But this isn't confusing, Theo. You know what this means."

"I know what it means," Jaime said. "If this note was written by *that* Ava, and if it's meant to be a clue . . ."

He trailed off because he didn't have to tell them. They all knew. If this note was meant to be a clue, then the next one could be hidden at Ava Oneal's New York City home. The building left to her by the Morning-starrs before they vanished more than a hundred fifty years ago. The one where she was the sole resident until her own disappearance in 1888.

Their home, 354 W. 73rd Street.

Suddenly, the air seemed so much heavier, so much more humid, thick, and swollen. Jaime wiped at his forehead and pulled at the collar of his T-shirt. "It's hot, and it's late. We should probably take Ava's advice and get off this island."

They hopped the bus south, this time headed for the F train on the Underway, which would get them home faster than the tram over the river. Theo said that a lot of people thought that the Underway tunnels in upper Manhattan were the deepest in all the city, but Roosevelt Island's Underway tunnel was deeper—a hundred feet below street level. The river that had looked so shiny and peaceful from above had been cut into the earth nine thousand years ago by the movements of glaciers, was anywhere from thirty to a hundred feet deep, flowed faster than four knots, and could pull anybody straight out to sea.

"Who needs sharks with a river sitting on top of your head?" Jaime mumbled. He felt the whole river pressing down on him, the whole world. It wasn't Ava's building and it wasn't theirs anymore; it was Slant's. And if they couldn't find the clue, maybe Slant would. And then what would happen?

He was starting to sound like Tess when she was in a mood. "Let's see that book again." Theo handed it to him.

Is it insane to defend yourself against disreputable men, Doctor, or insane not to? I'm going home to find my heart. I hope you find yours.
—Ava O.

He touched the border around the inscription. The ink wasn't black or blue or even . . . ink. "I think . . . I think this might be written in blood," he whispered.

"Really?" Tess whispered back, squinting at the writing.

"There was a story that Grandpa Ben once told me," Theo said. "He found some newspaper item about 'a female employee of the Morningstarrs' getting in trouble for attacking her boyfriend. Though they had cooks and some household help, they only had one full-time employee. Grandpa never found any evidence that Ava even had a boyfriend and there weren't any records about an arrest."

"Maybe it was a lie. Or maybe the Morningstarrs hushed the whole thing up," Tess said. "But getting committed in that place . . . it must have been horrible. She had to have been so desperate to get out."

Desperate enough to write in blood.

Tess glanced up at the stone-eyed Guildman sitting in his glass box and crossed her hands over the book as if the man could read the writing from that far away. And for all they knew, he could. The Guildman scanned the passengers, his hard, appraising gaze lingering on Jaime, lips twisting ever so slightly.

Jaime was grateful when they got off the F train and caught the 2. He was careful not to make eye contact with the Guildman on that train. Soon enough, they were out of the Underway and out on the street, standing outside 354 W. 73rd, staring up at the building as if it had just burst through the skin of the sidewalk like a new molar. Because this was one of the original Morningstarr buildings, it was one of the places that people heavily investigated after the twins disappeared. Decade after decade, it had been scoured from basement to roof by treasure hunters, examined by historians and TV hosts, x-rayed by X-ray machines, scanned with scanners. Even if there was a clue hidden somewhere in the building, how were they supposed to find anything new here?

As if he heard Jaime's thoughts, Theo said, "Grandpa Ben knew a guy who spent forty-two and a half years going over every inch of this building with a magnifying glass."

"We don't have forty-two and a half *days*," said Tess. "There has to be something else in the book, some other clue or puzzle or something." She pushed through the doors and into the cool of the lobby.

That was when four-year-old Otto Moran charged around the corner, brandishing his Wiffle bat like a sword. He stopped inches from Tess's legs. He was dressed entirely in camouflage print all the way down to his sneakers and was wearing one of his father's ties as a headband.

"State your business!" Otto yelled.

"We live here, Otto," said Tess.

"That's not business!" said Otto.

"Yes, it is. Where's your mom? Does she know you're down here alone?"

"The president is napping!" Otto said. "She is tired of this nonsense!"

The tie around Otto's head, Jaime noted, was black with tiny little happy faces all over it. "So, who's watching you, Otto?"

Otto waved the bat. "I am the one who's watching YOU!"

"You're just a dumb baby, Otto." Cricket Moran came motoring toward them on her three-wheeler. "*I am watching you.*"

"I. AM. A. NINJA!" Otto yelled. When his sister got close, Otto swung the bat. Cricket stood on the pedals of her trike, snatched the bat from his hands, held it over her head. Otto jumped for it, whining that he was going to wake up the president if Cricket didn't give the bat back. Cricket's pet—part-raccoon, part-cat, if Jaime was remembering right—chittered from his basket on the front of the trike. The cat-coon was wearing a tiny hat with antlers.

Jaime pried the bat from Cricket's hands. "Nobody needs to wake any presidents."

Cricket stared up at him through giant sunglasses. "He's not a ninja, he just thinks he is."

"Is that so bad?" said Jaime.

"Hmmph," Cricket said. Unlike her brother, Cricket was wearing a perfectly normal pair of denim shorts and a yellow shirt with a sparkly cartoon dragon on the front. Jaime had never seen her wear *anything* perfectly normal. She was usually wearing scuba gear paired with a tiara or rubber fishing boots that came all the way up to her armpits. Once, she "borrowed" her mom's wedding gown and accessorized it with a hockey mask.

"So, your brother's a ninja. What are you today, Cricket?"

Cricket's mouth curled at the corners. "Guess."

"You are a rich lady on her way to the beach."

"Who likes all that sand everywhere?" said Cricket.

"You're a movie star on her way to go shopping."

Cricket sucked her teeth. "Movie stars have people to shop for them."

Jaime guessed again. "A famous athlete on the way to a photo shoot?"

Little brows shot up over the frames of the glasses. "Seriously?" said Cricket.

"Hmmm," said Jaime. "I'm stumped. Who could you be?"

"You tell me," said Cricket, "I'll wait." She slid the heart charm on her necklace back and forth, *zip-zip, zip-zip*.

Just then, the elevator doors opened, and Mr. Stoop and Mr. Pinscher emerged pushing some kind of cart covered with a thick tarp. Next to him, Tess clenched her fists. Theo turned all the way around and presented the men his back. Otto sidled closer to Jaime. Cricket sat up straighter in the seat of her trike and . . . smiled, sweet as pie.

"Children!" said Mr. Stoop. "How lovely to see you all again."

"Good afternoon!" Cricket sang. "How is your work going?"

Mr. Pinscher grunted. Mr. Stoop said, "Our work is moving along just fine, young lady. Thank you for asking. And how is your raccoon?"

Cricket smiled even more sweetly. "Karl is doing just fine as well. Do you need any help bringing things down from the roof?" She pointed at Jaime. "He is very strong."

Mr. Stoop's filmy, colorless eyes skated over Jaime, sliming him. Jaime resisted the urge to scratch at his skin.

Mr. Stoop looked back at Cricket. "No doubt Mr. Cruz is very strong for a boy his age. But I think Mr. Pinscher and I have things under control."

"Okay," said Cricket, in a sugary voice that belonged to some entirely different child. "You have a nice day!"

They watched as Mr. Stoop and Mr. Pinscher wheeled the cart through the lobby and out of the building. They pushed the cart to a white van parked—illegally—right in front. Two other men wearing dark suits hopped from the van and opened the back doors of the van. All four men rammed the cart into the back of the van, and the cart's legs collapsed like a gurney's, allowing them to slide it easily inside. Then they slammed the doors shut, leaped inside the van, and drove off.

"What was that about?" Tess said.

"They think the building is going to give them something, but they're wrong."

"Huh?"

Cricket didn't answer. She tucked her necklace under the collar of her shirt, put her hand in the basket, and rooted around underneath Karl. She pulled out a notebook and a pencil. She licked the tip of the pencil and scratched a few notes. Then she shut the notebook and tossed it back into the basket.

"So," said Jaime, "you're just a regular kid today."

"Am I?" said Cricket.

"A regular kid keeping an eye on certain people, maybe?"

Cricket lifted her glasses and peered up with big dark eyes. "The word is *INCOGNITO*."

"That's a big word," said Tess.

"Maybe for you it is." Cricket lowered her glasses. "Come on, Otto. Karl needs his snack."

"I'm a ninja?" Otto said.

"Whatever," said Cricket.

Once the kids were gone, Tess tugged at Jaime's arm. "Did she say that those guys were bringing things down from the roof?"

"That's exactly what she said."

"What was up on the roof that could be loaded onto a cart and taken out of the building?"

They didn't bother stopping at either Jaime's or the Biedermanns' apartment, they went right up to the roof. The elevator took a leisurely route, drifting sideways, then rising, then falling, then rising again till it reached the penthouse. Once they were on the penthouse floor, they had to climb a short set of cement stairs that led to the rooftop garden, a lush green space that mocked the ugly air-conditioning unit as well as the beat-up, graffitied water tank that loomed so large on the roof of the building next door. All of the tenants were welcome to plant things here, but the tomatoes, vegetables, herbs, and flowers mostly belonged to Mima and Mr. Biedermann, the only people who could be counted on to make things grow in places they weren't supposed to.

To Jaime's surprise, Mima was sitting in a lounge chair facing the Hudson. She nodded when she saw them but didn't say anything.

Finally, Jaime said, "Mima, what are you doing?"

"Those men asked me to bring them up here. You know who I mean. The tall one and the short one. Those terrible people. I could have told them to come up here all by themselves. They didn't need me. But I did it because I wanted to know what they were looking for."

"What were they looking for?" Tess said.

"Do you remember that optical viewer that was in that corner? The one bolted down? Like the ones they have at the Empire State Building?" She gestured to the edge of the roof. "They took it. They tore it right out."

"My grandfather used that all the time!" Tess said. "It's been here since our family moved in. The left lens was always blurry. Why did they want that old thing?"

"Who knows? They ripped this seal right off the hallway window on the fifth floor." She gestured to the small medallion in her lap, encrusted with old white paint. "The tall one said that I didn't have to worry about the building or anything in it anymore, but I took this right back. I said this is my building until it is not. They didn't care."

Tess tugged at the end of her braid, and Nine nudged her fingers. "Are they allowed to do that? They shouldn't be allowed to do that!"

Mima sighed but said nothing, which meant she was saying, Yes, those men are allowed to do whatever they want to do and who can stop them? She lifted her chin toward the river. "Do you know what kinds of things have been found at the bottom of the water around New York City over the years?"

Jaime glanced at Tess, who glanced at Theo, who shrugged. "No, we don't," said Jaime. "What kinds of things?"

"Shipwrecks," she said. "No one official will tell you exactly where they are because these wrecks are considered archeological sites. There are also a lot of stripped cars in the water. A lot of rebar just lying around. A grand piano. A complete set of table and chairs sitting on the bottom as if someone were coming to tea. A giraffe."

"A *giraffe*?" said Theo.

"It escaped a zoo and ran right off the island, probably trying to get back to Africa, and who could blame it? Some ice cream trucks, a bunch of slot machines, a whole train, more than a thousand silver bars that fell off a barge and got buried in the silt. A *lot* of dead bodies." She took a deep breath, released it. "That is all very sad to me. What's been lost."

This time, Theo glanced at Tess, who looked at Jaime, who raised his palms—*I don't know what she's going on about either.* Mima was not the cryptic sort; she always said what she meant and meant what she said, no matter what language she was using. But Jaime had no idea where she was going with this.

"And there are also some strange creatures down there. I'm not talking about giraffes or even things like sharks. I'm talking about teredos, four-foot-long worms with nasty teeth. And *Limnoria tripunctata*—gribbles—tiny, tiny little bugs. The teredos eat wood and the gribbles eat wood and concrete both—amazing if you think about it, except they're eating away at the pilings that hold up the city. Worms and bugs taking one tiny bite at a time until the whole place slides into the water. Another thing that makes me very sad."

Theo reached up to scratch his neck, but his hand never made it, hung in the air, frozen. Jaime wasn't frozen; he shifted from one foot to the other as if he couldn't quite reach equilibrium. Nine walked over to Mima and put her head on Mima's lap.

Tess said, "That's not going to happen, Mrs. Cruz."

"No?" Mima said, idly petting the cat.

"No," Jaime said. "Someone will figure out a way to stop the bugs. Or protect the pilings. Or both."

"Well, maybe you're right. But sometimes it feels like we're about to sink into oblivion." Mima finally looked at Jaime, eyes so tired, so very tired, that Jaime felt his own lids going heavy. "Your father's company told him that they would help us with a new apartment. A better apartment. Three bedrooms. A view."

Jaime swallowed hard. "Well, that's not so bad, is it?"

"In New Jersey."

Tess and Theo said, *"Oh."*

Mima murmured to herself in Spanish, something about her parents not wanting her to come to this city, they already had to leave Cuba, why would anyone leave Miami, too, they were so angry, but one visit to New York City and she realized she'd found her place. At least, that was what Jaime thought she was saying. He opened his mouth to tell Mima about their possible discovery of a new line of clues, but then, they hadn't discovered anything yet, not really. What if he told her and it didn't pan out? What kinds of bugs would they be talking about then?

"We still have weeks, Mima," he said.

"True," she said.

"Anything could happen in a few weeks," Tess said.

"Things I probably can't even imagine," said Mima, smiling just a little. "I am not the one with the imagination in our family."

"You could win the lottery," said Tess.

"I'll have to start playing, then," Mima said.

"We could dig up the silver bars at the bottom of the river," said Theo.

"You have a submersible lying around?"

"Darnell Slant could be abducted by aliens," said Tess.

Mima nodded. "I would very much like to see that."

"A new superhero could capture him and lock him in a jail in outer space," said Jaime.

"As long as it's very, very outer."

"Or Slant could join a cult and give all his worldly possessions to the teredos and the gribbles," said Theo.

Mima was silent for a moment and Nine started to purr, a low rumble. Then Mima said, "I'd rather he left them to someone who knew what to do with them."

Jaime looked from their own green roof garden to the top of the building next door. Someone had impaled a disco ball on the top of it. On the side of it, someone else, or maybe the same someone, had spray-painted the words: YOU GOT IT ALL WRONG, TOOTS.

Well, Jaime thought, *I hope not.*

He sat on the deck next to the lounge chair. Theo and Tess did the same. Mima put her hand on the back of Jaime's neck, and they all watched the water together, imagining giraffes loping gracefully beneath the surface, making their way home.

CHAPTER SEVENTEEN

Tess

As they sat up on the roof with Jaime's grandmother, all Tess could think about was what she didn't want to think about: Do not think about teredos or gribbles eating the city. Do not think about teredos or gribbles eating the city, TEREDOS AND GRIBBLES ARE TOTALLY NOT EATING THE CITY RIGHT NOW.

"I should have named my hamster-hogs Teredo and Gribble," said Jaime.

"Ugh," said Tess.

"Are you guys getting hungry?" Jaime said.

"Ugh," said Tess.

"I'm hungry," said Theo.

"UGH," said Tess, holding her stomach.

"I'm making arroz con pollo for dinner," said Mrs. Cruz.

Tess let go of her stomach. "You are?"

"You guys want some?" said Jaime. "Mima always cooks enough for an army."

Tess said, "We should go see our dad. My mom's probably working late again, and Dad gets all mopey when he's by himself."

Mima stood and dusted herself off. "I'll bring the food to your place, then. It's bigger than ours. We can all mope together."

Tess was right; their mom was out catching burglars, so Jaime carried his grandmother's giant red pot already filled with chicken and vegetables into the Biedermanns' kitchen. On the stovetop, Jaime's grandmother added rice and a little beer, letting it cook for a few minutes before putting the whole thing in the oven. As soon as she smelled the food, Tess's appetite killed any remaining images of teredos and gribbles. She ate three helpings of chicken and rice as Mr. Biedermann practiced his chewy, New York–accented Spanish with Mrs. Cruz, and Mrs. Cruz practiced her wincing. Mrs. Cruz tried to teach him German instead. Which went just as well. Instead of speaking, Mr. Biedermann sounded as if he were sucking things out of his teeth.

Tess thought about the clue left by Ava Oneal. Home for Ava Oneal was this building, but *which part* of this building? Where were her rooms? She had owned the entire structure but had lived here alone. No personal items or papers had ever been found, no evidence that she spent more time on any floor or in any particular area.

"You are very quiet, Tess," said Mrs. Cruz, spooning some rice onto Tess's plate.

"Yeah," said Mr. Biedermann. "Usually she's asking all sorts of questions. What if right was left and left was right?"

Theo said, "What if a person could grow an extra arm?"

"Or an extra head?" said Mrs. Cruz.

Mr. Biedermann said, "What if cats could talk?"

Nine mrrowed for her share of rice.

"Cats *can* talk," said Tess. "It's not their fault some of us don't speak their language."

Jaime said, "What if cars could talk?"

Theo said, "Cars already talk."

"What if they understood?" said Jaime. "What if the *walls* could talk?"

Even though Tess's mouth was full of chicken, the words popped out: "Then maybe we'd know how to solve the Cipher."

No one said anything for a full minute.

Then Mr. Biedermann said, "This chicken is muy bien." *Moo-ee bee-in.*

Mrs. Cruz winced.

There was a knock on the door. Everyone stared at it.

"Those men again," Mrs. Cruz spit.

"I'll get it," said Mr. Biedermann. He started talking as soon as he stood up. "We are not legally required to leave for weeks, so I suggest you stop this harassment." He threw open the door.

"Edgar! Omar!" said Mr. Biedermann. "Come in!"

Edgar Wellington held out a box. "We were working upstairs and decided to take a dinner break. We brought back cupcakes."

Jaime said, "I wouldn't say no to a cupcake."

Mr. Biedermann pulled up some chairs for Edgar and Omar and introduced them to Mrs. Cruz. Without asking, Mrs. Cruz piled plates high with chicken and rice and set it in front of the men. "This looks delicious," Edgar Wellington said.

"It *is* delicious," said Mrs. Cruz.

Omar sampled the rice. "You are right about that," he said, smiling. Mrs. Cruz beamed.

To Mr. Biedermann, Omar said, "We managed to catalog some of Benjamin's items today. Not as many as we wanted to, of course. His collection is magnificent."

Tess didn't want to hear about what they were doing in Grandpa's apartment. She busied herself with the box of cupcakes.

"We found opera glasses that likely date back to the nineteenth century," said Edgar. "But the glasses can be transformed into a small pellet gun."

Vanilla, chocolate, red velvet, carrot.

"And a lipstick case that doubles as high-powered microscope," said Omar.

Lavender, caramel, peach, something beige and unidentifiable.

"Oh! And what appear to be the original plans for the Morningstarr caterpillar."

Tess plucked the beige and unidentifiable cupcake from the box. She imagined her grandpa's opera glasses and his lipstick case and his plans for the Morningstarr caterpillar in the display cases at the archives and popped the whole cupcake into her mouth.

Later, she didn't remember what the cupcake tasted like.

That night, Tess pretended to sleep. Her mom came home after eleven, rummaged around in the kitchen, and went to bed. When she heard the soft snores coming from her parents' room, Tess crept from her room to Theo's, where he was turning the pages of *Penelope* and picking at the Morningstarr seal on the window.

"Are you actually reading that book?" Tess asked.

Theo turned a page. "It was good enough for Ava Oneal."

"If you keep playing with that seal, Mrs. Cruz will have to fix it. Or Stoop and Pinscher are going to come up here and steal it for their collection."

"You really want to lecture me about the seal?"

"Have you found anything else in that book?"

"Not yet." When Tess didn't leave, Theo sighed. "I'm going to finish this chapter. And then I'm going to get some sleep. You should, too."

"I can't."

"You've got that zombie look. Like your eyeballs are going to cave in and your face is going to fall off."

Standing there, all gushy and loose on the outside, all tense and hungry on the inside, Tess *felt* like a zombie. It wasn't always this way. When they were little, Theo was the zombie, so plagued by nightmares that he used to come into Tess's room in the middle of the night and curl up on her floor, soothed by the sound of her breathing. She didn't know how they'd switched places, when exactly she'd become the nervous one and he'd learned to calm himself, learned to read nineteenth-century novelists with their nineteenth-century worries until his mind quieted and he could drift off, content that things were better now. She wondered if they would switch places again and again the whole of their lifetimes, which of them she'd rather be, if she even had a choice.

Nine nudged Tess's fingers, and Tess's own insistent, zombie energy nudged her out of her reverie. "I'm getting a snack," she told Theo, who merely turned another page in the book.

In the living room, the light of the moon shone through the windows, illuminating the streamers of toilet paper that festooned the furniture. Beneath those windows was Lancelot, who was "sleeping" in a pile of towels, looking a lot like Theo had when he was curled on her floor, stunned silent by his latest nightmare.

Lancelot didn't stir when Tess entered the space or when she rummaged in the box for one of the leftover cupcakes. Every once in a while, he'd let out a sigh so human that it froze Tess in her tracks.

"You miss him, don't you?" Tess whispered.

Her answer was a tiny metallic creak as Lance shifted slightly under the towels.

"I miss him, too. I miss the way things were." She went to Lancelot and pulled one of the towels up to his chin. She had no idea if this would soothe the machine. What soothes a machine? The question sounded like a clue to one of Grandpa Ben's crossword puzzles. Puzzle makers believe in misdirection, Grandpa said—was the clue "dentist's number" talking about the dentist's phone number or her social security number or her license plate number or her anesthetic? Number or NUMBer? NUMBer or number? You need to look at the clue from every angle, consider every possibility. When he worked the Sunday puzzle, he told Tess how to do it: Write in pencil; pick out plurals and fill in all those easy *s* boxes. Relax—how can you think, he'd say, if you're wound up tight? When the puzzle stops being fun, walk away, come back to it later, sleep on it, you'll feel better in the morning.

But when she woke up, she didn't feel better. And she didn't feel better the next night, or the next. They scoured every page of *Penelope* but found no more information, and they still didn't know where in the building to look or what to look for. After being so sure that they were on the right track, so sure that the Cipher was both reading them and guiding them, Tess now felt *farblunget* herself, lost and confused, even abandoned. Maybe the book wasn't a clue. Maybe a story was just a story. And the more time went by, the harder it was to believe that they'd ever found anything of significance, that the Morning-starrs would have hidden clues in a letter that could be lost or a chair that could be misplaced or a painting that could be destroyed. Her mood only worsened when she went out to take a walk with Nine and came back to find some random guy, white and round and bald, slapping a notice to the front door of the building:

THE CITY OF NEW YORK

DEPARTMENT OF INSPECTIONS

THIS BUILDING IS CONDEMNED

FOR THE PURPOSES OF PUBLIC SAFETY, A CONDEMNED

BUILDING MAY BE ORDERED VACATED.

THIS BUILDING LOCATED AT: 354 W. 73RD STREET

IS TO BE VACATED BY: JULY 31ST

DO NOT OCCUPY

PERSONS OCCUPYING THIS BUILDING PAST JULY 31ST OR

REMOVING THIS NOTICE ARE SUBJECT TO A $1,000 FINE

OR 90 DAYS' IMPRISONMENT OR BOTH.

"What is that? What are you doing?" Tess demanded.

The man barely glanced at her. "I'm knitting a sweater. What do you think I'm doing?"

Tess's chest heaved as if she'd just run a marathon. "This building is *not* condemned."

"Whatever you say, kid," the man told her. "I just hang the signs."

"It's not!"

"So, call city hall and argue with them."

"Take that sign down!" Tess shouted, but the man was already marching off, as if Tess were about as consequential as a stain on the sidewalk.

Tess ripped the sign off the door, balled it up, and threw it to the nearest Roller tidying up the street. She didn't want to go back to her apartment, so she went to Jaime's apartment instead. It took only one knock for Mrs. Cruz to throw open the door and say, "What is broken?"

"Nothing, Mrs. Cruz."

"Good! Jaime is in his room drawing his pictures." She saw Nine and immediately her voice got an octave higher: "Hello! Are you a kitty?" In response, Nine pranced around her ankles.

Tess went to Jaime's room, which was a shrine to

every superhero of every type of comic book ever written. Enormous floor-to-ceiling bookcases were packed
with figurines: Spider-Man, Batman, Wolverine, Wonder Woman, Wasp, Captain America, Hulk, Supergirl,
Super Indian. And those were only the ones that Tess
remembered. There were hundreds of others, probably
packed in some of the boxes that littered the bedroom
floor.

Jaime looked up from his drawing—the Octagon as
it would be viewed from the top of the stairs. Jaime had
captured the place perfectly. There was a figure at the
bottom of the stairs, barely sketched in.

Tess said, "Who's that?"

"Nobody yet," said Jaime. "Are you okay?"

"Theo says I have that zombie look."

"Now that you mention it . . . ," Jaime said.

Tess bent to see Napolean and Tyrone in their cage.
Napolean was curled up in a tight ball, napping, while
Tyrone was a blur of fury on her wheel. Nine was mes-
merized.

"She's not going to try and eat my hamster-hogs, is
she?"

"No. She just likes to be intimidating."

"So does Tyrone."

"Who's Tyrone?"

"The hamster-hog. When she's mad, she poops green."

Tess slumped in the chair by the window. There was a Morningstarr seal on the molding, but this one was on the upper right side, freshly painted white as the rest of the trim. "Theo has one of these seals by his window, too. But his is on the bottom of the sill."

"Yeah," said Jaime. "Mima says that certain apartments have the seals on the window moldings, sometimes two or three seals, and certain apartments don't. And some of the seals are on the left or right, some in the middle. She thinks that all the windows had them at one time, and probably a lot more of them, but people pulled them off or painted over them or whatever."

"Huh," Tess said. She stood to touch the seal, the raised star encircled by a sun. She'd been seeing this seal her whole life, but suddenly it seemed weird that some of the windows had the seals, and some of them didn't.

"Toss me your pencil," Tess said.

He did. She jammed it into the wood.

"Hey! What are you doing?" said Jaime. "Mima is going to kill me!"

The seal that had looked like nothing so much as a

stamp in the molding, popped out of the frame. Tess hefted the piece in her hand, scraped some white paint off with a fingernail, revealing a flash of silver.

It had the look and the weight of a coin.

"How many of these are left in the building?"

Jaime stared at the coin in her hand. "I don't know."

"We need to find out. And we're going to need something else, too. It's not going to be easy to get."

Jaime said, "What's not?"

"Your grandmother's key ring."

CHAPTER EIGHTEEN
Jaime

Jaime said, "Oh, sure. And while we're at it, let's steal Thor's hammer."

But he was only half listening. This morning, his dad had called to talk, the first time Jaime had had a real conversation with him in weeks. If you could call it a conversation. Jaime's dad was there, smiling, tanned dark from all his work in the Sudanese sun, but what he was saying was terrible. "You'll love Hoboken! My friend Jorge said the apartment is even bigger than it looks in the pictures I sent you. Did you see? Three bedrooms! The building is new, so that's less work for Mima. Fewer repairs."

"Mima doesn't want less work," said Jaime.

"Sure she does," said his dad. "She's getting older."

"So now she's some frail old lady?"

"What? When did I say that? I just said she's getting older."

"And that means we should just let Slant take the building that Mima has lived in for most of her life? Let him push us right out of the city?"

"Stop whining. If you want to feel sorry for someone, feel sorry for the people who don't have beautiful new apartments," his father said. "Did I tell you the math and science academy is right at the edge of town?"

"Math and science academy?"

"It's so close you won't even have to take a bus."

"I like the bus!" Jaime had roared, which was dumb, because he didn't really care about taking the bus. But his dad was talking about this move like it was nothing because, for his dad, it *was* nothing. His work assignments took him all around the world and he loved every minute of them, was always trying to get Jaime to come to Egypt or Brazil or Russia or wherever, like Jaime could jump into a whole different world, just like that. His dad could never understand wanting to stay put. Every move was an adventure.

But Jaime wanted to have his adventures here, right here, on this skinny island, in this ramshackle building. What's a superhero without his city? What is he supposed to protect, if not his home? It didn't make any sense to Jaime. Which is why he said the thing he couldn't have known, shouldn't have said:

"Mom would have understood."

The video quality was good enough to show the slight twitch at the corner of his dad's eye, the only indication of pain he ever showed. "Yes," he said. "Your mom understood a lot of things."

"Papi," Jaime began.

"It's late. I need to eat my dinner. Look at the pictures of the apartment. Maybe it won't be such torture, eh?"

And the video cut out.

Jaime dragged his attention back to Tess. Her knee was bouncing and her cat was frantically rubbing against it, trying to make her stop. "There are a bunch of these around building, I know it," she was saying. "And I bet they're not in random places. They're in some sort of pattern. The clue in *Penelope* isn't the inscription, it's those seals drawn around the inscription."

Jaime tried to remember what Mima had said about the seals. "All of them are located on the windows in the front of the building. And they're only on the middle floors." He closed his eyes and pictured the entire front wall of 354 W. 73rd, as if it had been torn free from the rest of the building—seven rows of windows, five windows across. There were seals in Tess's apartment, Jaime's apartment, and the hallway on the fifth floor, but Mima had also found seals on the third and fourth floors. He turned to a fresh page in his sketchbook and drew the rows of windows to show Tess where the seals had been found.

"We could ask your grandmother to let us into the apartments facing the street to check it out," said Tess.

Jaime groaned. "Even if she agreed, which she wouldn't, there's no way she's going to let us gouge things out of the window frames. But we can go knock on doors. Ask if anyone needs a patch or something."

"I don't think we want to tell anyone what we're up to. Even if they could be trusted, we don't want to get anyone's hopes up."

"Not even our own," said Jaime.

Tess said nothing. Jaime took off his glasses, rubbed the bridge of his nose. "Mima takes an hour nap every day around one. As long as we get the keys back before she wakes up, we should be okay."

"That's good," said Tess. "People usually work during the day. No one should be home."

"Except Mr. Perlmutter."

Mr. Perlmutter was approximately a thousand years old, rarely left his apartment, and sprinkled conversations liberally with one of three sentences: If you think I'm paying for this garbage, you're nuttier than a squirrel in September. Stop that caterwauling/screeching/yammering/hammering, we're not living in a zoo! You think I can do that with my sciatica/cataracts/rheumatism/hemorrhoids/corns?

"We should save Mr. Perlmutter's place for last," Tess said.

"Ya think?" said Jaime.

They called Theo and told him to bring Ava's book. To kill time before Mima got home, the three of them watched a movie about some people who used giant robots to battle giant monsters, which Tess said needed more girls to be realistic.

"Maybe the monsters are girls?" said Theo. When Tess glared at him, he said, "What? What did I say?"

Mima came home around a quarter to one, tired and dusty. She set her toolbox on the counter. "Hello, children. I see that you are having a good time staying inside on a beautiful day instead of going outside and getting fresh air."

"We're going out when this movie's over," said Jaime.

Mima set her keys next to the toolbox, muttered something about movies warping the brains of young people, and went to her bedroom. As soon as he heard the door shut, Jaime stuffed his sketchbook in his pocket, grabbed the keys and the toolbox off the counter. Then they slipped out the door. First, they checked the window in the hallway. Sure enough, Mima had already replaced the seal on the molding, but in the middle, on the right-hand side.

He hesitated before prying it off. But they were desperate, so . . .

With a screwdriver, he levered the seal out of the molding and handed it to Tess. He spackled the hole as neatly as he could. Then he marked the location of the seal in his sketchbook.

In the elevator, Theo said, "Let's start with the Schwartzes on the fourth floor They both work in an office somewhere. Nobody should be home."

Jaime said, "Knock first, just in case."

Tess knocked. "Hey, Ms. Schwartz? Wondering if you have, uh, an egg I could borrow?"

Theo mouthed the words, *An egg?* Tess put her fingers to her lips, but there was no reason to be quiet. No one was home.

Jaime flipped through the key ring until he found the right one. He opened the door and the three of them slipped into the apartment. The Schwartzes hadn't started packing yet, but it wasn't going to take them long. They had no books and barely any furniture, and what furniture they had was odd: a low, skinny orange couch and two purple chairs shaped like giant hands. They also had a machine—not a Morningstarr invention—that cleaned the floors, a plain flat disc that resembled nothing so much as a flying saucer whirring about, banking off walls and feet.

"What would you call this style? Modern?" said Jaime.

"Strange," said Tess.

In the bedroom, the Schwartzes had a bed, a dresser, and a couple of side tables. "No books in here, either," said Theo. "How can you not have any books?"

"Lots of people don't read," said Jaime.

"Why not?" said Theo.

"Let's discuss literacy rates later," said Jaime. He went to the window and found two seals close together in the bottom left-hand corner of the molding. He pried them out. This time, Tess spackled while Jaime noted the location of the seals in his book.

Once they were out in the hallway, they checked the window in the hall. Here they found no seals, and no evidence that the molding had been patched.

"Okay, whose apartment is across the hall?" Tess said.

"The Hornshaws," said Theo. "But they have a dog."

The Hornshaws' dog was a basset hound that spent twenty-three hours a day in a coma. Tess said, "Nine is more of a dog than that dog."

Again, Tess knocked, waited to make sure no one was home. Jaime let them in. Woody the basset hound didn't even lift his head off his doggy bed long enough to yawn. They all ran to the Hornshaws' bedroom, where they found another two seals on the right side of the window molding, right in the middle.

Tess checked her watch. "We still have fifty minutes till your grandmother wakes up."

They took the elevator to the fourth floor and were in and out of the third apartment—the Moran family's—in a few minutes. Jaime tried not to focus on the alphabet blocks and teddy bears and trucks strewn about, tried not to think about where Cricket and Otto would play, who would watch over them, if they couldn't solve the Cipher in time. This time, the seals were on the upper left-hand corner of the molding, two of them. The hallway window yielded three seals on the lower right side.

"I'm surprised that Stoop and Pinscher didn't take these," said Jaime.

"Oh, I'm sure they're coming back for them." Tess

checked her watch again. "We have forty-three minutes."

"I'm not sure that's going to be long enough to get Mr. Perlmutter to let us in," said Jaime.

"Only one way to find out," Tess said. She took a deep breath and knocked.

"I'm coming, I'm coming! Stop all that hammering! What is this, a zoo?"

Jaime was wondering how many zoos Mr. Perlmutter had actually been to, because he didn't remember any particular animals making hammering sounds, when Mr. Perlmutter cracked the door. His rheumy eye swam in the opening.

"Who are you?"

"I'm Tess Biedermann, Mr. Perlmutter," Tess said. "And this is Theo and Jaime. We live upstairs?"

"Well, do you or don't you?"

"Pardon?"

"Live upstairs?"

"Yes. I live upstairs. Theo and I live with my parents. The Biedermanns. My mom's a cop?"

The rheumy eye blinked. "Well, is she or isn't she?"

"What?"

"A cop."

"Yes. Yes, she's a detective."

"Then stop asking if she is. What do you want?"

"I was wondering if I could borrow an egg because I'm baking—"

"An egg? Do you think I can digest eggs with my stomach? What do I look like, a snake?"

This was going about as well as Jaime had expected, which was not well at all. "Sugar?" he suggested.

The rheumy eye rolled up to Jaime. "What are you, a comedian? I'm ninety-two years old. I can't eat sugar. You want me to get the diabetes?"

Tess gritted her teeth. "No, of course not. We'd love for you to stay around for another ninety-two years."

"Ha! Listen to you! Attitude all over! You kids! You think I've never heard a smart mouth before? I was born with a smart mouth!"

"No kidding," Theo said.

"Is that a question?"

"No."

"Are you going to tell me what you really want or are you going to keep on with the smart mouth?'

"Oh, I thought I'd keep on with the smart mouth," Tess said.

"Ha," he said. "Go on home to your mother. Maybe she'll arrest you and let the rest of us find some peace." The door started to close.

Jaime slapped a palm to the surface and said what they should have said in the first place, the truth: "We need to look at your bedroom wall. Under the window. We need to see if there's a seal there, and we need to take it with us. It might help to solve the Old York Cipher. Or part of it. Maybe."

The eye blinked some more. It blinked so long that Jaime thought Mr. Perlmutter had fallen asleep blinking. Then, gnarled fingers fumbled with the chain and the door opened.

"Fair enough. Come in, if you must."

Mr. Perlmutter was stooped over a walker, three hairs combed over his freckled head. He backed up and did a wide turn into the apartment. Tess followed him inside, Theo and Jaime behind her.

"Oh, look. A crowd of teenagers. It's my lucky day," said Mr. Perlmutter.

"Thank you for letting us in, Mr. Perlmutter," said Jaime.

"Yeah, yeah," he said. "Do what you have to do. But don't touch anything! I got everything where I want it! Only took me seven decades."

Jaime ducked into the back bedroom. Another three seals in the middle of the top of the molding. He pried them off, spackled it smooth.

"Thanks again," Tess said when he got back to the living room. "We'll get out of your way."

Mr. Perlmutter maneuvered himself toward a well-worn armchair the color of yams. He carefully lowered himself into it. "Whatever you're doing, you might want to do it faster. Some of us aren't getting any younger."

"Okay, Mr. Perlmutter."

As they walked out the door and into the hallway, Jaime thought he heard Mr. Perlmutter say, "And some of us have nowhere else to go."

CHAPTER NINETEEN
Tess

As quietly as they could, they crept into Jaime's apartment to find Jaime's grandmother standing in the kitchen, pointing a knife at the three of them. "Have you brought me my key ring and toolbox, you bad, bad children?"

Jaime stopped short just inside the doorway, and Theo slammed into his back. Tess maneuvered around them both.

"Is that dough for pastelitos, Mrs. Cruz?"

Mima made a sharp cut in a sheet of pastry on the table in front of her. "Yes," she said, "guava and cream cheese. My mother's recipe. Not that you will have any, because children who steal people's keys do not deserve any pastelitos."

"Mima," Jaime began.

"James Eduardo," Jaime's grandmother said, "did you think I wouldn't hear you swipe the keys from the counter?"

Jaime frowned. "I was quiet!"

"Yes! Like a polar bear is quiet! Or maybe a dinosaur on a Starrboard is quiet!" Mima made another sharp slice in the pastry and then aimed the knife at the kitchen counter. "Keys. Box."

Jaime pulled the ring from under his shirt and laid it and the box on the counter.

She jabbed with the knife. "Talk."

"If we talk, can we have some pastelitos?"

"Bad, bad children are not in a position to make bargains, but I will think about it."

Jaime pulled out his sketchbook and showed her the grids, explained what they were looking for. "There are seals just around the windows in certain apartments."

"Yes, yes. I know. You could have asked me. I am not so scary. Well, maybe I am. Anyway, why not check the other apartments on all the floors?"

Jaime looked at Theo and Tess. They'd told Mr. Perlmutter the truth. Why not Mrs. Cruz? Didn't seem like they had anything to lose, not at this point. They didn't tell her the whole story though, the entire new line of clues. All they said was that the seals near the windows could mean something.

"Mean what?"

"It's a cipher," said Jaime, opening his sketchbook. "One that I've seen before." He handed the book to Tess. "What does this look like to you?" On the page, Jaime had sketched what looked like a tic-tac-toe grid with dots.

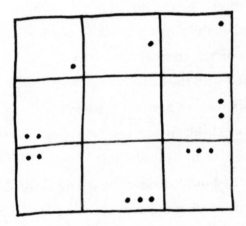

"It looks like that cipher they had at the archives!" Tess said. "A Rosicrucian cipher?"

"That's why I remembered it," said Jaime.

"Rosi-what?" said Mima.

"A type of secret writing used by some secret guilds or clubs. Freemasons, guilds like that," said Theo.

"Silly men and their silly secret clubs. Who needs a

club to feel important? Ben Franklin needed a club? George Washington needed a club?" She rolled her eyes.

Jaime said, "You belong to a bowling league."

Mrs. Cruz's dark eyes narrowed, and she sliced another triangle into the sheet of dough. "Did you check all the other apartments for the seals?"

"Are there more seals?" Theo asked.

"No," said Mrs. Cruz. She wiped her chin with the back of her hand, leaving a stripe of flour. "I would still check the other apartments."

"Why?" said Jaime.

"Because I would like you to get caught by one of the tenants and have to explain this kooky stuff to them."

Jaime said, "It's not kooky."

His grandmother put down the knife. "The whole thing is kooky. Who leaves the fate of so many people in a puzzle none of the people can solve?"

"Good question," said Theo.

"We're going to do it," said Tess, lifting her chin. "And the Morningstarrs didn't make a puzzle no one can solve—they made a puzzle only the *right* people can solve."

Jaime's grandmother's sharp eyes took Tess in. "You can have some pastelitos, but only if you help to fill them."

They spooned the guava-and-cream-cheese filling onto the triangles of pastry and then sealed the pastry into little pockets and placed them on cookie sheets. After the sheets went into the oven, they sat in the living room and went over their chart. Jaime paged through his sketchbook and found the key he'd seen at the archives:

"Hmmm," said Theo. "This isn't quite the same, though. According to this key, the lines in the grid are important. They help form the cipher text. See?" He pointed to Jaime's name, which Edgar had enciphered using the key, and which Jaime had scribbled in his book.

"But here in this building," Theo continued, "the seals—or dots—are all technically inside individual squares. So how would this work? A number of letters would look the same."

"Maybe they wanted to make the puzzle harder," Jaime said.

Tess said, "Or the lines aren't important,"

At the same time, Jaime and Theo said, "They're important."

Tess's eyebrows flew up like window shades.

"But maybe not important in this puzzle," Jaime said. "What if we only need to read the position of the dots?"

They compared the locations of the seals to the locations of the dots on the key. Jaime said, "That gives us *A, D, G, L, M, R, S,* and *Z.* The blank spot in the center could represent a vowel, maybe."

Theo said, "The *D* could also represent a vowel. Like an *O.* But that's only if this is a transposition cipher and not a substitution cipher. I think we have to assume it's both, though. Maybe with more than one cipher alphabet."

"Sometimes listening to you guys talk is like listening to strange music from a foreign country," Jamie said. "Weird and interesting, but not something everyone can dance to."

"In a transposition cipher, you basically take the letters in your message and just mix them up according to some pattern or scheme," Tess explained.

"Yes. But in a substitution cipher, you substitute each letter for some other letter in a cipher alphabet. It used to be that people would use one cipher alphabet to encipher a message," said Tess.

"Julius Caesar did a lot of this," said Theo.

"It's amazing how often people like Julius Caesar come up in conversations with you guys," said Jaime.

Theo said, "Julius Caesar encrypted his messages with an alphabet that shifted three places to the left, like this."

Theo wrote:

A	B	C	D	E	F	G	H	I	J
D	E	F	G	H	I	J	K	L	M

Jaime said, "So, you just stick *A*, *B*, *C* at the end, which stand in for *X*, *Y*, and *Z*?"

"Right," said Theo. "If I wanted to use the Caesar shift to encrypt the word *high*, I would write *KLJK*."

Tess said, "But it turns out that this kind of encryption is easy to break."

"For who?" said Jaime.

"So people had to come up with something that was

harder," said Theo. "You want something hard to break, but easy to translate if you know the way the message has been encrypted. You could make up a cipher alphabet by jumbling up the letters of the alphabet, but unless the person you're sending the message to has an exact copy of the cipher alphabet memorized, they won't be able to figure it out."

"Couldn't a computer do it?" said Jaime.

"I guess, but if the cipher alphabet was totally random, there are something like four hundred septillion possible keys."

"Even if you could check one key every single second, it would take a million times the lifetime of the universe to go through all of them," said Tess.

"A *billion* times the lifetime of the universe," said Theo.

"Million, billion, whatever," said Tess.

Theo ignored her. "But let's say the cipher alphabet wasn't totally random, that you jumbled the letters using a certain key word or phrase. Like—"

"Julius Caesar!" said Jaime.

"—Ava Oneal," said Theo. "You write out the key phrase, taking out all the spaces and any repeated characters. Then after that, you write the rest of the alphabet in order." He wrote:

A	V	O	N	E	L	B	C	D	F
A	B	C	D	E	F	G	H	I	J

"Well, if the key were Ava Oneal, instead of *A, D, G, L, M, R, S, Z,* we'd have *A, E, C, I, J, R, S, Z.* That doesn't seem to work. Three of the letters aren't even ciphered."

They tried Morningstarr for a key. They tried Old York Cipher and then just Cipher. For the heck of it, they tried Theresa and Theodore, Octagon, and Ava.

The smell of the pastelitos filled the apartment, rich and sweet and doughy. Tess's mouth watered. Jaime's stomach growled.

Jaime said, "What if it's just a bunch of letters jumbled around?"

"We could try anagramming them. A computer might help us. Still an insane number of permutations, but maybe we'll get a hint from an anagram solver site," said Theo.

Jaime pulled his phone from his pocket and handed it to Theo. Theo found a site and entered *ADGLMRSZ.* "Nothing," Theo said.

"What if that blank space is a vowel?" said Tess.

Theo tried that. Again, nothing.

"Look at the answers that contain only some of the letters. Maybe a partial answer will give us a clue," said Tess.

"I have *dogma* or *a dog. Molars.*"

"Speaking of chewing," said Jaime as his grandmother placed a tray of pastelitos and three glasses of milk on the table.

"Oh, Mrs. Cruz, these smell so good I could eat the air," said Tess.

"I hope you will eat the food instead," said Mima. "That is the normal thing to do." She studied their notes, leafed through the pages with all the permutations of the letters, the different keys and alphabets. "You said this Rastafarian cipher—"

"Rosicrucian," Theo said.

"This language of dots," continued Mrs. Cruz, "was used by silly men in silly clubs. What about the guild that runs the Underway? They are silly. They don't have any women. And they have secrets to keep, no?"

Theo said, "People have been questioning the Guildmen for more than a hundred years. They're not talking."

Jaime dropped his pastelito. "Mima, you're a genius!"

"Yes, but what's your point?" said his grandmother.

Jaime grabbed his phone, punched something in.

"What?" said Tess.

"A, D, G, L, M, R, S, Z isn't a cipher at all." Jaime flipped the phone so they could see. "These are train routes. All of them are train routes." He pointed to the spill of coinlike seals on the table. "And these are tokens."

CHAPTER TWENTY
Tess

O f course Theo asked his usual robot questions: Trains? (Yes, trains.) Where are we supposed to ride them? (Until we find out why we're doing it.) Should we take Nine? (We'll leave her with Mrs. Cruz for this one.) How can we be sure of this? (We can't.) But what do we do once we're on the trains? (We'll pay the Guildmen.)

"Mrs. Cruz gave us the hint," Tess said. "They're the ones the Morningstarrs charged with the secrets of the Underway, right? And the clue in this building points to the Underway. I think they're keeping the secrets of this clue."

"People have asked the Guildmen about the Morningstarrs before," said Theo.

"Maybe they didn't ask the right questions," Jaime said.

"What are the right questions?"

Jaime added a few more lines to whatever he was sketching. "Or maybe they didn't understand the answers."

"Who says *we'll* understand the answers?" said Theo.

"We have the tokens," Tess said.

But Jaime and Tess didn't answer Theo's question about questions or his question about answers, because they were too busy trying to figure out what to do next. They couldn't take a long ride just then, because it was too late in the day, and because Tess and Theo's parents would be expecting them home for dinner. And they couldn't go first thing in the morning either, because they had to spend another morning adding to the teetering piles of boxes and bags filling up their living room, as if Darnell Slant were a train that nobody had the power to stop.

So, it wasn't till the next afternoon that Theo and Tess met Jaime in the lobby, and they headed for that first train. They agreed they would take the A train all the way up to the end of the line—or the beginning, depending on how you looked at it—Inwood, 207th Street. They would ride the A train down the length of Manhattan, cross into Brooklyn, stopping at Ozone Park, and then on to Rockaway Beach if they had to. And then they'd switch over to the D train and ride that whole route for as long as it took. Then G, then L, and so on. Since they had more tokens than trains to ride, they would simply offer the tokens to the Guildmen and see what happened. They had not told their parents or Mrs. Cruz the particulars of their plan, understanding that they would never be allowed to travel so far from home, from one borough to the next, through neighborhoods they didn't know and stations they'd never been to. And they didn't talk about what they would do if they didn't have time to complete the routes, or if the Guildmen had no information to offer, or if they simply refused to talk, or if their answers didn't make sense and would lead exactly nowhere, or if they were all thrown off the train and banned from riding forever.

They found seats in the front of the train and waited. The stops flew by—people getting on, people getting off—the normal ebb and flow of humanity. Tess wondered how many of them were even thinking about the train they rode, how many of them understood what a marvel it was. How it had been born in the imaginations of the Morningstarrs when most of Manhattan was forests and farms, horses and carriages, muddy trenches where pigs roamed.

And then she looked at the guildmember in his box, white apron crisp, the wheel symbol of the guild right over the man's heart. To the Guildman's right, there was a panel of buttons and gears and levers, but his fingers didn't touch the mechanisms. Even seated, he seemed large and immovable, stone-faced and stony-eyed, his dark brows drawing to a sharp V shape on the ridge of his skull. Tess had her own questions: How long had he been in the guild; was it a family tradition; did his father and his father's father and his father's father's father keep the secrets of the Underway; and what it would take to reveal them—to her or to anyone? She hoped she could ask him.

The train quickly passed Central Park, bursting out of the ground at 116th Street and onto an elevated track darning neatly in and out of the tapestry of buildings. People stood in windows of the buildings, drank coffee, laughed, and talked. She was too anxious to sit, so she stood by the doors, rested her forehead against the glass, and looked down where people walked the streets below, brown and black and yellow hair shining in the afternoon sun—168th Street, 175th, 190th. Theo tugged at his lip. Jaime held his sketchbook and pencil but the page remained blank. When the train tunneled into the earth once again and pulled into Inwood, the guildmember's stone face rolled slowly toward Theo and Jaime and then rolled away, as if they held no more interest than the dog-sized rats that ran up and down the Underway tunnels. Tess's eyes strayed to the white tile wall just outside the train. Laid into the tiles were the words *At the start . . . at long last.* She hoped so.

The train idled a few more minutes, a few people stepped on. The doors closed. The train began its journey south. Tess swallowed hard, then stumbled toward the glass booth. Nobody else in the car noticed. The Guildman ignored her. Tess pressed her hands on the glass. He looked past her.

She did what they'd all decided she would do: she offered the pile of tokens to the Guildman.

The train stopped. The people filed off; the people filed on. The train inched forward. Tess glanced back at Theo and Jaime. So, maybe their theory was wrong and the Guildman knew nothing. Or Theo and Tess and Jaime knew nothing.

The Guildman turned his stone face toward her, expressionless as the Sphinx. He opened the window and plucked a token from her palm, his fingers dry and scratchy. He said, "Your journey is just beginning."

Tess's heart spasmed. "What? What was that?"

But he wouldn't look at her again, no matter how much she waved her hands. She stumbled back to Theo and Jaime.

"Now what?" Tess said.

Theo said, "We switch to the next train on the list. D. Get out at 145th."

Tess sat next to Theo, bouncing with so much excitement that she would have bounced herself right onto the floor if Theo hadn't gripped one of her knees. But he was gripping her knee so hard that she knew he was just as excited. A grin split Jaime's face.

They got off at 145th Street and caught the next D train going downtown. They walked up to the first car, found seats. The Guildman in this car was as small and wiry as the one in the first had been large and beefy. His brown skin shone like oiled wood rather than stone, but his expression was just as blank and unknowable. This time, Tess didn't wait until they hit the end of the line. She positioned herself by the glass and offered the tokens.

He opened the glass door, took a token. His brown eyes met hers. He said, "Your journey continues."

She ran back to Theo and Jaime. "Where can we catch the G?"

Theo pulled out a pocket map and opened it across their laps. The G line was a Queens–Brooklyn line, and they would have to make a few transfers to reach it. As they traced the route, the train jerked and the map slipped to the floor.

"Is it me," said Jaime, "or is the train going faster?"

Theo said, "They always go the same speed unless there's some sort of emergency."

"Feels faster," said Jaime.

And it did. Tess's thoughts raced through the various what-ifs—what if they went too fast to stop, what if they drove all the way down to Brazil, what if they crashed through one Underway tunnel into another, what if they burst through a wall and pitched into the sea—until Theo interrupted.

"We'll have to get off at 53rd, transfer to the E train, go to the Court Square stop, and then catch the G there."

It was a quick trip to 53rd. They hopped on the E train, not bothering to work their way up to the front. They took the E train across town and over to Queens and then found the G line. Unlike the trains in Manhattan, this train was strangely empty. When they arrived in the front car, there were no other passengers. Tess approached the booth and spoke to yet another wooden-faced man in a white apron, paid a token, and got the same message as the last: "Your journey continues." She turned to go back to her seat, but the train jerked again, and she lurched into one of the poles and nearly tumbled into Jaime's lap.

"He said the same thing the last guy did," she said.

Theo said, "You might be right."

"Of course I'm right," said Tess.

"No, I meant Jaime. I think the train *is* going faster."

"But this is a different train," said Jaime.

"Yes, it is," said Theo.

Tess's stomach lurched along with the train, but she tried to ignore it. "Where do we catch the L?" Tess said.

"Metropolitan Avenue," said Theo, and then grabbed for the pole as the train lurched again. When it stopped, the brakes squealed in protest. They ran for the L line. On the L line, the Guildman took two tokens from Tess's outstretched hands. Tess had just gotten the next message from the Guildman on the L—"Your journey continues"—when the Guildman took hold of a lever and pushed down hard. The train took off, the passengers gasping as they hung on to poles and straps. Protests rang out in the car—*What's going on? Who's driving this thing? Why is it going so fast? Is he trying to kill us?*—but the Guildman had turned his seat forward and was facing the black hole of the tunnel. The train screamed to a stop and pitched Tess forward, the tokens spilling to the floor. As the terrified passengers ran out through the open doors, Theo and Jaime helped her gather the tokens and pushed her into an empty seat.

"We have to stay on this awhile, to Myrtle-Wyckoff."

What if he won't stop? But he did, barely. The train jerked forward and braked, jerked forward and braked so abruptly that Tess held her knuckles to her lips to keep back her lunch, then tried not to think about the word *lunch*. And then the sign overhead was blinking MYRTLE—WYCKOFF AVS L—M, and the three of them were staggering down the platform to catch the next train. She had a small pile of tokens left. Theo looked green, Jaime looked gray, and though Tess had no idea what color she was, she was sure it didn't look too healthy. Crowds parted as if the three of them were zombies and what they had was catching.

Once on the M, Tess maneuvered herself to the seat closest to the Guildman. When she was informed that their journey, yes, continued, the train bucked so hard she whacked her temple on the glass. Cold, dead eyes regarded Tess and then the train sped up again. It was supposed to stop at Knickerbocker and Central, Essex Street, West 4th, and more, but it blew through them all, chewing up the tracks, going so fast through three boroughs that the force pulled them all sideways. *They're communicating,* Tess thought. *They know we're here; they know we've figured out the next bit of the puzzle. But aren't they supposed to be helping us? What's going on?*

The train stopped. Tess looked up at the blinking sign—Jackson Heights—exactly where they were supposed to catch the R train.

"It's like the trains are running just for us," said Theo.

"Yeah," said Jaime. "But they don't seem happy about it."

Her stomach scuttled into her mouth as they got on yet another train car to hear "Your journey continues."

Right before the lights cut out.

The train hurtled through the dark. Tess gripped the seat, screwed her eyes shut. The darkness and the movement of the train toyed with her, telling her up was down and left was right, and she would never get off, she would be trapped in this whirling, hurtling blackness forever.

And then the lights blazed on, the train stopped and spit them out, dizzy and stumbling, toward the S shuttle. Their journey continued.

"Two . . . more . . . ," she said, breathing heavily.

"Three," said Theo. "The S, then the 4, 5, or 6 to Canal, where we catch the Z."

She swallowed hard, but kept moving, afraid that if she stopped, she would never get on another train for the rest of her life. But they did get on the S shuttle, a short, bone-jarring ride over to Grand Central Station. This ride cost Tess three tokens. The train rocked as if something huge and monstrous were trying to punch it off its tracks, the train tipping to one side only to crash back down again, over and over. Tess bit her tongue, and her mouth flooded with the tinny taste of blood.

At Grand Central Station, they hopped on a crowded 6 train headed for Canal Street. The 6 screeched past every stop between Grand Central and Canal, turning the vague grumbling to hysterical shrieks weirdly muffled in the tight space. When the train stopped, it stopped so short that entire groups of people tumbled like dominoes.

"I'm calling the police!" someone screamed.

Tess gripped the three remaining tokens in her palm so hard that they left imprints on her skin.

And then it was time for the last train, the Z, suspiciously empty, except for the caterpillar zigzagging back and forth over the floor of the car. The Guildman was older than the others had been, shaved bald, small features crowding the middle of a pale face. He took the last tokens out of her hand and said, "It's the end of the line," and then turned away as the train started to move.

Finally, thought Tess.

And then, *What kind of end?*

"I think we're the only people on this train," Jaime said as Tess sat down.

"How is that possible?" said Theo, but this was the Underway and who knew what was possible?

The train gained speed. Unlike the last train, which had rocked and rolled down the tracks, this train barreled straight ahead as if it had been shot from a gun. The force pulled at their hair and their cheeks, a strange wind whipping through the empty car. The train plunged through the darkness of the Underway tunnels, lights buzzing and flickering, making everything appear like a series of terrible snapshots, moments lost between them—first the Guildman's bald head was turned away, then he was staring right at them, then turned away again, the back of his head like a face wiped clean of eyes, nose, mouth. Tess's head pounded, and her ears popped as the train broke free of the rock under Manhattan and into a tunnel at the bottom of the East River, this one made of some sort of transparent material. Outside the tunnel was a vast green murk stained here and there with shadowy and unrecogniz-able things that swam in the dark, tentacled things that Jaime's grandmother had never mentioned were below the surface. Maybe she didn't know about them, maybe nobody knew, maybe they weren't real, maybe this whole thing was a dream. And then the train charged back into the rock under Brooklyn, churning with impos-sible speed toward who knew where. A terrible thought pierced her brain.

"It's not going to stop!" she said.

"What?" Theo yelled.

"What if it doesn't stop?"

Jaime said, "It has to . . . doesn't it?"

The train jerked upward, the track leading them to the surface. The car emerged from the tunnel and accelerated on an elevated track. The train got higher and higher, level with the tops of the highest buildings in the borough, the speed of the train making the peo-ple walking below look like rain-smeared chalk scrawled on a sidewalk.

The Guildman slipped out of his glass box. He stood regarding them with a detached, clinical expression, as if he were unaffected by the motion of the train, the screaming wind, or the fear of the kids huddled on the seats in front of him. He walked toward the caterpillar still cleaning the floor, scooped it up the way you scoop up a baby, and whispered to it. Then he put the caterpillar back on the floor, strode past them like any other commuter anywhere looking for a comfortable place to sit. When he reached the door at the end of the car, he turned. In a low voice that should not have carried over the screeching of the wheels and the howl of the wind, he said, "To read the map, you'll have to look into the lights."

"What map?!" Tess shouted. "What lights?"

The man didn't answer. He kicked at the door at the other end of the car, stepped through the opening, and shut the door behind him. He hovered on the platform between cars, bald head floating in the window, before he disappeared.

"Where did he go?" said Theo.

Strange thudding sounds came from overhead.

"He's on top of the car. But why would he climb on top of the car? How can he even stay on?" said Jaime.

Even though it seemed impossible that the train could go any faster, it picked up speed.

Jaime said, "This thing is driving itself."

"But to where?" said Theo.

"The end of the line," Tess said.

Theo slid to the floor, crawled to the glass booth, reached up yanked on the door. "It's locked. I can't get to the controls."

"Nah, don't like that. I don't like that at all, nope. NOPE," said Jaime, and pointed. Outside the car, the Guildman dangled, face still wearing that same clinical expression.

And then the man let go.

Tess's breath caught.

Through the back window, she saw the Guildman rolling to his feet on the top of a nearby apartment house.

"We're not going to do that, are we?" said Tess. "Tell me we don't have to do that."

"We don't have to do that," said Theo. But the train only picked up more speed. More stops without slowing.

"I think we're going to have to do that," said Jaime.

"Look for an emergency brake," Tess said. "There! On that wall."

Jaime staggered over to the red lever, pulled it. Sagged when nothing happened.

Tess's skin prickled with sudden cold. "They disabled the brake?" People had been investigating the Cipher for decades, but no one had ever risked anything more deadly than a paper cut before. No one imagined surging across the borough in a runaway train, no brakes, no way to stop.

As they rounded a rather sharp bend in the tracks, the train tipped, landing back on the tracks with a crash. Tess, Theo, and Jaime crouched on the floor. The caterpillar passed within inches of their noses.

Theo said, "We need to get off this thing now, while there are still buildings to land on. If we get past the populated areas, there could be nowhere to jump."

They crawled to the door the Guildman had taken. Using one of the poles, Jaime hauled himself to his feet. He wrenched open the door. A rough wind plowed through the car, an invisible hand shoving at them. Jaime used the chains that attached one car to the next to pull himself outside. "There's a ladder out here!"

Tess and Theo looked at each other, then at Jaime. The Guildman was gone, the brake was disconnected, there was no reason to believe the train wouldn't keep going until it fell into the ocean. They didn't have a choice.

Theo nodded. Jaime began to climb, Tess right behind him. The wind tore at her hair, whipping her braid against her back. Her sweaty palms slipped on the ladder, and then her sneaker slipped, too. Theo gripped her calf, set her foot back on the rung. She would not think of the what-ifs, she would only think that this would all be fine, some funny story they would tell after they had solved the Cipher and they were back in their home with their families and they would laugh and laugh and laugh.

Jaime crawled onto the top of the train and flattened himself, inching forward. When Tess crawled up after him, she found a wide trench running down the center of the train car with two thin rails on either side. The wind was so strong it stung her eyes, so she kept her head down as she inched forward. She risked pressing herself up to her knees, saw the buildings flying by, some with roofs only a few feet away. If the train would just slow down a little bit.

The train hit another bend, and the force pulled Tess to the right and jammed her against the railing. Another bend, and she hit the left rail and flipped over the side of the train car. A shriek tore out of her throat as Jaime's hand clamped around her wrist and hauled her up again. She'd barely breathed her thanks when the train hit another bend and *Jaime* pitched over the side. Theo lunged forward and caught Jaime's arm just before he fell, pulling him back. The three of them dropped to the top of the train, panting. The train jerked again, and *Theo* slipped backward off the end of the car. Tess pounced on his outstretched arm, landing on her stomach with an "oof!" The impact of his body flopping against the back end of the car nearly wrenched her shoulder out of the socket but she held on. Theo's eyes rolled in his head as his feet scrabbled, but the train swerved so wildly he slipped again and again.

Behind her, Jaime said, "Hold on, Tess, I'll help you!"

"NO!" Tess yelled, just as the train rocked, and Jaime was tossed over the side of the train once more. With her free hand, she grabbed for him. Her shoulders screamed as she was pulled in two directions, Jaime on the side of the car, Theo at the back, both of them scrabbling for purchase. The what-ifs crashed in her head—what if Theo fell, what if Jaime fell, what if they all fell? Pasted to the top of the train, feet hooked over the thin rails, she looked for a safe place to let go, any place to let go—the top of an apartment building, a rooftop garden or pool—but they had entered a long stretch of tiny suburban homes, and the drop was long and terrifying and impossible. Her thin gibbon arms were stretched to their limit, her legs quivered and burned. The wind slapped at her and the blue skies mocked her and the what-ifs punched her when the wheels locked. The train screamed, and she screamed with it, using every molecule of strength to hold on.

And then, when it seemed as if the train would enter orbit, it shuddered and shrieked to a stop, nearly pitching them all into the sea of tiny houses before it pulled into the last stop, the end of the line. Theo and Jaime dragged themselves onto the top of the car and the three of them lay there, lungs heaving, the smell of scorched metal in the air. Slowly, they sat up in the late afternoon light. Theo opened his mouth to speak, but Tess punched him in the arm.

"Ow!" he said. "What was that for?"

She kept socking him, punctuating each word: "Don't you EVER say ANYTHING bad about MONKEYS or GIRLS again!"

And then she hugged them both as if she would never let them go, as if she hadn't just proven that very thing.

CHAPTER TWENTY-ONE
Theo

Theo let Tess hug him for as long as he could stand it; he was still too shocked to move. But she was squeezing him so hard his eyes popped open, and what he saw all around them was nothing but blue sky, as if the train were suspended in midair by the clouds alone.

"Yo," said Jaime, apparently noticing the same nothing. "Where's the station?"

Tess let go. The three of them carefully slid to the edge of the train and looked down. The train was stopped next to a narrow, uncovered platform many, many stories off the ground, with a spindly staircase that zigzagged down to street level. It was so windy that Tess's braid kept smacking Theo and Jaime in the face.

"That platform doesn't seem big enough to unload

more than one person at a time," said Jaime.

"Doesn't even seem finished," Tess said. "Maybe they abandoned it before it was done? The city does that."

"Why would they build a platform so high up anyway? They'd need forty escalators to get everyone back to earth," said Jaime.

"Or solarpods."

"Or parachutes."

There was a brief shudder beneath them. Theo grabbed for Tess and Tess grabbed for Jaime. They all held their breath, sure that the train was about to take off again, heading straight up to the moon.

But no. The train didn't move. A faint *whish* sounded from below.

"The doors," Tess whispered.

As they watched, the metal caterpillar scuttled from inside the train out to the narrow platform.

"What's it doing?" Jaime said.

The caterpillar stopped. It rose up on its hind legs, scanning, or sniffing, or . . . ?

It seemed to be looking right at them, swaying just a little. Then it scuttled its way across the narrow platform toward a lone metal lamppost missing a bulb, skittering up the post till it reached the empty socket at the top. Somehow, it attached itself to the socket, leaving most of its metal body dangling like a streamer in the wind. More faint noises—the scrape of metal against metal, the clicking of dozens of tiny feet—more twitching.

"What's . . . what's wrong with it?" Jaime said.

Its metal skin seemed to be *rippling* somehow, as if it were made of liquid and not metal. It expanded, then contracted, expanded again, rounding into a great silvery ball. But cold metal couldn't do that.

Could it?

The ball that once was a caterpillar quivered and clanged against the pole. A thin buzz cut through the air, a buzz that turned into a high-pitched whine that made Theo's teeth ache.

"What the—" Tess began.

The ball burst in a shower of sparks. They mashed their faces against the top of the train as fine bits of metal rained down like glitter. When the whining and sparking and raining subsided, Theo risked a peek.

Where the caterpillar had been, a sphinx moth the size of an eagle perched. It rested for a moment, cooling its molten metal wings, then took off toward Manhattan in a fluttering, silvery blur.

"It's official," Jaime said. "Things have gotten really weird."

"And scary," said Tess. "Those stairs look like the

only way to get down from the platform."

"Scary or not, I'm not staying up here another second." Jaime carefully slid down onto the platform, walked over to the flimsy staircase, and tested his weight on the first step. When it held, he started down. Tess and Theo followed. Theo focused on his hands gripping the rails and his feet connecting with the treads; he didn't look left or right, up or down. He didn't focus on the ground or how far away it was.

They'd been zigzagging for what seemed like forever and had almost reached the street when a cop's angry, reddened face appeared between the treads below.

"Sweet peanut butter and jelly! What in the name of Starrbucks do you kids think you're doing up there?"

It had been a while since Theo and his sister had been in police car.

He remembered it being more fun. That last time, Tess and Theo had been around nine years old. His mother and her partner, Syd, drove them around Manhattan, telling them wild stories about crazy crimes, like the guy who tried to use a burrito to beat up his cousin, or the woman who got caught dragging a big blue mailbox down the street, or the car thief who crashed into a news van, or the teenager who tried to steal a Roller only to get rolled to the nearest police station, or the burglar who fell asleep on the couch of the apartment he was attempting to burgle, with the family's fer-otter curled up on his chest.

This time, there were no stories. Just a lot of questions that they really didn't want to answer. The three of them sat in the backseat with one officer crouched in the open door on one side of the car, and his partner crouched in the open door of the other side.

"So," said the red-faced officer, whose name was Clarkson. He was white and doughy and blond. "What you're telling me is that this train was a runaway train, and you three were stuck on it alone? And the only way you thought you could escape was by jumping off that train onto the top of a building?"

"Yes," said Tess.

"And you're telling me that you saw a man, a Guild-man no less, jump off the top of the train onto the top of a building?"

"Yes," said Tess.

"Except we checked with the guild," said Clarkson's partner, a small, lean Asian officer named Chin. "And they tell us that this particular train has been waiting on that particular abandoned track for repairs since last night. Hasn't been in operation all day. And to their knowledge, no GM, and I quote, 'would be so stupid as to jump off a moving train,' end quote."

"Huh," said Theo.

"Huh? What's that supposed to mean?" said Clarkson.

"Just thinking," said Theo.

"Thinking of a better story?" said Clarkson. "Because this one's full of applesauce." Clarkson was making Theo hungry. He continued, "Are you kids going to tell us what the butterscotch you were doing up on top of that train or do we have to take you down to the station?"

Jaime wriggled between them. If they sat here with the two officers, there was a good chance their parents would be called. If they were taken to the station, their parents *definitely* would be called.

Chin added, "Look, we know who you are. At least, we know that you and this girl over here belong to a certain member of New York City's finest. You think she'd be happy to hear about this?"

Tess blurted, "It was a dare."

Theo turned to stare at her.

"Theo is always talking about how much stronger and braver and more adventurous he is than me, just because he's seven minutes older." She stared back at him. "It's not true."

Theo pressed his lips together. He'd never said he

was more adventurous, just smarter about choosing his adventures. There was a difference.

She said, "We were coming home from our aunt's house and we saw this empty train just sitting on the tracks. So, we got off the train, circled back, and climbed one of the service ladders to the tracks. We just wanted to see the train. We weren't going to do anything else."

The lies rolled off her tongue so smoothly that even Theo believed her. He hoped the cops did.

"Please don't tell our mom," Tess said. "We've never done anything like this before, and we'll never ever do anything like it again." She shuddered as if reliving the horror, and Theo knew she wasn't faking that. Theo rubbed the wrist that Tess had held—the skin burned raw—then stopped doing it when he saw Tess's slight shake of the head.

Clarkson looked across at Chin; Chin gave a one-shouldered shrug.

"All right, listen," said Clarkson. "I don't want to get you guys in trouble, and to tell you the truth, I don't want to spend the next two hours doing a bunch of forking paperwork and babysitting a bunch of kids. But don't let me catch you or even hear of you doing something so cornnuts ever again, okay? Because if I do, I'll have to tell your mom what happened here, and then

we'll *all* be in a whole lot of hot mustard."

"We won't do anything like this again, sir, we promise," Theo said. As long as the Cipher didn't demand it.

It probably would.

The cops drove them to the nearest Underway station. Theo, Tess, and Jaime waited a few minutes to make sure the cops had left, then walked right back to the curb to hail a cab.

They got back to 354 W. 73rd Street so exhausted that the word *exhausted* seemed inadequate (maybe Officer Clarkson would have a better substitute—cream-cheesed? roasted?). Theo's wrist ached. His shins and knees were bruised where he'd banged them against the train. He hadn't fallen off the train, but he felt as if he had.

"My arm is killing me," Theo said, rubbing his shoulder.

"I can't even feel mine anymore," said Tess. "Are they still there? Or did I leave them in the taxi?"

Theo's whole body winced. "Um, about that."

"If you're going to thank me, don't, because the shock would be too great," said Tess.

Jaime said, "Thanks."

Tess said, "Thank *you*. You pulled me up when I fell off first."

Jaime put out his hand, maybe to touch one of the arms Tess couldn't feel anymore; Theo didn't know. But Jaime dropped the hand and shoved it in his pocket. Theo liked Jaime's hand in his pocket better than on his sister's arm. And then he wondered why he was thinking about Jaime's hand or his sister's arm (beyond the obvious and undeniable fact that she had saved his life with that arm).

Jaime cleared his throat and pressed the elevator button. "What do you want to do about the next clue?"

"I love clues," said Tess. "Except right this second. Right this second, I love aspirin. And food. And then I will love sleep, if I can ever sleep again. Tomorrow, I will love clues."

The elevator drifted up, the left, then down, then up once more, as if giving them some time to gather themselves before they had to go to their respective apartments and start lying to their family members about how they had spent their day. Theo didn't think "Oh, I was dangling from a runaway train while my sister kept me from hurtling to certain death" was going to cut it. And though Tess could lie as smoothly as she could tell the truth, Theo couldn't. Especially not to his mom.

"What happened to you two?" Mrs. Biedermann said

as soon as they walked into the door.

Theo froze. Tess said, "Frisbee in the park. I'm starving. What's for dinner?"

Mrs. Biedermann frowned at Tess. "What's wrong with your arms?"

"Nothing. Why?"

"You're holding them funny."

Tess laughed. She held her arms out in a T. "Maybe they've just gotten longer. Because of the Frisbee." She dropped her arms her sides again. "Dinner?"

"Your dad's picking up falafel and kabobs. Oh, and don't make any plans for tomorrow. Aunt Esther is coming."

"Aunt Esther? Why?"

"We're going to load up some of these boxes in her van and take them to her home in Queens," said Mrs. Biedermann. "So I really do hope your arms are okay, both of you. You're going to need them."

Theo was dreaming of a bald man with no face on his face when his dad yanked on the shade and it snapped up with a clatter.

"Your aunt's just called," Mr. Biedermann said. "She's on her way."

"What time is it? Five a.m.?"

"Try eight," said Mr. Biedermann. "And try getting out of bed, lazybones."

Theo attempted to rise, flopped back down when every single one of his lazy bones shrieked in protest. Apparently, his whole body was broken. Which wasn't convenient.

"Are you all right?" said his dad.

"Peachy."

He had just hauled himself into the kitchen and flopped down next to Tess when Aunt Esther arrived.

"Greetings, Biedermann family!" she announced, marching into the apartment with a box of doughnuts and a container of hard-boiled eggs. "I have brought carbohydrates and protein." She set the food on the table and sat. Nine immediately jumped onto her lap and started purring.

Theo picked a chocolate doughnut. Tess reached for one, winced.

Aunt Esther said, "I have also brought tiger's balm. But not for the tiger," she said, scratching Nine between the ears. She reached into the large bag she referred to as a "pocketbook" and pulled out a tube of ointment. She slid this to Tess.

"Why does she need tiger's balm?" said Mrs. Biedermann.

"I found tiger's balm to be very soothing back when I was working for the post office," said Aunt Esther.

Mrs. Biedermann said, "She hasn't carried any boxes yet."

"A preventative measure," said Aunt Esther. "You should select a carbohydrate before Theo eats them all."

Aunt Esther was pushing seventy, but she didn't look it. She was medium height and sturdy, with short brown hair and a no-nonsense manner a little like his mother's but not quite. As far as Theo knew, Aunt Esther had never married, but she had done just about everything else. Each time he saw her, she mentioned some piece of her past that he'd never heard before, as if she were just remembering it herself. Or making it up.

"When did you work for the post office, Aunt Esther?" Theo asked.

Aunt Esther stroked Nine's striped back. "Right after I managed the game preserve in Botswana. Tiger's balm?"

It took hours to load up Aunt Esther's van and another one his dad had rented, so many hours that they stopped to eat lunch before they left. If Theo's body was broken, he couldn't imagine what Tess's felt like, but she seemed too tired to complain. She slumped against the window of the van as they drove along the Hudson River, crossed the Bronx on the Cross Bronx Expressway, and curled south toward Flushing and Aunt Esther's house. Theo wondered if Tess was thinking about the moth, what the moth was supposed to mean, what they were supposed to do next, how they were supposed to find the map that the Guildman talked about. His mind was as tired as his body; he had no idea what to think.

They arrived at Aunt Esther's house forty-five minutes later and spent the next couple of hours carrying the boxes from the vans to the house and then trying to find places to store them. Aunt Esther's home was tiny, with more rooms than it had a right to, each of them painted a different color—purple, red, yellow, green— and decorated with ornate masks, creepy puppets whose gaze seemed to follow them around the room, and a stunning array of knives and swords. Aunt Esther also liked plants, and the house was riotous with them, twisting vines pinned up along the moldings, potted trees so tall they bent where they met the ceiling, slack-jawed orchids gaping from the top of a dusty piano. Tess once said it reminded her of the lair of Poison Ivy, if Poison Ivy had been a senior citizen fond of toys, cardigans, and sensible shoes.

After they were done unloading the boxes, Aunt

Esther mixed up a batch of iced tea with lemon and brought the pitcher to the living room with the announcement: "I have brought you some iced tea and some Fig Newtons." They sipped their drinks as Mrs. Biedermann took a work call out on the front porch.

"I have already cleared out the attic for Tess and Theo," Aunt Esther said. "I will clear out the red room for you and Miriam by the end of the week."

"Thanks, Esther," said Theo's dad. "I know this is a lot of trouble, and we really appreciate it."

"Trouble can't always be avoided," said Aunt Esther. "Right, Tess?"

Tess, who was rubbing her shoulder, said, "What?"

"Have a Fig Newton. I think your blood sugar is low."

Theo grabbed a cookie for himself. There were a lot of strange things moving around Aunt Esther's apartment, not least the numerous mechanical spiders that pruned and watered the plants and the mechanical ladybugs that ate the real aphids.

No moths the size of eagles, though.

He should have been pondering the Guildsman's riddle: *To read the map, you'll have to look into the lights.* He should have been asking himself: What map could the Guildman have been talking about, and what lights? But he was more intrigued by another riddle: How could a caterpillar made of metal—a robot whimsically designed to look like a natural creature—have the kind of transformation that only flesh-and-blood caterpillars can have? How could a robot be . . . alive?

This was not adorable.

Not adorable at all.

Which was why, for the first time since they'd started on this quest to solve the Cipher, Theo was convinced they'd stumbled onto something important, really important. Along with the mystery of the Cipher, here was a real mystery, a *scientific* mystery. And maybe one that hinted at the real power of the Morningstarrs. Because he didn't think the Guildmen were men at all. And he didn't think the Morningstarr Machines were just machines. The Morningstarrs' creations were alive.

And they were thinking for themselves.

CHAPTER TWENTY-TWO
Jaime

When Theo shared his theory with Tess and Jaime—
that he believed the Guildmen were actually
Morningstarr Machines come to life—Jaime thought it
was the most awesome thing he'd ever heard. But then
he remembered that, machines or not, the Guildmen
had probably tried to kill them so they couldn't solve the
next clue. And then he realized that they had no idea
how to solve the next clue anyway. They went over the
riddle a million times—*To read the map, you'll have to look into
the lights*—but they didn't know which map the Guildman
was referring to or where to find it. And though they
racked their brains, looked in books, and searched the
internet, they didn't know which lights they needed to

look into. Did it refer to a Morningstarr invention? Some forgotten inventor?

Maybe it was the "condemned" notice posted on the glass doors downstairs or the creeptastic presence of Stoop and Pinscher, who continued to chisel off tiles and doorknobs and light fixtures with increasingly sadistic glee, but the rest of the residents of 354 W. 73rd Street weren't consumed with an incomprehensible clue; they seemed to be afflicted with packing mania. At all hours of the day or night, doors were propped open and the occupants inside could be seen sorting clothes, stacking up books and dishware, stuffing bags full of sheets and towels, sitting on suitcases just to get them to close. Tess and Theo were dragged to and from their aunt's apartment in Queens.

While they were gone, Mima gave Jaime a new job: remove all the photographs from the walls, wrap each carefully in brown paper, and set them in a box. They had hundreds of photographs on every surface of their place, and it would have taken Jaime forever to finish the job even if he'd been moving quickly. But he wasn't moving quickly. He was so used to seeing these photographs every day that, except for his few favorites, he had never taken the time to stop and look at them. Until now. Here was his great-grandfather Daniel, astride a motorbike in

Havana in 1949, dark and brooding and mustachioed. Here was his grandmother Mima, then just Estefanía, posing with a group of grinning girls in downtown New York City. Here was his father, dark brown, muscled, hard-hatted but shirtless—fearless—standing on top of the skeleton of a Mexican solar plant. And here was his mother, Renée, as a doctoral student at T&T University, long 'locs coiled so tall on the top of her head that she looked like some kind of scientist-queen.

All of them had been in this apartment. The walls had heard their wishes. The floors had felt their foot-steps. How could he leave this place when so many of the people he loved had left the last of themselves here?

It was the same for the twins. But maybe they wouldn't have to leave. If they just could figure out which map the Guildman had been talking about, and which lights.

"Is this all you've done? Two rooms? Are you moving in slow motion?" Mima said, hands on hips.

"I keep looking at the pictures," Jaime said.

"You haven't seen them before? They've only been hanging in this apartment your whole life."

"I know. I just . . ." He shrugged.

"Okay," said Mima, taking from him an old photo of her as a child with her favorite cat, Beets. "Shoo."

"What?"

"Go take a walk around the block. Get some fresh air." She held out some money. "And pick up a pizza for dinner on your way back."

Jaime took the folded bills. He hadn't told her what had happened on the train, hadn't told her that if he and Tess and Theo hadn't been able to save one another, he'd be just another picture on the wall.

"What?" said Mima. "Why do you have that strange look on your face?"

"Just hungry."

She waved her hand. "What else is new? Get two pizzas."

Outside, the sun was just setting, which meant it was late, after eight o'clock in the evening. The sky was so wild with purples and pinks and oranges that even New Yorkers couldn't help but stop and look up. High above, the white belly of a solarship floated past. He wondered what the people on the ship saw when they looked down, all the people skittering around the streets like tiny little Rollers. After walking awhile, Jaime sat on a bench in Riverside Park. He pulled his sketchbook from a pocket and sketched—not the river in front of him or the dazzling sky and the solarship above, but Tess on top of a train, head thrown back, roaring like a liger. Tess didn't have any superpowers—she was as skinny as a chicken wing—but Mima always said that you could never tell how strong a person was just by looking at them, especially girls skinny as chicken wings. Mima said that when she was just a teenager, skinny as a chicken wing, she'd knocked out the front teeth of a boy who'd tried to kiss her after she told him no.

He was just wondering if he should give Tess a pair of wings when the lamps in the park went on. Or one lamp went on. The rest stayed dark. Which was weird. Weirder when he saw the buildings across the water and saw only a smattering of lights over there, too.

But the city had had brownouts before, especially in summer. Anyway, it was too dark to keep sketching. He tucked the book in his pocket and made his way over to Mima's favorite pizza joint, Dangerous Pie, and ordered two pizzas with everything. He sat down to wait. While he was playing Angry Bots on his phone, a large man charged into the pizza shop and ordered a pie with a quarter cheese and tomato sauce, a quarter no cheese *or* tomato sauce, and half pineapple and peppers. He paid, turned around.

"Jaime!"

"Hey, Mr. Moran. How are you?"

"I've been apartment hunting all day. How do I look?"

He looked like a ham with under-eye bags. "Fine?" said Jaime.

"I look terrible. We all look terrible."

The pizza man said, "Maybe some of the lights will go out uptown, then. We won't be able to see you all looking so terrible."

"That's not funny. Why would I want a brownout? Out-of-control machines aren't a joke."

"What do you mean, out-of-control machines?" said Jaime.

"A Morningstarr Machine was caught on video in a bunch of different power stations messing with the circuits," Mr. Moran said. "It was all over FaceSpace. They haven't caught it yet."

The pizza man was shaking his head. "I saw that video. It looked fake. And that ain't no Morningstarr Machine."

"Of course it was!" said Mr. Moran, growing even pinker.

"Morningstarr Machines don't break. And anyway, they didn't make a machine that looked like that."

"That looked like what?" said Jaime.

"Butterfly," said the pizza man. "My kid has the

complete Lego collection of Morningstarr Machines. You got your Rollers, you got your SqueeGees, you got your anteaters, your caterpillars and dragonflies. Oh, and Lancelots, too, but those don't really count. Anyway, they didn't make a butterfly."

"I don't care what kind of toys your kid has!" Mr. Moran shouted. "That butterfly is a Morningstarr Machine. It has to be."

"I'm just saying, I know those machines, and that screwy machine ain't one of them."

"What else would it be, then, huh? Huh, tell me that!" said Mr. Moran.

The pizza man scratched his big belly. "Okay, okay. Maybe you want to sit down."

"Why should I sit down?!"

"Because you look like your head's going to pop like a balloon."

"MY HEAD IS FINE! WHY IS EVERYONE ALWAYS BURSTING INTO HYSTERICS?"

The pizza man plopped two boxes on the counter. "Pies are ready, kid. Get out while you can."

"WHAT'S THAT SUPPOSED TO MEAN?"

"Thanks," Jaime said. He grabbed the pies. They smelled delicious, but his mind wasn't on his stomach.

His mind was on the "butterfly" that was flying around turning off the lights.

But turning off the lights for what?

Turning off the lights for *who*?

When Jaime got home, he and Mima did something they never did: ate dinner in front of the TV. They watched the amateur videos of a fluttery silver object so blurry you could barely identify it, and listened to witnesses and reporters:

"Look, I'm telling you, that thing attached itself to one of those there circuit breakers and zapped it. Lights haven't been right since."

"It was only a matter of time for those machines to go kablooey. Darnell Slant knows. Out with the old, in with the new, am I right?"

"The machine seems have rewired the system somehow, because some lights work, some don't."

"It's a conundrum for city workers and for authorities, too, who are trying to figure out who or what is behind this sabotage, if it is sabotage. But officials say they expect to have full power restored by tomorrow morning."

Mima put a slice of half-eaten pizza back on her plate.

"This is a strange story. A strange story for a stranger city."

Maybe not so strange, Jaime thought. What if the moth wasn't sabotaging the lights? What if it was trying to send a message with the lights? But what kind of message? Morse code? No, then the lights would have to blink on and off. Maybe not a message. Maybe a picture or a pattern.

A pattern like . . . a map?

But then how would they see the whole of the map? From his vantage point, Jaime could only see a few lights here and there in the buildings closest to him. They'd have to plot the map light by light on a computer or on paper, and there were hundreds of lights. That would take forever. They could climb the tallest building in New York City, but even that might not be high enough to see the whole of the city, might not show them all the lights at once.

Then he remembered the white belly of the solarship he'd seen earlier, floating gently across the clouds, and he knew what they'd have to do.

"*Fly*," he whispered.

"Yes," said Mima. "If I was going to make a machine to mess with this city, I would not make a butterfly. I would make a wasp." She nodded to herself. "Yes. Something that stings."

Later that night, while Mima was washing the dishes, Jaime whispered into his phone: "You guys know anyone with a solarship?"

There was a long silence on the other end, and then Theo said: "I think we might."

CHAPTER TWENTY-THREE
Tess

"Uncle Edgar!" said Tess loudly. "What are you doing here? Look, Dad, it's Uncle Edgar!"

"Yes," said Tess's dad. "I heard that. And so did the entire building. Hello, Edgar. Great to see you again."

Edgar stepped inside the apartment, took in the boxes and the bags and the general chaos, Nine guarding her pile of socks like a dragon over an egg. "I know it's last-minute, but I thought I'd take the kids off your hands for a couple of hours."

"Now?" said Tess's dad, looking at his watch. "But it's so late."

"For you and me, maybe. But not for these two." He patted Theo's poufy hair. "There's a showing of *The Glorious Vision of the Morningstarrs* at the planetarium. I figured we could catch it if we hurry."

Tess's dad tapped his chin thoughtfully. "Well, they *have* been packing and moving all day."

"And yesterday! And the day before that!" said Tess.

"I don't see why not. They deserve to have a little fun."

They told the same story to Jaime's grandmother, who told them they'd probably have more fun going to see *Wonder Woman: Revolution*, but to each his own. Uncle Edgar packed them in a cab and told the driver to take them to the Croton Fountain. In the front seat, Uncle Edgar kept up a steady stream of chatter with the driver about politics and about the best baseball player on the New York City Starrs and whether or not the team would make it to the series, while Tess's leg vibrated with nerves until Theo clamped his hand down on her knee.

The driver dropped them off at the fountain, where a group of teenagers crowded around listening to a kid in braids and jeans rapping: "I grew up a warrior in the Seminole Nation, resisting the brutality of colonization. . . ." Otherwise, it was quiet, and the society's building was dark, as were most of the buildings on the street. Edgar led Tess, Theo, and Jaime through the oak-paneled lobby and the steel door beyond, down the filigree staircase, and into the belly of the archives.

Auguste Dupin, sleeping in his cage with his head under his wing, didn't even look up.

As soon as they reached the ground floor, Uncle Edgar pulled out his phone, typed in a code. Two enormous bookcases opened up to reveal a cavernous room.

In the center of the room was a yellow inflatable ship with solar panels on top and a gondola underneath for the pilot and passengers.

"Kind of looks like a pat of butter you'd get at a fancy restaurant," Jaime said.

"It's small but powerful. And it's safer than riding in a car," said Edgar. "Wouldn't be a great idea to tell your mom, though."

"Or my grandmother," said Jaime.

"Or anyone else," said Tess. "Since when can you fly?"

"A number of members got our pilot's licenses when the society purchased the ship. We keep it inflated and ready to go at all times. But we're not going to have much air time before air traffic control notices us. So, we're going to have to get up in the air, see what we need to see, and then get back inside as quickly as possible. Someone could get a picture or a video, but I can always explain that away later. We society members are considered quite eccentric, so if I told them that I wanted to fly to the moon on my pat of butter, I'm not sure they'd be surprised."

They got inside the gondola and strapped in. Uncle Edgar told them that though it was an antique, it ran as well as a new ship, but didn't feel much different from strapping into the car of a Coney Island roller coaster.

Uncle Edgar pushed a bunch of buttons and controls. The ceiling above the ship split, then yawned wide. But instead of the herky-jerky motion of a roller coaster, the airship rose gently as a balloon. Once they were hovering over the courtyard, Edgar pushed another button, and the doors below them closed tight again, so tight that you'd never have known they were there in the first place.

The airship lifted straight up. The ground below got smaller and smaller, the society building turning into a miniature of itself, a model among a line of models, rows and rows of models, like the worlds Theo built with his blocks. The air flowing through the open gondola windows was crisp and cool, and the sky revealed more shades of blue—midnight and cornflower and periwinkle—all streaked with traces of silvery cloud.

Jaime said, "I want to draw this, but I don't have the right colors."

"I wish you could draw the smell." Tess inhaled the smells of carbon and the briny scent of the sea, but also something sharp and metallic that tickled the back of her nose. She wondered if stars had a smell. If the moon did.

"Now," said Uncle Edgar as the ship kept rising, "why don't you kids tell me what we're looking for and how you knew to look for it?"

Tess took a deep breath, then told him what they had all decided they could finally reveal to him, especially now that he had agreed to help them: that their grandfather had gotten a letter written by Theresa Morningstarr herself the day that Slant had announced his purchase of 354 W. 73rd Street, that it was the start of a whole new branch of clues, that it had led them from the Liberty Statue to the Tredwell House, the chair of George Washington to the painting of William Waddell, the grave of Eliza Hamilton to the Octagon on Roosevelt Island, and finally to 354 W. 73rd itself, and what came after.

Uncle Edgar was quiet for a long while, and Tess wasn't sure if he believed them. Then he said, "Ava Oneal's house. Your grandfather always wondered if she was the key to the Cipher."

"He did?"

"She was such a cipher herself. Maybe a bigger mystery than the Morningstarrs."

"So you believe us? That there's a second line of clues?"

Edgar's voice was kind when he said, "Does it matter what I believe?"

Tess bit her lip, then shrugged. Though it stung a little to think that Edgar might believe that this was nothing more than a solarship ride, Tess believed, Theo and Jaime believed. That would have to be enough.

Theo popped his head out of the window and craned up. "You can see the stars. You can never see stars in the city."

Edgar said, "That's because of the lights. There are always too many lights on. They overpower even the light of the stars. But not tonight."

"Tonight we have to look down, not up," said Jaime.

Higher and higher they rose, the air getting colder and colder, until Tess was shivering, until the whole of the city spread like a blanket below them, studded here and there with winking diamonds. Even in the dark, the spire of the Morningstarr Tower poked at the clouds; the ribbon of the Underway laced all the buildings together. Just beyond the edges of the city, the water glimmered.

All four of them hung their faces out of the windows, trying to see a map in the lights below, something that would tell them what to do next. Tess stared at the winking lights and darkened buildings and glimmering water, and frustration knitted her brow, knotted her guts.

"I'm not seeing anything," Theo said.

"Me neither," said Jaime. He looked up overhead and down below. "Kind of looks the same. Like a bunch of random stars."

"It can't be random," Tess muttered, but nobody seemed to hear.

"I'll take some photos anyway, just in case." Uncle Edgar pressed a button the console. Jaime sketched furiously.

"How long do we have till the police or whoever figures out we're up here?" said Theo.

"This airship is somewhat special. It's invisible to radar, but not invisible to the eye, so we could get reported anytime now. I think we have enough pictures."

He maneuvered the airship around and floated them gently back to the society's building. Another press of the controls opened the courtyard, and Uncle Edgar lowered the solarship inside.

"You're really good at this, Uncle Edgar," Tess said.

"You should see your aunt Esther fly," said Uncle Edgar. "Your grandfather invited her out here last year."

"Aunt Esther is a pilot?" Tess said.

Theo said, "Why not? She's done everything else."

The gondola touched the ground and the balloon above shuddered. Uncle Edgar said, "Okay, let me just send these photos to the computer inside. Good. Everyone out!"

They left the hangar and went back inside the archives. Uncle Edgar sat at an antique rolltop desk with a decidedly *not* antique computer on top of it. They all huddled around the giant screen. Uncle Edgar typed some commands, and one of the pictures he'd taken popped up on a screen.

Theo tipped his shaggy head. "Could we put this picture on top of a picture of the city? Maybe the lights are referring to certain buildings or monuments?"

Edgar did as Theo asked. "We've got a few lights on some of the bridges," he said, "and here's one at the main branch of the library, but most of these"—he clicked more keys, checking—"are in or on buildings built after 1855."

"What if you superimposed the map onto buildings built before 1855?" Jaime said.

"Good idea," said Edgar. He called up a map of New York City in 1855 and layered the photograph of the lights on top of it.

"Looks like a lot of the lights are sitting on farmland or in the woods," said Theo.

"Maybe there are clues buried on those spots," said Jaime.

"There are buildings on top of them now. We'd never be able to get to them," Tess said. Uncle Edgar glanced at her, his expression as kind as his voice had been earlier. Tess yanked at her braid hard enough to hurt. There had to be something else to this "map." Or they had to read it in a different way.

"Maybe it's not a map of the city or even things in the city," said Tess.

"What does that mean?" said Theo. "What else could it be a map of?"

"I don't know!" Tess said.

Edgar pushed back his chair. "Did you bring the original letter with you? And the copy of *Penelope*? Why don't we look at those?"

Tess didn't know what good it would do, but she pulled the letter and book out of her messenger bag and handed them over. Uncle Edgar read the Morningstarr letter, muttering, "Fascinating, just fascinating. So, you'd already gotten this when you came to see us?"

Tess's ears went hot. "Yes. I'm sorry we didn't tell you. We weren't sure we were on to something, and we thought that if the society got involved, Slant might figure it out."

"'Trust No One,'" Uncle Edgar said, pointing to the warning on the envelope. "I understand. I'd have done the same thing." He set the letter aside and picked up the book. "Now, this is even more fascinating. We know so little about Ava Oneal. Records show that she worked as a nurse at a hospital for sick orphans—one of Eliza Hamilton's projects, I believe—which was where Ava met Theresa Morningstarr. But we don't know where she born or who her family was. People have speculated whether she was a runaway from a plantation and was living under an assumed name, but, again, we have no evidence of that. Apparently, she didn't have a Southern accent." He thumbed through the book. "By all accounts, she was as smart as she was beautiful, but I don't think either condition made life any easier for her."

"What do you mean?" said Jaime.

"Excuse me a moment." He strode to one of the shelves and scanned it with a finger. He found what he was looking for, some sort of leather-bound journal, and brought it back to the desk.

Tess edged closer to look. "What is it?"

"Notes of a physician from the New York City Lunatic Asylum."

"I think Ava Oneal was in that asylum!"

Edgar said, "Yes, she was. All sorts of scribbles here, some difficult to read. Here we have 'Young man admitted. Caught stealing a pig. Claimed the pig was his brother, Charles.' And a few pages after that, we have 'Mrs. Roddington still claiming her husband had her locked up because he didn't like her cooking.' Unfortunately, more than a few people were locked up simply because they were nuisances and not because they were insane. And here's something about a boy who had an unfortunate incident with a Roller; that's a bit gruesome, so I won't read that one. Ah! Here are the notes that are more interesting."

He pointed to some notes dated April 1853. "'A most interesting case. Ms. Ava Oneal. Servant to the Morningstarrs. Abused a would-be suitor for trying to kiss her.'"

"My grandmother did that," said Jaime.

Uncle Edgar grinned. "I've met your grandmother, and that doesn't surprise me a bit. About Ava, the doctor writes that she 'seems in good physical condition. Incredibly strong for a woman.'"

"Yes, because women are weaklings," said Tess, rolling her eyes.

"The people of that time were not known for their egalitarianism, Tess," said Uncle Edgar.

"Tell me about it," said Jaime.

Theo said, "What else does it say?"

"That she spoke a lot of nonsense. 'Today she asked me if I remembered the old fable "The Man and the Lion," where the lion asserted that he should not be so misrepresented when the lions wrote history. When I asked her who was the lion, she laughed and laughed and would not stop.' And that she spent three days repeating these sentences: '"For it is not light that is needed, but fire; it is not the gentle shower, but thunder. We need the storm, the whirlwind, and the earthquake." I'm afraid she's desperately, irreversibly ill, and possibly dangerous. I recommend she be confined indefinitely.' This doctor didn't seem to realize that Ava was quoting the abolitionist Wendell Phillips and the writer and orator Frederick Douglass."

"That's actually pretty funny," said Theo.

"If it wasn't so horrible and sad," Jaime said.

"Yes. And it turns out that this doctor, a Dr. Chauncey Welborn, quit the profession after it was discovered he had quite the problem with whiskey."

He closed the volume, turned his attention back to the computer screen. The lights of the city really did look like a gentle shower of stars, Tess thought. But what could you read in a map made of stars? Real stars were never still, never fixed in place; they moved across the sky. Every time you looked at them, the stars would be different.

"A map made of stars," she said out loud. "Or a star map?"

Theo's brows bunched, then flew up in surprise. "I think you might be right!"

"Wait, how is a star map different from a regular map?" Jaime asked.

"The stars look different depending on the exact date and time you're looking at them. If Tess is right, then the star map will give us a specific date. Maybe another clue." Theo turned to Edgar. "Is that something your computer can calculate?"

"Well," said Edgar, leaning back in the chair, considering. "Yes. I think it can." He slid the chair closer and typed in some more commands. "This should identify the positions of the lights, er, stars, and tell us what day we need to pay attention to. It should also give us the vantage point from which the stars need to be viewed. It will take a minute or two."

Nobody spoke as the computer calculated.

And calculated.

And calculated.

Tess tapped her foot. Theo pulled his lip. Jaime's fingers drummed a rhythm on his leg.

The computer gave a soft *ding!*

They all leaned forward.

December 3, 1844. Brooklyn.

Edgar leaned back in his chair, blinking.

"Brooklyn?" said Tess. "What happened in Brooklyn in 1844?"

"Brooklyn wasn't even a part of New York City then, was it?" Theo asked.

"No, it wasn't," said Uncle Edgar. "Let's see, 1844, 1844." Into the computer he typed the date and place. On the screen appeared inventions from the nineteenth century, notations from history books, photos and bios of dead presidents, endless lists of information. He frowned at the search results, lips working, fingers scrolling, until he stopped, took in a sharp breath, let it out with a long hiss.

"What?" said Tess.

Uncle Edgar didn't answer but again walked over to

one of the towering bookshelves. He consulted one volume, then another. Then he pulled a third. He opened the book.

"What is it?" Tess said.

Uncle Edgar spread the volume out on the desk, showing them a yellowing newspaper article. "On December 3, 1844, the Atlantic Avenue Tunnel officially opened in Brooklyn."

Tess looked down at a drawing of a train entering a dark shaft. "What's the Atlantic Avenue Tunnel? I've never heard of it!"

"That's because it was only open for twenty years, and then it was closed, buried, and forgotten," said Edgar.

"Until now," said Tess.

Uncle Edgar laughed, and his laugh was equal parts shock and delight and belief. "Yes. Until now."

CHAPTER TWENTY-FOUR
Theo

They only had a few minutes to celebrate the discovery of the Atlantic Avenue Tunnel, because they soon found out that only way to access the tunnel was through a manhole cover smack in the middle of Atlantic Avenue in Brooklyn. If they didn't want to be seen, they would have to make the journey in the middle of the night and would only have a few hours to find the next clue. And since the tunnel was seventeen feet high and some 2,500 feet long, it was way too much ground to cover in so short a time, especially if you had no idea what you were looking for.

So, they would have to be prepared before they went anywhere, Edgar insisted. And to be prepared, they had to find out everything they could about the tunnel. Edgar Wellington dug up books and articles in the archives. Jaime searched the internet. Tess helped Omar and Priya and Ray continue to pack up Grandpa Ben's apartment, just in case Grandpa had a relevant letter or a book or an artifact stashed somewhere, something that might describe the precise location of a new clue in the tunnel. She did this with the energy of a squirrel searching for a nut.

A few days into their research, however, Theo's mom announced that they would be making a trip out to Long Island, and it was as if someone had stuck a pin in Tess and all her excitement and energy drained out. She sat deflated in the car next to Theo as Nine nibbled at her fingers and Mom issued her normal warnings: Grandpa could be having a good day, or he could be having a bad day, or he could be having an in-between day when one minute he was good and the next he was bad. They had to be ready for anything.

They were never quite ready.

The drive to Grandpa's took about an hour. The place was a smallish white building situated on a wide lawn so green you might think it was spray-painted. Maybe it was. It also had lots of trees, winding paths for walking, and benches for sitting. If it was one of Grandpa's good days, they could stroll around the grounds, maybe even go out to dinner. If not . . .

Well.

They found him in the sitting room, a sunny space decorated with gauzy curtains that let in as much light as possible. He was sitting by one of the windows, white hair swept back from his brown, regal profile like a bust you'd find in a museum. When Theo's mom knelt next to Grandpa's wheelchair and kissed Grandpa on the cheek and Grandpa said, "Hello, Rabbit," they knew it was a good day, or at least a day with some small good in it, because Rabbit was Grandpa's old nickname for Theo's mom—no Yiddish for her. "I call you Rabbit because you're so easily spooked!"

"Not so much anymore," Theo's mom said, her voice thick.

Grandpa patted her hand. "Sometimes, though?"

"Maybe," Theo's mom said.

Grandpa turned to Theo and Tess. "Look at you! So tall!"

"Hi, Grandpa," said Tess, bending to give him a hug.

Grandpa held Tess by the shoulders, beaming at her fondly, his eyes still clear and blue as ever. "And what do they call you?"

Tess swallowed hard. "Tess. And *Gindele*. You always called me that."

"Ah," said Grandpa. "Rabbit is a rabbit and you are a deer. That's nice."

So maybe a bad day, too.

Grandpa turned to Theo. "And you, young man? Are you a rabbit or a deer or something else entirely?"

"I'm Theo," he said. "Just myself."

"Hmmm," said Grandpa. "Are you sure?"

"Yes," said Theo.

"Because Rabbit has had imaginary friends before, right, Rabbit?"

Theo stuck out his arm. "Not imaginary, Grandpa. I'm real."

Grandpa squeezed his hand. "So, you are," he said, still smiling. "The other man was real, too."

"What other man?" said Theo's dad.

Grandpa Ben looked surprised, as if he hadn't expected Theo's dad to speak, as if he were a painting that had suddenly offered an opinion. "The tall man. Very tall. Had to look up so far I hurt my neck."

Theo's mom said, "What was his name? Did he tell you?"

"Oh, I'm sure he did. He was very polite," said Grandpa. "He sat and helped me with my crossword." He gestured to a puzzle that lay on the table next to him. The puzzle was blank.

"What color was his hair?" said Theo's mom.

"Hair?" said Grandpa. "He had hair. I told him that you had what he wanted."

"What? What do I have?" Theo's mom said. She looked as if she were about to cry.

Grandpa Ben laughed. "Not you, Rabbit, *you!*" He pointed at Tess. "The little deer that isn't so little. Little deer grow up so fast."

"But I don't have anything," Tess said.

"You have everything you need," Grandpa said, nodding wisely. "You just don't know it yet."

But they didn't have everything they needed, not according to Edgar Wellington. Theo wished he could ask Grandpa about all the other companies competing with the Morningstarrs to modernize and expand New York City, about the trains that caused so many accidents that the people of Brooklyn demanded a tunnel be built. And he wished he could talk about all the rumors about the tunnel after it was sealed: that pages from John Wilkes Booth's lost diary were buried there. That German terrorists were making bombs down in the tunnels during the First World War. That bootleggers had taken over the tunnel and made gin in the 1920s. That spies hid in the tunnel in the 1950s. That a whole locomotive might be buried in the rubble. He wished he could ask: What do you think we're looking for, Grandpa? Is this the end of the line? Is the real treasure of the Morningstarrs buried in this tunnel? Is Tess right, and the treasure has been waiting there for us to discover? Or are we somehow creating the puzzle ourselves, building it out of the choices we make?

But Theo didn't ask any of this. He played checkers with Grandpa while Tess took Nine around to the other patients in the sitting room, letting them pet the cat. One very old man held on to Nine and cried into her fur. He missed his dog so much, he said. The younger woman sitting next to him said that he'd never had a dog.

The man kept crying. "I miss the dog I never had."

"You can't miss what you never had," said the woman, irritated.

"Yes, you can."

Could you miss what you never had? Theo wasn't so sure. One of his earliest memories was unwrapping a Hanukkah present from his grandfather and finding a paper dictionary so heavy that he could barely lift it. His mom asked his grandfather why Theo couldn't just use the internet, but Grandpa said the paper version was better because you could write in it. You could interact with the words, make them your own. Every time he came upon a word he didn't know, he and Grandpa Ben would look it up. When he got older, they would write sentences using that word in the margins. "The boy's bathroom was as *fetid* as a swamp." "I am all *agog* to hear your latest story." "He used several *malapropisms* when he said that Michelangelo painted the Sixteenth Chapel." Grandpa Ben showed him three-letter words useful for crossword puzzles: *ore, era, zuz.*

But one day, he lost the book. Or rather, the book was taken. He and Tess were playing with the dumb-waiter, putting things inside it and sending them for a ride through the building—one of their mom's frying pans, a cactus, even Nine (who liked it so much she rode it ten times in a row). They put Theo's dictionary in the dumbwaiter, but when the dumbwaiter returned, the book was gone. They put Nine in the dumbwaiter to find the book, but then Nine was gone. They ran and told their mother, who called Mrs. Cruz, but Mrs. Cruz had no idea where the items disappeared to. Tess was in tears over Nine, until Nine showed up on the roof, basking in the sun. They never did find that book.

Grandpa Ben said that the building sometimes did that—"borrowed" things it liked and offered other things as gifts. Grandpa said he'd buy Theo another dictionary, but Theo knew it wouldn't be the same. Mrs. Cruz locked up the dumbwaiter and disabled the power. No one had used it since.

Theo missed his dictionary still. And he didn't see how you could miss something as ordinary as a dictionary in the same way, if you'd never spent hours sitting with Grandpa Ben, poring over the new words, tasting them on your tongue, then pressing those words into the paper, shaping them into sentences that you made up yourself, with your grandpa laughing at your malapropisms.

"Young man!" said Grandpa.

"What?"

"Isn't it your turn?" He tapped the edge of the checkerboard.

"Yes. Right." Theo made a move. Grandpa grinned and jumped a black checker over three red ones, though Grandpa was supposed to be playing red.

After a couple of hours, Grandpa Ben, tired from all the checkers and the chatting, yawned, his white head drooping.

Theo's mom stood, kissed Grandpa on the cheek. "Okay, Dad, I think you need to go back to your room and get some rest. We'll be back soon." She motioned for an aide. A round woman with milky skin and a pouf of blond hair came over and took the handles of Grandpa's wheelchair.

"I'll take it from here," the aide said.

"Thanks so much, Gladys," said Mrs. Biedermann.

Gladys began to push the chair, then stopped. "Oh! I meant to ask you if you got the letter."

"What letter?" Mrs. Biedermann asked.

"There was a letter that your father needed help mailing a few weeks ago, but he wanted to mail it to himself. Or at least, to his post office box. I figured that since you were the one picking up his mail, he meant to send it to you. I hope you got it. He was very agitated about it. Made me cross out the address and rewrite it more clearly so that it didn't go to the wrong place. Said it was top secret. For his eyes only. Or yours."

"Trust no one," Grandpa whispered as he fell asleep.

All the way home, Tess gripped Theo's wrist tight enough to crush the bones. Grandpa Ben had sent the original Morningstarr letter to himself. But where did he get it? Who sent it to him? When he told Tess she had everything she needed, was he talking about the letter?

Theo's mind was spinning by the time they got home to find Mr. Stoop and Mr. Pinscher in the lobby. The two men had some sort of metal detector that they were sweeping across the tiles.

"You're not going to find anything," said Theo. "People have been scanning and x-raying and examining this building for decades."

"Not with this device, they haven't," said Mr. Stoop. "This is a new invention. A *modern* invention. Notice the elegant design?"

"Elegant?" said Tess. "It looks like a plate attached to a stick."

"Right. It looks exactly like what it's supposed to be and not a . . ." He twirled his hand in the air.

"A grasshopper?" offered Mr. Pinscher.

"Or a cockroach," said Mr. Stoop.

"Who would design a scanner to look like a cockroach?" Tess said.

"Who indeed?" said Mr. Stoop. When Tess stared up at the man, frowning hard, and Nine growled, Mr. Stoop's smile only got wider. Mr. and Mrs. Biedermann glared and steered Tess and Theo toward the elevator.

Theo sifted through his conversations with Grandpa Ben. Did a man come to see him to ask about 354 W. 73rd Street? It was possible. Grandpa Ben had lived in this building longer than anyone else they knew, and had had family that had lived there long before him.

Grandpa Ben would be the person to ask, if a man had questions.

A man so tall Grandpa's neck hurt looking up at him.

Mr. Stoop.

CHAPTER TWENTY-FIVE
Jaime

The funny thing about time was that when you were running out of it, it only seemed to go faster. Not that long ago, it had felt like they had weeks to figure out the Cipher, and now Jaime felt the ticking of the clock in his bones. Even Edgar Wellington seemed to feel it. After they'd read everything they could find about the Atlantic Avenue Tunnel, even found an old engineering survey of the tunnel, Edgar decided that they were as prepared as they could be, and they'd just have to take a chance, especially if Mr. Stoop was desperate enough to go to Long Island to pump the twins' poor, sick grandfather for information, as the twins had claimed.

"We need to stay ahead of these people," said Edgar, jaw set. "They will not win."

He convinced Mr. and Mrs. Biedermann and Mima that a sleepover at the archives would be great for the kids and a nice break for the grown-ups. Since they needed to wait till at least midnight before going to Brooklyn, they passed the time telling more stories of the Atlantic Avenue Tunnel. It was filled with poisonous gas! (Not true.) It was filled with albino alligators! (Maybe one or two but that was a long time ago.) It was filled with ghosts! (Please.) It was filled with rats! (Likely.) After the stories, they packed up some equipment: flashlights; water; a screwdriver; a crowbar; a set of lock picks; a ladder that collapsed into the size of a serving tray; a whole bunch of other tools that not even Theo could identify. Uncle Edgar said that the tunnel should be safe enough, but that you couldn't be too careful.

A little after midnight, they headed out. No cabs this time; the society had its own van. Twenty minutes later, they were parking. The streets of Brooklyn were busy enough. As Jaime had said, this was New York City, and there were always people around. But it was also true that the people of New York were good at minding their own business and excellent at refusing to be surprised. Want to perform Shakespeare on the Underway in your bathing suit? Eh. Want to dress up like a toucan and tap-dance in the park? Whatever. Roller-skate through the department store? Don't let the security guards catch you. Want to hold a philosophical debate with a piece of Swiss cheese, make a mask out of peach pits, stick raisins up your nose? Looks pointless/painful/ugly, but it's your cheese/face/nose.

Sure enough, when Edgar went to the middle of the street and set up a bunch of traffic cones around the manhole, the cabs and cars simply swerved around him, the people on the sidewalks barely sparing a glance. Edgar waved the kids over. They ran across the street, barely avoiding a man on a unicycle flying a flag that said, WHAT GOOD IS A STORY YOU ONLY WANT TO READ ONCE? Edgar levered up the manhole cover. He pressed a button on the side of the ladder and it shot down into the darkness with a snap.

"Wow," said Jaime. "That's some Batman stuff right there."

"Let's hope it all works," Uncle Edgar said. "Now, who wants to go first?"

They all wanted to go first. Three games of rock-paper-scissors later, Jaime went in.

He hit the floor and then stepped through an opening that had been broken into the concrete wall. Another dusty, ladderlike stairwell—this one not as steep—led into the tunnel. The tunnel itself looked like, well, a

2,500-foot-long tunnel that had been built in 1844. Back at the archives, they had read Walt Whitman aloud:

> *The Tunnel, dark as the grave, cold, damp, silent. How beautiful look earth and heaven again, as we emerge from the gloom! It might not be unprofitable, now and then, to send us mortals—the dissatisfied ones, at least, and that's a large proportion—into some tunnel of several days' journey. We'd perhaps grumble less, afterward.*

Jaime wouldn't grumble at all if they found something. He'd seen Slant's workers setting up wire fences, cordoning off 354 W. 73rd Street, getting it ready for the wrecking ball, whenever that would come. He hoped they could stop it in time. But he wasn't sure he could stop anything else: Mima's sadness; the fact that they had to leave 354 W. 73rd Street. They were too far gone now, one foot out of the door, a deposit on the apartment in Hoboken, a new job for Mima, a new school for Jaime. But maybe saving their own homes wasn't the point anymore. Maybe the point was to save a piece of history. At least, that was what he told himself.

He rubbed his arms to warm them, and then his nose. Sneezed. Said, "I thought this place would be spookier."

"It would be if the stories were true," Theo said.

"Ghosts. Pirates. The pirates were supposed to have an entrance to the tunnel from a bar nearby, guarded by a pair of seven-foot-tall Turks with scimitars."

Jaime said, "Turks with scimitars would be awesome."

Edgar said, "So, according to the survey we found, there are a few things buried down here. A twenty-foot-long metallic structure between the middle and the south side of Atlantic Avenue, which the engineer thought was a steam engine or some sort of digging machine. There's a smaller geophysical anomaly on the northern side."

"What do they think the smaller anomaly is?" Theo said.

Edgar shrugged. "No idea. They didn't dig because the government pulled the funds and permission. Closed everything up indefinitely."

"I wonder if that's what we're looking for," Tess said.

"We won't know till we get there," Edgar said. "Come on. Let's head to the other end. Keep your eyes open."

They walked. The floor of the tunnel was dirt, with large rocks here and there. The lights bounced off the stone walls, illuminating writing that had been carved into the surface:

Lynch put first electric light in this subway.

"Subway? Not Underway?" said Tess.

"Weird," said Jaime, and scribbled it in his sketch-book, right next to an imaginary seven-foot-tall Turk. It was hard to sketch in the dark, but he did it anyway, quick lines that limned his thoughts.

They found the remnants of an old phone, with a long coiled cord and a rotary dial. Jaime picked up the handle and pretended to talk to John Wilkes Booth. Tess took the phone and pretended to talk to the ghosts until Edgar told them to quit fooling around.

They reached the end of the tunnel, a pile of debris in front of a wall. "This is where the locomotive is supposed to be hidden. And over there"—he pointed the beam of his light—"is where the other anomaly is located."

He took the pack off his back and unzipped it, remov-ing various tools. He pulled out a silver cylinder the size of a drinking glass and popped off the cap, exposing a bit an inch in diameter.

"A drill?" said Theo.

"Not just any drill. The Morningstarrs designed it. This little darling could drill through cobalt plates if we needed it to." He put the tip of the drill against the wall and started up the machine. A high-pitched whine echoed through the tunnel, dust puffing in the air like a cloud. After about five minutes, Edgar turned off the drill, blew on the new hole.

"Theo, could you shine your light over here?"

Theo moved to stand next to Edgar. The tiny drill had made a hole big enough to see through. Behind the rock was suitcase.

A shiver chased up Jaime's spine. "Can you make this hole bigger?"

"What's in there? What is it?" Tess said.

They took turns peeking into the hole, Tess nearly jumping up and down.

"Okay, okay," said Edgar. "Let me work on this wall for a while longer, and then we'll open that case."

He drilled new holes at intervals, which took so long that Jaime, Tess, and Theo sat down in the dirt to wait. Then Edgar tried to kick down the weakened wall. Even as big and strong as he was, the wall didn't budge.

"Now what?" said Tess.

"We're going to have to get a little more dramatic," said Edgar. He dug around in the pack again and came up with a flat disk that sort of looked like a doorbell.

Theo's eyes widened. "Is that . . . ?"

"An explosive. But a very small one. Won't be louder than a passing Underway car. That said, you should probably move back."

They got to their feet and moved to the other side of the tunnel. Edgar put the device in the middle hole and pressed the button. Then he jogged to where Theo and the others were standing.

"Turn your faces away," he said. "One . . . two . . . THREE!"

Behind them, a dull *boom*, and then a shower of falling rock. When the dust cleared, the hole was now a doorway to a hidden chamber. They tossed and kicked the stones out of the way and dragged the suitcase out of the chamber.

"Heavy," said Edgar.

They brushed it off. Some kind of bright metal skin, welded in patchwork. Finding this here felt almost magical, like some robot wizard or alien left it just for them. Even through the dust, it gleamed like it was made of stars.

"Silver?" said Theo.

"I don't know," said Edgar. He ran his hands over the top and then tried to lift the lid. Nothing.

Thud.

They shone the light on the back wall of the chamber, where the sound had come from. Nothing.

"The explosion must have loosened some rocks," said Edgar. "It's fine."

"Are you sure?" said Tess.

"Tess, this tunnel has been sitting here since 1844. I don't think one little explosion is going to hurt it."

"'Little explosion' is an oxymoron," said Theo.

"Can I have more light here?" Edgar said.

They all shone their beams on the suitcase.

"How do you open it?" said Jaime. He knelt and felt for the latch. He pressed it, but pressing did nothing. When he looked closer, he saw there was a keyhole next to the latch, a heart etched around it.

Edgar took the suitcase, prodded it, tugged it, smacked the top of it to try to get it to pop open.

"What about the hinges in the back? The case might be more vulnerable there," Tess suggested.

"Good idea." Edgar grabbed the drill, flipped the case, and placed the bit on one of the hinges. The drill squealed, caught, and sparked in Edgar's hands. He dropped it to the dirt.

"What the . . ." He picked it up, examined it. "It . . . broke the drill."

"There's got to be a way to open it," said Tess. "Maybe we should take it back to the archives, where we can see it better."

"Maybe you already have the key," said Edgar.

"What do you mean?" Theo asked.

"Well, you've been helping pack up your grandfather's things. Does he own any kind of artifact or key or mechanism shaped like this heart on the front?"

"I don't remember anything like that," said Theo. He turned to Tess. "Do you?"

She shook her head. "No. But you have most of Grandpa's stuff now. Let's go back and look."

"He said you'd have it," Edgar muttered. "He said you had everything you needed."

"What?" said Tess.

"Are you sure you've never seen any kind of key that would open this? Maybe it doesn't look like a key."

Crack.

Again they turned their lights on the back wall. Dust snaked up from a small pile of stones.

Jaime said, "I think we broke the tunnel."

"This is all very exciting and mysterious, but maybe we could get out of here now?" Tess said.

Theo ignored his sister and the not-awesome rumbling sounds echoing through the tunnel. "Who said we'd have the key with us? Who said we'd have everything we needed? Wait." He stuck his hand in his ginormous hair, took a step back. "It was *you* who went to see my grandfather?"

Jaime had a bad feeling. A very bad feeling. Dust was

raining down from the ceiling of the tunnel. Edgar Wellington packed up his tools and picked up the silver suitcase. When he straightened, his face was drawn and white. But he didn't look angry. He looked resigned and a little sad.

And that's when Jaime saw it, when they all saw it. Another disc shaped like a doorbell in Edgar's free hand.

"Uncle Edgar," said Theo, his voice careful and slow, "what are you going to do with that?"

"Nothing drastic," Edgar said. "I just need you to stay down here for a while."

"What?" said Jaime.

"Stay down *here*?" said Tess.

Theo said, "What's a while?"

"That's not drastic at all," said Jaime.

Thud. Thud.

Behind them, a bit more of the wall crumbled to the ground. Jaime's stomach dropped along with the rocks.

Theo said, "What are you doing?

Tess said, "Why are you doing this?"

The flashlight cast an eerie glow onto Edgar's face, shadowing his eyes. "You know why. For the Cipher. For the most amazing treasure known to man. Cipherists have been going in circles for more than a hundred and fifty years. And to find out that it was because they were working a false Cipher? A whole line of red herrings? The Morningstarrs were more amazing than anyone ever imagined."

Theo said, "What if there's a third line of clues? A fourth or a fifth or a dozen? What if my grandpa was right and the Cipher was designed with no solution? What if the search *is* the treasure?"

"Your grandfather is a brilliant man way too satisfied with his own brilliance," said Edgar. "No, the Cipher has a solution. And I'm going to find it. Please understand. I've been searching for this my whole life."

While the twins argued with Edgar Wellington, Jaime figured their odds. There were three of them, but Wellington was a large man, and he had that doorbell thing in his hand and probably other Batman weapons in that backpack of his. Maybe a baton or a cattle prod or a gun. Maybe nets or ropes to tie them down. If he could just creep behind the man, maybe knock him down, take the pack and the suitcase.

Quietly, Edgar's pale gaze lasered to Jaime. *"Don't,"* he said.

Tess's angry eye twitched in the same way it had that day in the elevator, the day in which they learned they would have to leave 354 W. 73rd Street. "You don't even know what to do with that suitcase."

"Are you saying that you do?"

"Maybe you're right, maybe Grandpa does have the key. Maybe it's with his other stuff, the stuff you didn't take. If you leave us down here, you'll never know," Theo said.

Edgar said, "Technically, you're not much of a poker player. Plus, I have more powerful tools at the archives." He pulled a blanket and a smaller parcel from his pack, tossed them to the ground. "Some food and water. The blanket should cover the three of you."

"But this makes no sense!" Tess shouted. "You'll get in trouble! My mom will arrest you!"

Edgar Wellington said, "No one will get in trouble. You won't remember what happened."

"What are you talking about?" said Tess. "Of course we'll remember!"

"There are certain drugs that can interfere with that. You'll be fine."

THUD, THUD, THUD.

Every brain cell in Jaime's head screamed that they had to get out, all of them, *now.* He said, "Except for the fact that this tunnel is going to collapse. Look, let's all go. You can use your drugs or whatever to erase our memories once we're up there. But we need to go, we all need to go."

Edgar took a few steps backward. A flicker of uncertainty passed over his face, then was gone. "The tunnel is solid. It's stood since 1844, and it will stand another day or two. I'm going to seal it temporarily, but I'll come back for you."

"Wait!" yelled Tess.

And then the wall exploded *behind* them. They hit the ground and put their arms over their heads. Edgar stayed on his feet and grunted when a stone hit him in the shoulder. He staggered. Coughing, waving away the clouds of grit, he turned toward the opening in the now-crumbling wall behind them. A giant metal machine looked right back them, black as a train, but not a train.

Because trains didn't have mouths.

"Get up, get up," Jaime bellowed, scrambling to his feet and shoving at Tess and Theo. Theo got up, but Tess didn't move. The great black machine lurched forward, saw-toothed mandibles clanging, legs churning, a segmented body almost wide enough to fill the entire tunnel. A loud clanking filled Jaime's ears and rang in his brain. He and Theo pulled at Tess's arms, but she was heavy and limp. A trickle of blood traced across her brow where a rock or something must have hit her. They tried to push her, to roll her, but the machine was coming. *It was coming.*

Jaime wasn't a superhero boy, but he flung Tess's arm over his shoulder and hefted her off the ground. And she wasn't a skinny little chicken wing at all—she was heavy as fourteen bags of cement, *forty* bags; but Theo took hold of her feet and they staggered over to the hole in the wall where they'd found the suitcase and ducked through it.

Edgar—stunned by the sight of the beast erupting from the back wall, the train that was not at all a train—ran for the stairs. And the beast undulated after him, nimble as a whale in the ocean. The black expanse of the beast's carapace filled their view. They heard a scream. Jaime risked a peek through the opening and saw that there were jaws on the hind end, just as vicious as the ones on the front.

And then, and then, the beast stopped moving, its honed black plates rippling to a halt. It raised its mandibles, and Jaime could have sworn it was tasting the air. It scrabbled back from where it came, marching through the opening in the wall and plunging into the blackness and beyond.

They sat in the dark of the chamber, panting, feeling

the reverberation of the beast as it tunneled under Brooklyn on its way to wherever such beasts went.

"The explosives must have woken that monster up," said Jaime.

"A digging machine," said Theo. "We always thought the Morningstarrs used the cut-and-cover method to dig the tunnels for the Underway but could never figure out how they completed the work so fast. There were stories, but . . ."

"The stories were true," said Jaime.

Theo's eyes were glazed and shocked. "Do you think he's dead?"

"Wait here," said Jaime. "There's a flashlight over there." He hefted himself through the hole and walked cautiously over to the flashlight. He picked up the light and shone it toward the entrance of the tunnel. He had walked only a few steps when there was a new noise.

The tapping of numerous tiny feet.

Four Rollers clicked and clacked toward the dark form of Edgar Wellington slumped on the ground. Whatever he had done, or almost done, Jaime didn't want to see him *Rolled* like garbage. But instead of turning around, they backed up, and two of the Rollers heaved the limp form onto the backs of the other two. And then the four

Rollers made a solemn procession through the tunnel, past Theo and Tess and Jaime, and out the way the giant beast had gone, vanishing into the underbelly of the city.

Jaime didn't know what to feel. His chest was like the tunnel, dark and filled with rubble. This was not the way it was supposed to go; this was not the way things were supposed to be. Things like this happened in comic books and movies, not in real life. He couldn't imagine what Theo was feeling. That was a man they thought they could trust. A friend.

Jaime tried to see into the tunnel the beast had made. "Where do you think they took him?"

Theo's voice was high and thin. "I wonder if we'll ever know."

"Come on," Jaime said. "We have to get your sister out of here."

They tried to wake her, but it was no use. They picked her up again and started back toward the entrance of the tunnel. The suitcase lay on the ground, half buried in a pile of rocks. So, it hadn't been crushed; it hadn't been scooped up with Edgar's body. Jaime hooked it with his foot, flipped it up onto his wrist, but could feel no happiness, just a grim satisfaction that made him wonder about the world, that made him wonder about himself.

They got moving again. The ground felt unsteady, his knees bending this way and that. More strange rumbling sounded throughout the tunnel. Thunderstorm? No, they were too deep to hear a storm. The earth beneath his feet seemed to hum somehow. Small stones dropped from the walls next to them.

Jaime said, "My feet are vibrating."

"I don't know if this tunnel is stable anymore."

"Maybe that one monster isn't the only monster down here," Jaime said. "Hurry."

They walked faster. Jagged cracks unzipped the stone walls beside them; above, rocks punched from the surface by an unseen force. They gathered Tess closer and half hobbled, half ran. Small stinging stones cut Jaime's skin, and the clouds of dust choked him, made him cough. Flailing and coughing and close to blind, arms burning, they made it to the stairwell. They stumbled up the stairs and raced for the ladder that would take them to the street level. Theo shoved Jaime toward it. When he protested, Theo shouted, "Help me from the top!"

Jaime left Theo with his sister, climbed the ladder, the suitcase tucked under one arm making his movements slow, too slow. The thundering grew louder, like a thousand digging monsters behind ready to chew them up and spit them out. Jaime reached the manhole cover and pushed, but it was like trying to move a mountain. He ducked his head, pressed his back into it, and heaved with everything he had. The cover lifted and then fell over into the street, but he wasn't the one who had moved it, at least, not alone. He looked up.

A woman like a human stick bug held out her hand.

CHAPTER TWENTY-SIX

Tess

The world spun around and around and around, like the Rollers were rolling her through the tunnel. And maybe they were. She saw nothing but blacks and blues, a kaleidoscope of nowhere. It should have hurt, but it didn't. *Where are we going?* she asked the Rollers.

Home, they said.

And she said, *Yes, but where is home now?*

"Come on, Tess!" someone shouted. "This whole street is going to go."

Tess fought the fuzzy feeling in her head, the tumbling and the spinning, the blue-black nowhere. She opened her eyes. Three faces floated above her. Theo, Jaime, and . . .

"*Delancey DeBrule?*" Tess said. "What . . . what's going on?"

"Where's Edgar?" said Delancey.

Theo just shook his head. Delancey stared one moment, then set her mouth. "Get her on her feet." Theo and Jaime had just pulled her upright, half walked, half carried her to the sidewalk, when the entire street seemed to shake itself off and caved in right down the middle. Parked cars slid sideways into the trench, people pointed and screamed, dogs everywhere erupted in a frenzy of barking, a pipe burst and sent a plume of water into the sky. Sirens sounded in the distance.

Now it hurt. Tess gritted her teeth against the throbbing in her head. Delancey said, "Keep walking. Priya's waiting in the car on the next block."

"Priya?" said Tess.

"Yes. Who did you expect?"

"I didn't expect any of this," said Tess.

They walked around the block, rushing against the tide of humanity pouring past them. Here was something big enough and strange enough and inconvenient enough to surprise even the unsurprisable New Yorkers, and they all wanted to see it for themselves.

Priya Sharma was at the wheel. Once they'd gotten

into the solar-winged car and were on their way, Theo said, "How did you know where we were?"

Priya drove grimly, deliberately, hand over hand, in a hurry but trying hard not to look it. "Auguste told me."

"The *bird* told you?" Tess said, then winced, rubbing her head. From the front passenger seat, Delancey rummaged in her bag and handed back a tissue so that Tess could dab at the blood still trickling from her wound.

"Edgar's been acting very strange the past few months, staying late at the archives nearly every night," said Priya.

"Things have been going missing from the collection," Delancey said. "At first I thought . . . I thought maybe your grandfather had walked away with them. Without knowing what he was doing, of course. But then Edgar got so secretive."

Priya said, "I decided to stop by the archives to see if Edgar would talk to me, tell me what was going on. Instead, Auguste did. I drove right over here with Delancey to see if I could find him."

"And you found us," said Tess.

Delancey said, "Something else that Auguste told me: Edgar was convinced that your grandfather had finally figured out the Cipher on his own but got sick before he could share the information with the society.

What happened down there?"

Tess pressed the tissue harder against her wound. "Why should we trust you?"

Priya and Delancey were quiet for a moment. Then Priya said, "I was your grandfather's friend for a long time. But so was Edgar. So you shouldn't trust me at all. Or her." She nodded at Delancey. "You should trust no one."

Trust no one.

Tess looked at Jaime and Theo. "It's okay. You can tell them what happened."

Jaime and Theo told Delancey what they thought they could, which wasn't very much. Only that they'd found something among Grandpa Ben's papers, and then gone exploring in the tunnel. Only that Edgar was certain they knew more about the Cipher than they did, that the tunnel collapsed when he threatened to leave them there.

Numbness spread throughout Tess's body. "So . . . so Edgar is dead?"

Jaime shook his head. Theo said, "Maybe. We can't be sure."

Tess leaned back in the seat. What kind of world was this, anyway? Where your grandfather could get sick and slowly lose bits of himself until he couldn't remember the people he loved? Where a man you trusted, a man you called Uncle, your grandfather's *friend*, wanted to keep you trapped in an underground tunnel so he could find a treasure?

It was an awful kind of world. A blue-black nowhere of a world.

Priya said, "I'm going to take you back to the archives. You'll stay there overnight just like you planned so that no one is suspicious."

Delancey said, "I can take a better look at your head there, anyway. I'm a little worried you have a concussion."

"What can you do about it?" Theo said, apparently still annoyed with Delancey for her attitude back at the archives.

Delancey's mouth quirked up on one side. "When I'm not researching ciphers, I'm a doctor. Just like Edgar is."

"Oh," said Theo.

"If Edgar doesn't . . ." Priya hesitated, then began again. "If Edgar is really gone, I'll report him missing in a couple of days. The story is that he was with us till the morning, and then he went out, okay? We don't know where he went and we haven't seen him since." When none of them answered her, she said, "*Okay*?"

"Okay," Tess and Jaime said together. Jaime only nodded.

"I guess you'll want to take a look inside this suitcase, too," said Theo. "Uncle . . . I mean, Edgar said that he had special tools to open it."

Again, Priya's dark eyes flicked to the mirror. "No. The Cipher couldn't have stayed unsolved for as long as it has unless there were very powerful forces in play that didn't want it to be solved. But I think your grandfather was right about the Cipher, that it solves you as much as you solve it. It meant for you to find it, and it meant that only you should open it, if that makes any sense."

"How could that possibly make any sense?" said Theo.

Priya's mouth twisted into a rueful smile. "I don't think the Cipher is much concerned about making sense or not."

They did exactly as Delancey and Priya advised: they stayed overnight at the archives, barely sleeping a wink; Delancey checked Tess for dilated pupils, slurred speech, numbness, nausea, and about a million other things, and then shook her awake every hour, which made Tess so nervous she was a twitching mess. In the morning, Priya drove them back to 354 W. 73rd Street armed with alibis about Edgar, about the book that fell off the shelf and hit Tess in the head, leaving a small cut, about the extra suitcase that Edgar figured might come in handy for packing up their stuff, about Edgar telling them he'd see them again soon.

But they needn't have worried about alibis. Every person in the building over the age of thirteen was so distracted by packing and apartment hunting that they probably wouldn't have noticed if Tess, Theo, and Jaime had sprouted antennae and wings and turned into butterflies themselves. That made it much easier to sneak up to Grandpa Ben's apartment with the suitcase in order to open it in private.

If only they knew how to get it open.

Which they didn't.

But by the time they were settled in Grandpa's squashy, comfortable furniture, ready to wrestle with the suitcase, the strange and horrible night caught up with them; they all fell asleep, waking only when Tess and Theo's parents charged in and started banging things around.

"What? What?" said Tess, sitting up so fast that Nine slid off her lap.

"You are supposed to packing up here," said Tess's mom. "And instead I find you all asleep like . . . like . . . like"—she gestured to Nine—"like a pile of kittens! You promised that if I let you stay overnight with Uncle Edgar, you wouldn't stay up all night and you'd be ready to help today. This doesn't look like helping."

Tess rubbed her eyes. "We were helping. We will help."

"Are you going to tell me that you *didn't* stay up all night?"

Tess opened her mouth, shut it. She didn't want to lie to her mom, she didn't, but Mrs. Biedermann was a little too angry. They'd been betrayed, they'd witnessed the death of someone they thought was a friend. Grandpa's friend. After that, falling asleep for a couple of hours wasn't a crime. And if they could only figure out the Cipher, no one would have to leave this place. That was the whole point. The reason why they had risked so much.

"You're not even listening to me," her mother said.

"I'm listening!"

Mrs. Biedermann put her hands on her hips and glared. The fact that she was wearing sweatpants and a T-shirt that said "I found this humerus" with a picture of a bone did not make her any less intimidating. Even Mr. Biedermann's normally calm and placid expression was angry, his hair in weird little ropes like the snakes of Medusa.

"We just—" Tess began.

Mrs. Biedermann put up a palm. Stop. "What were you thinking?"

"You know what we were thinking," said Theo quietly.

"No, I know what you were *doing*, I have no idea what you were thinking. There's a difference. My children should not be up all night on a wild-goose chase!"

Tess said, "It's not a wild-goose chase, it's a—"

"I know what it is. It's a stupid puzzle that some people invented a million years ago. It's a stupid puzzle that obsessed my own father. And you know what? That's fine. I like puzzles. Who doesn't like puzzles? But this is enough. It's *enough*."

"Mom," Tess began.

"No. I will not listen to any more of this. It was one thing when we weren't about to be tossed from our home. But now we have more important things to think about. We *all* have more important things to think about. We have to pack up and we have to get our stuff over to Aunt Esther's and we have to find a new place to live. That's the beginning and the end of the story."

Despite the fact that they weren't to trust anyone, this was her mom! And she should understand. "Mom, we found—"

"More clues?" said Mrs. Biedermann. "That's

amazing. That's wonderful. I'm so glad to hear it. In the meantime, *we are being evicted from this building.* We are leaving, with all of our stuff, which will be entirely packed up in the next week. Do you understand me?"

Tess shut her mouth.

"Do you?"

Tess nodded; so did Theo. Even Jaime nodded, and this wasn't his mother talking.

"I took the week off," Mrs. Biedermann said. "And that means you and you will be here in this apartment every day packing along with your father and me. And every night, you will go to bed at a reasonable hour and you will stay in bed till you get up in the morning and do it all again."

Tess couldn't help it. "But—"

Her dad said, *"No."*

"Dad, please," she said.

"We shouldn't have to beg for your help here, Tess," he said, his voice low and even. "We shouldn't have to beg you to be responsible."

Tess thought of the movie they had watched together, the one about the man whose life was just a computer-generated dream, and how he had to be brave enough to release himself, face reality. "What about the black box, Dad?"

The angry expression dropped off her father's face. He knelt in front of her, took her hands. "Tess, honey. I'm sorry. This *is* your black box."

They ate breakfast, they packed. They ate lunch, they packed. They ate dinner, they packed some more. And every second they could spare, they tried to open the suitcase. They tried to pick it with a paper clip. They tried to pry it open with a screwdriver. Chisel it open with a chisel. Crack it with a hammer. Nothing worked.

The hours and the days ticked by—July 23, 24, 25. Priya Sharma, Imogen Sparks, Ray Turnage, and Omar Khayyám carted away books and maps and artifacts from Grandpa Ben's penthouse, sometimes stopping by the Biedermanns' for lunch or for dinner, trying to make small talk, even mentioning Edgar's mysterious and sudden disappearance. When small talk got too hard for everyone, Mrs. Biedermann turned on the radio. And when Darnell Slant came on the radio, talking to reporters about progress, talking about making the city even greater than it was already, Mr. Biedermann kicked the wall so hard he left a hole.

No one bothered to patch it.

July 26, they ate breakfast, they packed, they soaked the suitcase in a bath. July 27, they ate lunch, they packed, they threw the suitcase down the elevator shaft. July 28, they ate dinner, they packed, they tossed the suitcase under the wheels of a delivery truck.

And still they couldn't open it.

Every minute, they were consumed with erasing all the evidence of the life they had lived in this building, and the passing of every day felt like a hand around Tess's heart, squeezing, squeezing, squeezing. But time would not stop ticking away.

July 29

   July 30

      July 31

         Till there was no time left at all.

On their very last day at 354 W. 73rd Street, two burly men took four hours to load the couches and the chairs, the beds and frames, the dressers and end tables, the shelves and the filing cabinets from the two Biedermann apartments, all in a hot, rainy mist that made it hard to see. And then the apartments were completely empty except for a few boxes they would have to cram in the van. The Biedermanns ate a dinner of calzones while sitting on the floor. Nine didn't know where to sit, what to do with herself. Where was her coffee table? Where was her sock collection? She ran from room to room, chirping in confusion. Theo didn't blame her. Without their books and shelves and tables and photographs, the walls looked dingy and bare; this could be any apartment anywhere. Not theirs, not anyone's. Anonymous as a skeleton.

Mr. Biedermann said, "We'll load up the rest of the boxes and then . . ." He trailed off, took another bite of calzone, chewed. "A home isn't a place, you know. It's not an apartment or a building. It's not the stuff you have. Home is with your family. We're going to be fine, even if it doesn't feel that way right now."

A million questions flooded Tess's mind. Fine? FINE? What about school? What about the wandering elevator? What about Jaime? What about his grandmother and Mr. Perlmutter and the Morans and the Hornshaws and the Adeyemis and the Schwartzes? What about New York City, the city of the Morningstarrs?

More than that, what about fairness? What about justice? What about right and wrong? What about Grandpa?

What about us?

When Tess leashed Nine, Nine lunged for the door as if she couldn't wait to get out of a place that was no longer theirs. The whole family got on the elevator, pressed the down button. It took them on a tour of the building, the doors opening on each floor, though they had only pressed the one button. In the lobby, they saw the Ms. Gomezes, the Hornshaws, the Adeyemis, the Yangs, and the Morans—some resigned, some fierce and determined, some blinking back tears. They saw Mr. Perlmutter, small and hunched in a wheelchair, a sweater around his shoulders, being pushed by a tired-looking man in his own worn cardigan. "Some of us have nowhere else to go," Mr. Perlmutter had said.

So where was Mr. Perlmutter going to go?

"Well," said Mr. Biedermann. "This is it." He patted the cameo walls. "Good-bye, 354 W. 73rd. We'll miss you."

Mrs. Biedermann didn't pat the tiles. Tess didn't either, and didn't, *wouldn't*, say good-bye. To come this close and fail filled her with such a deep despair she could barely pick up her feet, as if gravity had suddenly become ten times more powerful. She and Theo trailed behind their parents, the luggage cart they were pushing as heavy as a city. They nearly ran over Cricket, who yelled, "Watch it! You almost ran over me!"

"Sorry, Cricket," Tess said. "We didn't see you behind the boxes."

"Nobody sees me anymore," said Cricket. And she shouldn't have been hard to miss because of the Miss

Marvel nightgown, the striped tights, and the clogs.

"I thought you were going incognito?" Tess said.

"Incognito is boring. Even Karl thinks so." Cricket poked at the raccoon in the basket of her tricycle. The raccoon was wearing swim trunks and eating from a bag of Cheez Doodles. "I'm not incognito anymore, but everyone is too busy to notice. I told Dad that his face was as red as a riding hood this morning and he didn't even tell me to bridle my honesty." Cricket seemed genuinely disappointed by this turn of events. She played with the heart charm on her necklace, left, right, left and right.

A heart with an arrow thrust through it, the fletching just like the cuts of a key.

Ava Oneal's words echoed in Tess's head. *I'm going home to find my heart. I hope you find yours.*

"Cricket," said Tess carefully, casually, "where did you get that necklace?"

CHAPTER TWENTY-SEVEN
Cricket

Cricket gripped her necklace and backed her trike away from the Hairball Twins: *beep-beep-beep*. She didn't want anyone looking at her necklace, because it was SINGULAR and it was HERS and also NONE OF ANYONE'S BEESWAX. The building had given her this necklace, and no matter how many times her mother told her that she'd have to learn, Cricket did not enjoy sharing, just like she didn't enjoy being nice or quiet or any of the things her parents said little girls were supposed to be.

Little girls weren't supposed to be spies, either.

But that was what she'd been doing for the last few weeks, spying on Mr. Stoop and Mr. Pinscher. It wasn't difficult. They weren't even trying to hide. People who thought they were the boss of everything never tried to hide what they were doing. They were too proud of themselves. (Obviously, Mr. Stoop and Mr. Pinscher didn't have moms who told them not to be too proud of themselves, because people who were too proud of themselves ended up with no one to play with at recess. Mr. Stoop and Mr. Pinscher only had each other to play with, and Cricket assumed neither of them much liked the arrangement because who'd want to play with either of them? Yuck.) Anyway, Mr. Stoop and Mr. Pinscher thought they owned the place, so they took pieces of it whenever they wanted to, no matter who was watching. And Cricket was always watching. She watched them chisel tiles from the floors and the walls, remove light fixtures from the ceilings, pull doorknobs from the closets and storerooms, cut solar glass from one of the hallway windowpanes, carry off the wooden desk that had sat in the lobby for a million, jillion years. She followed them down to the basement and took notes as they picked through the residents' belongings as if those belongings belonged to them, watched as they poked around the giant row of Lion batteries in the basement. (To Cricket's irritation, the massive Lion batteries that kept the building powered were not shaped like lions as much as giant pain capsules with feet.)

And she watched them as they returned to the dumb-waiter again and again, trying to pry it open, trying to get it to work. But they were too dumb to work the dumbwaiter. So dumb they didn't know how dumb they were. The dumbest of dumb babies.

"Our shadow has returned, Mr. Pinscher," said Mr. Stoop, just a couple of weeks before, when they were once again attempting to drill out the lock on the dumbwaiter.

"Uh-huh," said Mr. Pinscher.

"And she has brought her little pet with her."

"And her little notebook."

"Should we be worried, Mr. Pinscher?"

Mr. Pinscher made a rude noise.

"What do you think, little girl?" said Mr. Stoop, stooping low to look Cricket in the eye, talking to her as if *she* were just another dumb baby. "Do you think we should worry about you?"

"Nope," said Cricket, who was nobody's dumb baby. "I'm just playing a little game."

"What kind of game?"

"A game of pretend," Cricket said.

"What are you pretending to be?"

"A writer," she said. "I'm writing an adventure story. With villains and monsters and heroes and people who steal things that don't belong to them."

"My favorite kind of story," said Mr. Stoop. "Do you think we could read it when you're done?"

"You can buy it in the bookstore," said Cricket. She was watching them very carefully now, because she wanted another glimpse of the little leathery hand thing that she'd seen with them before, a creature they let out of its bag when they thought no one else was watching. It was so metal, the little leathery hand thing. And also, the tiniest bit scary.

"Where's the LLHT?"

"Pardon?" said Mr. Stoop.

"The little leathery hand thing."

"Ah. So you like our friend, do you?"

"I didn't say that," Cricket said. "It's PECULIAR, that's all."

"It's a new invention. Cutting-edge science."

Cricket didn't understand how little leathery hand things could be inventions or science, so she said, "Hmph."

"Our friend senses things we don't," said Mr. Stoop. "Would you like to know what it's made of?"

"Nightmares and leftover meatloaf," said Cricket.

"You are an imaginative little person, aren't you? Wouldn't you agree, Mr. Pinscher?"

Mr. Pinscher snorted. "Sure."

"How would you like to do a job for us?" said Mr. Stoop.

"What kind of job?"

"Well, you seem to enjoy watching people. How about you watch other people?"

"Which other people?" said Cricket.

"The other residents in this building. Maybe you can observe them. Ask them if they've ever found anything interesting in their apartments. Hidden under the floorboards, say. Or in the closets. Watch what they do when they think no one is looking. Then you can tell us what you've seen, and we will give you a prize."

Cricket doubted that Mr. Stoop and Mr. Pinscher had any sort of prize that she would want. Still, she asked: "What kind of prize?"

"What would you like?"

"A rocket ship."

"I'm afraid I can't help you with that. How about something smaller?"

Cricket thought a minute. "A million jillion dollars."

"That might be a little out of our range as well. Anything else?"

"A secret."

"Ah, secrets are the best sort of currency, it's true."

Cricket did not like that she didn't know what the word *currency* meant. "Hmph," she said.

"All right," said Mr. Stoop. "If you spy on the other residents of this building, and report back to us, I promise that I will tell you a secret."

"It has to be a real secret," said Cricket. "A *secret* secret."

Mr. Stoop smiled.

It was not a good look for him.

"A secret secret it is," said Mr. Stoop. "You have a deal."

"Hmph," said Cricket.

And she and Mr. Stoop shook hands like real spies.

Which meant that both of them were lying.

But Cricket *did* watch the other residents, because what else did she have to do while her parents packed up their apartment and tried to find a new one (though they would have to spend some weeks at Cranky Cousin Gordon's house in Bayonne, New Jersey, which made her dad APOPLECTIC). She followed Mr. and Mrs. Adeyemi and the Hornshaws and the Schwartzes. She wrote down what they did and what they said, even when what they said wasn't very interesting. She even followed Mr. Perlmutter once, but when he offered her a sugar-free lollipop if she'd stop, she agreed, because eating a lollipop, even a sugar-free one, was much more fun than following Mr. Perlmutter, who kept perlmutter-ing that she should be outside playing in the park like a normal kid instead of annoying old men. As if she could be out in the park SOLO, spy or not.

But she spent most of her time following the Hair-ball Twins and their friend, Jaime Cruz. They were much more interesting. They were always huddled close together, whispering, as if they were the ones with the secret secret, one that they had no intention of sharing with anyone else. As good a spy as she was, Cricket never heard more than snatches of their conversations: *letter, chair, cemetery, octagon, Ava, Ava, Ava*. Whoever Ava was. And now they were dragging around a janky old suitcase as if there were a million jillion dollars in it.

Mr. Stoop wanted to know what they talked about.

Cricket opened her notebook and read from it: "'Bet-ter,' 'bear,' 'cement airy,' 'concoct a gong,' and 'flavor, flavor, flavor.'"

"You can't concoct a gong," Mr. Pinscher pointed out.

Cricket shrugged. "I can't help it if they talk a lot of nonsense."

"Maybe you're the one who is talking nonsense."

"Now, now, Mr. Pinscher. I'm sure our friend

wouldn't invent things, would you?"

"Hmph," said Cricket.

Mr. Stoop peered down at her. "So, that's what they said. What have they been doing?"

"Counting the tiles," said Cricket. "And eating. They eat a lot."

"Counting the tiles?" said Mr. Pinscher. "There's nothing special about the tiles."

"Then why do you keep taking them off the walls?" Cricket said.

Mr. Stoop laughed.

It wasn't a nice sound.

"I've told you everything that's been happening," Cricket said. "So, I'd like my secret, please. A *secret* secret. Just like you promised."

"I suppose you're right. I did promise. And a promise is a promise." He took a step closer to Cricket, and his long shadow fell over her. "Once everyone in the building has moved out," he said, his voice low, "I will release my friend from this bag. The, uh, little leathery hand thing, as you so charmingly named him. I've told him that he will be free to roam the halls of this place, and anyone that he finds inside, he's allowed to eat." Mr. Stoop took another step forward, and Cricket had to crane her neck all the way back to see him. "But that's not the real secret, not the *secret* secret."

"What's the secret secret?" Cricket whispered, unable to keep herself from asking.

"The secret secret," said Mr. Stoop, "is that he has no mouth."

"How . . . how does he eat with no mouth?"

"I don't know," said Mr. Stoop. "But when he's done, there's nothing left behind but a few scraps. An ear. A toe. A single nostril. He can be, er, a bit messy."

Cricket heard Mr. Stoop and Mr. Pinscher laughing as she raced her trike all the way back to her apartment.

She didn't like the twins much and she liked their friend, Jaime, only a little bit more, mostly because he had famous hair. But they were better than Mr. Stoop and Mr. Pinscher, that was for sure.

Cricket liked her ears. She liked all her toes and both nostrils.

She liked all these things exactly the way they were.

"How can you eat with no mouth?" Cricket asked the twins.

"Is that a riddle?" Tess Biedermann said.

"No," said Cricket. "It's a serious question."

"About that necklace," Tess said.

"It's mine," said Cricket.

"I know. I'm just wondering if I could borrow it for a second."

"I do not enjoy sharing," said Cricket.

"Nobody enjoys sharing," said Theo. When his sister gave him a look, he said, "What? It's true."

Tess bit her lip. Then she said, "Listen, Cricket, can you keep a secret?"

"What kind of secret?" Cricket said.

"A *secret* secret," Tess said.

Cricket stood perfectly still. Maybe Tess had been spying on *her*.

"You see this suitcase?" Tess asked, pointing at the cart.

"Everyone does," Cricket said. "It's janky."

Tess's eyes darted to her parents, who were just outside the lobby doors, loading up their car. "We can't open it. We need a key. And it looks like the charm on your necklace might be that key. Did you happen to find it somewhere in this building?"

Cricket stared.

Tess *was* a spy.

DOUBLE CROSS.

"I found it in the dumbwaiter," said Cricket.

"I thought that didn't work anymore," said Theo.

"It only works for Karl. He has monkey fingers."

Everyone looked down at Karl, who waved a cheese curl in triumph.

"If you let me borrow that necklace for a second, and it is the key we've been looking for, we'll let you see what's inside the suitcase," said Tess.

Cricket thought about this. She wanted to see inside the suitcase, but maybe she didn't. What if there was a little leathery hand thing in the suitcase? Or a little leathery *foot* thing? Or an actual face with an actual mouth?

With actual teeth?

Cricket was suddenly very tired. This was a weird place filled with weirder people. Sometimes, the most metal thing you could do was to spy on them all. Other times, the most metal thing you could do was get in the car and take a long nap.

Cricket pulled the necklace over her head, handed it to Tess. "Keep it." Who needed to share like some dumb baby? Giving a gift was *better* than sharing. Besides, she didn't need some cheap necklace. She had her word book. And that was way more important. The most important.

PARAMOUNT.

Tess Biedermann held the necklace in the palm of her hand as though she were cradling an egg. "Are *you* okay, Cricket?"

"I'm fine," Cricket said. And she would be. Even if she had to go to Cranky Cousin Gordon's house in Bayonne, New Jersey, with her tired mom, her screamy dad, and her not-so-ninja brother.

Bayonne, New Jersey, wouldn't know what hit it.

She hoped Cranky Cousin Gordon had lots of Cheez Doodles.

As Zelda "Cricket" Moran rode her trike slowly through the lobby of 354 W. 73rd Street, so intent on taking that nap, she forgot to warn the Hairball Twins: Beware little leathery hand things with no mouths.

Who knew what they were hungry for?

CHAPTER TWENTY-EIGHT
Jaime

As Cricket three-wheeled her way toward an epic car nap and possibly a whole new future, Jaime returned to 354 W. 73rd Street to get the last of his things. The new apartment in Hoboken was as big as his dad had said, with enormous floor-to-ceiling windows that faced the wrong side of the Hudson. The rooms were bright and white and clean, with some exposed brick along one wall, polished wooden floors, a sparkling new kitchen with all sorts of fancy appliances. Nothing needed to be painted or grouted or sanded. Nothing needed to be fixed or patched or welded. It was a nice place. An excellent place. Mima had taken one long look around and slumped on their lumpy old couch. She'd stared off into space until Jaime made her a cup of tea and promised to go to 354 W. 73rd alone. As the Underway trundled under the river back to Manhattan and then uptown, he felt like he'd abandoned her. Or failed her. Or failed his mom and dad. Or something.

In front of 354 W. 73rd, Mr. and Mrs. Biedermann were wedging more stuff into the trunk of an ancient van, one solar panel like a broken wing. The twins' aunt Esther was there, too, telling Mr. Biedermann how best to pack the van in order to get the most into it. There was a lone reporter trying to get a statement from them all, but Mrs. Biedermann gave the reporter a look of such loathing that the reporter stuffed the microphone in his pocket and ran away, the camera operator loping after him.

"Hey, Jaime," said Mr. Biedermann, noting him standing there. Mr. Biedermann's hair and beard hadn't been trimmed for so long, they looked as if they might engulf his whole face. "I thought you and your grandmother had already left. Everyone else has."

"We had a few boxes that couldn't fit in the cab, so I came back for them myself. We have until midnight. Technically."

"Technically," Mr. Biedermann echoed.

And then Tess and Theo Biedermann burst through the lobby doors. Tess had a strange expression on her face. She jerked her chin at the suitcase on the cart, eyes wild. She touched her neck, where a key on a chain now dangled.

Aunt Esther grabbed the twins' cart and jammed the boxes into the backseat of the van. She rested the suitcase by Jaime's feet.

Mrs. Biedermann protested: "How will the kids fit in the van with us with all that stuff in the backseat?"

"Oh! They won't," said Aunt Esther. "But it looks to me like they need a little more time to say good-bye to their home."

"I don't think that's a good idea," said Mr. Biedermann.

Mrs. Biedermann gave Tess a long, appraising look, a look that said *I love you*, a look that said *I'm sorry*, a look that said *I understand*. "Just don't stay too late. It will be dark soon. Well, darker."

"Thanks, Mom," Tess said, her eyes now glinting with tears. Or maybe it was just the rain.

Mrs. Biedermann got into the passenger seat of the van while Mr. Biedermann squeezed into the backseat with the boxes.

Aunt Esther said, "You should probably keep Nine Eighty-Seven with you. She might be able to help."

"How can she help?" said Theo.

"How do you know she can't?" Aunt Esther asked.

She winked and climbed into the driver's seat. Jaime, Tess, and Theo watched as the van eased onto the street, turned the corner, and was gone.

Then they were alone. Jaime looked up at the building, squinting into the rain. Maybe it was the gloomy weather, the unseasonable chilly drizzle, but 354 W. 73rd Street seemed shrouded in shadow. It looked—there was no other word for it—dead.

But maybe not just yet.

Back in the empty penthouse, Tess unclasped Cricket's necklace and slid the key off the chain. She slipped the tail end into the lock and turned.

Click!

This was it.

This was it.

This was—

The silver case popped open. And nestled inside a nest of red velvet—

"—a walking stick?" Jaime said. Long, black, with an ornate pewter handle shaped like a dragon. Engraved on a pewter ring underneath the handle were the words *All that opens is not a door.*

"There's a letter, too," Tess said, pulling a piece of

thin paper from inside the suitcase, unfolding it. She read:

SO, MY FRIENDS, YOU HAVE COME TO THE BEGINNING OF THE END (OR THE END OF THE BEGINNING, IF YOU WILL). HERE YOU FIND NOT A PUZZLE AS MUCH AS A CHOICE: YOU CAN CHOOSE TO MOVE FORWARD, OR YOU CAN CHOOSE TO WALK AWAY. THINK CAREFULLY: IS ANY TREASURE WORTH ANY PRICE?

YOUR TASK IS BOTH SIMPLE AND MONUMENTAL: TAKE THE ELEVATOR TO THE 12211514511 2TH FLOOR. SET THE CANE IN THE CLOCK, AND YOU WILL FIND WHAT YOU'VE BEEN LOOKING FOR.

BUT REMEMBER, ONCE THE DRAGON IS AWAKENED, THERE IS NO GOING BACK.

AT LEAST, NOT FOR A VERY, VERY LONG TIME.

Jaime said, "So, I'm guessing '12211514512' is a code?"

"The letter says it's simple, so the simplest thing would be to punch that number into the keypad on the elevator," said Theo.

"And then?" said Jaime.

"And then we see what happens," said Tess. "What the Cipher wants us to find."

Jaime tugged at one of his 'locs. "Why does it sound like a warning?"

"Because it is," said Theo. "I think."

"But a warning about what?" Jaime said.

"Maybe we won't like what we find," said Theo.

"How could we not like it," Tess said, "when the treasure could save our home?"

Jaime didn't remind her of what had happened in the Atlantic Avenue Tunnel—that Edgar Wellington had not been saved. That maybe the Cipher didn't care about what they wanted. That it might be bigger than them all.

Jaime hefted the cane. "Okay, so what do you think the letter means by 'dragon'?"

Tess stood. "We're going to find out. The whole world is going to find out."

They went to the elevator and pressed 122115145112 into the keypad. For a second, the elevator didn't move, but then it began to hum. It trembled and then lifted upward, then over, up and over, up and over, stairstepping through the building on a steep diagonal. Then it flew in a horizontal line all the way to the back of the building, way past what Jaime thought of as the back of the building.

"Has it ever moved like this before?" Theo said.

"No," said Tess, who was watching the doors as if they would open up onto another world.

And then they did.

The elevator stopped, still humming, rotating 180 degrees. There was brief *whoosh* and a slight wind. Nine mrrowed, jerked at her leash. The doors flew open. Beyond the threshold of the elevator was a long, wide marble hallway, as long and wide as an Underway train, a hallway that Jaime had never seen before, with beautiful chandeliers winking like stars in the dim light.

Without saying another word, they stepped into the corridor. All along the hall, there were paintings of magical creatures: a winged horse; a sort of lion-snake; and giant bird blocking the sun.

"The Ziz," said Tess.

"The what?" Jaime said.

"This bird. It's from Jewish mythology," said Theo. "Kind of like a griffin, but bigger. He has another name, Renanin, which means 'singer.'"

They kept walking, allowing Nine to sniff in front of them like a dog on a scent. The cat led them into a large sitting room with arrangements of antique furniture in front of a giant marble fireplace, a dining room with a long table and twelve chairs, another sitting room, a bedchamber with a four-poster, canopied bed. They saw nowhere to set the cane, nowhere obvious at least, until they reached a library with two reading chairs, a table and lamp between them. Jaime scanned the volumes. Washington Irving, Frederick Douglass, Charles Dickens, Jane Austen, Nathaniel Hawthorne, Harriet Beecher Stowe, Frances Harper, Mary Shelley, Paul Laurence Dunbar, Lydia Maria Child, Edgar Allan Poe, Phillis Wheatley, Publius, Balzac, Dostoyevsky, various volumes by a writer known only as A Lady, author of *Penelope*, as well as volumes in Arabic and Spanish and many other languages that Jaime couldn't identify, all shelved in no particular order, or maybe an order only the librarian would understand.

Who was the librarian?

But then he knew.

"This is her place," Tess breathed. "Ava's. For all this time, people thought she'd left nothing here, but she left everything. That's why the building is so big. Not just because the elevator needed room to move, but because her apartment was hidden here."

Jaime picked up a saucer sitting by the table, the dregs of tea dried at the bottom of the cup. "What happened to her?" he said. But he could have been talking about so many people—Ava Oneal, for sure, but also all those other people who were servants and secretaries and wives and spies and prisoners and lunatics, all those people that history forgot or hid or deliberately erased, because they were not a part of the story that history wanted to tell.

"Look at this," Tess said. She was standing in front of a large grandfather clock, but a clock that didn't look like any other clock Jaime had ever seen. Stained black, it had a dial within a dial—both blue and green and yellow—and two different hands, one with a small golden sun, and another with a smaller silver moon. Small carved figures flanked the larger face of the clock: one man holding a mirror; one man holding a flask; one man playing some sort of lute; and lastly, a grinning skeleton lifting a bell. All along the top of the clock, more figures, these even more fantastical—like the paintings in the hallway—griffins, gargoyles, sphinxes.

"Creepy," said Jaime.

"No, I'm talking about this," said Tess. She pointed down. On one side of the base stood a tall black post topped with a pewter dragon, but on the other side, just a hole in the wood.

Jaime set down his duffel, pulled out the dragon-topped cane they'd found in the Atlantic Avenue Tunnel. "It's the same."

"This is where we set it," Tess said.

Jaime took a deep breath. "The last clue said that

once we do this, there's no turning back."

"We have to set it. We don't have a choice," said Tess.

People always had a choice, Jaime thought. But then, if they didn't do this, weren't they letting Darnell Slant write the story of this building, write *their* story, write them right out of it?

Before Jaime had a chance to change his mind, before any of them did, he took the cane and set it in place, twisting until he heard a small *thunk*. Immediately, the hands of the clock began to spin around and around. Nine meowed. The clock chimed. One, two, three, four, five, six, ten, twelve, fourteen . . .

"What is going on?" Theo said.

Nine meowed again and pulled on the leash.

"Clocks don't chime seventeen," Theo said.

Nine scrabbled backward, her claws scratching for purchase on the marble.

"I don't like this," Jaime said.

Nine howled a long terrible howl.

"It sounds like a . . . like a . . . timer," Theo said.

Tess leaped forward, tried to wrench the cane out of the base of the clock, but the dragon snapped off in her hand. She stared at it dumbly as the clock chimed on and on and on.

"I think we should go," Jaime said. "I think we should go *now*."

There was a sharp *bang*, and then a sound like the drum of rain on a roof. The big face of the clock popped open. Out flew something—what? A fluttering, silvery something.

Jaime stared at it, watching it dance like silver fire in the air.

And then it hit him right between the eyes.

"Ow!" he yelled, knocking it away, forehead and hand stinging. But then Tess and Theo were knocking away more of the moths, an enormous cloud of them, a great heaving shudder of them, all streaming from the face of the clock and heading right for them.

"Run!" yelled Jaime.

They tore from the library, skidded down the marble corridor, flung themselves into the elevator, frantically slapped at the keypad. L for Lobby, 1, 2, 5, close, close, close, please close already. The doors shut so slowly, so slowly, as the air beyond them shattered with the sound of a million metal wings. And then the doors were shut and the elevator was dropping, dropping, dropping, straight down, no detours, no melancholy twists and turns, just a stomach-churning plummet from top to bottom, so fast that for just one moment they were weightless as moths hovering in the air. Then the car landed so hard it slammed them all to the floor, but they didn't have one second to catch their breath before the doors opened again, pitching them into the lobby.

Right at the feet of Mr. Stoop and Mr. Pinscher.

CHAPTER TWENTY-NINE
Tess

"Well!" said Mr. Stoop. "If it isn't our old friends!"

"They're not my friends," said Mr. Pinscher.

"Now, now, we shouldn't be rude, Mr. Pinscher."

"Why not?" said Mr. Pinscher.

"That," said Mr. Stoop, "is a good question. Another good question: What is that you have in your hand, Miss, Miss . . . What was her name again, Mr. Pinscher?"

"Pain in the Butt," said Mr. Pinscher.

"I don't believe that's her given name."

Mr. Pinscher shrugged. "That's the name I gave her."

Up until that moment, Tess had forgotten she had anything in her hand, but when she looked down, she was still holding the dragon handle of the cane. She sat up.

"Why don't you toss that to me," said Mr. Stoop, "and we'll let you all go without any further fuss."

Tess didn't want to give these men anything. Not the dragon, not anything.

"Listen," she said. "My mom knows where we are and she's coming to pick us up in a few minutes."

"Liar," said Mr. Stoop, in a singsong sort of voice.

"Children always lie," said Mr. Pinscher. "Little lying liars."

"You didn't tell your mother what you were going to do. You wouldn't dare. Give me what you've found," said Mr. Stoop.

Ever so faintly, Tess heard the chime of the clock. Or maybe she was imagining it.

What she didn't imagine: the elevator doors closing behind her. She scrambled to her feet.

"No . . . ," she began. But how to explain that they put a cane in a clock and were chased away by moths? What did that mean? And why should she tell them?

But she needed them to let her and Jaime and Theo go. "Listen, I think something is going to happen. Something is happening right now."

"We all have to get out of here," Jaime said.

"*You* do," said Mr. Pinscher.

"Who is controlling the elevator?" said Theo,

watching the numbers flash over the doors.

"I will not be distracted by this ridiculous, malfunctioning, crumbling old hut!" shouted Mr. Stoop.

Theo said, "Technically—"

"We have been here all month searching this, this, this"—Mr. Stoop twirled his hand in the air, searching for the right word—"this pile of bricks and I am done. Done! So, young lady, you'd better give me what you have in your hand and tell me exactly where you found it or I will have to call in reinforcements."

"We're allowed to be here until midnight," Jaime said. "The cops won't do anything."

"Who said I was going to call the police?" said Mr. Stoop.

Theo was still watching the elevator. "Abi thabink thabe maboths abare cabomabing abon thabe abelabevabatabor."

Jaime said, "Mabe taboo."

"What are you two yammmmering about?" said Mr. Stoop.

Jaime's expression was pure innocence. "What?"

"Mabovabe abawabay frabom thabe daboabors," said Tess. "Gabet rabeadaby tabo rabun."

"Stop mumbling!" Mr. Stoop said.

"Why do you work for Slant?" said Tess. "Why are

you doing this to us? Why do you want to toss people from their homes? This isn't fair."

"Fair?" said Mr. Stoop. "Oh my goodness! Didn't they teach you in kindergarten that the world isn't fair? Nothing is fair, stupid girl. Do you think this is the worst thing that could happen to you? The worst thing that will ever happen?"

Tess said, "What happened to *you*?"

Mr. Pinscher rolled his creepy eyes. Mr. Stoop checked his watch. "It is a little early, but I don't think this can be helped. What do you think, Mr. Pinscher?"

"I think he's probably hungry by now," said Mr. Pinscher.

"Who's hungry?" said Tess.

Mr. Pinscher pulled a bag off his shoulder and set it on the floor. He opened the flap and gave a low whistle. Inside the bag, a flutter of movement. More moths? thought Tess. But no, a weird leathery-looking thing about the size of man's hand crawled out of the bag. Not a bat, not a spider, not a machine—a many-legged thing, reddish and scarred. It had no eyes that Tess could see, no face.

What kind of creature has no face?

"He doesn't have a mouth, either," said Mr. Stoop, his teeth gleaming in the dim light. "But he does love to eat. I gave him a whole cow once. It was gone in an hour. Except the feet. He doesn't much care for feet."

Nine lowered her head and growled.

"I'd be careful with your kitty," said Mr. Stoop. "Our little friend here loves kitties, but not in a way you'd appreciate."

The leathery thing raised one leg in the air, tap, tap, tapped the floor.

It seemed like a challenge.

Nine growled again, hackles rising, straining against her leash. Impossibly, she seemed larger.

The leathery thing tapped. Tapped again. *Bring it.*

Nine panted, showing her incisors. *Are you sure?*

"No, Nine," said Tess. She risked a glance at the elevator. How many loops around the building was it going to make?

Mr. Stoop held his hand out. "Give me what you're holding, Miss, and I'll call off my friend."

"No, you won't," said Mr. Pinscher.

Mr. Stoop clucked his tongue in annoyance. "Mr. Pinscher, I do wish you'd stop with the spoilers. It ruins the suspense for everyone."

There was a loud metallic *bang*. They all looked around.

"Okay, now it's the dumbwaiter," said Theo.

Mr. Stoop shook his head. "The dumbwaiter is welded shut. It hasn't worked in years. *Nothing* in this building has worked properly in years. Why people are so determined to stay here I simply don't understand when there are perfectly lovely apartments in Ohio."

"If the dumbwaiter is broken, what's it doing?" said Jaime, pointing. The brass door of the dumbwaiter quivered, as if it were straining against its own lock.

"What did you foolish children put in the dumbwaiter?" said Mr. Stoop.

"Nothing!" said Tess.

"Then *who* did you put in the dumbwaiter?" said Mr. Pinscher. "Is it that raccoon again? I don't like that raccoon."

"The abelabevabatabor abis cabomabing dabown nabow," said Theo.

"We really need to go," said Jaime, glancing from the dumbwaiter to the elevator and back again. "Even you guys." He took a step back from the little leathery thing, which was twitching and shivering, as if it was getting ready to spring.

"No, I think it's time for you to go," said Mr. Stoop.

"Bye-bye," said Mr. Pinscher.

The little leathery hand thing jumped up. Nine charged, wrenching her leash right out of Tess's fingers.

"No!" Tess screamed.

"Yes," hissed Mr. Pinscher.

Nine caught the thing in her teeth. Like a bear catching a spawning salmon. Or a giant serval-wolf-cat catching a little leathery hand thing.

"No!" said Mr. Stoop.

"Yes," hissed Tess.

The cat bit down.

As it turned out, a mouth was a fairly useful thing to have.

And so was a cat.

Mr. Stoop moaned. "Cecil! Not my little Cecil!"

Mr. Pinscher said, "Stop whining, you sentimental fool. We'll have to do things the old-fashioned way." He was reaching for Tess when the doors of the elevator flew wide and a hurricane of silver wings flooded out. Mr. Stoop and Mr. Pinscher batted at the moths but they only came faster, hitting the men in the face and the shoulders and the back, shoving them both toward the dumbwaiter. Suddenly, the dumbwaiter yawned wide. The moths balled up together, one rolling, shimmering mass of wings and fury, and hit the two men like a wrecking ball, shoving them into the waiting maw of the dumbwaiter. Tess heard their brief screams before the dumbwaiter slammed shut.

And then she was shaking the little leathery hand thing from Nine's mouth and they were all running to the door. The raging ball of moths blasted past them, blew out the windows in a shower of glass.

"Go, go, go!" Jaime shouted.

They climbed out the broken windows, trying not to cut themselves on the jagged edges, trying not to scrape their hands on the pavement, failing.

"Wait!" said Tess.

"No waiting!" Jaime said, hauling her to her feet and dragging her across the street. Tess's thoughts scrabbling and scratching like squirrels trapped in a wall. They were supposed to find the treasure—where was the treasure? What was happening? Where did Mr. Stoop and Mr. Pinscher go? Theo was saying something to Jaime, but Tess couldn't even make out their words; everything was a furious blur in her head and in her vision. Her breath came hot and fast, her feet dragging until someone—Jaime?—literally lifted her off her feet.

"Wait!" said Tess. "Stop!"

A high-pitched whine cut through the humid summer air. Then a series of muffled *WHUMP*s like the beating of drums in a marching band pounded Tess's ears, *WHUMP*, but she didn't know what it was, *WHUMP*, where was it coming from, *WHUMP*. It was only when she saw the bright bursts of flame in each of the windows at 354 W. 73rd Street that she herself understood, that they all did.

Explosives.

For a moment, nothing else happened, the building's many eyes seeming to look down upon her with a placid sort of calm, the way mothers regard crying children.

And then, all at once, the floors collapsed in on themselves, falling and falling, imploding into a gray cloud of dust.

The shock of it punched her in the throat and in the chest, odd strangled, wordless sounds bursting from her lips. No. No. No. This was not supposed to happen. Not after everything they'd done.

Everything *they'd* done.

They had done this.

They had set the cane.

They had started the clock.

They had set the building off.

Is any treasure worth any cost?

No.

No.

No.

But the stinging dust that filled the air said that it was, that the worst had come to pass, said that it was over now, that everyone else had been right, that a bunch of kids could never solve the Cipher, that the Cipher itself was as fanciful as any fairy tale, and who but little kids could believe in fairy tales anyway?

There was no treasure.

And now there was no 354 W. 73rd Street.

She couldn't help the sobs that racked her body. Adults had gathered around—from where she had no idea—they were all suddenly there, a small crowd of them, patting her and Jaime and Theo awkwardly, saying, "There, there," and "You're all right," "Everything will be okay," like they must have seen people do in movies. She wanted to hit them all. She wanted to tell them nothing would ever be all right.

But there was a hole in the landscape just like there was a hole in her gut. In her heart. When the dust started to clear, Tess could see all the way to the river. She saw the raw, naked walls of the buildings on either side, exposed for the first time in a hundred and fifty plus years. The stupid water tower on the roof of the building next door mocked her: YOU GOT IT ALL WRONG, TOOTS.

Eventually, the crowd grew bigger. The cops showed up. The fire trucks and the ambulances, the firefighters and the EMTs. The reporters with their vans and their microphones.

All of them ignoring three kids and their giant, dust-covered cat.

Still, Tess and Theo and Jaime stayed. Tess felt rooted to the spot, like she could never move. The moon burst through the clouds, silvering the dust, so bright that they had to shield their eyes. The beams hit the water tower on the nearby building, sending an arrow of silver down through the dust, where it hit the wall of the building on the other side of the demolition site.

Tess's breath curled, caught.

For there, on that newly exposed wall, was a rectangle of shadow in the shape of a door.

CHAPTER THIRTY
Theo

Implosion, the opposite of explosion. Technically, instead of energy and matter released outward, implosion was a bursting inward, a situation where matter collapses in on itself. A method often used in building demolition in order to spare the surrounding buildings.

He could almost hear Tess's voice in his head: Theo, you *robot*.

Except he didn't feel like a robot. He felt like he himself had imploded along with 354 W. 73rd Street, the very center of himself plummeting straight down, all his outsides cascading in.

And then Tess whispered, "A door."

"What did you say?" said Theo.

She leaned in. "But look at the wall of the building

next door. There's a door on it. Or there's a shadow in the shape of a door."

She was right. On the expanse of dull-colored stones was a hazy rectangle of shadow made when the moon shone through the water tower on the opposite side of the rubble that was once their home.

Theo's mind was churning. "The building had to come down. We wouldn't be able to get to that door if it hadn't. We would never have seen it."

"That means they knew," said Jaime. "The Morningstarrs, I mean. They knew people would be too curious not to set the cane and start the timer. That we'd have to do it."

Maybe Theo should admire this, admire them for their ingenuity and their cleverness and their insight into people, their ability to plan a building's implosion long before implosion was invented, their completely impossible ability to predict the future, but he couldn't, not with his home collapsed in front of him. "The Morningstarrs were jerks," he said. "If they were so smart, they would have figured out a different way. They would have known people lived here, that this was someone's home. They would have anticipated every possibility. They could have made it so the building could stay. But they didn't." He searched for a stronger word, a better word, but he was too angry. "Jerks," he said again.

They watched the firefighters pick through the rubble, the cops take statements, the reporters report. They didn't ask Jaime or Tess or Theo any questions. What would kids know about this anyway? It was obvious that someone was going after Darnell Slant's buildings, the reporters said. But how did they plant all those explosives in the first place without being seen? How did the implosion occur so neatly, to the point that it left the sidewalk intact? Why was there so little debris? What kind of new technology had done it?

Theo almost laughed.

A clock had done it.

But that wasn't exactly true. Theo stuck both hands in his hair, watched the too-small curls of smoke twisting up toward the stars. What if the Cipher really was alive? Then it wasn't still and static, just a series of clues waiting for someone to follow them. It shifted, it responded.

If they hadn't set the clock, what would it have done? What would it have asked *them* to do?

What if they weren't discovering the Cipher as much as building it for themselves as they went along? Goading it and challenging it?

"We need to see what's behind that door," Theo said.

"There are way too many people around right now,"

Tess said, her voice dull as a butter knife. "And our parents and Jaime's grandmother and father will be worried. They might have heard about this already."

"We'll be grounded for life," said Jaime.

"Wouldn't be the worst thing that happened today," said Theo.

"Jaime, how about you come home with us now and go back to Hoboken in the morning?" Tess suggested.

"Yeah, that way my mom won't have to go too far to arrest us all," said Theo.

"Sounds good," said Jaime. "But . . . I don't want Mima to wake up alone."

"Right," said Tess. "Okay." And her eyes got that glassy look again, because this was good-bye. Not forever, but still. Good-bye. Good-bye, Jaime, good-bye, 354 W. 73rd Street.

Good-bye.

Tess threw her arms around Jaime and hugged him. Theo patted Jaime on the back, and Jaime slugged him on the shoulder. They went their separate ways, Jaime traveling to one Underway station and the twins to another. The twins took a train across town and then over to Queens. The Guildman in his glass box wore the same inscrutable expression every Guildman wore, paying Theo and Tess and Nine no more mind than he paid anyone. The people swaying in their seats with the rhythm of the train read books or listened to music or stared off into the distance thinking about whatever it was people thought about: work, bills, the chicken they would make for dinner. It was like any other ride on the Underway and also unlike any other ride because Theo wasn't the same. He had been betrayed. He had seen a man carried off by Rollers. He had seen two others swallowed whole. He had watched his home crumble. That had to mark a person, but no one looked at him any differently. Their eyes flicked to his hair and then skirted away. To them, he was not a human whose life had changed forever, he was a kid who needed a haircut.

They got off the train. Their steps slowed; no one was in a hurry to get to Aunt Esther's, not even Nine. They would probably be grounded for a month. Or a year. It might be a while before they could get back to the building with the shadow door. It was just as well. Theo had a sinking suspicion that opening that door wouldn't be an end to anything, but yet another beginning.

Tess unlocked the door in front of him and swung it open cautiously, as if she were afraid Mr. Stoop or Mr. Pinscher were lying in wait. But the only thing lying in wait was Aunt Esther, who sat in her chair in the living room. The house was quiet.

"Well!" she said. "Hello, you children! How was your evening?"

Theo sat on the couch. "Somewhat eventful."

"Hmmm," said Aunt Esther. "We had a few adventures here ourselves."

"I can imagine," said Tess.

"Can you?" said Aunt Esther, knitting needles clicking.

Tess said, "I imagine Mom is furious that we took so long."

"Furious isn't the word. Sleeping is the word. She was so exhausted that she and your dad lay down for a nap a few hours ago and that was that. I don't think they'll wake up till tomorrow."

"So, you guys didn't hear the news?" Theo said.

"The only thing I heard was snoring," said Aunt Esther. Nine nudged her knee and Aunt Esther scratched the top of Nine's head. "Well! I think we've all had enough adventures for one day. I've made the beds in the attic and you should be comfortable enough. I shall wake you all in the morning. Or rather, Lancelot shall. He's been practicing his pancakes. I rather think he likes it here." Aunt Esther held up her knitting, which appeared to be outfit for a very small octopus. "And I rather hope that you two come to like it as well."

◆ ◆ ◆

As Aunt Esther had predicted, the smell of pancakes woke Theo and Tess.

Also, the sound of yelling.

Tess and Theo got up, rubbed the sleep from their eyes, and wandered downstairs in their pajamas. Their parents were in the living room, hands around mugs of coffee, shouting at the TV. As soon as they saw Tess and Theo, Mr. Biedermann quickly shut it off.

"Heeey," said Mrs. Biedermann, drawing out the word. She put the coffee on the table, hugged Tess tight. And then she did the same thing to Theo. "I'm so glad to see you two."

"What were you watching?" said Tess.

"Oh, nothing," said their dad, again, too quickly. "Who wants pancakes?"

"Dad?"

Mr. Biedermann put his coffee cup on the table, rubbed his forehead. "You guys might want to sit down. Something happened last night."

"Our building imploded," said Theo.

Mrs. Biedermann's mouth hung open. "You knew?"

"Jaime told us. He has a cell phone. He gets news and stuff. It must have happened right after we left. We missed the whole thing."

"Oh!" said Mr. Biedermann, her eyes moving from Theo to Tess. "Are you okay?"

Nine shambled over to Tess, pressed her big body against Tess's leg. Tess didn't say anything for a minute. Then she said, "I'll live."

"So is that what was on the TV?" Theo said. "The news?"

"Oh, that jerk Slant was going to have a press conference and I just want to arrest him right now for being such a *schmendrick*!" their mother erupted.

"So, let's watch it," Theo said.

"Are you sure?" said their dad.

"Yeah," Theo said. "Let's see what the *schmendrick* has to say for himself."

Mr. Biedermann punched the button on the remote and a reporter's face filled the screen. "We're waiting at the site of 354 W. 73rd Street, where Darnell Slant is expected to make a statement after he's seen the damage from last night's mysterious implosion that destroyed his latest investment. Luckily, no one was hurt in the event that took down this landmark building. But people everywhere are wondering whether this was simply a wanton act of sabotage, or whether Slant himself planned this all along. Aaaand, here we go live."

The camera panned away from the reporter over to a

tall, pale man with thick, dark hair buzzed on the sides, a man who would be handsome except for the lipless slash that matched his name. Jaime couldn't have drawn a better villain.

"Thank you all for coming," said Darnell Slant in his nasal accent. "This is an important day for all of New York because this is about the survival of New York. I know that some of you are upset. Some of you will probably protest what I've done here."

Wait, what *he* had done?

"And that's good. That's what we do in this city. We fight for what we think is right. I'm fighting, too."

Tess stiffened, and Nine licked her knee.

"Some of you see here the engines of destruction. I see engines of progress. The Morningstarrs were geniuses, the earliest architects of our city. I have said before that they should be honored in museums, in history books. We should think of them every time we ride the Underway. But the world in which they lived is history. And we need new heroes."

Theo tugged at his hair, wanting to stuff bits of it into his ears to muffle the sound of Slant's words.

Tess was squeezing her fists so tight that her knuckles went white.

"We have been trying to solve the Cipher for more

than a hundred years," said Slant. "But the solution is not in the streets or the buildings of this city, but in us, in its people. *We* are the magic. *We* are the treasure. And we are going to keep moving forward. The world stops for no one, and neither do we. We will rebuild. Thank you."

He thrust the microphone at the nearest minion and was swallowed up by the buzzing, yammering crowd.

"*Schmendrick*," said their mother.

"*Liar*," said Tess.

"So, according to Darnell Slant himself," the reporter said, "this was a planned demolition. But with residents barely out of the building, was it a legal demolition? Will charges be brought? And what are we to make of the fact that two men that reportedly worked for Slant, a Mr. Sinscher and a Mr. Poop, were found wandering in their underwear in Riverside Park, with no memory of the last six months? And what of the disappearance of Edgar Wellington, the current president of the Old York Puzzler and Cipherist Society, who vanished from the society's headquarters a week ago only to show up last week at a Miami bar dressed like a Starr Punk?"

"Edgar is back?" said Mr. Biedermann. He turned to his wife. "Did you know?"

Mrs. Biedermann sighed. "I didn't want to upset

anyone even more. But yes. He doesn't remember anything either, apparently."

Theo didn't have a name for what he felt about Edgar. Relief. Rage. Sadness. Disappointment. All of the above? "That's . . . weird," Theo said carefully.

"Yes. Very," said Mrs. Biedermann. "All of this is very, very weird."

"Weird," said Aunt Esther, "is relative."

And then there was nothing but the sound of Lancelot banging pots and pans in the kitchen, the scrape of coffee mugs on the table, the click of Aunt Esther's knitting needles, Nine's furious and insistent purr.

Slant had said, "We are the treasure." Not so different from what Grandpa Ben always said.

Slant was so wrong about so much, but what if he was also just a little bit right?

Their world had been torn apart, but they were still here.

What is the city but the people?

"It's very, very weird," said Tess. "But we're safe. And we're together."

"Yes, we are," said Mrs. Biedermann, smiling, taking Tess's hand. "We're together."

They hadn't found the treasure, not yet.

But maybe they'd had one all along.

CHAPTER THIRTY-ONE
Jaime

It was a long ride from Hoboken. A short walk and two different trains, the Path under the Hudson and the No. 2 uptown. He wasn't worried about the Guildmen anymore. They gave him no more attention than they gave anyone else, as long as he wasn't littering. (He did, however, give the centipedes that cleaned the Underway cars a wider berth. Who knew when they would explode?)

Now he was sitting in his favorite spot across from 354 W. 73rd Street, or rather, the empty lot where the building used to be. He'd gotten over the shock of it. Mostly. He'd even gotten over the shock of living in Hoboken (though he would never stop bugging his dad to find them an apartment somewhere cool, like Harlem or Seneca Village). Even Mima had adjusted,

joining another bowling league, going out salsa dancing, and starting her own handyman business, which
she called the Handy Woman. She was even busier than
ever. Bought herself her own white van so that she could
drive around and see her clients. Sometimes, Jaime went
with her. He was getting pretty good with tools himself.

"Watcha drawing, kid?" said an older man, who
stopped to tie his shoe. He was wearing a brown suit
that nearly matched the brown of his skin.

"A building," said Jaime, flipping the sketchbook so
the man could see.

"Ah, that building. They never did figure out who
did it, did they? Not for sure."

"Nope," said Jaime. "Not for sure."

The man stood up straight, mopped his brow with a
handkerchief. "A shame about all those people, though.
Nobody should be pushed from their homes. It's not
right."

"No," said Jaime. "It isn't."

"Probably going to build some kinda fancy hotel or
something. Some condos with an amusement park on
the roof. Some restaurant that serves tiny food that only
makes you hungry."

"Probably," said Jaime, smiling a little.

"Cheer up, kid," the man said. "Who knows? Maybe

in twenty or thirty years, you'll be the guy who owns the city and you can do whatever you want with it."

The man walked off, whistling. Jaime sketched the familiar lines of 354 W. 73rd Street, the windows like eyes watching over him, always watching over him, waiting for the twins to come.

Tonight was the night.

The crews had cleaned up the site. The rubble was gone. Slant was all over the TV talking about the tower of condos that he planned to put in the space, each of those condos with a view of the Hudson. The neighbors on either side of the lot were fighting him. They didn't want a tower with views of the Hudson, a tower that would dwarf their buildings, send rents skyrocketing.

But they would lose.

Unless.

Someone cleared her throat. Someone else meowed. Jaime grinned before he looked up. Theo and Tess and Nine stood in front of him. They waited as he stood and tucked his sketchbook in his pocket. They walked all the way around to the back of the construction site, where there was a gap in the chain-link fence. There were earthmovers and caterpillars (the construction kind), but no one was working, no one was around. They slipped under the fence and crept over to the building next to the empty lot. You could only see the strange arrangement of brickwork in the shape of three pyramids when you got up close, the shadow door right under it when the full moon shone just right.

Tess took one last look around, then pulled the pewter dragon from her pocket, the one that had once topped a black cane they had found in a tunnel.

"Do you think it will work?" she said, touching a strangely carved brick right where a doorknob would be.

But it was a silly question and she was only thinking out loud. Jaime took the dragon from her, pressed it into the brick, hesitated. Tess put her hand on top of Jaime's. Theo put his hand on top of his sister's. The three of them turned the handle. There was a low groan and a long scraping sound as it opened. A waft of musty air drifted out like the gasp of an ancient tomb.

"Well?" Theo said.

"What's the worst that could happen?" said Jaime.

Tess laughed.

They stepped across the threshold.

February 13, 1861

Charles L. Reason walked the city streets uptown, his stride long, the tap of his walking stick on the cobbles like a metronome. It was late, and the air had a wicked bite that sank its teeth into his thick wool coat. He paid it no mind. Nor did he acknowledge the strange looks he got from the few passersby out at this ungodly hour. For many of these people, New Yorkers though they were, the combination of his fine clothes, confident gait, and brown skin was a surprise they could not keep off their faces. He tipped his hat, a brief smile touching his lips. Then he left them where they were, standing in the middle of the street, gaping like lake trout.

What would they say if he spoke to them in Greek? Latin? French? What would they say when he introduced himself as a mathematician? If he confessed that he'd returned to the city of his birth to improve the schools here? That he could teach them a thing or two or many? That he'd be a teacher always?

Of course, that wasn't all he was.

As if a man were any single thing.

He patted the pocket where he had tucked his latest poem. A competent effort, but not up to his usual standards. He would have to try again when he had a moment to spare. Those were becoming fewer and farther between. A new president had been elected but not yet inaugurated. There were meetings and demonstrations. Seven states had already seceded from the union, clinging to the barbarism of slavery, and more states threatened to the do the same. The nation was in turmoil, and there were rumblings of war. There was so much work to be done.

Yet here he was, on this odd errand. *Please come,* she'd written in her precise hand, *when the clock strikes midnight. I would make an entreaty on behalf of our lost friends.*

And friends they had been, at least for a short time. So, though there was so much work to be done, though the hour late and the air spiteful, though his body wished for the release of sleep, he would meet her and hear her entreaty, even if a hearing was the only thing he could offer.

He walked faster, the metronome ticking to a quicker tempo. He was so far northwest that the fine brownstones turned into estates surrounded by frost-stiffened lawns and bare, creaking trees. The Underway had brought more and more people to this area, but it was still a world of wealth and privilege; the shoemakers and barmen and tailors forced to hunker downtown. Here, on the upper west side of Manhattan, ladies learned to embroider cushions and play the piano rather than how to turn cream into butter or how to pluck a chicken. Men took over their fathers' shipyards and banks, their farms and estates, and did not have to scratch to put food in the bellies of their children. (The governesses and brown-skinned cooks did that.)

He reached the trio of buildings that hugged the Hudson. He wondered if she was lonely here, no servants of her own, with just the river for company. But she was not one to express such feelings as loneliness.

He entered the grandly tiled lobby unannounced. She didn't keep a manservant either, which would have been a terrible scandal—and a terrible risk—if she were any other woman. She had told him where she'd be, in the large apartment on the fifth floor. She claimed it was her favorite, but then, she enjoyed moving from room to room, apartment to apartment, occupying every space in this grand building, far too large for any one person, and yet too small for such a one as she.

He took the elevator, remembering his first ride on the miraculous contraption, how he'd idly wondered if it would just keep going until it reached the stars themselves.

As it had on that first ride, the elevator drifted in verticals and horizontals, its own special geometric poem. They had a shared passion, a kinship, he and this machine. He hoped it would live on forever.

He entered the hallway on the fifth floor, his walking stick striking the tiles with less force, softer than the tick of a faraway clock sounding the midnight hour.

"Always so punctual," she said, from her seat by the window. "Thank you for coming."

He nodded, laid his gloves on the small table near the settee. She had set out a tray with tea and biscuits, though she would partake of nothing herself. She held out a slim hand, gesturing for him to warm himself in front of the fire, which he did gratefully. The tea was hot and eased the chill of the evening, as well as the strange prickle of apprehension that crawled across his skin.

"I would not have asked you here if it was not of vital importance," she said. "Though I fear that when I make my request it might sound quite . . . mad."

"If your request does sound mad, and I offer such an opinion on it," he said, taking a sip of the tea and replacing the cup, "it is nothing you haven't heard before."

She laughed. In the firelight, her dark eyes burned like the wood that warmed him. He had surmised long ago that she was . . . special, but he had also learned not to be afraid of her.

Most of the time.

She placed the book she had been reading on a nearby table and picked up a large envelope. "I would ask that you take this letter for me. Keep it with you. Arrange for its transferal to your kin after your . . ." She hesitated.

"Death?" he said, smiling at her sudden delicacy.

"Yes," she said. "You'll find instructions tucked in with the letter. The letter must be bequeathed to your kin, then your kin's kin, and so on. It needs to find its way to certain people . . . in the future."

"In the future?" he asked, perplexed. "How many years in the future?"

"Many," she said.

"But how—"

"I've worked out the details. It shouldn't be too much trouble."

He was quiet for a moment. Then: "You wouldn't want to perform the task yourself?"

"I'm afraid I have too many other things to do. And I'm afraid I don't have much time."

He put the cup and saucer on the table, surprised. Was she ill? But if she was, she would never say.

"And," she added, "it will help *them*."

He exhaled. They had been gone for six years. He couldn't see how they could be helped now. But they had been supporters of education for all people, no matter what color their skin. And he had spent quite a few evenings in front of their hearth.

"Yes. Yes, I will make the necessary arrangements if you think it important."

"Thank you," she said. "There is also a donation in the envelope."

Suddenly, the fire was too warm, his cravat too tight. He had come as a friend, and he was to be treated as a paid employee. "Pardon me?"

"A rather large donation. For your school."

"*Their* money?" he said.

"No. Mine."

"Money they bequeathed to you."

She laughed. "They did bequeath plenty to me, it's true, but not what you think. It is my money I give to you. I have my own investments. My own interests. My own profession. I always have."

"Interests," he said. "Yes. I did hear tell of a fearsome man come to New York City some months ago looking for a runaway from Virginia. He claimed a woman had divested him of all his coin and other valuables, warned him that if he dared to meddle with any runaways or anyone else, he would be dealt with most harshly."

"How curious," she murmured.

"And then this woman tossed him into the Hudson. Of course no one believed him. Eventually he stopped speaking of it, for the shame was too great."

"Shame over the wrong thing, I'd wager."

"But that was before he disappeared entirely. Some people said he went back to Virginia. Other people believe he did not escape so easily."

"Fascinating."

He chose his words carefully, as he always did. "Have you heard the stories as well? About this man, and others like him?"

Her lovely mouth twisted into a smile. "Why do you

ask? Do you think anyone misses men like them?"

The uneasiness had come over him again. His eyes roved over the bookshelves, the table in front of him. A sheaf of paper was stacked neatly there. On the top page, in an elegant hand, were the words: *The Lost Ones*, a story by A Lady.

"Are you the lady in question?" he asked.

"Oh, I am always and forever a lady."

Though he did not believe that was an answer, he nodded. He took another sip of the tea despite the fact it was already going tepid.

She said, "I have one more request that might prove a little more painful."

"Oh?"

"Your walking stick. It was a gift." A statement, as she knew exactly who had given it to him.

"Yes," he said, running his fingers lightly over the dragon's head.

"Do you think you could part with it?"

"Part with it?"

"They didn't tell you when they gave it to you, but it has more than one use. It is not just a walking stick."

"Pardon?" he said, his voice growing an edge. This was too much. This sounded mad.

"Let me make their apologies now that they cannot.

There is much they couldn't say to anyone, even to you."

"And giving up my walking stick will help them?"

"It will help others."

"How?" he said, the edge getting even sharper.

"It is a beginning," she said.

"Excuse me?"

"They knew they could trust you with it," she said.

"Not enough to explain," he said, standing. He picked up the walking stick. He had carried it for years, liked the weight of it, the feel of it. But he was not a man who would keep a gift that hadn't been given freely. He was not a man who needed a crutch.

He held out the walking stick, and she took it. "I'm sorry," she said.

He considered her and wondered if the gleam in her eyes wasn't as bright as he had known it to be, if her spark was truly fading out. "I'm sorry, too."

After that, there was nothing left to say.

A few moments later, he was outside. He tucked the envelope inside his coat, trying not to feel naked without the walking stick, the reassuring message engraved on the ring below the handle: *All that opens is not a door.* True. A heart opens. A mind.

Well, he still had those. And he wanted to get them home to his own hearth, his own bed. The wind had picked up, an icy curtain wafting off the river. A shadow appeared in front of him, startling him, but it was nothing but the moonlight passing through the trees. The streets were empty now, and the windows dark. He heard creaks and moans, and he told himself that this was just the wind in the bare branches, the guttural utterings of discontented ghosts. And yet, sneaking underneath the creaks and the moans—a whisper, a cough, the heels of furtive boots. Not just from one direction, but from every direction. Behind him. To the east. To the west. From everywhere at once.

A shiver chased down his spine. The uneasiness he had felt in Ava Oneal's parlor grew and grew till his open heart was fit to beat out of his chest, his open mind a flood of revelation that threatened to drown him.

Someone was coming.

And some*thing* was coming. War, yes, a long and bitter war that would shake the nation to its very soul.

But something else, too. Something bigger, something that could swallow the whole of the world, bones and all.

Charles Reason lost all reason, and ran.

ACKNOWLEDGMENTS

I want to thank my indomitable agent, Tina Wexler; my incredible editor, Jordan Brown; and the always fabulous Debbie Kovacs at Walden Pond Press for shepherding *York* from its rocky beginnings some four years ago through to its current form. Thanks to Sasha Vinogradova for the gorgeous cover art, designer Aurora Parlagreco for the beautiful design, and art director Amy Ryan for her vision. And thanks to Danielle Smith for getting the word out. I'm lucky to have you all on my side.

Thanks to Swati Avasthi for letting me talk through the *entire* outline with her one cold day in Minnesota; to Sarah Aronson, Brenda Ferber, Carolyn Crimi, Jenny Meyerhoff, and Mary Loftus for reading this book in its early stages; and to Anne Ursu for reading it in every stage and listening to me whine about it. Thanks also to Ebony Wilkins and Hannah Gómez for all their amazing insights, and to copyeditors Renée Cafiero and Anne Heausler for their tireless efforts to keep me from repeating words, contradicting myself, and generally screwing things up. Any errors of fact or representation are mine.

To my colleagues and my dear friends at Hamline University, including Mary Rockcastle, Anne Ursu, Swati Avasthi, Emily Jenkins, Jackie Briggs Martin, the Marshas Chall and Qualey, Phyllis Root, Sherri L. Smith, Claire Rudolf Murphy, Ronald Koertge, Coe Booth, Gary Schmidt, Gene Yang, Matt de la Peña, Megan Atwood, Christine Heppermann, and Miriam Busch: you guys rock. Thank you so much for the conversation and the inspiration. A special shout-out to Sarah Park Dahlen, who knows where to get the best cupcakes and the best pho.

Thanks, too, to Ellen Oh, Will Alexander, Katherine Paterson, and Valerie Lewis. Our intense but friendly debates about books helped sustain me through a difficult and tumultuous year. I'm so proud of our work and happy to know all of you.

Huge, huge thanks to my ladies: Anne Ursu, Kelly

Jensen, Sarah McCarry, Justina Ireland, Tessa Gratton, Leila Roy, Miriam Weinberg, Laurel Snyder, Tracey Baptiste, Olugbemisola Rhuday-Perkovich, Kelly Barnhill, Martha Brockenbrough, Kate Messner, and Linda Urban for keeping me sane (and keeping me in funny animal pics) when I thought I was losing my mind, and to Annika Cioffi, Melissa Ruby, and Tracey George for not letting me forget where I come from. Tanya Lee Stone, you always know when to call. Linda, I think about you every day.

And finally, thanks to Melissa, Jessica, and Steve for putting up with my endless obsessions and distraction while I worked on this story. Love you.